CONTENTS

REFRACTION

by

Terry Geo

To Ken
For making my dreams
become a reality

THE PRESENT

INTRODUCTION

We all dream.

Every time we sleep, we enter our own, personal world of endless possibilities.

Some people dream of fame and fortune; others want simply to spend time with a lost love. We dream of changing our appearance; to be slimmer, taller, or to sprout wings. There are even those of us who wish to travel through time, to change some unfortunate moment in the past, or try to shape the future.

We dream of a place where restrictions don't apply and even the most grandiose of wishes are granted. We only have to close our eyes to be whisked away via the power of our subconscious; to travel anywhere, to any time and to be whoever we want to be.

But alas, these are only dreams. Sooner or later, we all have to return to reality.

CHAPTER 1

Abby was running as fast as she could. The young girl couldn't remember why, but with her heart pumping, the quickening of her breath and the fear that coursed through her body; all her senses knew it was the right thing to do. She was being chased. Abby swerved around the trees of the darkened forest, her mind racing and not knowing where she was nor how she could escape from her unknown assailant.

It was the noise that first alerted her to the ocean, and as she neared the edge of a cliff, the sound of the waves could be heard, crashing on the rocks far below. If Abby stopped now, she would be giving herself to the Shadow Man, a prospect that filled her with even more fear than falling into the moon-lit ocean below.

The girl continued running, and without thinking twice, as she neared the edge of the cliff, she pushed off from the side and jumped high into the air, much higher than she ever would have thought possible. She felt as light as a feather, her white nightgown billowing ever so gently, as if pushing her farther up towards the stars. Abby felt as if she were flying and ascending higher into the night sky. She glanced back to the cliff edge, where the dark shape of a man with burning red eyes was standing, motionless, staring directly at her. Abby was safe. He couldn't follow her up here.

As she rose higher, a gust of wind caught her long, dark hair, blowing it in front of her face. Scrambling to clear her view, she felt a jolt in her stomach as gravity kicked in, causing her to drop out of the sky. She was falling fast now, plunging towards the ocean below with no way of slowing her descent. Panic surged through her as she kicked her legs violently; a futile attempt to propel herself back to safety. It didn't work. She tumbled clumsily through the air, her young body falling downwards until her face was mere metres from the crashing water.

Abby bolted upright and let out a small scream as she scrambled to untangle herself from the duvet and blankets wrapped around her. She was back in her bedroom, lit only by the light of a small lava lamp at her side. As she readjusted to the familiar surroundings, a second, ghost-like girl also sat upright and occupied the same space as Abby, now staring at the trembling reflection of herself in the lamp.

The bedroom door burst open and the harsh light from the hallway filled the room as her flustered mother came in to check on her. Out of breath, wiping sleep from her eyes and visibly shaken, Shira pulled her daughter close to her in an embrace which comforted both of them.

"My darling, are you OK?"

"I was being chased, I fell and, and —"

"It's all right, it was just a bad dream. You're safe now. I'm here to look after you. No-one will chase you while I'm here, or they'll get this." Shira clenched her fist and shook it comically in the air.

A small tear escaped Abby's eye; a tear brought on from the fear she had felt, the relief that the dream had ended, and the comfort brought by her mother. She wiped her eyes, smiled, and settled back down into bed.

After a long while, with her mother gently stroking her hair, Abby finally fell back to sleep.

Bedford

"The most upsetting part is that she won't even look at me." Terrell was walking along the school corridor with his best friend, Cody, talking about the same girl he had been obsessing about since before he knew what the word 'obsession' meant.

"I've seen her look at you, mate."

"Really?" Terrell's face lit up.

"Quite often, actually, but it's more of a scowl." Cody pulled a face, mimicking the look of disgust from the object of Terrell's affections.

"Great. Thanks for that." Terrell's shoulders returned to their slumped position as they continued through the school. "I'm crazy about her, the least she could do is be nice to me. The occasional smile, asking how I am, leading to us grabbing a slice of pizza together, working on some homework in the library and then, when the time is right, she leans over for a kiss —"

A bag swung into Terrell's back, snapping him out of his temporary lapse in concentration.

"Stop dreaming, mate. She's never going to fancy you. You're a geek and she's . . . well, she's Lindsay Coppard — the hottest girl in school."

Terrell straightened himself up and looked at Cody.

"Dreaming's preferable to the reality of her hating my guts."

"Can you blame her? You did puke over her bag in chemistry."

"That was in year seven. How was I supposed to know that burning sulphur was going to make me hurl? Can people really still hold that against me? It's been six years."

The boys turned into the lunch-hall, where a group of girls spotted them.

"Hey, Pukey!" the tallest of the girls called as Terrell passed by, eliciting a cascade of muffled giggles from her friends.

Cody hugged Terrell's shoulder and quickly ushered him away.

"Mate, don't take this the wrong way, but maybe girls just

aren't for you?"

Yorkshire

Daylight was breaking through the clouds as Jake donned his filthy, worn-out wellington boots. Yet another long day lay ahead, tending to his land and livestock. Upper Malham Farm had been passed down through many generations; it had been his father's dying wish that Jake continue in the family footsteps. His father had always been a strong, proud man and on seeing him frail and failing as he took his last breaths in a hospital bed, Jake had held his hand and agreed to take over the farm. Being an only child and the last remaining family member, there was really no-one else who could.

That had been two years ago, and now this remote farm in northern England had become his prison. The prospect of doing this for the rest of his life filled him with dread. At twenty-six years old, he rarely ventured away from the farm and his computer had become his only window to the outside world.

Agriculture was no longer a booming business and the low turnover meant he could only afford to employ a skeleton staff. Jake worked seven days a week; hard, relentless, tiring, physical work. He wished for a different life but could see no way out of his current one.

The young farmer's boots sloshed through the soft mud. The cool air of a new day chilled his face as he made his way across the field. In front of him was a battered, old tractor. Jake pulled himself up into the driver's seat and stared through the windscreen. The sun was rising behind the old birch trees in the distance, casting wild patterns over the valley floor and the huge puddles of water on the track in front of him. A flock of birds soared through the air, moving in perfect formation, disappearing towards the horizon. They left behind an eerie

4

silence.

Still half-asleep, Jake's mind began to wander and he closed his eyes, breathing in the moment. A few seconds later, his body was slumped over the steering wheel, fast asleep, yet a ghostlike version of him was still sitting upright in the cabin, eyes open and staring straight ahead.

◆ ◆ ◆

Kent

Ryder was the illegitimate child of Lord and Lady Braighton's only daughter, Maria. After a near-fatal accident in Afghanistan, Ryder had been medically discharged from the army. Wheelchair-bound, he was finding it difficult to adjust to everyday life, especially having no money to support himself. He hoped his estranged family would be able to offer some financial stability, at least for the immediate future. His mother had passed away some years before and he hadn't been back to Braighton Manor since.

Ryder waited patiently in the sitting-room. The name belied the room's grandiosity. Priceless works of art adorned the walls, but the one that really stood out was the oil painting of his mother, positioned above the open, stone fireplace.

Heavy footsteps echoed in the distance; the louder the sound, the closer the footsteps and the stronger Ryder's heartbeat. The pounding in his chest seemed to match the pace of the steps, until they stopped right outside the room. There was a pause where no sound could be heard for a few seconds, then a creaking of hinges announced Lord Braighton's arrival.

Carrying a stern look on his face, the lord walked towards Ryder and held out his hand.

"Ah, Ryder, so good of you to come. It's been too long since you were here last." Lord Braighton shook his grandson's hand and then stood back to survey the wheelchair. "I see the army's left its mark on you, but as they say, 'what doesn't kill us makes us stronger', and all that."

The two men regarded each other in an awkward silence before Lord Braighton walked across to the antique sideboard; his Italian leather shoes tapping on the mahogany floor beneath him. He fixed himself a neat brandy without offering one to his guest.

Ryder opened his mouth to speak but no sound came out. With a dry throat, he swallowed hard in an attempt to regain composure.

"Good afternoon, sir. I'm sorry to arrive unannounced. I realise we haven't spoken since Mum died. I'm sorry for not keeping in touch. I hope being here today isn't an inconvenience?"

"Not at all. Good of you to come, good of you to come."

There was another awkward silence. Both men glanced around the stately room in a bid to avoid the other's gaze. The lord drained his glass as both men's eyes came to rest on the painting above the fireplace. A pang of emotion hit Ryder's chest. He hated himself for coming here, but he was desperate. So desperate, in fact, that he was about to ask for help from the person he believed was responsible for his mother's death.

CHAPTER 2

Bedford

Terrell had a vivid imagination. It was the reason he excelled in creative studies at school; it was also the cause of his broken and restless sleep.

Recently, his dreams were more intense than usual, causing him to wake in the middle of the night, unable to differentiate between reality and dream. Usually, he would fall back to sleep, but occasionally, his brain would keep him awake, making him tired the next day. This didn't go unnoticed.

"No, you can't call in sick just because you're tired. We're all tired, that's life." Mrs Prince was preparing breakfast and bustling about, tidying the kitchen. "I blame those awful computer games you play. They're too violent. I wouldn't sleep, either, with all that blood and gore on the screen."

Terrell instantly regretted telling his mother.

"It's fantasy, Mum, it's not real blood. And anyway, I wasn't on the computer last night." He played with his spoon in the soggy cereal absentmindedly, sloshing around the contents of the bowl in front of him.

"Then it's those awful comics you read. They're just as bad."

"You mean graphic novels, Mum."

"*Too* graphic, if you ask me." Mrs Prince turned around from the sink, dishcloth in hand, and proceeded to clean the table Terrell was sitting at. "Now, hurry up and finish your breakfast. You'll be late for school."

Terrell dismissed what his mother had said, something that came easy for the teenager to do. He loved her, but they rarely saw eye-to-eye on anything, especially when it came to his love of comics and video games. The fantastical characters he watched and read about were never the source material for his waking dreams; if anything, he wished they were.

Terrell had started reading graphic novels at a young age, and so began a fascination with all things fantasy-related, spawning countless years of creating fan fiction and artwork. After much begging, he had received a computer for his eleventh birthday, which brought with it an introduction to online role-playing games. This was total immersion; teaming up with gamers from all over the globe as they battled mythical creatures together.

Over the years, his online friends gradually dissipated as his obsession with fantasy began to evolve into a morbid fascination with death. It was one thing killing a fictitious ogre for character experience, but another to revel in the graphic details of the creature's demise. For Terrell, it was harmless fun; to everyone else, it was weird.

As the years passed, his macabre thoughts won him very few friends in the real world and, try as he might, he had never had a girlfriend. His handsome, dark-skinned face and beaming smile simply couldn't outshine his social 'otherness'.

He had consoled himself with his writing. Creating worlds and creatures was euphoric, yet the theme of death was always prevalent in his work. Though beautifully crafted, he would kill off the main protagonist in every story he wrote, whether it be a reimagining of Chaucer's Canterbury Tales or for a competition to write a new children's book. When questioned by his teacher, he had reasoned that original children's fables had always been written as cautionary tales, but his behaviour worried the school and his parents were called in to see them.

That was the first year he wasn't awarded a prize in the

annual literary competition. He was twelve at the time and couldn't understand what the problem was. He had read countless books and felt they were all too predictable; by killing off the lead character, he was adding a dramatic twist to his own stories.

His parents didn't approve, and when he saw the worried look in his mother's eyes, he agreed not to kill off any more people in his stories. From that point on, he only killed off their pets.

News of the incident quickly circulated around the school. Rumours that he was dying surfaced, which when proved false, made everyone question why a healthy boy was so morbidly obsessed with death. That was something Terrell himself couldn't answer. He had never faced death; he wasn't a child of trauma; he'd never even lost a family member he'd been close to. Yet for some reason, death had always played a part in everything he thought about.

His parents and teachers blamed video games. His mum and dad had tried limiting access to his computer when he was younger, but many years and countless tantrums later, they'd realised that restricting access to the things he loved, had no positive effect on his behaviour at all. Now, they reasoned that however different their son might be, it was simply who he was.

He may have tempered his dark thoughts on paper, but they were never silent in his head. Every time he slept, he saw a new wave of unknown people killed off in numerous, sometimes extravagant, ways. Terrell's dreams frightened him, taunted him, and left him with the foreboding sense that it was his brain conjuring up these horrific scenes.

Everyone knew he was different, but only Terrell himself knew the extent of what he imagined. He feared that if anyone found out, he would be slung into a padded cell, never to see daylight again. He couldn't even tell his best friend, the one person he had always confided in.

Cody was, in some ways, Terrell's polar opposite. The two

boys had lived on the same street and had grown up together since pre-school. He may have been six months younger, but Terrell looked up to him like an older brother. Cody was always the one to get them into trouble, but to his credit, he would always take the blame for whatever scrapes they had gotten into.

When they were young, Terrell would follow his friend everywhere, like a doting puppy. Cody had grown quicker than anyone else and had always been the tallest and strongest kid in school. He loved playing sports and excelled in all physical activities. With his carefree personality and charm to spare, he was never short of friends or admirers. Yet despite their many differences, Cody and Terrell had remained best friends throughout.

Growing up was an adventure. The boys would climb trees, build dens and camp outside in the summer; but try as he might, Terrell never seemed to enjoy these activities as much as Cody. As their teenage years arrived, their adventures began to dwindle. Terrell found he enjoyed writing more than playing in the mud. His young mind flowed with ideas, thoughts and dreams that he desperately tried to articulate on paper. He had kept a diary every day from the age of nine, which now took the form of an online vlog. His website rarely got any visitors, but that didn't matter; he had a need to share his thoughts and feelings and this was his way of expressing himself.

Worried he was losing his friend, Cody insisted Terrell join his five-a-side soccer team at the local sports centre.

"But no-one likes me," Terrell had protested one Friday evening.

"Of course they do. They wouldn't play with you if they didn't."

"They only play with me because you're there. No-one will tell you that, because you're twice the size of any of them."

"What's your problem, then? You're safe as long as you're with me."

That wasn't really the point. It was obvious that no-one other than Cody wanted him around. The sniggers from girls, the muffled insults from boys and the way people looked at him as if he were a circus freak. He didn't believe he deserved the treatment his peers gave him, but no matter how hard he tried, he couldn't change their opinion of him.

There was no doubt in Terrell's mind that if it wasn't for his personal bodyguard, life would be a lot harder. For Cody, everything was easy; boys wanted to be like him, and girls wanted to be with him. Terrell longed to have that life, to be popular and live without the constant fear of rejection and ridicule. In his teenage years, Terrell changed his appearance many times in a feeble attempt to win the favour of his class-mates. He grew out his afro before shaving it all off; he saved up for the latest designer trainers and even tried smoking to look "cool" - nothing worked. He simply couldn't change the core of who he was, despite his attempts to do so.

A year ago, Terrell's panic attacks started. In those first few moments after he had been shaken out of sleep, he actually believed there were two of him in the room; as if his dream-self had been pulled back to reality with him, if only for a brief moment. The more frequent these early morning wake-ups happened, the more he could focus on his second self. At first, he thought he was still dreaming; once his eyes had adjusted to his surroundings, the image of the other person disappeared. As the panic attacks increased, so, too, did the visions.

Frightened yet excited, he needed to share this information with someone. Against his better judgement, he approached his parents. Either through lack of understanding or simply not knowing how to respond, they were less than helpful. Cody had a similar reaction and used it as yet another reason why he should spend more time in the real world, but Terrell was convinced this was real and not just a fantasy he was living out in his head. He needed proof, not just for his parents or Cody, but for himself.

At breaktimes, while everyone else was outside in the playground, Terrell was in the school library. He scanned through biology books and texts on dream analysis in the hopes of finding the answers to his waking dreams. Nothing. He turned to his computer, reading papers and theories written by and for the scientific community, yet nothing matched his experience. There was one paper he read though which suggested a person could manipulate their own dreams through a process of lucid dreaming. He learned that this was a complicated procedure which many struggled to achieve, yet on his first attempt, it worked. He couldn't entirely stop the onslaught of death, but he had managed to reduce its impact. This didn't, however, temper his panic attacks, and he saw his dream-self even more frequently. It was then Terrell began recording himself while he slept. Placing a video camera by the side of the bed and setting it to record in night-vision mode, he hoped it would capture the evidence he needed. However, after months of reviewing his night-time awakenings with no results, he had come to the conclusion that either he really was imagining it all, or this wasn't something which couldn't be captured on film.

Terrell was up late one Friday night, engrossed in the pages of a book on neuroscience when he glanced at the clock and saw it was past one in the morning. He placed the book on the floor by the side of his bed and followed the same routine he had followed every night previous; turning on his video camera before turning off his bedside lamp.

His head sank into the pillow, but his mind was still racing. He tried to relax, but his mouth felt dry, and he knew he wouldn't drift off without first quenching his thirst. In darkness, he reached out his hand and fumbled around until he found the glass of water. After taking a sip, he placed the glass on to his bedside table, right in front of the running video camera.

As Terrell drifted off to sleep, he was unaware that he had just set into motion something which would change his life for ever.

CHAPTER 3

Kent

Ryder shifted uncomfortably in his seat. He had rehearsed this speech in his head a thousand times before today, but all the preparation in the world couldn't make this any easier. He cleared his throat abruptly.

"Sir, I've been bound to this wheelchair ever since the accident. My condition has meant that I had to leave the military. I've been struggling to adjust ever since, especially financially. I accrued a lot of debt, sir, and the banks refuse to help me any further. As regrettable as the situation may be, I need money to survive, and I'm afraid I have nowhere else to turn." Ryder looked up towards his grandfather with a cautious expression on his face. That was not how he'd rehearsed it at all. He had planned to ease into his financial problems rather than blurting out that he was broke and desperate.

His grandfather remained stonily silent. He appeared older than Ryder remembered. A stern, weathered face peered down at him. It was hard to gauge the old man's reaction thus far, which made Ryder's plea all the harder. He didn't want to beg but knew his options had run out.

"I have only manual skills, sir. Skills I can no longer use. I have no usable qualifications and although I plan to rectify this, I'm currently without funds and soon to be evicted from my home. I had hoped for a loan, of sorts; if only for the short-term."

Lord Braighton ruffled his moustache and drained the contents of his brandy glass. He gazed at the painting of Maria.

"Your mother was quite a handful, lad. Many a conversation like this one took place between she and I, in this very room. Each plea for money was more extravagant than the last, yet every time I relented, giving in to her . . . well, blood is thicker than water and all that. Unfortunately, nothing ever changed and no amount of help from me or her mother could stop her from —" he paused for a moment, staring into the painted eyes of his daughter "— it destroyed your grandmother, you know. And I vowed I would never make the same mistake again."

"But I . . ."

"Please, Ryder, let me finish." Lord Braighton poured himself another generous brandy, this time filling a second glass. He handed the drink to his grandson and sat down on the leather chesterfield opposite him.

The lord drank slowly as he stared at the burning embers of the large open fire, transfixed by the flames.

"Your grandmother hasn't slept properly in years, you know," he said, turning to Ryder. "She still blames herself for Maria's death. Of course, we knew she had gotten in with a bad crowd but what could we do? We'd heard stories — mere rumours, really — about the excessive drinking and drugs and so forth, but we tried to ignore it as idle gossip. After all, this was our daughter, our only child . . . we believed her to be responsible and couldn't imagine for a second she would be in with those sorts of people." He looked away, obviously trying to recompose himself. "I'm aware you have no idea who your father is. I very much doubt if your mother really knew, but we've always loved you, Ryder. You were, and still are, our only grandchild and every time I helped your mother financially, it was under the proviso that you were fed, clothed and looked after.

"I'm not sure how much you remember from that time, but you stayed here for a lot of your youth, and it was I who steered you on to the path of the army, a far more obtainable goal than the astronaut you were so hell-bent on being when you were younger." The old man smiled. "I felt you would benefit from the structure and stability of the military, something that had been so lacking throughout your young life."

Ryder looked at his grandfather with a new appreciation. So much had happened since joining the army at eighteen that his childhood had become a forgotten memory. Speaking to him brought a flood of memories racing back into his conscious mind. Only now did he realise how much of his past he had blocked out.

Ryder had only seen his mother twice after joining the army. In his first year of service, he had received a phone call from her, begging him to come home after what she described as an attack on her life. Taking compassionate leave, Ryder discovered there had indeed been an attack, but it had been self-inflicted. Her doctor told him that if she had cut any deeper, they wouldn't have been able to save her.

Maria started using crack cocaine and heroin heavily. Without Ryder at home, she only had herself for company, and that was something she had never been comfortable with. After a life living in a grand manor with a constant stream of visitors and waiting staff, she never had time to be alone growing up. After leaving the family sanctum, Maria realised quickly that she couldn't cope with being alone.

With a family fortune tucked away in the bank, the then young, slim and attractive woman discovered nightclubs open until dawn and all the people who frequented them. She threw lavish parties for her new friends, who were only too happy to spend time with someone so generous with their money.

Maria felt alive in these moments, yet when the parties ended and the caterers had packed up and left, she found herself alone once again. In those times, she considered moving back to Braighton Manor, but felt she was too old to be under the watchful eyes of her parents. She needed her independence, to make her own friends and her own way in life, believing the loneliness would pass in time. She dabbled with work, but nothing seemed to stick. Maria lived for the nightlife, not the grind of nine-to-five.

Nights were quiet and made her uneasy. It was difficult finding new friends who wanted to stay awake with her, so she entered the dating scene. At first, men were taken aback with how quickly she wanted to sleep with them. For Maria, it was less about sex and more about companionship. She was soon sleeping with a handful of different men on a regular basis. Having someone's arms wrapped around her as they slept made her feel safe and loved, although, deep down, she knew that it was mostly unrequited.

These relationships fizzled out fast and she found herself visiting the bars and clubs more often. It wasn't long before she was offered drugs and even though all her senses told her not to, she justified it as a means of keeping people around her for longer. Cocaine, amphetamines and ecstasy brought in a new wave of people; caterers were replaced by drug dealers and her parties went from two days a week to almost seven.

Ryder was conceived in the midst of these drug-fuelled and sex-filled parties. Maria had no girlfriends but plenty of male companions who were only too willing to satisfy her seemingly never-ending desires. As for the true knowledge of Ryder's biological father, Maria could barely remember her own name in those moments, let alone the men she slept with.

Through the nine months of pregnancy, Maria moved back to Braighton Manor. In a rare moment of clarity, she had reasoned this was the right thing to do, as she didn't want to expose her unborn child to the seedy, party world. Lord and Lady Braighton were only too happy to take their daughter in. Close friends of the family warned of a potential scandal an illegitimate child could cause, suggesting abortion as being the best course of action, but her parents wouldn't hear of it. This may have been unexpected, but the unborn baby was already a Braighton, and the child of their only daughter.

The first two years of Ryder's life were spent on the grounds of Braighton Manor. A nanny had been on-call, twenty-four hours a day, but was rarely required; Maria never wanted to leave her son's side. He was her true treasure and the reason she awoke with a smile on her face every morning.

Ryder and his mother moved from the family home into a luxurious garden flat in Kensington. Maria no longer felt alone while Ryder was with her and her sordid past seemed like a distant memory. The next three years were the best of Maria's life. She developed friendships with local mothers and regularly had coffee mornings while their children ran around the large home.

It wasn't until Ryder started school that Maria began to fall back into her old ways. The other mothers returned to work as their children no longer needed them throughout the day, and Maria found herself alone once again. Despair and loneliness enveloped her as she counted down the minutes until her son returned. Art classes, bicycle rides, museum exhibitions — what was the point of anything unless she had someone to share them with? On weekends, she spoiled her little boy, taking him all over London, enjoying every moment she could.

As Ryder grew, he developed his own friendships, leaving Maria alone again.

On his seventh birthday, Ryder was dropped off with his grandparents for the weekend. He was going through what his mother called his "space phase" and would only wear a NASA costume he had received as a present. He argued with his mother when she tried to get him to change clothes, reminding her that she had said he could wear anything he wanted on his birthday.

With tensions running high, neither spoke on the drive to Braighton Manor and when Ryder refused to kiss his mother goodbye, Maria drove away in floods of tears. Five days passed, and when she returned the following Wednesday evening, she looked weathered and worn-out. To explain her extended absence, Maria said that she had been struck down with a bout of flu. Lord Braighton wasn't convinced, but naively chose to believe his daughter.

As the years passed, Ryder grew up watching his mother's exuberant lifestyle from a distance. He spent a lot of his childhood with his grandparents at the Manor or was shipped off on extended school trips to keep him out of sight of his mother's recreational activities.

He became introverted, pushing potential friends away before they could learn the truth about his family life. Braighton Manor became his playground and the only place he could really relax, although as he entered his teenage years, he began to resent his grandparents for not doing more to help his mother. Until today, he had not known about the money and support given to Maria by his grandfather and he'd totally forgotten his childhood initiation into the army and just how close he and Lord Braighton had once been.

For years, Ryder watched his mother bring countless men back to the house, injecting and smoking anything she could get her hands on, totally forgetting about her son, sometimes for days on end. He learned to feed and dress himself from the age of eight. His schoolwork suffered and his mood declined, never recovering until the day he left for the army.

When he arrived at his mother's flat after his first year of service, he regarded the once-beautiful garden, which was now an overgrown mess of weeds and unkempt bushes. Opening the door to her apartment, he was met with a build-up of uncollected post and newspapers jamming the entrance. He pushed his way through and looked around his childhood home.

The floors were filthy, piles of shoes had been kicked off and left where they'd landed, bins were overflowing, and the kitchen sink was full of dirty dishes and decaying food. There was a stale smell of smoke emanating from the drawing-room and as he entered, he could see from a glance that his mother's overindulgent lifestyle had finally taken its toll.

Taking leave from the army to witness his mother once again

in this state angered Ryder as much as it upset him. Regardless of everything that had happened, he still loved her. With matted hair, filthy clothes hanging loose from her emaciated body and the distant look in her eyes which didn't even register his presence, it was clear she needed professional help.

Ryder checked her into a rehab clinic and contacted his grandfather to pay and keep her there. After spending the whole day together, she began to brighten up. She was happy to spend time with her son, although Ryder suspected she would have been just as happy for anyone to be paying her attention again. Satisfied with the facility and the clinical staff, he informed his mother that he had to go back to work.

As he leaned in to kiss her goodbye, she spat in his face and told him to leave her, just like all the other men in her life. As the nurse led her away, she screamed at him, calling him a bastard. As Ryder walked out of the clinic, wiping saliva and tears from his face, he promised himself he would never be dragged into her world again. For thirteen years, his mother's phone calls and letters went unanswered as Ryder concentrated on his life in the army.

Throughout his service, he had been promoted many times and was now Captain and second-in-command for over a hundred soldiers in Afghanistan. Just six months after this promotion, he was called home to attend his mother's funeral.

Years previously, she had been diagnosed with schizophrenia and moved to a psychiatric hospital. Her doctor believed this was likely due to her heavy drug-use. With therapy, counselling and a concoction of prescription medication, she had begun to reach a state of equilibrium.

Maria had tried many times to contact her son but had never succeeded. She wanted to make amends for the years of neglect and to ease her own guilty conscience, but he never responded. Maria's letters had gone unread and Ryder avoided all of her calls. It was only when a telegram from Braighton Manor was handed to him that he knew the day he had been dreading had finally arrived.

When he saw his mother for the final time, she was lying in a coffin, dressed in a high-necked blouse to hide the rope marks. Ryder was overcome with emotion. She looked still and peaceful and, for the first time since Ryder was an infant, she actually looked like a mother. A tear slipped down his face and landed on her cheek, making it appear as if she were crying, too. He bent down and kissed her forehead.

"I forgive you, Mum, and I love you. I hope you finally find peace."

After the funeral, Ryder had taken a few days off to sort out his mother's belongings before heading back to the army, all without a word to his grandparents. He blamed them for her death as much as he blamed himself for not being with his mother in her last few months.

He decided that work would take his mind off everything, but he couldn't concentrate on his job. The more he tried to put the thoughts of his mother to the back of his mind, the more they resurfaced and distracted him from his work. Work which put his life and the lives of a hundred cadets at risk.

It was this lapse in concentration that had almost gotten him killed when he drove his Jeep into an area covered with landmines. Luckily, no-one else in his battalion had been near the blast and he was the only person injured.

Doctors told him that he was lucky to be alive, but Ryder wished he wasn't. The army was his life; all his friends, his colleagues and his future had been taken from him that day. Now, he was doomed to live out a new, unwanted existence. Ryder's legs would never work again, and he had no training or experience that didn't involve them. The pay-out from the army was decent for a thirty-five-year-old, but he hadn't counted on his disability restricting him as much as it did.

For a long time, he was in too much pain to leave his home. He had his shopping delivered and "gourmet" microwave meals became his everyday fuel. Through sheer boredom, he started online gambling.

Star Wheel Casino opened up a new life for Ryder. At first,

he didn't notice the amount of money he was wasting on this new source of entertainment and social interaction. By the time he did realise, he no longer cared. He couldn't stop playing now; he would lose the only shred of existence he had left. That's when the drinking began. Alcohol numbed the pain, both physically and psychologically.

Excessive drinking may have been the fuel to continue this destructive lifestyle, but it was also the one to take it away. Falling asleep at his keyboard one morning, he knocked over an open bottle of vodka which drenched his computer, rendering it useless. It took five days for a new PC to be delivered, during which time Ryder had sobered up and realised that his life was spiralling out of control.

He had squandered his money and savings and was now massively in debt. He thought of his mother in her coffin and understood how easy it was to slip into a life beyond control. It was at that moment he knew he needed help.

His doctor had contacted a charity for former military workers with disabilities. Four years ago, Ryder had refused their help. As he blamed himself for his accident, he didn't believe he deserved it. Now, with a clear head and no real friends to talk to, he let the charity worker into his home. Once a week, someone bought his shopping, prepared meals and cleaned his flat.

After spending the majority of his life in the army, Ryder was used to having people around him which was why he had opted to live in central London. A city with millions of inhabitants, yet total anonymity. No inane conversations, no looks of pity; just people dashing around and looking through him like he wasn't there, just the way he wanted them to. He felt comforted by the mass of people but didn't need their intervention.

Now, with three months' rent arrears, it was a terrifying thought that he may have to move into the suburbs or even out of London altogether. His disability had bought him a little more time, but there was only so much goodwill his landlord would show. It was now Ryder realised just how much of his mother's phobia of being alone he had inherited.

After everything that had happened, he was once again back at the Manor, looking into his estranged grandfather's eyes with all the pain and suffering he had borne throughout his life, knowing his entire future was balanced precariously on this one conversation.

CHAPTER 4

San Francisco

On her ninth birthday, Abby was still a regular girl. She excelled in school, had lots of friends and was the loving and loved daughter of Shira and Oren Rosenberg. Everything was perfect until six months later, when her father disappeared, and the nightmares began.

She would often dream terrifying and disturbing images which would jolt her back into the real world and keep her awake for the rest of the night. The Shadow Man. At first, he was harmless and intriguing; a dark silhouette whom Abby wanted to reach out and touch. As the months passed, the man appeared more frequently and became a welcome and comforting figure.

She remembered the first time he became malevolent. The dream had begun benignly enough, with a visit to a local funfair. She looked up at the Ferris wheel, where people were laughing and enjoying themselves as the cars whizzed by. Abby was mesmerised by the big, colourful structure towering above her and desperately wanted to ride it.

With her head tilted to one side, she recognised the Shadow Man passing in one of the cars. He was sitting on his own and looking out, surveying the fair. Abby waved to catch his attention and tried to focus to see him more clearly; her hard gaze set on that one carriage. The man turned his head suddenly towards her, and instead of a face, all Abby could see were the man's red eyes burning menacingly into hers.

Fear overtook her and she tightened her grip on her mother's hand for protection. Closing her eyes, she tried desperately to erase the vision of the man and bring back the feeling of joy she had felt just moments before. She waited a long time before she dared to open her eyes again and look up at the Ferris wheel. The Shadow Man was gone. Relief swept over the young girl and she exhaled a long, slow breath. It was just her imagination, she told herself.

Smiling, she looked up at her mom, still holding her hand, but instead of Shira's face, she was met with the burning eyes of the Shadow Man staring down at her. Abby tried to run away, but he held on to her hand tightly, restricting her movement. He pulled her towards him more closely and it seemed like he wanted to bear down and envelope her. Abby screamed at the top of her lungs, and the next thing she knew, she was back in her bedroom with her mother by her side.

From that moment, the Shadow Man became a regular visitor to Abby's dreams; sometimes as the main character, other nights simply a presence in the background, tainting even the most pleasant of moments.

Concerned for her daughter's wellbeing, Shira had taken Abby to see their family doctor.

"I'm quite confident that these dreams will pass in no time. Try not to worry too much and if that nasty Shadow Man keeps bothering you, tell him if he doesn't behave, your mother and I will tell him off."

Abby smiled at the doctor, who had looked after her all her life.

"Now, if you could wait outside for a few minutes, please, Abby, while I chat to your mommy. If you speak to Janine at the front desk, I'm sure she'll have a lollipop for you." The doctor winked.

Abby, reassured, bounced out of her seat with a smile on her face.

Once the door had closed behind her, Dr Wanda Philips turned to Shira with a concerned look on her face.

"How are you holding up?"

Shira sighed slowly and allowed a small tear to escape her eye.

"I'm a mess," she admitted. "I'm hurting over losing Oren, but I can't give myself time to grieve because I'm too worried about Abby. Every night, sometimes more than once, I'm woken up by her screaming. It's terrifying. Sometimes I can't wake her, and I don't know what I'm supposed to do. Do you really think these dreams will stop soon?"

"Honestly, I don't know. She's at a very impressionable age. This is almost certainly a reaction to losing her father the way she did — the way you both did — but it's quite an extreme and rare symptom. I did some research into it after you called last week. I found some information that might help." Wanda riffled through some papers on her desk and handed some printouts to Shira. "But I'm also worried about you," she continued. "We've known each other a long time. It's not a good idea to bottle up your feelings. It's understandable to be concerned for Abby, but you need to give yourself time to grieve and heal, too. Can I set up an appointment with the counsellor here at the clinic? She's very good."

"Thank you. I know you're right, but I can't think about myself while Abby's going through all this. Once everything's settled down, I promise I'll see someone."

"OK." The doctor didn't sound convinced, but knew better than to pressure someone who was clearly struggling. "In the meantime, you can always talk to me." Wanda gestured to the papers in Shira's hand. "And hopefully these will help with Abby. It's only been a few months since the funeral. Give her some time to adjust. If these dreams persist or they seem to be getting worse, come back here and we'll look at other options."

Shira smiled and stood to leave the office.

"Thank you."

"It will get better, you know," Wanda said reassuringly as Shira left the room, walking straight into the arms of her beloved daughter.

Abby's dreams got worse. After a year of troubled sleep, she was too afraid even to go to bed, keeping herself awake throughout the night and then, inevitably, falling asleep at school. Many more visits to the doctor were scheduled until Wanda reluctantly prescribed Abby mild sleeping pills to help her rest at night. The dreams were diagnosed as night terrors, but Wanda was still certain they would go away naturally, given time.

Soon after her twelfth birthday, Abby was reaching breaking point. Wanda had referred her to a child psychiatrist and, although her mother could barely afford it, Shira was taking her to see Dr Richmond on a weekly basis. Although the therapist came highly recommended and had helped many children in the past suffering from grief and disturbed sleep, Shira feared that it was too little, too late.

The Shadow Man was no longer contained to the dream world; Abby had begun to see him even when she was awake. He was in the supermarket; he was on the swings in the park; and he rode the cable-car with them every day. Abby was even convinced that he had taken up residence in the attic, right above her bedroom, waiting for her to fall to sleep so he could attack her. Nowhere felt safe for Abby, and Shira felt powerless to protect her.

A year ago, in yet another attempt to try to improve things for her daughter, Shira had taken Abby out of the public education system. Abby suffered frequent panic attacks in class or fell asleep at her desk. Her teacher sympathised with the situation but believed it would be better for everyone if Abby was home-schooled. Shira had been worried about how she would be able to afford a private tutor, but Miss Templeton had suggested her friend and former student.

"Lidia's a lovely girl. She's just finished her training and she's been looking for work. I've told her all about Abby and she would love the opportunity to tutor her. I've also had a word with Dean Braxton, and he believes we can use school funding to pay part of Lidia's salary," Miss Templeton told Shira.

"I don't know what to say. Thank you so much."

"We're all aware of the situation. We want to help as much as we can," Miss Templeton offered with a sincere smile.

As Abby no longer felt safe on her own, it was comforting for Shira that her daughter and Lidia had hit it off so well. Being home-schooled appeared to benefit Abby, as had been hoped. Lidia was a patient tutor who helped improve the young girl's grades and start to rebuild the confidence she had lost in her mainstream classroom. It also meant that Shira could find part-time work during the hours when Lidia was with Abby. This gave them just enough money to afford the ever-rising medical bills.

"How was school today?"

It was Friday evening and Lidia had just left, leaving behind a stack of homework for Abby to complete over the weekend. Shira had found a part-time job in a restaurant on Fisherman's Wharf. The pay wasn't great, but being situated in a tourist area, the tips mostly made up for the low wage. With her husband gone, money had been extremely tight, and Shira was pleased to find a job to support her and her teenage daughter.

Abby looked up from the book she was reading.

"It was good, thanks, Mom. Although I'm not sure if I will ever understand the difference between a noun and a pronoun."

"Don't ask me," Shira laughed. "It's been a long time since I learned all that stuff. Actually, I've never really known what the difference is and I'm doing OK. But don't tell Lidia that! A good friend once told me that language is fluid and ever-changing, so who knows; maybe someday, someone will pop them together to stop them being so confusing."

Abby laughed. Her mother could always make her smile. The little things she said or did could always brighten even her darkest moods.

Shira hung her jacket behind the door and put the shopping bags she had been carrying on the dining-table.

"I popped into the supermarket on my way home and bought us some nice veg to go with that brisket you like."

Abby tried to hide the dismay on her face. She may have liked her mother's stew the first few hundred times, but now it was more like a punishment. Abby knew how tight money was, though, and would never complain about what her mother provided for them.

"But then as I was walking through Chinatown —" Shira continued as she emptied the bags "— I thought, how about having take-out instead . . ."

Abby's face lit up as she saw her mother produce small boxes hidden inside one of the supermarket bags. She set the table hurriedly as Shira laid out spring rolls, Kung Pao chicken and fried rice on to two plates. They sat down, ready to start their meal, just as the phone rang.

"Isn't it always the way? You sit down to enjoy dinner and the phone rings." Shira stopped serving, stood up from the table and walked over to the phone. "Hello?"

"Hello, could I speak with Mrs Rosenberg, please?"

"Yes, this is she. If this is a sales call, I'm currently in the middle of dinner. Could you call back later?"

"Oh, I do apologise. Of course, we can talk some other time, but this isn't a sales call. My name's Doctor Sharma and I work for a company called Silicate. We're based in London."

"Silicate? I've never heard of it."

"I'd be surprised if you had. Let me get straight to the point, Mrs Rosenberg. We believe we can help your daughter."

CHAPTER 5

Yorkshire

"Well, bugger me! How much have I been drinking, Betty? I think I'm starting to hallucinate. I swear I just saw Jake Hampton walk in here, but that can't be right, can it? He doesn't mingle with us common folk any more." The rugged farmer moved away from the barmaid and over to Jake, who was standing at the door with a huge smile on his face. He greeted his old friend with a manly hug. "What are you doing in here, Jake? I haven't seen you in bloody ages."

"Hey, Toby, it's good to see you. Sorry I've not been in sooner. I've been working flat-out since Christmas."

"Well it's bloody good to see you, how about a pint?"

"Would love one, thanks, mate."

The Hayward Arms was Jake's local, though he'd rarely had the time to visit since his father's death. Frequented predominantly by farmers, this was a typical country pub. Open fire, cask ales and burly men and women laughing and joking while an Eighties CD played on repeat in the background. The digital age hadn't made a big impact on this rural community in the heart of the Yorkshire Dales.

His pint was light on the head and heavy on the alcohol, just the way he liked it. Jake downed a quarter of the glass in one gulp.

"Bloody hell! Looks like you needed that," Toby observed.

Jake wiped the froth from his upper lip and smiled. He'd been so focused on running the farm that he'd forgotten about taking time for himself. He may have only been twenty-six years old, but his hair and beard were already showing signs of grey. Working long hours, having little sleep, and the daily stress of not knowing if he had enough money to pay the bills had aged him prematurely.

As a boy, he'd looked up to his father, but it was only now that he realised just how incredible a man he had been. If it hadn't been for the tumour, Jake was sure that his father would still be working the land at sixty-seven years old, and somehow managing to stumble back from the pub every night, too.

As a child, Jake's parents were everything to him. He'd wanted to work the land and stay in Malham for the rest of his life, just like generations of his family before him. He'd fully expected to raise his own family on the farm and live a happy and productive life, just like his parents and grandparents.

All that seemed impossible now. He was on his own, and the land which had once appeared so green and promising now felt stark and depressing.

Two weeks ago, he'd fallen asleep at the wheel of his tractor and not woken up until past midday. Missing the morning on a farm was akin to not working for a whole week, his father used to say. As he awoke from that much-needed rest, Jake realised none of this mattered any more. His father's final words had echoed around his head for years, and in response, Jake had done everything in his power to live up to the promise he'd made.

Now, a new voice grew in his head, one he hadn't heard before, but one which seemed to speak the truth. His mother and father were dead; their savings had been wiped out and Jake was living hand-to-mouth, desperately trying to survive on the paltry sum his farm turned over. Over the next few days, as this new voice developed in his head, he believed, if he stayed any longer doing what he had been, he would surely be reduced to watching his beloved home rot and decay in front of his eyes. For two years he had given Upper Malham Farm everything he had and received nothing in return. Something needed to change.

Jake was a little apprehensive as he picked up the phone, but after speaking with the local property realter, he felt the massive weight he had been carrying on his shoulders suddenly lift.

Things moved quickly and soon a date was set to sell the farm and all its assets. Mr Peatree, a short, stout man with a heavy, tobacco-stained moustache, was acting as seller and auctioneer. As he looked around the farm, he rubbed his hands together enthusiastically.

"I knew your father, young man. Made him an offer on this farm many times after your poor mother died, but he wouldn't have it. I told him he could make more money selling than he ever could working it, but he was too sentimental. I'm glad to see you've got more sense. Upper Malham Farm's a prime piece of land, my boy. We'll both do well from this."

Jake thought Mr Peatree was an odious little man who only cared about money, but he was good at his job and was certain to deliver a good return. Trying to decide where he'd live after the farm was sold, one place kept coming to mind: London.

It was a city so far removed from the life he knew that he questioned his own judgement; yet, every night in bed, as he tried to picture his new life, he kept feeling that London was where he was meant to be. Where he *needed* to be. The more he thought about it, the more attractive London became. Maybe it was the place where he could finally be himself.

Jake had always known he was gay, but with the hopes and dreams of his parents weighing heavily upon him, he hadn't allowed himself to even consider a lifestyle which didn't include the farm and a family of his own. Jake had forced himself to believe that being married to a woman would break his desires, but as he grew older, he realised that wasn't the case.

At thirteen, he spent the summer in a state of confusion.

He couldn't stop looking at the topless farmhands as they worked the land and couldn't understand why. As his obsession grew, he became aware of what he was, but was too ashamed to tell anyone or act on his instincts.

To try to squash these unwanted thoughts and desires, he worked longer and harder than he ever had before in the vain hope of leaving his mind too tired to stray to the places he felt uncomfortable with. He tried praying the gay away, but this, too, was a fruitless endeavour.

If he could have chosen not to be gay, he would have. As an adult, he accepted that his sexuality was as much a part of him as the colour of his skin or the size of his hands, realising sexuality is not something we get to choose.

He may have accepted this, but thought no-one else would. He couldn't tell anyone for fear of embarrassing or upsetting his parents. As much as they loved him, Jake believed they would never understand. And so, he buried who he was from them.

Now that they had passed, he could have announced to the village that he was gay; two years on, he still hadn't. Perhaps he had used his parents as an excuse — maybe he was simply too scared to tell anyone. The more time passed, the more frustrated Jake became. He wasn't being true to himself, but what would — or even could — change by telling people now? Instead, he poured all his time and energy into the farm, following his father's final wish.

He knew now was the time to move on from this place, to discover himself and build a life which was truly his own.

Not that he could say any of this to Toby, of course. His old school friend and fellow farmer was a great guy, but not the worldliest person. Toby had married the girl he had dated in high school; ten years later, they had two children together with a third on the way. To tell Toby he was selling up, moving to London and on the hunt for the perfect man was a concept Jake believed he wouldn't understand. Instead, they enjoyed a few drinks together, reminiscing nostalgically and enjoying each other's company.

Before heading back home, Jake stumbled over to the local graveyard to say a final farewell to his parents. The moon shone brightly in the night sky as he walked over to the plot of land directly behind the small, parish church. Only slightly inebriated, Jake sat in front of the simple gravestones. It had been a while since his last visit, and the flowers he'd placed on his mother's grave had wilted and dried out. He read her slightly faded epitaph and smiled. *To a beautiful wife and mother. Wait for us while you sleep. When the time comes, we shall all be reunited for eternity*. He remembered helping his father with the inscription; his dad had struggled to find the right words. Without his help, Jake had found it even harder to write an inscription on his own eight years later. *To a loving father and husband. Be at peace in your eternal sleep.*

Jake's heart felt heavy. He had been worrying about this moment for weeks, but the alcohol had temporarily given him the confidence to finally speak to them.

"Hi, Mum. Hi, Dad. I'm leaving Malham tomorrow, and I'm not planning on coming back for some time. I'm sorry I didn't live up to your expectations, Dad. I really have tried. But the farm's losing money and I know I'm doing more harm than anything else. I'm just not as good a farmer as you were.

"Tomorrow, our old home's being auctioned off and then, in the evening, I'll be on a train to London. I know this isn't what you expected of me, and I'm sorry. I just can't do this any more. The world's changed, there's no money in agriculture. I feel totally alone here with you both gone. Selling up is my only option.

"Hopefully, whoever buys the farm will be more cut out for it than I am." Jake struggled to contain his tears as he stared at the gravestones. "Mum, you always told me that I could be the best at whatever I wanted to be. When you were both alive, I wanted to be a farmer and carry on the family line. I realise now that I only wanted that for you guys. In all honesty, it's just not who I am. I don't want this life.

"You both loved me, and I love you still, and I know I'm letting you down, but I hope you realise that I'm following my own path. The last thing I want to do is not live up to your expectations, but I also know that you would want me to be happy. And now, by doing this, I think I can be. If I can find someone to love and be half as happy as you were, I know I'll have lived an amazing life."

Jake wiped his eyes and looked up at the clear, night sky.

"There's so much I don't know, so many places I haven't been to and so much I haven't done. Now I can. I love you both."

The short walk back to the farm was slow as the heavy, emotional weight returned to his shoulders. It seemed that with every step he took, a new worry to obsess over sprung to his mind. Why was he selling his home? Why was he going to London, of all places? Why hadn't he given himself more time to think this through? For two weeks, he'd been gung-ho about everything; but now, he wasn't sure if he was making the right decision or not. Eventually, he wrapped himself tightly in the bed-sheets and stared at the ceiling for a long time before falling into a restless sleep.

He awoke to the sound of banging. Standing only in boxer shorts as he opened the farmhouse door, Mr Peatree burst inside without saying a word. Clipboard in hand, the man nodded and ticked boxes on a sheet of paper as he surveyed the contents of the property. Jake had decided to sell everything except for the clothes on his back and a suitcase containing a few sentimental memories.

"I'll get dressed, then, shall I?" Jake's question was met with barely a grunt in response from the stocky, middle-aged man, who continued to check the boxes on his list without looking up.

Showered and dressed, Jake stepped outside to see a gathering of people milling around the outhouses. Mr Peatree stood by the first barn, talking excitedly to a group of farmers, one of whom Jake recognised.

Toby walked over to him.

"Why didn't you tell me you were selling up?"

"I thought you'd try to talk me out of it," Jake replied apologetically. He didn't want to upset his friend, particularly before leaving.

"Mate, I'm surprised you stuck it out this long. There's no way I could've managed this place on my own. When your old man passed, I was sure you'd have to pack it all in. Well done for sticking at it this long."

Feeling reassured, he and Toby walked over to the group of farmers waiting for the auction to start. For the first time, Jake knew that he was making the right decision. It was time to start living his own life.

◆ ◆ ◆

Kent

The old man's eyes were grey and filled with pain. Ryder knew that he, too, blamed himself for Maria's death.

"I'll help you, Ryder, but I won't make the same mistakes again. By handing you money, it would feel like history repeating itself. I accept and can see for myself that your needs are genuine, but you must understand that I lost my only daughter, and I'll be damned if I allow the same thing to happen to my only grandson. I'll pay the rent on your apartment for the next year, including any arrears you've gotten into. I'll also employ a driver to help with transportation. I imagine that your movements are somewhat restricted at present — I can see no better way of getting you motivated.

"Finally, Ryder . . . I'm going to give you a job."

Lord Braighton waited for his words to sink in before continuing.

"I once proudly served in Her Majesty's Royal Airforce and I know the military's much more than guns and running for your life. I presume you're trained in weapons and explosives as well as dealing with potentially dangerous situations?"

"Yes, of course, sir."

"Then you're just the man I'm looking for."

"Thank you, sir." Ryder was confused yet grateful.

Lord Braighton nodded and picked up a telephone which rested next to the bottle of Cognac.

"Hello. Yes, we're ready for you now. We'll be out shortly." He put down the phone. "That was Charlie, my driver. He'll take you to Saville Row in London, where you can pick out some new suits and clothes. Best to make a good impression on your first day, eh?" The old man smiled.

Ryder was about to launch into a series of questions, but without missing a beat, the lord continued.

"We have an account with a store there, so don't worry about money. In time, you'll be earning a regular income and I'm happy to help you on to that path, any way I can."

He opened the doors and led the way out of the living room and into the high-ceilinged hallway. The driver was waiting patiently, ready to help Ryder into the car. Once the clumsy manoeuvre was complete, Lord Braighton bent down next to him, waiting until Charlie was out of earshot before speaking.

"You won't understand this now, Ryder," he whispered, "but I expect you to take care of them. You're one of the few people I can trust with this assignment. You'll understand what I mean when the time comes."

The lord closed the passenger door and waved his confused grandson farewell as the car travelled down the driveway.

The events of the next twelve hours progressed quickly. Ryder's shopping trip had ended with a trunk full of brand-new clothes, including several suits costing more than a thousand pounds apiece. Charlie drove him to his flat and informed him he would be waiting outside for him the following morning.

As soon as he was alone, Ryder switched on his computer and began searching for any information he could find. His grandfather owned many companies, but only one of them was based in London: Silicate. The information was sparse and was of little help to him, especially as he had no idea what role he was being hired for. He discovered Silicate had been registered shortly after his mother's death and was already worth several billion pounds. They didn't seem to manufacture nor sell anything; they didn't list their investors, and none of the staff were credited. Why all the secrecy, he wondered. It wasn't likely that his grandfather had recreated Willy Wonka's chocolate factory, was it? Ryder smiled wryly to himself at the thought.

As promised, Charlie was parked outside Ryder's flat at eight in the morning the following day, a letter waiting for him inside the car with further instructions from his grandfather. He was to meet a doctor in the reception of Silicate at nine a.m. Why all the secrecy and lack of information, Ryder wondered as they drove the short distance to The Particle, a huge glass building towering into the sky, high above central London.

As he wheeled himself through the main doors, Ryder couldn't quite believe the size of the place. Created to look like millions of glass particles bonded together, every room was spherical. The huge, domed windows of the foyer appeared to continue through the walls and ceiling, simulating the feeling of being an electron moving around inside. It was an impressive feat of engineering that wasn't lost on the former soldier. He marvelled at the architecture as he moved towards one of the many glass elevators. Maybe this is Willy Wonka's factory, after all, he thought to himself with a smile.

As the elevator raced up towards his destination, he watched the lower floors disappear beneath him. Looking around, he noticed a gold plaque above the door, it informed him that The Particle was the largest man-made structure in the world.

The doors opened on to Silicate's reception. Positioned near the top of the building, this, too, was built to resemble a glass bubble. As Ryder entered, he was overwhelmed by the number of people moving around him. Suited men and women rushed in and out, never averting their gaze from their phones and tablets. Ryder wondered how they didn't crash into each other.

Managing to advance through them unscathed, he admired the beautiful surroundings. Silicate had impressive views of the city below through its circumference of glass.

He pushed his chair over to the large seating area and positioned himself at the side of a red, wrap-around sofa. He fidgeted in his brand-new suit as he waited. Looking around, he saw huge packages being carried through a door marked *Deliveries only*, while the four receptionists answered calls and tapped away frantically on their keyboards.

What did this company do, Ryder wondered. A huge, digital clock above reception displayed the current time in ten different countries; the central clock was GMT. Just ten more minutes until I find out, Ryder thought.

CHAPTER 6

London

Jake stepped off the train and surveyed the sea of people around him. Kings Cross was bigger and busier than he'd imagined. The high-roofed structure echoed noise from the passengers and trains moving through the busy station. Before today, the furthest he'd travelled was to the west coast as a boy. He remembered thinking, back then, that Blackpool must have been the busiest place on Earth; he now realised just how sheltered his life had been. He threw his rucksack over his shoulders and carried a small, battered suitcase in his right hand. He disguised his nervousness as best he could as he walked to the end of the platform.

The sale of Upper Malham Farm had gone well. Mr Peatree had smiled widely when he saw the final total, no doubt calculating his ten per cent cut. The money would take a few months to filter through to Jake's bank account; in the meantime, he had procured a bridging loan through Mr Peatree, which would last him until the end of the year, if needed.

As he followed the signs towards the taxi rank, Jake dug into his pocket and fished out a scrappy piece of paper with the address of his new home written in pencil. An estate agent was to meet him there in thirty minutes. His mother had always been a fan of Abba's music, and so, in memory of her, he rented an apartment in Waterloo. He wouldn't find out until many years later that the Waterloo Abba sang about was actually in Belgium; not that it would have mattered. Knowing very little about London, this seemed as good a place as any to begin his new life. He put the note back into his pocket and joined the long queue for a black cab.

The taxi ride was invigorating. Seeing the famous landmarks of the nation's capital for the first time was exciting; the British Museum, Leicester Square, the London Eye . . . He stared up in awe as they drove past the Palace of Westminster. It all seemed so surreal to actually be here, seeing these familiar sights with his own eyes. As the cab crossed over Lambeth Bridge, the Thames appeared tranquil in the soft, evening light. Boats sailed by on the water below whilst tourists snapped pictures of their friends on either side of the bridge.

A smiling, well-dressed woman was waiting at the entrance of Westminster Apartments. Jake had chosen this modern, curved-glass building purely on its aesthetics. Moving from a rundown farmhouse in the middle of the Yorkshire Dales to this futuristic tower overlooking the capital seemed to mirror his own dramatic change in life.

"Mr Hampton, welcome to London."

The estate agent was everything her voice had portrayed; dyed-blonde hair pulled tight into a bun, a smart, navy-blue dress suit and a gleaming, white-toothed smile. He shook her hand firmly as the taxi driver pulled away.

"It's good to finally meet you, Marion."

The estate agent looked down at the small suitcase by Jake's feet.

"Are the rest of your belongings in transit?"

"Nope. I've left everything behind. New home, new me. The only clothes I have are the ones I'm wearing, and I doubt the 'farmer grunge' look is in this season."

"You'd be surprised. You'll fit right in around Shoreditch." Marion chuckled as she led Jake into the building.

"Here we are — floor twelve, apartment fifteen. Unfortunately, the penthouses are all occupied at the moment, but

I don't think you'll be disappointed with the view from this height."

Jake walked through the plush, minimalistic living space towards the room-length windows. Dusk was settling over the city and streetlights were flickering on across London.

"It's breath-taking!" Jake could hardly contain his excitement. "I can't believe I get to look at Big Ben every day."

Marion joined him at the window.

"Actually, Big Ben's the name of the bell inside of Queen Elizabeth Tower. Only tourists call the building Big Ben because they don't know better. As you're a resident now, it's good you know these things." She smiled warmly before continuing, "Across the river, behind Parliament, you can see Westminster Abbey and, beyond that, Hyde Park and Paddington in the far distance."

"As in the bear Paddington?"

Marion laughed.

"Yes, I suppose so." She moved to face the opposite direction. "And from your bedroom window, on a good day, you can see Canary Wharf Tower."

Jake spun around and peered through the glass.

"Today is definitely a good day." As he looked around his new home, a burst of excitement rippled through his body, washing away the knots in his stomach. He looked at Marion with a beaming smile. "You did well. This place is perfect."

Once the paperwork had been signed, Marion left Jake to settle in to his new home. She had given him a map with several shopping locations marked in the city centre. His new housekeeper had fitted new sheets to the bed and fully stocked his fridge. That was something Jake would have to get used to — having his own housekeeper. He took a beer from the fridge and sipped it while leaning against the balcony rail. He watched people walk around below him. This was his first night in London; the first night in his new home; the first night of his new life.

After showering in the black, slate bathroom, he collapsed

on to the Egyptian-cotton sheets of his brand-new, king-size bed. He had wrestled with the idea of exploring this — *his* — new world, but exhaustion won out. As he closed his eyes, he smiled; this would be his first, restful night's sleep in years.

◆ ◆ ◆

"Mr Braighton?"

Ryder looked up to see an Indian man in a doctor's white coat smiling down at him.

"Sorry, I didn't mean to startle you. I'm Padman Sharma, thank you for waiting."

Ryder shook the man's offered hand.

"Good morning, Doctor Sharma. Please, call me Ryder."

"As long as you call me Padman."

"It's good to meet you, Padman. Sorry, I was lost in thought when you arrived. There's so much activity. Is this place always so busy?"

"Pretty much." Padman smiled. "Where we're going will be a lot quieter, though."

Padman had been top of his class at school, college and university. He had pushed himself hard to achieve the highest levels of education; gaining distinctions, honours and a position with a then-new company, Silicate. His father had been friends with Lord Braighton for many years and was one of the founding board members, but it was his son's knowledge and academic achievements which had earned him a place here, not his connections. Padman had proved time and again he was the best person for the job. Now in his forties, he was the facility's lead doctor and researcher.

His hair had started thinning in his late twenties. Rather than go for the balding teacher look, he shaved his head and grew in a designer stubble beard. He also spent a lot of his free time in the company gym. With so much responsibility on a daily basis, he found that loud music pumping through his headphones while he worked up a sweat on the treadmill was the best way for him to switch off from work. Years of this routine had toned his muscles, and his well-defined body was visible, subtly, beneath his clinical uniform.

Padman's father had objected to his less-than-traditional look, but his mother had said he reminded her of a young Arjun Rampal, her favourite Bollywood star, and that had let Padman off the hook. It wasn't easy being a modern, young man with a traditional Indian heritage, but he knew he could always count on his mother to have his back.

Padman led Ryder through the double doors into a smaller, sunlit room. The elevators were guarded by a security station with two stern-looking men sitting behind a desk.

"Good morning, Doctor Sharma," one of the guards said as they approached.

"Good morning, Sam. This is our new recruit, Ryder Braighton. He's to be our new head of security."

Padman noticed Ryder's eyes had widened into a look of shock.

"Could you print him up a security pass, please? He'll need clearance for all sections, including Archeus."

"Sure thing, Doctor." The guard tapped away at his computer keyboard. "Could you look into this camera, please, Mr Braighton?"

Still reeling from the information he'd just learned, Ryder peered into the small lens of the webcam mounted on the desk in front of him. He waited for the sound of a camera click but was instead greeted with the whirring of a printer starting.

"All done. There you are, Mr Braighton." Sam handed a card to Ryder: it was a white, credit card-sized piece of plastic with Ryder's name on it alongside a rather startled-looking photograph of him.

Padman chuckled as he led them to the first elevator.

"If you think that's bad, you should see the picture of me on my first day. I couldn't find the camera in time, so I'm looking off to the side with my mouth open. Before you ask, I updated the picture a few years ago once I knew where to look."

Ryder responded with a smile as they entered the lift together.

"I'm guessing from your reaction; you didn't know what position you were here for today?" Padman asked.

"You guess correctly."

"We do have tight security here, but your grandfather takes it a little too far sometimes." Padman smiled. "I've read your service record; you have every requirement we need for the position and I'm sure Lord Braighton wouldn't have offered you the job if he wasn't confident you were the perfect candidate."

The doors opened on to a smaller room with yet another security station, albeit with only one guard on duty. Beyond the desk was a large, white door. Engraved on a metal plate positioned at the upper portion of the door was the word *Hygge*.

"Here, you just need to scan your pass on this electronic reader by the desk so the guard can verify you have the correct clearance. You should register instantly and come up on Ted's screen." Padman motioned to the lone guard sitting behind the desk. "There's also a second reader by the side of the door to Hygge, which you'll also need to scan to get through. I did mention we were big on security here. Speaking of which, I have some legal documents for you to sign."

The security guard handed Padman a tablet which he clicked on and gave to Ryder. The file was labelled *Laboratory Staff Contract.* The bottom of the screen told him that this was page one of ninety-seven. Ryder stared in disbelief as he flicked through the electronic pages, reading words he could hardly pronounce.

Ryder was lost within the first few paragraphs; he was never one for reading documents, medical warnings or fine print. His brain clouded over as he stared vacantly at the contract.

"I doubt my grandfather's trying to get me killed, so I don't think I have anything to worry about." He flicked through to the final page and then, with Padman's assistance, to the end of the confidentiality agreement, and scrawled his signature with an electronic pen.

Padman took the tablet and emailed the documents to him-self before handing it back to Ted.

"Excellent. I promise you there's nothing to worry about in there, it's just highly secretive. You'll understand why very soon."

Padman scanned his security pass and Ryder followed suit.

"Thank you, Doctor Sharma, and good morning, Mr Braigh-ton." Ted smiled at them both as he read Ryder's name from his computer monitor.

"Thanks, Ted," Padman responded.

Ryder simply nodded with a smile as they moved towards the door. He felt a strange twinge of anticipation and un-steadiness which was an unfamiliar feeling for someone with his background and training. This all seemed rather surreal. He'd accepted a job, not knowing what the company did or what part he was to play in it.

"What is it you actually do here?"

"To answer that, seeing really is believing." Padman touched the security panel with his card and the door swung open. "This is the nerve centre of our entire operation."

"It's an empty room!" Ryder stared in bewilderment. There was nothing inside except for the four walls surrounding them and another door at the far end.

"This is just the buffer room, to protect against sound and light." Padman and Ryder moved forward through the silent space. White padding on the walls eliminated every sound, in-cluding footsteps and the wheels turning on the chair.

The twinge of anticipation grew in Ryder's stomach as they neared the far door. Padman scanned his card and the doors opened, bringing noise back into existence.

Rushing air was the prevailing sound here, followed by run-ning water. The expansive and dimly lit room was lined with a vast array of large, glass pods emanating light which projected in waves on to the sleek, metal walls. Each pod had what looked like a small diving board on the top, but no ladders to reach them. As they passed through the centre of the room, Ryder counted ten rows of two, lined up side-by-side, filling the entire space. The only light here was from each of the pods, with a rippling water effect bouncing out on to every surface. It reminded him of being submerged in the London Aquarium, without any of the fish.

In this tranquil setting, Ryder wondered why they were the only two people here. Then he spotted something. At first his brain disregarded it; but the more he focused, the more he realised he had not been mistaken. Of all the questions racing through his brain, only one escaped his lips.

"Is there someone inside that pod?"

"There is indeed. It looks like she's overslept again."

"There's someone asleep in there? But how? Wouldn't she drown?"

Padman let out a small chuckle.

"Ah, I see your conundrum."

Ryder followed Padman around to the far side of the pod. As they neared, Ryder could see the glass wasn't a solid mass at all. Up-close, he could now make out a rectangular-shaped groove running the full height of the pod and by the side of that was what looked like an entry security panel.

"It's a door!" Ryder exclaimed, almost to himself.

The doctor pressed his card against the electronic panel. A doorway emerged from the solid glass and glided open with a light hiss. Instinctively, Ryder shielded his face from the expected gush of water, but nothing came. Instead, a cool breeze of fresh air escaped the pod and the person inside began to stir.

"Good morning, Isabell, how did you sleep?" Padman asked as he walked into the pod.

An attractive woman with long, dark hair yawned, stretched and sat upright on what Ryder could now see was a bed.

"Good morning, Doctor Sharma. Did I oversleep again?"

"It appears so," Padman responded with a smile. He turned to a wide-eyed Ryder. "As you can see, the room is hollow. Each pod has two thick pieces of glass, half a metre apart, all the way around. They're held together by heavy-duty glass bolts, and the three hundred and sixty-degree gap in the middle is pumped full of water from an inlet on the roof."

A million more questions surfaced in Ryder's head and he stumbled with the most obvious. Padman had seen this look many times before. With Silicate's tight security measures, no-one knew what to expect before they entered Hygge and saw the pods for the first time.

"Before I answer any of the questions I'm sure you have, let me see to Isabell and then I can explain what it is we do here."

Isabell was still perched on the side of the bed, drinking from a bottle of water.

"What time is it?"

Padman checked his watch.

"It's almost ten. Why don't we pop into the Blue Room and we can wait while you freshen up?"

Isabell hopped off the bed and the three of them made their way past the other rows of pods to a small door at the end of the room. Inside, everything was coloured in different shades of blue. Even the lockers, sofas and changing facilities complimented the blue décor.

"The research guys advised that blue's the most calming colour and helps the volunteers relax before getting into the pods. Although they said the same about pink a few years ago. If you ask me, the contractors keep changing it so they can get more work." Padman turned to the woman, who was still yawning. "Isabell, if you want to get your clothes out of your locker, we can wait here until you've showered and dressed."

Ambling to the lockers, she pulled out a bag and headed off to shower.

"Each of our dressing-rooms is equipped with its own bathroom. Our volunteers' comfort is of utmost importance. Equally important is their having an empty bladder before entering the pods. We did try a catheter in the early days, but found that put unnecessary stress on patients and disturbed their sleep patterns. Now, we ask for them not to eat or drink for at least an hour before they arrive, and to spend another hour in here before they enter the lab. A bottle of water is provided for emergencies, but it's more for when they wake up. We minimize the number of 'accidents' that way."

"I have so many questions it's hard to know where to begin."

"I'd be surprised if you didn't. Once Isabell's away, we can go to my office and discuss everything in detail."

Isabell stepped out of the dressing-room; she was showered and changed. With a towel in hand, she rubbed the last remnants of water from her long hair and smiled.

"That's better; I feel human again. I can't believe you guys let me sleep in. Not that I'm complaining — I feel great for it." She turned to Ryder. "Hello, I'm Isabell. Are you a patient here? Or joining Doctor Sharma in watching me sleep?"

"Nice to meet you. I'm Ryder." He shook her hand. "It's my first day. I'm not entirely sure what it is I'll be doing yet."

"Ah, of course — the security measures. I've been coming here for six months and I still don't know exactly what this place does. But I get a good night's sleep on my visits, so that keeps me coming back."

"Do you sleep here every night?"

"Just once a week and then a therapy session a few days later. I've suggested they just install a pod in my bedroom so I can sleep there every night, but they haven't gone for that yet." Her smiled then faded to one of worry. "Every once in a while, I do get asked to visit Archeus, but luckily not too often..."

Padman rose from the aqua-blue sofa abruptly, cutting the conversation short.

"We should be getting on. Why don't we escort you out, Isabell?"

"Sounds good."

The three of them proceeded down a long corridor. As Isabell chatted with the doctor, Ryder watched the medical staff milling around. Two of them were holding what looked to be X-ray films, but he couldn't be sure. Three other people in lab coats were talking animatedly but quietly about something, stopping abruptly as they walked past. With nothing else to look at, Ryder listened absent-mindedly to the conversation continuing above him.

"... and as soon as we get the results back, we can arrange an appointment with Doctor Spelling."

"Cool. As always, I'll be at home writing, so whenever is fine with me. I'm sure I can pull myself away from Detective Oslo for you."

"How's the book coming along?"

"It's going OK, though the more time I spend here, the less I remember about my dreams. It's a good thing for my health, don't get me wrong, but not so good for a written account of what's been happening to me. I've started making up new characters that I haven't experienced before and trying to make them believable is proving difficult."

"I'm sure you'll make it work." Padman looked at Ryder. "Isabell is a very successful author of crime fiction. She bases her characters on people from her dreams."

"Meeting them in your dreams is one thing, but meeting them in real life? That's when I knew there was something wrong. No-one wants to find Vincent sitting at the end of their bed with a knife in his hand."

They exited the corridor and stood beside a waiting elevator.

"This is a private elevator with only three stops — here, the floor below, and The Particle entrance foyer," Padman explained to Ryder. "Lord Braighton had it designed into the plans so that the volunteers and staff would have easier access to the lab. It comes in most useful when you want to bypass reception. You've seen how busy it can get." He turned to Isabell. "Do you have your security pass with you?"

She looked through her handbag.

"I do somewhere. Ah, here it is. It's always hiding in the bottom." She looked up at Padman. "Give me a call when you want me in next. Like I said, I'm available every day next week and the deadline for my book is miles away, so I won't have my agent pestering me for pages.

"It was very nice to meet you, Ryder. I hope to see you again. Don't get scared off by all the craziness around here." Isabell grinned as she entered the lift.

"Thanks. I'll try not to," Ryder replied, smiling, as the doors closed.

As the lift descended, Isabell looked in the mirror.

"Look at your hair, girl," she muttered to herself. "When was the last time you got it cut?" She tried to coax some volume into her hair but was unable to achieve the look she was after.

The elevator doors opened and she walked through the foyer of The Particle and outside into the morning air. A gust of wind hit her in the face and forced her eyes closed.

"Issi, I know you're lying. I know you're sleeping with someone behind my back and this is the only way I can make sure you never cheat on me again."

Isabell's eyes shot open. She was strapped down and bound into the passenger seat of a moving car. Her mouth was taped and she was struggling to breath. Terrified, she looked around her, immediately recognising the driver. She knew she was about to die.

CHAPTER 7

Bedford

Terrell groaned. Without opening his eyes, he reached over to silence the irritating buzz of his alarm clock. Searching with his hand, he accidentally knocked over the glass of water which was placed precariously on his bedside table. At the sound of the smash, he bolted out of bed still half-asleep, staring at the shattered remains of the tumbler.

"Terrell? What was that?"

"Nothing, Mum, it was just a glass, I'll clean it up now . . . Don't come in—I'm naked!" He scrambled for his boxer shorts as his mother entered the room. "Mum!"

"Stop it! It's nothing I haven't seen before. I was just cleaning the bathroom so I can clear this up in no time." She knelt down and swept the pieces of glass off the floor with a dustpan and brush and mopped up the remaining water with a fresh cloth. "What are you doing up so early? Did you forget it's Saturday?"

"I forgot to turn my alarm off last night. Believe me, I'll be going back to bed in a minute."

"Teenagers! You'll miss the whole day if you go back to sleep now." Beth finished cleaning the floor. "There, all done. Just watch your feet in case I've missed any bits of glass."

"Thanks, Mum. Please could you wait next time? I don't want you seeing me without clothes on."

"Got it. Next time I hear smashing sounds coming from your

room, I'll just stand behind the door and wait, shall I? Even if I'm wondering if my son is hurt or not? Yes, of course I will, Terrell." Mrs Prince's words dripped with sarcasm as she left the room. He knew privacy wouldn't be awarded to him any time soon.

He was about to get back into bed when he noticed the video camera was still running. Picking it up, he checked for any water damage. Luckily, it was dry. He switched the machine off and climbed back under the duvet.

Unfortunately, Saturday was cleaning day and now she knew her son was awake, Mrs Prince didn't silence her noise. No-one could sleep to the sound of the vacuum-cleaner bashing against the skirting-boards or, indeed, his mother's out-of-tune rendition of "Dream A Little Dream" by the Mamas and Papas.

Terrell laughed to himself; most people his age had never heard of Mama Cass, but he knew every word of every song she'd ever sung, thanks to his mother keeping the Sixties' singer's spirit alive.

He had earplugs for situations like this, but now wide-awake, he decided to check last night's film instead. Picking up the camera, he hopped to the end of the bed and plugged it into his computer, shifting from his bed to his swivel chair.

When the picture came up on his PC monitor, the usual green, night-light image greeted him. Seconds later, he saw his hand move the water glass right in front of the camera.

Well, that's that ruined, then, he thought. Terrell was about to stop the playback when he saw the water settle and the camera refocus, bringing his bed back into view. This time, the picture looked elongated and wavy, as if looking up at someone from underneath a still lake. It was quite amusing to see his head pulled and stretched on the screen as the lens focused through the water. He carried on watching, amused by this new view of himself falling asleep when suddenly something happened to make him jump back and fall off his chair.

Mrs Prince bounded into the room, this time to see her

son and his chair toppled over on to the floor. Terrell's first thought was to shout at her for once again barging in, but the video footage he had just witnessed was far more important.

"I've done it! I've actually done it," he exclaimed, pulling himself and his chair back towards his desk.

"What? Managed to fall off your chair without breaking your neck?"

"Mum, shush, please, and come look at this." He rewound the video camera to the beginning.

"You're not still recording yourself sleeping, are you?"

"Mum! Just watch."

Mrs Prince settled on the edge of Terrell's bed and viewed the recording with her son. Her mouth fell open and she screamed for her husband to join them.

"Ghalen! Ghalen! Get up here now!"

Mr Prince bounded up the stairs and into Terrell's room.

"Beth? What is it? I have to get to the shop."

"Sit here and watch this."

"What's going on?" Ghalen asked, sitting down next to his wife while Terrell restarted the recording. "Not again. I thought you'd stopped doing this, Terrell."

"Ghalen, just shut up and watch," his wife replied sternly, placing her hand on top of his.

After a few minutes, Terrell turned around to see his parents' startled faces. His father's dark skin appeared pale.

"Terrell. You did it. You actually did it."

London

"Hello. I'm Shira Rosenberg, Abby's mother. We have an appointment to see Doctor Sharma."

The receptionist tapped on her keyboard until the relevant information appeared on the screen. She looked up and smiled at the well-groomed American woman.

"Doctor Sharma will be with you shortly, if you would like to take a seat over there please."

Shira led her daughter to the plush, red sofas the receptionist had gestured to. As they took their seats, she held on to her daughter's hand and noticed she was trembling.

"You'll be fine, darling, I promise. There's nothing to worry about."

Abby smiled tentatively, holding her mother's hand tightly. Why was she the one having to go through all of this? Her happy, carefree childhood seemed so long ago, like a faded dream or another life entirely.

As a young girl, San Francisco was a magical place. Most weekends, she would visit different parts of the city with her mother and father. School holidays would be filled with adventures; travelling to Yosemite National Park, taking a boat out on to the bay or driving through Napa Valley, where her parents would taste wine and buy a few bottles to take home.

On the family's last outing together, they had visited Alcatraz Prison. Abby had wanted to go for a picnic instead. She sulked as they toured the cells. Her father jokingly said that if she wasn't good, he would lock her inside. This had frightened her, and made her cry. When Oren tried to console her, she thrashed in his arms, screaming as she pulled away from him, running out of the building.

That memory had a profound impact on Abby after her father's death. Her developing brain couldn't understand why her daddy was gone; maybe if she had been better behaved, he wouldn't have left. Too ashamed to ask her mother and too embarrassed to tell her friends, she kept this belief bottled up; imprisoning her own thoughts akin to those past inmates on Alcatraz.

After Oren's funeral, the summer fog which rolled into the bay every evening no longer held an air of mystery, the bumpy rides on the streetcars were no longer exciting, and even the sea lions wallowing and singing in the sun on Pier 39 couldn't bring a smile to Abby's face.

At school, she learned about fault lines and the city's history with earthquakes. While this worried most of her friends, at times, she wished the ground would open up and swallow her. The only person who ever had the ability to make her feel better was her mother.

Shira was Abby's rock; a grounding point she could cling to, saving her from drowning in her imagined pit of despair. Shira knew that she had to be strong for both of them. It wasn't until Abby's teenage years when she understood just how difficult that must have been for her mother, but Shira had never once shown her daughter this strain.

The night Oren didn't return was the evening of his and Shira's wedding anniversary. He had taken the day off work so they could spend a long weekend together. Secretly, he had planned a trip to Las Vegas for all three of them. Shira loved Celine Dion and so he and Abby had booked a surprise three-day trip.

Abby had been secretly packing her small bag ready for the weekend and couldn't wait to see her mother's reaction when they got to Caesar's Palace, her father presenting Shira with the VIP tickets to see her favourite singer. Abby had been good at keeping the surprise in the weeks leading up to the weekend. She had kept her packed bag hidden at the back of her closet, waiting for her father to return.

The morning of the trip, Oren had been called into work for an early meeting. He apologised to his wife and promised to be back after lunch. By six, Shira was concerned when he hadn't returned home and wasn't answering his phone. She called Future Tech, the company he worked for.

"He was in this morning for the meeting, but I haven't seen him since. Let me check his office for you." The receptionist could hear the worry in Shira's voice and called Oren's assistant. After a few minutes on hold, she returned to the call. "Sorry about the wait, Shira. I've just spoken to Nathan, but he said Oren left the office around midday. I can check his GPS for you?"

"Thank you. Yes, please," Shira replied. It wasn't like Oren to be late, and certainly not like him to switch his phone off.

"OK, I have it on my screen now. The last GPS ping we got was at three-twenty on Lincoln Boulevard."

"That's strange. He would have to pass home to get on to Lincoln. Why would he do that?"

The receptionist paused for a second. "I'm not sure. I'll keep checking his GPS and will let you know if I hear anything."

"Thank you."

Shira put the phone down and stared at the wedding picture of her and her husband, hanging above the fireplace.

"Did you find him?"

Shira spun around to see Abby standing in the doorway, looking as worried as she felt.

"Not yet, honey. Apparently, he was on Lincoln Boulevard a few hours ago. I'm going to drive along there and see if I can find him. Want to come?"

Abby checked her watch. It was just past six.

"What if Daddy gets home while we're out?"

"I'll leave a note for him, just in case." She scrawled on a piece of paper, leaving it by the phone.

Shira didn't really know where to start. With Lincoln Boulevard stretching right from Lobos Creek to the Golden Gate Bridge, he could've been anywhere. She was hopeful they would be able to spot him walking along the sidewalk. Perhaps his car had broken down and his phone had run out of charge.

They scoured the street unsuccessfully for two hours. On the drive home, Shira tried to console her daughter.

"Don't worry, darling. You know your father — he's probably working on some new computer programme and lost track of time."

"But it's your wedding anniversary."

"We can go for a meal tomorrow night, instead. It's no big deal." As convincing as Shira had tried to sound, she was worried, but couldn't show her young daughter that.

Abby checked her watch; they had missed their flight. Her father was absent-minded sometimes, especially when it came to work, but he had been planning this trip for weeks. There was no way he would have forgotten. Abby was scared something terrible had happened.

Almost a week later, the police knocked on their front door. Oren's phone and wallet had been found stuffed into a bush on the Battery E Trail. Being so close to the bridge, they had deduced that her husband had most likely committed suicide, but Shira wouldn't accept that. There was no reason she could think of for Oren to take his own life. The man she married was happy and totally devoted to her and their daughter.

Abby was only nine years old at the time and as much as Shira tried to shield her from what was happening, this was impossible to hide. The search was reported on the local news, and when the San Francisco Police Department released a statement that his body had most likely been swept out to sea, Abby had been watching the TV at the time. That night, amongst others, she sobbed in her mother's arms for hours.

A large number of people turned out for the memorial service at San Francisco National Cemetery, just a few miles from where Oren's personal effects were found. A memorial plaque was unveiled in a plot near to where his parents were buried. Abby held her mother's hand throughout the ceremony. She didn't really understand what was happening, but she did know that her father was gone, never to return.

The months passed slowly; the trees started to shed their leaves and autumn turned into winter, as if reflecting the decay in the Rosenbergs' mood. Just before Hanukkah, Shira was wrapping gifts late at night after spending time soothing her troubled daughter to sleep. The phone rang and she answered it quickly, hoping that the sound hadn't woken Abby.

"Hello?"

"Shira, it's me — Oren."

The phone nearly slipped from Shira's fingers as her hands began to shake. She couldn't speak, her mouth dried up and a cold shiver ran through her entire body.

"Please, listen, I don't have much time. I didn't mean to leave you. I was taken, but I'm OK. I can't tell you where I am as I don't want to put you or Abby in danger, just know that I'm going to be all right."

"Oren, I can't believe it . . . I miss you. I love you so much."

"I love you, too, and I miss you both so, so much."

In shock, Shira stumbled over her words.

"What happened?"

"I discovered something I shouldn't have. I'm sorry, I have to go. Someone's coming and if they . . . You mustn't tell anyone I've been in contact or it could mean trouble for all of us. Just know how much I love you, Shira, and give Abby a huge kiss for me. As soon as I can, I'm coming home to you both."

The line went dead.

Bewildered and shaken, Shira put the phone down slowly, slumped to the floor and, for the first time since the memorial service, sobbed for her loss.

True to her word, Shira never told a soul about the conversation with her presumed-dead husband and, although she was terribly worried, she knew that he was alive and that he loved them and was trying to come home. From then on, she would tell Abby that her father wasn't dead and that, one day, he would return to them.

As Abby grew older, she believed that this was her mother's way of dealing with what had really happened; only Shira knew the truth.

That one phone call was the reason Shira could get out of bed in the morning; the reason she could be strong enough to raise Abby and carry on with everyday life. But as time passed with no word from Oren, she feared the worst.

It was too late to speak to the police about it, or to anyone, for that matter. Who would believe her now? If Oren were still alive, where was he? What could be so dangerous for him to make her promise never to tell anyone? And why hadn't he contacted her again? Oren had landed a job at Future Tech after being involved in white hat hacking in his youth — was that connected in some way? A million thoughts and scenarios ran through Shira's mind on a daily basis.

After the conversation with Dr Sharma just over a week ago, Shira had struggled to understand exactly what information he had found out about her daughter's nightmares, or why anyone in England would even care. Her first thought was that this must have something to do with Oren. Perhaps he was still alive, and this was his way of contacting her and maybe even meeting them, but in total secrecy.

She had questioned the doctor without revealing anything of her husband.

"I understand exactly where you're coming from, Mrs Rosenberg. I would be suspicious, too," Padman had reassured her on the phone. "I work for an extremely specialised facility that deals with people's dreams and, in cases like your daughter, their nightmares, too. We have links to hospitals throughout the world and when a case like Abby's is flagged, we investigate to see if there is anything we can do to help."

Shira was upset with herself for even considering the possibility that this was something to do with Oren. After all this time, why would he create such a convoluted story to make contact? Her thoughts now refocused on her daughter, and alarm-bells were ringing.

"You said 'tap into her dreams' — do you mean drilling holes into her head?"

"My goodness, no. The only thing touching her head will be a pillow. We just monitor her while she sleeps."

"I'm sorry, Doctor Sharma, but I don't understand what you'll learn from just watching her sleep."

"I understand your confusion, which is why I think it would be better for you to actually see the facility. Here, in London."

Shira scoffed.

"I'm a single mom on a low-income wage — I don't have the money to just hop on a plane to London. We barely have enough to keep the car running."

"The hospital would fund the totality of your trip — flights, accommodation and living expenses for you and your daughter."

"Why would you do that?" Shira was now thinking this was either some kind of practical joke or Oren really might be behind it.

"We believe Abby is a very special individual. After reading her medical file, I have learned she suffers from recurring nightmares, visualising the same man every night. I'm not sure if you're aware of this, but reoccurring dreams are extremely rare and something we would very much like to help with.

"If it'll help alleviate your fears, I can speak with your family doctor, who'll be able to vouch for our company."

Shira paused, trying to take in everything the doctor was telling her.

"I'll give you some time to think. I've sent you an email with information about Silicate. If you have any questions, please don't hesitate to call me."

"Thank you, Doctor." Shira put the phone down.

"Who was that?" Abby asked as Shira walked back into the kitchen.

"A doctor who said he might be able to help you with your nightmares."

Shira sat down and stared at her Kung Pao chicken but no longer felt hungry. The conversation with Dr Sharma had left her unsure whether to feel relief or worry. Thoughts of Oren began to resurface, thoughts that she managed to suppress — most of the time — in order to make the best of life. As cruel as it may have seemed, she often wished that he had never called that night. By now, she would have likely accepted his death and moved on; would that really have made life better for her, though?

"Mom, I don't want any more sleeping pills."

Shira snapped out of her internal musings and looked at her daughter.

"Of course not, darling. No more sleeping pills. The doctor who called was from England. They've read about your night terrors and would like to help, if they can. They want to monitor you while you sleep."

"You mean, I get to go to England?" Abby perked up, a stray noodle dangling from the corner of her mouth.

Shira pulled the noodle away, wiping it into a napkin.

"Now, don't get too excited. I've got some reading to do first and find out more about this company. Once I know they're legit, we can have a proper conversation about it and see if it's something we want to do." Shira pulled her cell phone from her bag and started scrolling through the list of contacts.

"In fact, I think I'll make an appointment to see Wanda in the morning, see if she knows anything about this company. If they really are as good as they say they are, who knows? They might be able to help you . . ."

Abby didn't look convinced, and as hard as Shira tried, she couldn't bring herself to pretend she felt any differently, though a chance to see London would be lovely, she thought.

Over the next few days, the two of them visited Wanda, who confirmed Silicate was a reputable company. They visited the hospital, who backed up their family doctor's view. Finally, they read through the information Dr Sharma had emailed, sparse as it was.

Now confident Silicate was a genuine company, Shira called Dr Sharma back. He was already poised to answer all her questions. Padman explained that on their visit, he would personally show them the whole facility, introduce them to the other staff members and explain the procedure in more detail, but he emphasised that this could only be done in person.

Shira thought it all seemed too good to be true; but she trusted her own doctor. If Wanda said the company checked out, then she believed her.

Shira had finished her second call with Dr Sharma and walked upstairs to Abby's room, tapping lightly on her daughter's bedroom door.

"Are you still awake, darling?"

"Come in, Mom, I'm just reading."

Shira walked in and saw that Abby was tucked into bed. She perched on top of her covers.

"I've just been speaking to that doctor in London again. He seems really nice."

Abby screwed up her face and laid her Kindle on the bed.

"I know you're tired of seeing doctors, darling, and I don't blame you. But this one specialises in cases just like yours."

Abby rolled her eyes and slumped down under the duvet, hiding her head.

Shira giggled as she pulled back the covers to reveal Abby pulling a funny face.

"I'm not going to make this decision for you. It doesn't really matter what I think, or even what they think — what matters is you."

Abby sat back up in bed to listen to her mother properly.

"I told him that I'd leave the choice up to you. All I can tell you is that they seem to be very confident in their ability to help you, and they'll pay for our flights and accommodation. What do you think, honey?"

Abby stared at her lava lamp, watching the gaseous liquids melt and mould into each other. She had been lost in thought many times staring at the lamp, but today she felt focused. She thought for a moment before turning back to her mother, frowning.

"But they're in London. What if I decide I don't want to go through with it once I'm there? Surely they'll be angry after paying for us to go all that way?"

"Not at all, Doctor Sharma says. They've promised that if we're not satisfied with them or the facility, we can leave at any time. At the very least we would have a nice vacation

— in London, of all places. Maybe we could have tea with the Queen. Would *one* like that, sweet pea?" Shira tickled her daughter, who laughed along with her mother.

"I'm sure the Queen will have better things to do than have tea with us."

"Nonsense. Nothing's more important than my beautiful girl." Shira enveloped Abby in a bear hug while her daughter tried, laughingly, to squirm out of her grasp.

"Mom! Stop it!"

Both laughing, Shira released Abby from her embrace and began to stroke her daughter's hair.

"Seriously, though, sweetheart — there's nothing in the world more important than you, whether the Queen knows it yet or not. This decision is yours to make, of course, and whatever you decide, I'll support you either way."

Abby sat upright and held her mother's hand.

"OK. Say we did go, and I decided to go through with the procedure, would I be stuck in a hospital bed the whole time we were there?"

"According to Doctor Sharma, they'd only need you at the facility for three days, giving us four more to go sightseeing before flying home. I've already been looking online, and we can see most of London in that time . . ."

Abby gazed into her mother's eyes and saw there a sad kind of longing. Her mother worked hard and worried constantly. She needed a break. The last time they'd been away together was just a few months before Oren disappeared. The memory of hiking around Yosemite National Park and camping under the stars popped into Abby's head for the first time in years. She smiled, only for that happy memory to be replaced with the painful one of the Las Vegas trip which had never happened. To this day, Abby had never told her mother about the anniversary surprise and in doing so, buried it away from her conscious mind, just like the bag which was still buried from sight, sentenced to an eternal state of limbo beneath clothes and toys at the back of her closet.

Shira had been an amazing mother and Abby knew she wouldn't have ever gotten through her father's tragic death without her. Of course, she had her doubts and fears about going to London; but on the other hand, what if this company really could help her? Would she finally be able to sleep properly again? The possibility seemed too alien to even imagine, but she couldn't stop the glimmer of hope which rippled through her.

"OK, let's do it. You're right, Mom — what have we got to lose?"

Shira held her daughter's hand and smiled.

"Fantastic. I'll let them know right away."

That conversation had been a month ago. Shira arranged leave from work and informed Abby's tutor they were going away. They received their plane tickets and hotel booking via email from Dr Sharma's assistant, and a town car drove them to the airport.

Having never flown business class before, they both dressed in their best clothes and were treated to the finest in-seat cuisine and entertainment. It was thrilling for Shira to experience this side of life, but Abby was too lost in thought to appreciate it.

"It's OK, darling — we'll be back home soon. And who knows, maybe in a week's time, we can put all the distress of the past few years behind us."

Abby smiled to appease her mother, but she couldn't stop her stomach from churning. As much as she wanted to relax, the fear of the unknown was just too strong.

Shira was giddy as they turned left upon boarding the aircraft, passing a bar on the way to their seats. A glass of champagne and a very attentive crew were enough to ease any doubts Shira had about this trip.

Eleven hours later, they landed at Heathrow Airport. Shira managed to catch a couple of hours' sleep on the plane; Abby had been awake all night, watching films.

One of the stewardesses had kept an eye on the teenager and, as well as making up her bed when she wanted to relax, she had also kept her well-stocked with drinks and sweet snacks while her mother was asleep. Abby's sugar rush crashed shortly before breakfast.

"Aren't you going to eat that?" Shira asked, pointing to her daughter's untouched meal.

"I can't. My stomach really hurts."

"It's probably just nerves, darling. You should try to eat something, though."

Abby bit into a slice of toast and took an age to chew and swallow it before pushing the plate away.

"Sorry, Mom, I just can't." Abby's stomach-ache intensified as they neared the airport and, as they left the plane, the extent of her exhaustion hit her, too.

The hour-long queue through security and the long taxi ride did nothing to ease Abby's symptoms, and as they finally checked into the Particle View Hotel, she was looking extremely pale.

"Mom, I really need to lie down."

"Just one second, sweetie. Let me get the room key and then you can rest."

As soon as they entered their lavish suite, Abby raced into the bathroom and vomited in the toilet.

Shira rushed in after her as the porter placed their luggage in the room and left quietly.

"Oh, darling! If I knew it would upset you this much, I wouldn't have agreed to come."

Tears ran down Abby's face as her mother wiped her mouth with a towel.

"I'm sorry, Mom, my stomach has been churning non-stop but as soon as we left the cab, I knew I was going to puke."

"Don't you worry about being sick. At least you made it to the restroom." Shira smiled. "Can you imagine the look on that snooty receptionist's face if you'd have done it all over the foyer?"

The two of them laughed as Shira acted out a panicked receptionist, mouth open in shock and waving her arms around.

"How do you do it?"

"Do what, darling?"

"Make me smile, even when my whole body tells me I can't. I have puke on my face and I'm laughing. How?"

"Because I'm your mother . . . and because I'm hilarious."

They giggled again as Shira cleaned her daughter's face and flushed the toilet. They both got up off the floor and hugged.

"Right, young lady. We've got five hours until we meet Doctor Sharma. I suggest you get some sleep. After you've rested, you can decide if you still want to meet him. Just because we're in London doesn't mean we have to do anything you don't want to. And if you're too ill to even be here, we can catch the next flight home and curl up with a good movie together. Whatever you want to do, that's what we'll do."

Abby smiled again.

"I love you, Mom."

"I love you, too, darling. Now, try to rest."

Abby lay her head on the pillow and fell into a deep sleep almost instantly.

Shira sat with her daughter for a while before resting on her own bed. She plugged her phone into the travel socket and began sending messages back home.

When Abby awoke, she found that her mother was already showered and changed, sitting in an armchair by the side of her.

"What time is it?"

"It's almost two, darling. I was going to wake you up in five minutes. How do you feel?"

"Much better, thanks. I think all the candy I had on the plane didn't help my stomach."

"What candy?"

"You were asleep and so I asked the nice flight attendant to bring me some."

"Abby! No wonder you were sick."

"Sorry, Mom." Abby sat up and wiped the sleep from her eyes.

"Is the hospital far away?"

"According to the map, it's just down the street." Shira displayed the short route on her phone. "It says here '*The Particle is the tallest building in the world, built to imitate millions of molecules stacked high, forming a particle of glass*'" Shira read aloud from the article on her phone. "Sounds a bit bizarre."

"It sounds awesome, and if it's walking distance, we can easily escape back here if they have any torture equipment set up." Abby grinned.

"Honestly. Where does your mind take you? Right, go and get showered and we'll make our way down there. I've left you a towel out."

Thirty minutes later, the two were exiting the hotel and walking down a cobbled street, following the directions on Shira's phone. As they turned the corner, The Particle stood in front of them, dominating the skyline.

"You're right, Mom — we couldn't have missed that, even if we tried," Abby said as they reached the huge, glass building.

"It's made up of different-sized bubbles."

"I guess those symbolise the atoms."

"I quite like it. It's a lot more elegant than it looks in the pictures."

"And bigger!" Abby was smiling as they walked up to the doors; it wasn't until they stepped into the foyer that her stomach began churning again. She felt like turning around and running back to the hotel.

Shira saw the troubled look on her daughter's face.

"Are you sure you still want to do this?"

They stopped walking and faced each other. The whole space was alive with people milling around them, but for Abby and Shira, at least for that moment, time stood still.

Abby looked into her mother's kind eyes. She was with the one person she trusted more than anyone; even more than herself, at times. Yes, they were thousands of miles away from home, but as long as she was with her mom, she felt safe. Abby calmed her breathing and straightened her shoulders, forcing a small, tentative smile.

"Yeah, why not. We've tried everything else and we've flown all this way. It would be stupid to turn back now. It's just nerves, I guess. But don't worry — I'm not going to be sick again!"

"At least that's something." Shira chuckled as they walked, hand-in-hand, towards the elevator.

CHAPTER 8

Ryder was led into a clinical yet comfortable-looking office. Stacks of papers were piled in an overflowing in-tray; a heavily used whiteboard with the remaining residue of various colours of pen contrasted the white of the room, while a few decorative plants lay here and there.

"And this is my office," Padman announced proudly as he manoeuvred himself carefully around the desk to his chair. "I spend a lot of time in this little room. Luckily, the cleaners also look after the plants for me. Otherwise, I fear they would've died long ago." He let out a small chuckle.

Ryder smiled politely in response. He had spent the past two hours chit-chatting with the doctor, yet was still confused about what Silicate actually did. He had very many questions and a very dry mouth.

I could kill for a cup of tea, he thought to himself, and as if he had accidentally said it out loud, there was a light knock at the door and an older woman entered, smiling, carrying a tray of tea and biscuits. As Ryder watched her place it on to the desk in front of him, he wondered if the company had mastered mindreading. As he bit into a custard cream, he decided they couldn't be telepathic, or they'd have known to bring hobnobs instead.

The doctor took a sip of tea and looked at Ryder purposefully.

"We weren't really looking for anything in particular when

we started this project."

Ryder was perplexed. The statement came from nowhere, but instead of interrupting the doctor, he stayed quiet, eager to learn about the company he now worked for.

"In fact, you could say that Silicate was born out of your own tragedy, or at least your family's tragedy. After your mother's death, Lady Braighton was plagued with terrible nightmares. Her dreams were so vivid that Lord Braighton feared for her life. Night after night, her dreams became more intense — to the point of emotional collapse.

"The dreams engulfed her. Not just while she slept, but in the waking world, as well. They saw doctor after doctor, but no-one could help. One of the psychiatrists they saw, spoke with Lord Braighton privately after the appointment. He was concerned that Lady Braighton might be on the verge of having a complete emotional breakdown."

"Wait, you're telling me that all of this was set up because my mother killed herself?"

"Precisely! Your mother's unfortunate death was the catalyst for all you see here today. At the time, there wasn't one single person or organisation on the planet that could help your grandmother. The only options presented were to either watch her deteriorate into an early grave or institutionalise her in the hope that that would 'fix' the problem.

"You must know your grandfather well enough to understand he would never allow either of those things to happen. Although he had very little knowledge of the medical world, he had contacts in the field. Between that and having the money to get people on board . . . well, that's how it started.

"In the days following that quiet conversation with the psychiatrist, your grandfather flew in medical professionals from all over the world. They observed your grandmother and came together to talk through options of what — if anything — could be done to help her."

Five doctors sat in the living-room of Braighton Manor. Lord Braighton had adopted his usual standing position, near the antique sideboard and beside an almost empty bottle of Cognac.

"I'm afraid conventional medicine can't help your wife, Henry. We need to think of something else. Something new," a well-dressed man sitting in an armchair facing the lord said.

"I agree with Doctor Mendes. After examining your wife, it's apparent she's grieving the death of your daughter. But to this level . . . it's extreme. I'm not sure I've seen this severity of symptoms before."

"No offence, Tim, but I know all this," Lord Braighton barked in reply. "I didn't fly you all here to diagnose my wife; I need to know what we can do to cure her. I may not be a doctor, but I do have money — I would spend every single penny of it to save Elena."

The five medical professionals shuffled uncomfortably in their seats as the grand man in front of them struggled to keep his emotions in check. His only daughter had taken her own life and now his wife was seriously ill; it was more than the old man could bear.

"Henry, we won't rest until we find a way to save Elena. And I know I speak for all of us here when I say that we're not doing this for the money. We've known you for years; you're our friend and we want to help."

"Thank you, Rajesh. That means a lot."

"Over the next few days, those five doctors took up residence in the Manor and spent every waking hour discussing and debating ways to treat Lady Braighton."

Padman looked over at Ryder, who was hanging on every word.

"It was actually my father who came up with the idea of what is now Silicate," Padman continued. "He proposed monitoring your grandmother while she slept. A specialised unit was set up by my father and his colleagues in the guest suite of the Manor.

"It was a primitive lab, from what my father tells me, but effective. Lady Braighton slept with electrodes attached to her head for EEG monitoring. They caught every second on video-recording equipment. They used a gentle light so the patient's sleep wasn't disturbed, but the team and cameras could still function.

"Have you been in the guest suite?"

Ryder nodded.

"Do you remember the fish tank at the back of the room? When the team were setting up the cameras, Lady Braighton requested that the tank remain — she found the light and sound soothing. With limited space, the fourth camera was placed behind the tank, looking through the glass. No-one knew at the time, but it was this camera which provided the results, inadvertently leading to her recovery and the formation of this company.

"It was because of its position, looking through the water and glass, that they were able to observe your grandmother's dreams emanating from her."

Ryder looked lost. He knew Padman was dumbing down the technical speak so he could understand it, but he was still struggling to comprehend the doctor's words.

"Let me show you what I mean." Padman walked across to his whiteboard and cleared the contents with the sleeve of his jacket. He picked up a pen and began to draw.

"This is the subject — in our case, your grandmother, asleep in bed. Her brain is full of sorrow and sadness from her daughter's death and her mind is highly active. When asleep, and especially when she hits her REM cycle, the electricity the brain produces is so strong that it emanates images from her subconscious and out into the ether." He drew a crude sketch of a fish tank with a camera sitting behind it facing the circle representing Lady Braighton.

"This is what was captured on the camera. These emanations are invisible to the naked eye unless under the right conditions—in this case, the perfect conditions just happened to be behind a fish tank full of water.

"This is why we have our patients sleep in the pods you saw earlier. They're the evolution of the original set-up. A huge, glass tank, surrounded by water, with cameras positioned on the outside looking in. Anything that the patient dreams, we can monitor."

"You can see people's dreams?"

Padman bustled back to his seat, looking at Ryder directly.

"That's exactly what I'm saying. But that's just the beginning. With this technology, we can do so much more than simply monitor and record dreams. Imagine, things that have been locked up inside people's minds finally being released — allowing us to analyse that data and help the patient.

"With your grandmother, this knowledge meant we were not only able to explain what was happening, but actually show her what she was visualising. This helped the recovery process by directly retraining her brain. It was a breakthrough for your family and for the entire neuroscience community.

"Your grandmother still suffers from sleepless nights, but now she's able to control them rather than them controlling her. The treatment worked and is continued today through Silicate.

"When looking for premises, Lord Braighton was already on the board of directors for The Particle, which was then in the early stages of construction. With his influence and financial backing, Silicate was the first company to move in, right at the heart of the brand-new building."

It took Ryder a few moments to catch up.

"If my mother hadn't died, Silicate wouldn't exist."

"That's probably true," Padman replied. "As we continue to see every day, Silicate's work is incredibly important. We've had to build the technology from the ground up. We're now at a point where we prevent loss of life on a weekly basis. That sounds like a big claim, but it's accurate.

"But we're still in our infancy, we know that. So, we still

channel all our efforts in developing our research and perfecting the technology in the hope that, one day, we'll be able to offer this service to everyone, anywhere in the world. This is why we don't charge any of our current patients."

"Why wouldn't you charge for this?" Ryder queried. "Surely it must cost millions to set up and keep this place running?"

"Believe me, we get just as much from them as they do from us. More, even. The plan was always to spend the first five years collecting as much data as possible. At first, we could only monitor people who displayed the same traits as your grandmother, so we've scoured the world for the most exceptional cases with similar brain activity.

"These tended to be the acute cases, the people most at risk. We found that personal tragedy causes a massive amount of cognitive activity, and so we were able to learn a vast amount from these patients while at the same time helping them recover. It's been a long journey, but we are finally having successes with non-cogs as well."

"Non-cogs?"

"Sorry — people who don't display cognitive trauma. This is only possible from the valuable research we have acquired from our previous patients. Pretty soon, we'll be able to treat everyone and will be able to go public with our findings."

"And then what?"

"At that point, we will start to charge our patients. This was always a long-term investment, it's just one which has helped a large number of people in the initial process."

"For a second there it seemed like this was all a big, expensive humanitarian project. I'm sure your investors are looking forward to finally making their money back."

"Not all of them are in it for profit." Padman smiled. "There are others — like your grandfather and my father, who've invested solely for the future protection of the human race. Regardless of what financial bonuses this technology may bring, I like to think we do a lot of good here. We have an almost one hundred per cent success rate. The more we learn about the brain, the more equipped we become to help everyone. This is one of the greatest scientific breakthroughs of the human age; not just seeing inside the physical brain, but actually seeing the patient's thoughts and dreams."

"And all you need to do is watch someone sleep?"

"In essence, although without the pods we wouldn't see anything at all. Hygge, the room we saw earlier, is currently equipped with twenty pods. Once Silicate goes public, we have space to increase capacity to well over one hundred.

"We also have more specialised rooms, of course, including Archeus, but that's on a different floor."

"What's Archeus?"

At that moment the phone on Padman's desk began to ring. The doctor held up a finger, indicating he would answer that question momentarily.

"Padman Sharma."

"Hello, Doctor. Abigale Rosenberg and her mother have arrived and are waiting in reception for you."

"Excellent, I'll come and collect them."

Padman was about to put down the phone when the receptionist continued speaking, in a quieter voice.

"There's something else you need to know. We found a woman passed out in front of the main entrance. Security alerted us because they found one of our passes on her person. Doctor, it's Isabell Porra."

Shocked, Padman turned away from Ryder and spoke quietly into the phone.

"Where is she now?"

"She's still unconscious. We've put her in the recovery room. We didn't know if we should call an ambulance or not?"

"Definitely not. Call Martin and have him take her to Archeus. Keep her monitored and make sure everything's recorded. I'll come down and meet the Rosenbergs and then join Martin as soon as I can."

"Understood, Doctor."

Padman put down the receiver and took a breath to gather

himself before directing a toothy smile towards Ryder.

"And as if by magic, a new patient has arrived and is waiting in reception."

"Is everything all right?"

"Everything's fine." Padman brushed off Ryder's concern. "From her file, this girl — Abby — appears to be an extremely special case. I'll tell you more about her on the way over there."

Ryder followed him out of the office, unable to shake the suspicion that Doctor Sharma was not being entirely honest with him.

"How's your stomach doing now? I have some antacids somewhere in my purse." Shira started sifting through the assortment of items in the bag on her lap.

Abby looked up at her and smiled.

"Are you sure you're not Mary Poppins?"

Shira stopped what she was doing; her hands stuffed full of items but no sign of the antacids.

"Whatever do you mean?"

"The purse, Mom! How do you manage to squeeze everything in there?"

"It's a Mom thing!" Shira smiled at her daughter and laughed.

"Mrs and Miss Rosenberg?"

Both women jolted their heads up towards Padman and Ryder, who had appeared at the side of them.

"I'm Doctor Padman Sharma and this is our head of security, Ryder Braighton."

Shira quickly dropped the contents back into her bag and shook both men's hands. Abby appeared a little apprehensive but smiled politely.

"Today's a chance for us to meet each other. Very informal. We'll try to keep it as fun as possible and see how you both feel about Abby possibly staying here tomorrow night." Padman turned to Abby.

The girl was clearly nervous. Her hands were stuffed tightly under her legs, which were jiggling up and down. Her eyes were open wide as if she was trying not to cry.

The doctor put on his biggest smile as he knelt down to Abby's level.

"I was worried that you might think today was a bit of a snooze-fest, so I've booked the Red Room for later. We've got every games console you can think of in there, even the classic ones, and books and films. And if that gets a bit samey, we've also got a huge swimming pool and a spa if you and your mum fancy a massage or a manicure."

Abby's face changed into a tentative smile as she looked over at her mother.

Padman stood up again before addressing them both.

"First things first, though — I'd like to show you and your mum around. After that, the place is yours. I also want to reiterate that whatever your decision is at the end of today, Abby, we'll totally respect that. If you don't want to come back tomorrow, that's absolutely fine. I just want you to know that there really is no pressure for you to do anything at all."

Abby's legs stopped shaking as she smiled at Padman, who now held out his hand.

"Shall we?"

Abby took his hand and stood up. Shira was full of admiration for how the doctor had managed to put Abby at ease. She slipped an arm around her daughter and nodded to Padman in approval. Ryder, who had purposely tried to blend into the background, now followed the small group as they walked through the main doors and over to the security station.

"You have a lot of guards here," Shira observed as she pinned a *Visitor* badge to her blouse. "And does everyone get a bodyguard to chaperone them through the building?"

"Bodyguard? Oh, you mean Ryder! He started here this morning, so I've been showing him the ropes before you arrived. As for the level of security, it's an unfortunate necessity. As I mentioned on the phone, most of what we do here is highly confidential and the security is more for making sure that your information stays inside the building as much as anything else.

"Speaking of which, before we go any further, I'll have to ask you to fill out the visitors' confidentiality agreement. It's standard procedure for anyone who enters the facility."

They had now arrived at the second security station. Ted was already standing with two tablets in his hand.

"Does Abby need to sign one, as well?" Shira asked.

"She does. All guests over the age of twelve must fill out their own forms. You can help her, by all means, but the signature must be Abby's."

"This is just to make sure that we don't blab to anyone outside the building about what we see?" Abby asked.

"Yes, that's the long and short of it," the doctor replied, smiling.

Abby looked over to Ryder.

"Did you have to sign one of these this morning?"

"Something similar." Ryder nodded. "Along with my contract of employment."

"And did you read through all of it?"

Ryder laughed.

"Not all of it, no."

"Cool." Abby signed the document and looked at her mother expectantly.

Shira appeared a little apprehensive, but also signed.

Padman took the tablets from them, handing them back to the security guard. He clasped his hands together theatrically and looked closely at Abby with a sly smile on his face.

"And now, Abby . . . are you ready to step into Wonderland?"

Abby raised her eyebrow.

"I know it's cheesy," Padman admitted, "but I've always wanted to say that."

The doors opened and all four of them moved into the airlock, heading towards Hygge.

CHAPTER 9

Jake was now living in one of the most densely populated cities in the world, yet he had never felt more alone in his life. One week since moving from Yorkshire and he still knew no-one. He found it difficult to communicate with people in London. Back home, everyone knew everything about everybody; there wasn't one person's name in Malham that Jake didn't know, and vice-versa. It was sometimes a little too intrusive and had been a big part of why Jake had suppressed his sexuality while living there.

He had expected the same curiosity for new arrivals in London and banked on this as a way to make friends; but unfortunately, London was the total opposite. People actually went out of their way *not* to get involved.

Jake had spoken to another resident in the elevator on his second day; the older woman had looked scared, as if Jake was going to steal her handbag and attack her. The woman abruptly exited the elevator at the next stop, without saying a single word, and left Jake wondering if they'd even reached her floor.

A similar reaction had occurred on a Tube station platform. Jake was marvelling at seeing the underground train network for the first time when he heard a man humming along to the music he was listening to. Jake had immediately recognised the song and tried to engage him in conversation. The meeting was brief and not without profanity.

Now in his new apartment, Jake was alone; sitting on the sofa and mindlessly staring at the oversized TV on the wall. He flicked through channels, not registering what was being shown. His mind was lost in a sea of thoughts, none of them positive. He was brimming with regret about moving to London. This bright, new Eden, this fresh start, this brand-new life he had created in his mind was nothing more than a fantasy.

He had believed this move would somehow transport him from his old, stale life and make him happy; but London was just a normal city where people lived and worked. With over eight million residents, who had the time to get to know an ex-farmer from a town they'd never heard of?

This sad realisation was sinking in fast, but rather than let it defeat him, he was determined to pick himself up and integrate into this scary, fast-paced, unfamiliar world. Besides, he had cut all ties with Malham; the farm had been sold, his parents were dead, and his friends were all but estranged. Perhaps London was too ambitious for a country boy to start his journey in, but this was his home now and there was no turning back.

He switched off the TV, grabbed his leather jacket and exited the apartment. He had wandered the streets every day since his arrival, taking in the sights and doing a lot of shopping. Thanks to Marion, he'd navigated through the tourist traps to some great clothes shops. The helpful store clerks in Covent Garden were more than happy to help dress Jake and take his money. He'd never binged on clothes before and loved being able to do so. He already had a wardrobe full of fashionable outfits that suited him and helped to make him feel more comfortable in this strange, new city.

As much as he wanted to distance himself from his former life, Jake had kept his old farm clothes, that one outfit he had arrived in the city wearing, in a bag at the bottom of the wardrobe. There was no way he would ever return to farming, but he wasn't ready to let go of everything that had made him the man he was.

Clothes were just the beginning. Furniture, TVs, laptop, tablet and the latest smartphone were all charged to his seemingly limitless credit cards; Jake saw these things as an investment. If he was to make a life in the capital, he needed to up his game. Tatty, muddy jeans with worn-out boots and a mobile phone that only connected to the WAP service weren't going to cut it here. He wanted to fit in as a resident, not a tourist.

It was the beginning of summer. A refreshing breeze followed him on his walk across the Thames, but the sun shone still, and the sky was cloudless. He walked past the Houses of Parliament, through Trafalgar Square and towards the West End. He had no particular destination in mind, but when he got to Old Compton Street, he decided this was where he needed to be.

It was Friday night and although it was still early, Soho was bursting with life. Men and women, young and old, of all nationalities, meandered through the busy street. Music from one bar cascaded into the next and people stood on the crowded pavements, spilling out into the street with their drinks in hand and smiles on their faces. This one road, buried in the centre of London, felt alive.

Jake stopped, standing in awe as he took in everything he was seeing. Men were holding hands with other men as families walked by. There were no sneers or signs of disgust, just human beings of all sexualities co-existing. Jake's stomach fluttered, both from excitement and nerves.

He walked to the end of the street, noting all the many bars that stood out as being tailored to the LGBTI community. Rainbow flags adorned the buildings, drag queens beckoned passing trade into bars and flyer boys handed out money-off vouchers to different events and club nights.

Overwhelmed by choice, Jake didn't know where to begin. He felt like the proverbial kid in a candy store. He decided to make Compton's Bar his first stop. It was named after the street, after all, and it looked busy and inviting. His attention was also drawn to the handful of handsome men standing outside, smoking and drinking. As he walked towards the entrance, he felt a thousand eyes looking at him. His stomach began to churn as the door opened and lights from the bar hit his eyes.

A week had passed since Terrell's discovery and he still had no idea what it meant. He instinctively felt that the glass of water in front of the camera had to be important for showing the ghost-like image of himself on the screen, yet he was no closer to understanding why.

His parents were as baffled as he was, though they were more concerned than excited. After re-watching the video many times, they had decided it was best not to tell anyone what he'd recorded until they could figure out what it was. As much as Terrell didn't agree, he respected his mum and dad and didn't tell a living soul, not even Cody.

He did, though, upload the video to his vlog along with a short description. This was his diary, the place he recorded everything of interest. It also received no web traffic, and he was therefore able to reason to himself that he wasn't technically breaking his promise.

Felix Oscroft was sitting at his computer when a message alert prompted him to visit Terrell's website. His computer was tasked with searching out key words and phrases which might be of interest to Silicate. After watching the video, he stood up, grabbed his bag and made his way immediately to the train station. There, he bought a return to ticket to Bedford.

Felix was Silicate's Public Relations Manager and in charge of keeping anything that connected to Silicate's work in any way, shape, or form out of the media and the public eye. What the company did and what the public actually knew differed greatly, and what he didn't need right now was someone potentially exposing classified secrets before Silicate chose to make their work public.

In the past, most of what was flagged was either fake or a trick of the light, but this was different. From the boy's video and description, Felix was convinced this was real. That was why he, himself, was travelling to the boy's home rather than tasking one of his assistants with the visit.

It was late on Friday evening when the doorbell rang at the Prince residence. After a tiring day at the corner shop, Ghalen answered the door, ready to shoo off any pushy sales person or religious fanatic who might be disturbing his peace.

"Hello, are you Mr Prince?"

"I'm an atheist, I have everything I could ever want, and my wife brings home all the unwanted crap we could ever need. Whatever you're peddling, I'm not interested."

"Very good, sir, but that's not the reason for my visit. My name is Felix Oscroft and I'm here to talk about your son, Terrell."

Ghalen's face changed to one of concern.

"What's he done now? Are you from the school? Social Services?"

"No, nothing like that. I'm actually from a company in London." Felix took out his business card and presented it to Ghalen. "Would it be alright for me to come inside so we could talk about this in private?"

Ghalen surveyed the man. He was short and scrawny with glasses and a balding head. His suit looked tailored and his shoes, though scuffed, looked expensive. Working in the shop his whole life, he prided himself on being able to take the measure of a person in the first few minutes of meeting. Satisfied the man standing in front of him didn't have criminal intent or the body strength to overpower him, he opened the door wider.

"Sure, come on in."

Ghalen guided Felix into the living-room and switched off the television. He returned to his seat on the sofa, while Felix perched himself on a chair opposite.

"I'm sorry for not calling ahead. I only received news about your son's discovery this afternoon and it was so compelling, I felt a personal visit was in order. My secretary had already gone home for the day and I only had your address to hand. Again, I do apologise for my late and rather abrupt arrival."

This was a lie. Felix worked in public relations; he knew how to soften situations, explain his abrupt appearance and garner a sense of trust. He did have the Princes' home phone number, along with the family's mobile numbers, email addresses and even work and school contacts. But that video had to be taken down *tonight*, and the contents couldn't be discussed over the telephone.

Felix was paid a lot to keep Silicate's secrets out of the public eye. Terrell's video had the potential to expose everything the company had worked so diligently to hide. This could destroy Silicate and, more importantly for Felix, his career. He appeared demur and unthreatening as he perched himself, uncomfortably, on the end of a mint-green armchair in the Princes' modest family home.

Ghalen observed the man.

"I'm a bit confused. You said this was about Terrell?"

"Ghalen! Are you going to sit there all night or are you going to — Oh! I'm sorry, I didn't realise we had company." Mrs Prince walked into the room looking flustered, drying her hands on a tea towel. The smell of food lingered in the air, suggesting they had recently finished dinner.

"Beth this is — I'm sorry, I've forgotten your name."
Felix stood and shook Beth's hand, smiling.

"Hello, Mrs Prince. My name is Felix Oscroft. I'm here to talk about your son's discovery."

Beth sat down nervously on the sofa, next to her husband.

"What discovery?" Her voice broke a little as she spoke.

"The video on Terrell's website. I'd really like to talk to him about it, with your permission, of course."

Ghalen looked at his wife with wide eyes before turning back to their guest.

"Excuse me a minute, please." Ghalen stood up and walked to the foot of the stairs. "Terrell!" Ghalen shouted. "Terrell, get down here right now!"

As he walked back into the room, a thunder of heavy footsteps was followed by a teenage boy bursting into the small living-room.

"What?" Terrell stopped and looked at the suited man in the corner of the room.

Felix rose to his feet again.

"Hello, Terrell, my name's Felix. I'm here to talk about the video on your vlog."

"Oh, shit," Terrell whispered under his breath. He turned his head nervously from the man and into the angry gaze of his parents.

"Terrell, what did we say? Don't tell anyone!" Ghalen bellowed.

"I didn't tell anyone; I just uploaded the video to my website. I didn't think anyone would see it."

"So why upload it, then? You know how we feel about this."

"I know. Sorry, Dad." Terrell turned back to Felix. "Are you from the police? Did I do something wrong?"

"No, you haven't done anything wrong."

Beth shot Felix a look only an angry mother could portray.

"Well, apart from not listening to your parents, of course. Actually, I think it would be best for all of us if you could, please, take the video down before we continue our conversation."

Beth smiled at Felix and then turned to raise an eyebrow at her son.

"You mean take it down right now?"

"Yes, Terrell — now. Go on," his mother coerced.

Felix's number one priority coming here this evening was to get the video off the internet and away from prying eyes, especially those connected to anyone working in the media. This was a task he had expected to take a lot more time. Luckily, with the boy's parents being so unhappy that the footage was online in the first place, Felix's primary task was already complete and he had fortuitously seemed to appease Mrs Prince in the process.

Within minutes, Terrell was back in the living-room and shoehorned between his parents on the sofa. Felix had been furnished with a mug of tea and an overflowing plate of biscuits.

Silicate had an official statement used for media cover-ups and non-disclosure agreement breaches. For this particular situation, that cover story wouldn't work. Terrell had seen too much and had the evidence to prove it.

Of course, there was little chance of the Princes knowing what it was that they had actually captured; even less likely that it would ever be linked to Silicate's work, but there were already too many conspiracy theories floating around the internet. If that footage was leaked, it wouldn't take too long for someone to piece everything together. Even if the evidence were confiscated, there was nothing to stop Terrell from recording himself again.

Felix cleared his throat before speaking.

"I'm sure you have a million questions, so let me start at the beginning." He leaned forward to engage the family in a relaxed yet professional approach. "I work for a company in London called Silicate. We specialise in dream analysis to help people with serious neurological health and social problems.

"What you discovered, Terrell, is called a dream apparition. It is you, in your dream state. We know this through years of research and observation of hundreds of patients who've displayed similar apparitions. This isn't public knowledge. Usually, we don't divulge any information outside of the company at all, but from the video I saw, it seems you've already discovered a small part of what we do."

Ghalen was listening intently to every word but struggled to understand what was being said.

"Are you monitoring ghosts?"

"Not ghosts, Mr Prince. The apparition you saw is your son,

just the dream version."

All three family members looked at each other quizzically.

"I'm sorry, we're still not getting it."

"I totally understand. When I joined the company, it took me a while to get my head around it, too. Unfortunately, for me to dive deeper into what we do, I have to ask you to all sign a non-disclosure agreement. It's pretty standard procedure, everyone at Silicate has to sign one."

"I'm not signing a bloody thing when I don't know what all this is about. Can't you tell us first and then we'll decide?" Ghalen asked.

"That would negate the need for the agreement, I'm afraid, Mr Prince. You seem like a lovely, tight-knit family. You didn't know what it was you saw on your son's video, but you accepted it. We don't believe everyone would have that same reaction. The idea that we can film someone's dream would scare a lot of the general population, and our research could be compromised."

The family shuffled uneasily. Ghalen was about to speak when Beth put her hand on his knee and leaned forward.

"Let me see if I understand this correctly. Terrell has recorded his dream-self, and this is something your company is currently working on in secret, so you need us to sign a confidentiality agreement so that we don't tell anyone what you do?"

"That's exactly right, Mrs Prince."

"OK. But until you arrived, we didn't even know your company existed. How could we have told anyone? If you hadn't come here tonight, surely your secrets would have stayed safe?"

Felix didn't want to explain to the Prince family about the online whispers and rumours; or how Terrell's footage could be linked to a leaked video a technician had captured on his phone two years early, and tried to sell to a tabloid newspaper. The story was stopped by Silicate, who had paid the paper a lot of money to keep the article from running. The technician was fired, and Silicate had fined him for breach of contract.

"You're right, Mrs Prince. I could've not come here at all, but what your son has discovered — on his own — no-one else in the world has managed to do, except for our company. On the way over here, I had a conversation with my boss. After reviewing the website, he agrees that Terrell is an incredibly talented individual and would like to invite him to Silicate with the possibly of working with us in the future." He turned to speak to the smiling boy directly. "I understand you finish your exams in two weeks' time. After that, you're more than welcome to visit our facility. We believe you've got a lot of potential."

Mr Prince sat bolt-upright next to his wife, leaving Terrell squashed into the sofa behind them.

"Wait a bloody minute, we don't even know who you are. You walk into our home after seeing Terrell's video, and now want us to sign some forms to shut us up and take our kid away to London?"

"I appreciate this is all coming at you pretty fast, Mr Prince, and I understand your apprehension. As well as offer Terrell a job with us, we're prepared to compensate you for your discretion."

"How much?"

"Dad!" Terrell sat straighter, giving his father a stern look before turning to Felix and speaking more softly. "This is a big deal, isn't it?"

Felix nodded.

"Yes, you could say that. The research we're doing right now is some of the most important and significant in history." He turned to Terrell's parents. "This is why we can't risk anything getting out to the public before we're ready to release it ourselves. Mr Prince, in answer to your question, we are prepared to pay one hundred thousand pounds for your discretion."

Beth dropped the damp tea towel she had been holding and clasped her hands over her mouth.

Felix opened his briefcase; all three of the Princes moved forward, expected to see stacks of £50 notes inside. Instead, Felix lifted out a leather-bound folder and the family slumped back into their seats, slightly disappointed.

"In here is everything you need to know about Silicate. All of our associated companies are listed, and on the inside page is a DVD. If you like, we can watch the film together and I can answer any questions you may have, but I will need the non-disclosure agreements to be signed — by all of you — before I leave. Terrell, I'll also need your assurance that you won't upload or show the video to anyone else."

Terrell nodded as he took the DVD from Felix and slipped it into the player.

The half-hour film was a high-budget production, clearly made for corporate use. When looking to obtain new investors or appease media outlets, this was the film they saw. It said a lot, without divulging any real information about what the company actually did.

Starting with aerial shots of The Particle, the camera worked its way through the building from the lush reception area through to the finer workings of Silicate. Expensive-looking equipment, busy workers and bright colours were depicted, intending to impress and dazzle the audience while deflecting from the lack of substantial content. A soft and welcoming voiceover guided the viewing, adding to the seduction and, ultimately, the deflection of the film.

When the DVD finished, Felix turned to the family expectantly.

"What did you think?"

"Was that Kate Winslet narrating?"

"Honestly, Ghalen, is that really the first thing you think to ask?"

Beth rolled her eyes.

"Yes, that was Kate Winslet. She was actually lovely to work with" Felix replied. "Terrell, do you have any questions?"

"Just one. Do I really have to wait until after my exams to visit?"

"I'm afraid you do. I'm sure your parents would rather you finished school before heading off to London."

"Yes, they would." Beth narrowed her eyes towards her son.

"To be honest, I'm a bit blown away by all of this." Ghalen was a proud and simple man. After leaving school young, he had initially resented working in his dad's corner shop. After marrying Beth, he matured and grew, willingly taking on more responsibility and being proud of the business which sustained his family.

He and Beth had never been interested in travelling, but Ghalen recognised a different draw for their only son. He had been obsessed with London from a young age. Any thoughts he had once harboured of his son taking over the family business had evaporated long ago.

Terrell was intelligent, ambitious and inventive — qualities Ghalen had never possessed nor craved. Although they were different people, he was proud of Terrell. He could be overprotective at times, but he would always try to support his son's decisions.

"I never realised such a company existed. I know I've seen the proof with my own eyes from Terrell's camera, but I still wasn't completely convinced that any of this was true. I mean, videoing dream apparatus — or whatever they're called — who knew that was even possible? I just don't know what to make of any of it."

Terrell loved his father, but he knew most of what had been discussed would have gone over his head.

"Dad, you don't need to understand it, you just can't *talk* about it. With anyone."

"And what happens if we decide we don't want to sign the confidentiality agreement."

You mean the worst-case scenario, Felix thought.

"That would be your choice, Mr Prince. I'm not here to force you to sign anything. Although, I'll be honest, it would make my life a lot easier if you did. Of course, you wouldn't get any money if you didn't sign."

Looking around the small, mid-terrace house the family shared, Felix knew that the financial offer he had made was more than enough. The house couldn't have cost more than £100,000, and was probably mortgaged up to the hilt. He surmised that the money would go a long way to improving the Princes' lives. Felix was highly regarded in the company as being a brilliant marketer and shrewd businessman. When it came to offers, pay-offs and hush money, he had proven himself time and again with many companies, journalists, websites and the occasional sneak photographer. Felix was the man who was trusted to offer the right amount to keep Silicate's secrets hidden, and the shareholders out of the scandal columns.

"It's not enough."

Felix snapped out of his all-knowing stare, looking surprised.

"I'm sorry, Mr Prince — not enough what?"

"It's not enough money."

"DAD!"

"Easy there, Terrell," Ghalen said calmly. "I'm thinking this would be a huge story for the papers and they'd probably pay quite a bit for something so secretive. If you can afford to get Kate Winslet to voice that promo video of yours, I'm sure you could afford to give us more for our silence."

Ghalen may not have achieved much at school, but he was a natural business man. When it came to money matters, there was always a better price.

Felix was stunned. This had never happened to him before.

Ghalen could see that he'd rattled him; he just had to hold his nerve and not push it too far. £100,000 was a huge amount of money. He could hear his own father's words echoing in the back of his mind, "If a man is trying to sell something fast, never accept the first offer — just don't get too greedy."

Felix was left with only two choices: calling Ghalen's bluff, which meant risking walking away without their signatures, or offering more money. He composed himself, straightened his tie and opened his briefcase.

"I appreciate what you're saying, Mr Prince. The economy isn't as good as it was, while the cost of practically everything keeps on rising. A few inches in the national press may very well fetch a fair price, but I doubt they would pay anything in the region of two-hundred-and-fifty thousand pounds."

Ghalen filled his cheeks with air and exhaled; Beth's face seemed to have frozen completely in a look of total bewilderment while Terrell's head was a messy mix of emotions.

Beth managed to compose herself, though she was once again fiddling with the tea towel.

"Would we get a cheque tonight?" Ghalen blurted out.

"We don't use cheques any more — it's all done wirelessly."

"Wirelessly?"

"It means that the money would be transferred from their bank to ours instantly, over the internet," Terrell explained.

"We'd have the money tonight?" Beth's eyes widened.

"As soon as the forms are signed, I'll transfer the funds immediately."

"Can I have a look, please? I want to have a read through this before we sign." Ghalen reached for his reading glasses from the coffee table. He took the tablet containing the lengthy agreement. It would take him a while, but he wanted to know exactly what was worth a quarter of a million pounds.

Felix was worried. The last thing he needed was to go through every clause with someone who didn't understand what a clause was. What if they wanted their own lawyer to read it first? Then he caught himself with the reassuring thought that they probably didn't have their own lawyer.

"Please, take your time, Mr Prince. I want you all to be completely satisfied. In a nutshell, as long as you don't talk about the video, Terrell's findings, or our company, you just get to enjoy being quarter-millionaires." He smiled widely, sensing the tension in the room easing as the family turned back to the contract.

It took over an hour for Ghalen to finish looking through the

NDA. He had little knowledge of legal documents but could find nothing potentially catastrophic or damaging to his family. He put the tablet down, took off his glasses and looked over at his wife and son to gauge their reaction.

Both were wide eyed and nodding. If Beth's hand could have gripped her husband's any tighter, there would have been blood trickling from his palm. Ghalen turned to Felix.

"OK, let's do this."

CHAPTER 10

"We're rich!"

Terrell's parents hugged each other, laughing hysterically. Hooking the teenager around the shoulders, his father pulled him into their embrace.

"You're a genius. I mean it, a bloody *genius!*" Ghalen and Beth kissed their squirming son's forehead before he managed to wriggle out of the bear hug.

Standing back, Terrell watched his parents continue without him, holding back their tears as they embraced each other, beaming from ear to ear. Terrell smiled, too. An overwhelming feeling of accomplishment washed over him; he opened his mouth wide, enjoying the sensation of air rushing into his lungs. A thousand tingles ran through his body, raising goose pimples across his arms and neck.

Exhaling again, Terrell felt his legs weaken, and perched himself on the edge of the sofa, awash with emotion. Was this what true happiness felt like? He had craved the affection and acceptance of those around him his whole life; instead, he'd been mocked, scorned and teased. Yet, as he watched his parents in this moment, tears of joy in their eyes, he felt proud that he had been responsible for it, in a way.

Beth gasped and stepped away from her husband.

"Ghalen, I've just had a thought. What are we going to tell the neighbours? Surely they'll ask questions if we suddenly go on holiday or buy a new car?"

"We'll tell them we won the lottery or something."

"Or a long-lost relative left us the money in their will," Beth suggested excitedly.

"It would have to be on your side, then, all my family escaped from Tanzania in the war, leaving everything behind."

"We'll stick to the lottery story."

"No-one's going to ask," Terrell offered.

"Well I bloody would." Beth chuckled. She walked over to her son, cupping her hands around his face.

"I am so proud of you, honey — we both are."

Ghalen looked on, nodding approvingly.

The next two weeks seemed to crawl at a snail's pace. While every other student was feeling the pressure of exams, Terrell was in high spirits. He knew he couldn't tell anyone what was happening, but he found it almost impossible to contain his excitement.

"Will you stop smiling, please? I know this stuff comes easy to you, but for the rest of us, exams are hard." Cody and Terrell were in the library, cramming for their English Literature final.

"I'm not smiling because of the exams. You really think I'm that much of a geek?"

"Yeah!" Cody looked at him, feigning a dumb look.

They both laughed, earning stares of disapproval from other pupils trying to study.

"Why *are* you so happy, then?"

"I've landed a work placement, of sorts, with a tech firm in London."

"No way! That's awesome news! No wonder you're smiling. When do you go?"

"A week on Saturday. I only found out a few days ago — I still can't believe it."

"And you're only telling me this now? How long are you going for?"

"Not sure yet. They said a few weeks to begin with, then see how it goes from there."

"That's bloody brilliant, no wonder you're walking around like the Cheshire Cat. You'd better keep in touch. If you do end up moving down there permanently, make sure there's room for me in your bachelor pad. I've always wanted to live in London."

Terrell knew that was Cody's way of saying he'd miss him and, though he felt the same way, this opportunity was too exciting to be apprehensive about leaving.

Exams and revision seemed to drag. On his final day, students filtered out of the exam hall, cheering. The school year was over and, for some of Terrell's school cohort, so was formal education. He watched as textbooks were thrown into bins along with school ties and blazers. Terrell had planned to go to college in the autumn and wondered if that would still happen. Perhaps they would let him study in London, or maybe he wouldn't need further education at all ... Distracted by a million thoughts and emotions, he almost collided with Cody.

"Oi! Have you gone blind after all those test papers?"

"Hey! Sorry — I was just thinking about London. How did you get on?"

"Probably failed, but who cares? It's party time!"

Cody wasn't wearing his blazer or tie, and Terrell noticed his school bag was absent, too. He smiled to himself, thinking that his friend had probably been the first to ditch his school attire as he left the exam hall.

"I'd love to, but I need to pack. I'm leaving for London in the morning." It was a bit of a white lie; Terrell had been packed for the past two weeks, but he knew Cody wanted to go to one of their classmates 'end of school' parties. Even with his best friend by his side, that was the last place Terrell wanted to be, especially on his last night in Bedford.

"I know you're leaving tomorrow, and that's why me and your folks are taking you out for a farewell meal."

Terrell was happily surprised. As he looked up, he saw his parents standing by their shiny, new car, waving at them. He waved back, smiling.

"It was your mum's idea," Cody said. "They're taking us to that fancy Italian place in town. There was even talk of letting us drink champagne."

"Really?"

"Well, maybe I brought it up and they just smiled, but that's as good as a 'yes' in my book. We're almost eighteen, anyway," he said, leading his friend over to the car.

A grand meal was enjoyed by all. After an emotional farewell, Cody hugged his best friend and said he would make his own way back, no doubt heading to the party while it was still relatively early. Mrs Prince opened the door to their home and made a pot of tea. The family stayed up talking until the early hours of the morning, theorising what Silicate really *did* and what Terrell's role might be. Ghalen was convinced that Silicate were real-life ghostbusters, while Beth felt sure the company was trying to prove the existence of the soul. Terrell didn't know what to think. One thing the family all agreed on was that it must be something big — massive, even — to warrant the level of secrecy and the £250,000 pay-out.

In bed, Terrell desperately tried to sleep. Everything had happened so fast, from all the boring waiting and wishing and dreaming, to this. In the space of two weeks his life — and that of his family's — had completely changed. He'd finished his exams, ending his five-year sentence at high school, and tomorrow morning, a car would pick him up and take him to his prospective new life in London.

He was excited, but it was also a bit scary to have such limited information about what he would be doing, where he would be living and most of all, when he would see his parents again — though Ghalen and Beth had insisted on riding in the car with Terrell.

"To make sure nothing funny's going on," his father had asserted.

Terrell smiled at the memory as he finally drifted off to sleep.

❖ ❖ ❖

Padman hadn't left the confines of Silicate's offices for recreational purposes in a long time, but after today, he needed the distraction. He was lost in thought as the elevator descended to the ground floor, paying no attention to the droves of people filtering in and out of the building's foyer. As he stepped outside The Particle, a warm, summer breeze danced before his tired eyes and nudged him out of his musings. Instead of hailing a cab, he decided to walk, giving him more time to clear his head.

He made his way through Borough Market and on to the South Bank walkway. The last of the day's sunlight was illuminating St Paul's Cathedral and transforming the shimmering waters of the Thames into waves of scarlet-red. Weaving through hundreds of tourists and the backdrop of iconic London landmarks, Padman smiled. On any other day, having to meander around gaggles of tourists would have been a chore; today, it made him feel alive.

His work at Silicate had taken over his whole life. Everything he did was linked, in some way, to the success and survival of the company and his patients. The Particle had become his home, spending more nights in his office than he cared to admit. There was always something that needed his attention, some emergency that required his help and a never-ending list of potential issues that only he had the clearance to resolve.

However, extended and excessive working hours, minimal sleep and a total lack of any sort of social life, had finally taken its toll. Padman prided himself on being efficient yet caring, but lately, he had begun to lose focus. He blamed himself for having discharged Isabell before she was ready.

At this point, he knew that the quality of his work was more important than ever before, especially so close to the launch. Very few people were trusted with the knowledge he held or the full extent of what the company did. Going out tonight would have been a small moment of respite for most, but to Padman it felt like a true vacation from work. He didn't know when he would have a chance to do this again; the next few months were going to keep him even busier than ever.

It was dusk when he reached Soho. Colourful lights illuminated the street and the people who had gathered beneath them. The usual parade of theatre-goers, drinkers and tourists crowded the road and bars, giving traffic little room to manoeuvre along the narrow, London backstreet.

He allowed himself to be moved along with the herd and into a bar he had once frequented. Usually, Padman would unwind with a few hours in the gym, but today, that faint holiday feeling had provoked a desire for alcohol. He needed to turn down the figurative heat building in his mind.

Inside the bar, he found no relief from the Friday night masses and as the need to anesthetise his brain intensified, he began to feel quite agitated. Taking a deep breath, he waited and then moved more slowly towards to the topless barman in front of him.

CHAPTER 11

Isabell's episode had been her most severe to-date. The clinical staff had, for a period, been fearful for her life, concerned she wouldn't be able to pull herself out of the dream state. For the first hour, she was placed in a recovery facility before being transferred to Archeus by Dr Sharma. There, in the specially designed room, she had been carefully monitored and treated.

Still unconscious following her treatment, she was moved to the hospital wing, where she was now recovering in the small ward. A team of nurses were monitoring Isabell, and although Padman knew she was out of danger, the experience had left him drained and uneasy.

He was still reeling from the experience as he moved away from the bar and stood in a corner of the room, pint in hand. In front of him, a group of muscular men with their tops off were parading around in a desperate attempt for attention. Whenever one of them tried to catch Padman's eye, they received an almost imperceptible shake of the head in return, communicating his desire not to engage. What is it about warm weather that makes everyone behave like over-sexed animals, he wondered to himself, as he sipped his beer.

It was then that he noticed a handsome, young man standing alone in the corner of the bar. He looked nervous; holding on to his pint glass as if it were an anchor. Padman may not have been a regular to the bar any more, but it was clear, even to him, that the man was new to the gay scene.

Wading through the many sweaty bodies, the doctor made his way across the bar.

Jake looked startled as the attractive Indian man approached him and offered his hand to shake. In his fitted suit and beaming, white-toothed smile, he stood out from the crowd.

Raising his voice to be heard over the music, the doctor introduced himself.

"Hi, I'm Padman. I saw you from the other side of the bar and thought I'd come over and say hello."

Jake took the doctor's hand, shook it, and returned the smile.

"I'm Jake. It's my first time in here."

"Yeah, I could tell."

"Is it that obvious?"

Padman laughed.

"You could say that. Are you new to London?"

"Yes. I've only been here a few days." Jake paused before admitting, "This is also my first time in a gay bar. I was doing OK until those guys started taking their tops off. Now I don't know if I should be looking at them or not."

"I always find it's best not to stare at the wild animals," Padman joked. "It could give them cause to pounce on you."

Both men laughed. Jake drank the last of his pint.

"Want another of those?" Padman asked.

"That would be great. Thank you."

When the doctor returned from the bar carrying two fresh pints, a small gathering of men had crowded around the fresh-faced northerner. As he passed the drink to Jake, Padman smiled.

"Looks like you've attracted your fair share of admirers already tonight."

Jake smiled back and took a sip of his beer.

"Aye, but there's only one guy buying me drinks.

"Cheers to that, then!"

The two clinked glasses and carried on drinking. The men

who had been pushing their way towards Jake now backed off, looking for another conquest.

"Come with me — there are seats at the back where we can chat properly, if you like?"

Jake followed Padman through the crowd until they reached a small area away from the noise. They put their drinks on a table and took seats next to each other.

"That's so much better," Padman said as he angled himself towards Jake.

"How come this bit's empty? Do Londoners not sit?"

Padman laughed.

"Usually we do, but in here it's because most guys are on the pull. You can't see the bar from where we are, so it's unwanted space, at least on nights like this."

"You're not on the pull tonight, then?" Jake smiled as he drank from his glass.

"Just here for the pull of pints tonight."

"Good answer."

"Your accent — you're from Yorkshire?"

Jake nodded.

"Beautiful part of the world. What made you move to London?"

"It *is* beautiful, but not known for its vibrant gay scene, at least not where I'm from."

"You did come here to pull, then?"

"I thought I already had!"

"Good answer." Padman smiled.

They both smiled and clinked their glasses together.

"Are you here for work?"

"No. It's a long story — boring, really — but I left my job, my home and my friends to come and experience life in the big city."

"I'm no stranger to long stories. How are you finding London?"

Jake's smile dropped.

"It's not really what I expected." He laughed nervously and drank more of his beer.

"Sounds like we've not made a good impression on you."

Jake scrunched up his face and gave a little sigh.

"To be honest, no, not really. I'd never even visited London before, so I didn't know what to expect. I obviously knew the streets weren't paved with gold, but I did expect people to be friendlier. London's not exactly welcoming to strangers. It's a bit of a culture shock. No-one wants to talk to me . . . well, apart from you. You're actually the first person I've had a conversation with in a week."

"I'm really glad I came over now." Padman smiled warmly. "Sorry you've had a crappy time. Where in Yorkshire are you from?"

"Malham — do you know it?"

"I know Malham very well. I've been hiking up there quite a few times . . . Malham Cove, Janet's Foss. Such a beautiful place. No wonder you're having a hard time adjusting. You've exchanged country life in a quaint village for one of the busiest cities in the world."

"I have. Still, people are people, wherever you go. At least, that's what I always thought."

"We're all the same species, but not all people are the same. I know London can feel cold to an outsider, especially one from the country. The problem is that there's so many millions of us living here in a relatively small area, so we adapt to make life work for us. It's easier not to notice strangers so we can get to and from work as efficiently as possible.

"On top of all the people who live here, there's all the tourists. Millions of them crowding the streets every day. Just getting to where you need to be on time becomes a bit of a battle. Commuting, even within the city, can be a nightmare. People tend to be a bit suspicious, too — they don't know who to trust . . . but once you make friends, in my experience, you can count on them for life."

"Wow," Jake breathed. "I never thought of it like that. I was working on the assumption everyone was just totally up themselves."

"Some people are." Padman laughed. "But most are a bit more complicated than that." He noticed Jake's glass was empty again. "Want another?"

"It's my round this time. Same again?"

"Sure. Thanks." Padman smiled as he passed his empty glass to Jake and watched as he disappeared into the sea of people gathered around the bar.

◆ ◆ ◆

"Ahhhhh!" Isabell bolted upright in her hospital bed, gasping for air. A nurse rushed over to check on her.

"You're OK, Isabell. I'm here."

She looked around the room, gathering her bearings, before focusing properly on the nurse flashing a small torch into her still-sleepy eyes. She smiled as a wave of relief flooded over her. The nurse returned her smile.

"My name's Sally. You're in the hospital wing at Silicate. You had another episode, but we've been treating you, and all your vitals have returned to normal. How do you feel?"

"I'm OK, I guess. Just a bit dazed."

It was then she realised there was someone sitting to her right — Ryder. She recognised the man in the wheelchair and gazed at him quizzically.

Recognising her confusion, he spoke.

"I was here when you were brought on to the ward. I decided to stay until you woke up. Sally told me this has happened before and not to worry . . . but what can I say? I'm a worrier.

"I thought it might be nice for you to see a friendly face when you woke up, but I can leave now if you want to get some rest." Isabell was touched that someone she'd just met had taken the time to stay with her. She sat up a bit straighter and smoothed her tangled hair, trying to restore composure.

"Thank you, that's very sweet. At least I made your first day eventful."

"It's certainly been different."

The nurse returned to Isabell's bedside, carrying a glass of water.

"Sorry to interrupt. I've just left Doctor Sharma a message. He asked me to call him as soon as you were awake, but I suspect he might have gone to bed already. He'll see you in the morning, though."

"Great." Isabell grimaced. "As if I hadn't been through enough, I'll have to relive it all tomorrow."

Sally looked apologetic.

"Sorry, not everyone gets my sense of humour." Isabell tried to reassure her. "This isn't my first time back from cuckoo land. I'm not actually worried about talking to Padman. He's a great doctor — these days, I think of him as a friend, too."

The nurse looked relieved.

"In that case, I'll leave you to try to rest. If you need anything at all, just push the button."

As Sally left the room, Ryder released his wheelchair's brakes and began manoeuvring around the bed.

"I should be off, too, then — let you get a decent night's sleep before your interrogation in the morning."

"I've only just woken up — I won't be tired for a while, so you can stay, if you want. I don't really fancy the idea of staring at the ceiling for the next few hours."

Ryder looked around. A huge TV hung on the wall, the shelves were crammed full of books, films and music, and a large stack of magazines lay on the bedside table. There was no shortage of distractions here; Ryder suspected that what Isabell really craved was company. For all her bravado, the episode must have been scary.

"All I have waiting for me at home is an empty fridge and a disconnected cable service, anyway. I'd love to stay."

"We can order food here." Isabell grinned. "I'm starving now you've mentioned it."

Ryder pulled himself back by the side of the bed as Isabell scanned the dinner menu.

◆ ◆ ◆

A mobile phone vibrated gently, lighting the darkened room, as a voicemail message registered. Padman reached for his phone and smiled as he heard the news that Isabell was recovering well.

Jake turned his head towards Padman, the phone having woken him up.

"Who was that?"

"Just work, but it can wait until the morning."

"Thanks for reminding me." Jake stumbled out of bed, scrambling around on the floor until he found his clothes.

"Leaving already?" Padman queried.

Jake pulled his mobile phone from the front pocket of his jeans.

"No. But if you want me to stay, I need somewhere to charge this."

The doctor smiled.

"There's a charger in the drawer and a plug by the side of the bed. I'm going to grab a glass of water; do you need anything?"

"Water sounds great, thanks," Jake replied, riffling through the bedside drawer.

Padman lived alone in a three-bed, Edwardian, terraced house just off Bloomsbury Square. It was family owned and given to him by his parents. As impressive as the house was, he rarely had the time to appreciate it or to put his own stamp on the place. The furnishings hadn't changed, the oven was never used, and his cleaner got more use out of the living-room.

Meeting Jake had been just the distraction the doctor had needed. The two had chatted and drank for hours, enjoying each other's company while sharing stories of their past. Padman's house was a short walk from Soho and when Jake offered to escort him home, both men knew what that meant.

Now, hours later, Padman smiled as he stood in the kitchen filling two glasses with water. He was still smiling when he walked into the bedroom, finding Jake had fallen back to sleep. He placed the glasses on to the bedside table, climbed into bed and snuggled up to the handsome Northerner, falling into a deep, restful sleep.

When Padman inherited the house, it hadn't felt right to adopt his parents' old bedroom as his own. He decided to commandeer the second-largest room, which was once his father's study. After the events with Lady Braighton, this had become a temporary clinic before the birth of Silicate. Here, Rajesh had treated those early patients using the primitive equipment he had developed.

The room had fallen out of use once The Particle was built. The equipment had long-since been removed, except for one modified camera positioned behind the two-way mirrored wardrobe, facing the bed. Padman hadn't thought about that camera in years; if he had, he would have removed it. Or, at the very least, unplugged it from the socket Jake had inadvertently switched on in a bid to charge his phone.

CHAPTER 12

"...And now there are reports of spaceships hovering over central London. Brian Jennings, our resident technology expert, has more on this bizarre story."

"That's right, May. Londoners have awoken this morning, looked out of their windows and seen spaceships. We apologise for the shaky footage you're watching — it was taken on someone's phone — but we can clearly see what looks to be the projection of a giant cube-type object hovering above Central London.

"As the film continues, we can see the sky is littered with space vehicles which on closer inspection, all appear to be from different films or TV shows: Star Trek, Star Wars, Flight of the Navigator, and, if we zoom in closely, we can see a police box, which can only be the TARDIS from Doctor Who.

"We think this is possibly some kind of promotion for a future crossover. We've reached out to the BBC and to Disney, but so far neither organisation has confirmed nor denied anything."

"Brian, do you think this is connected to yesterday's reports of dinosaurs in Hyde Park?" May giggled as she picked up the tabloid newspaper, holding the front page up to the camera. It showed a blurry image of what looked like a group of dinosaurs running through Hyde Park with the headline: Jurassic Lark!

"I think so, May. In recent years, we've seen many crossovers on the screen. This could be the latest. If it is, it's strange they chose to *advertise it in this way as it seems to be quite difficult for people to actually spot them or identify them clearly. The pictures used in the paper and online were taken by a professional photographer."*

"Do you think he was employed by Disney or the BBC or whoever to release these photos, then?"

"I believe so."

"What about the video footage we just saw?"

"There were a number of witnesses from the same block of flats, but when they opened their windows, the images were gone, indicating these are either projections or reflections."

"And what about the pictures of the dinosaurs?"

"According to the photographer's website, he was in Hyde Park yesterday shooting a magazine cover with Megan Hilty when it began to rain. He says it was then that he saw these dinosaurs and decided to shoot them with his camera."

"Are they still there now?"

"I've been to both sites, and I'm afraid they appear to have gone. But that's not to say we won't see any more over the coming days."

May turned to face the camera and smiled widely.

"Well, if you're in London this weekend, be on the lookout for dinosaurs, spaceships or anything else out of the ordinary. And, as always, as soon as we have more information, we'll bring it to you here first.

"Now, Vance is here with the weather ..."

A thud from upstairs tore Padman away from the video he was watching on his tablet. He removed his headphones and heard his guest ambling about in the room above him.

The morning sun shone through the window and dazzled Jake as he came round from sleep. Reaching for his phone, he checked the time; it was just past seven. He rubbed his eyes and surveyed his surroundings. A little disorientated, he slowly remembered coming back here the night before. He glanced to the other side of the bed, but Padman wasn't there. A sudden urge to use the bathroom came over him. Jake moved to the edge of the bed, stretched and pulled on his boxer shorts. As he left the room, he heard the doctor's voice calling from below.

"The bathroom is to your right. I'm downstairs in the kitchen when you're ready."

Padman's smile disappeared as he turned back to the paused video, wondering what he was going to do. A few minutes later, he heard footsteps coming down the stairs, indicating Jake's imminent arrival. He turned around and picked up the remote control for the television. Megan Hilty was sitting on the couch with the presenter talking about her new West End show. He made a mental note to try to get tickets to see it before switching off the TV.

As Jake entered the room, Padman was pouring boiling water into a teapot.

"Good morning, sleepy-head, would you like a drink? I've got tea or . . . well, it looks like we just have tea."

"That's good. I'm a true Yorkshireman — I only drink tea." "And beer, going by last night. I'm guessing you're a milk with ten sugars kind of a man, are you?"

"Oi! Less of the stereotypes. Just the nine, please."

They both laughed.

With caffeine in hand, Padman moved to the adjoining room and placed the pot and mugs on to the dining-table before taking a seat.

"How are you feeling this morning?" the doctor enquired as they sipped their drinks.

"I'm fine apart from almost being blinding by the sun when I woke up."

"Sorry, I must have forgotten to close the curtains last night. It was raining when I got out of bed, otherwise I would've closed them for you. No hangover this morning, then?"

"I don't get hangovers."

"How old are you again?"

"Twenty-six."

"Ha! Wait until you're in your thirties, then tell me you don't get hangovers."

"How old are you?"

"Older than twenty-six." Padman grinned.

Jake considered the doctor, trying to gauge his age. Sure, he looked older than him, but not *that* much. He sported no grey hair or wrinkles that he could see...

"Oi! Stop staring. I'll be forty-one next month, but I don't think I look it. Beard dye works wonders."

"I think you look great, whatever your age."

"I bet you say that to all the boys."

Jake gave a nervous laugh and looked down into his mug of tea. Padman noticed a flush colouring his cheeks and realised that Jake was more inexperienced than he'd led him to believe.

"Wait, am I your first?"

Jake remained looking down and silent, his cheeks glowing a deep shade of red.

Padman reached across and took hold of his hands.

"Last night was amazing. *You* were amazing."

Jake looked up with a nervous smile.

Searching the room for anything to deflect from the current conversation and his obvious embarrassment, Jake noticed a picture of a beautiful Indian woman hanging on the wall.

"Who's that?"

"That's Zoya, my ex-wife."

Jake almost choked on his tea.

"You were married to a woman?"

"I was. For a short while, at least."

"What happened? Did she find out you were gay?"

"She did — not long after the wedding, actually. It was an arranged marriage between my father and his best friend from university. They both came from traditional backgrounds, so it wasn't particularly strange for them to cement their friendship through a pact to marry off their future children.

"I'm quite a few years older than Zoya. By the time she'd

come of age, I already knew I was gay. I'd been in a relationship with a man for a few years at that point, but I was still very much in the closet."

"And you went through with the wedding?"

"I had to. It was around the same time that Silicate, the company I now work for, was formed. My father's friend, Zoya's father, Devansh Kapoor, had invested money in the company as a show of good faith for the upcoming wedding," Padman continued. "He had actually wanted to buy up a much larger proportion of shares, but Lord Braighton, the founder of the company, wouldn't let him," he recalled.

"Why not?"

"Whereas my father had become a respected healer, Devansh had used his degree in science to form a string of biotech companies in the US, becoming extremely wealthy in the process. He was known as a ruthless businessman and there even were rumours of money laundering, internal corruption and illegal human trials."

"And your father still pushed for you to marry that guy's daughter?"

"In his eyes, Devansh was still the same person he studied at Oxford with. To my dad, the rumours were just malicious lies spread by his competitors. Lord Braighton was more cautious and only allowed Devansh to buy a handful of shares."

"What happened with your wife?"

"My parents moved out and gave us this house so that we could make a home here together. They wanted grandchildren." Padman grimaced slightly. "That wasn't on the cards for me." He drained his tea and reached for the pot, refilling his and Jake's mugs. "It didn't take long for Zoya to figure out the truth."

"How?"

"A few months after the wedding, Zoya came home and found me crying in the living-room. I had just gotten off the phone with my partner of two years. He told me he couldn't be with me any more, now that Zoya was in the picture. He'd always hoped that, one day, I would come out to my parents and we could announce our relationship. Once I was married to a woman, that seemed impossible."

"I'm sorry, that must have been really hard."

"It was. Extremely. But I totally understand why he did it. We were so in love before the wedding. Afterwards, we rarely saw each other. It crushed both of us."

"When Zoya found you crying, did you tell her outright?"

"I fumbled, trying to make up some ridiculous cover story, but she'd caught the tail end of my conversation. My secret was out."

"She wasn't upset?"

"She must have been, but she didn't show it. Being gay is a big taboo in our culture, and I think that went someway to her understanding. We talked about the possibility of staying together to keep my secret, but we both knew that wouldn't work. It wasn't fair on either of us to live a lie; I respected Zoya too much for that.

"The following weekend, I came out to my parents."

"How did they take it?"

"They were angry at first, but Zoya was there, with me, for support. I just seemed to shut down. Confronting the years of repression brought out intense emotions and I couldn't handle it.

"When people say coming out's the hardest thing they've ever done, that doesn't do it justice. It reminded me a bit of Scooby Doo — as if my parents had only ever known Padman the straight guy, and when I ripped off the mask, they saw the real me, underneath. They'd never even considered the notion I was gay. They didn't know how to respond.

"I was so thankful Zoya was there. She helped calm them down and explained everything I couldn't. I don't think I would have had the courage to go through without her."

"More tea?" Padman stood up to switch the kettle on again.

"Please."

"We discussed so much that afternoon," Padman continued

as he refilled the teapot, "and once my parents had adjusted to this new reality, a bigger concern hit us — how was Devansh going to react? I offered to fly to America with Zoya to talk to him, but she convinced me it would be better if she went alone." Padman paused, gazing at Zoya's photograph on the wall, before taking his seat at the table again. "That was the last time I ever saw or heard from her."

"What? Why? What happened?"

"My father told me that Devansh had been furious when he'd heard I was gay. I'd brought shame on his family and *tainted* his daughter. The marriage was annulled, he pulled out the money he'd invested in Silicate and cut all ties with me, my father and everyone we knew."

"What about to Zoya?"

"I presume she's living in San Francisco now. I've tried contacting her on numerous occasions — but after five years, nothing. Her phone was disconnected, and I haven't been able to track her down on social media. I just hope she's all right. She never asked for any of this."

"What about her stuff? She must have had things here?" Jake queried, thoughts of leaving all his own belongings behind in Yorkshire still fresh in his mind.

"Devansh hired a removal company to take everything away. The only thing I have left is this picture, which I was able to save. I hang it here to honour a woman I truly admire. Without her, I would most likely still be living a half-life, full of lies and regret."

"Did you get back together with your boyfriend?"

"Once everything had calmed down, I got back in touch with him, but he'd already moved on. We still chat occasionally, and I've met his new partner. They seem happy together."

"Not so great for you, though."

"I guess, but life isn't always a bed of roses. It gave me time to concentrate on my work instead." Padman smiled as he sighed, gazing into Jake's eyes. "And I wouldn't have met you and had an awesome time last night." He poured the freshly brewed tea.

"How did you sleep?" Padman asked, changing the subject.

"Great! I fell unconscious as soon as my head hit the pillow. I didn't snore, did I?"

"Not that loud." The doctor raised an eyebrow and smiled.

"Sorry."

"Don't worry about it. I fell asleep not long after you, anyway. You didn't keep me awake."

"I tend to snore if I've been drinking."

"We won't drink as much next time, then."

"Next time? You want to see me again?"

"Absolutely! In fact, I was wondering if you'd like to spend the day together?"

"Sure." Jake beamed. "That'd be great. Don't you have to go to work, though? I remember you saying last night you had to go into the office today. I can't remember what you said you did for a living, sorry."

Padman walked over to the breakfast bar, picked up his tablet and sat back down, pulling his chair closer to Jake's.

"I'm a doctor, working in a scientific research facility." Padman paused, he felt nervous. He never talked about his work to anyone outside of Silicate; the strict security measures he had helped create didn't allow him to, but after witnessing the video on his tablet, he knew he had to break the rules.

"I work in a specialised field. It's highly secretive, because we're the only company in the world researching this particular niche."

"What is it you do?"

"In layman's terms, we monitor people as they sleep, and track their dreams."

Jake was a farmer of four generations. His education had finished after high school. Knowing that his future in agriculture was not only expected but required, he'd breezed through school taking in just enough information to pass his exams. He wasn't stupid; neither was he very learned.

"Have you ever had a nightmare?"

"Yes, of course," Jake replied, looking puzzled.

"Have you ever dreamed of something so real and terrifying or upsetting that it has woken you up?"

"Yes. Quite often, actually."

"And after you wake up, have you ever felt like there was someone else in the room with you? Someone who was actually in the bed with you, or the feeling that you were looking at yourself?"

Jake's mouth opened wide, his eyes staring into Padman's. He felt a shiver run across his right arm and goose bumps form all the way up to his neck.

"How could you possibly know that?" he breathed.

"This is what we research. We've monitored hundreds of people over the years. People who display these apparitions."

"Is that why we met? Did you know about me before last night?" Jake's mind was racing.

"Amazingly enough, we met by chance. I have a theory that we all share this phenomenon, though only a percentage of the population show outward signs of apparitions, like you."

"If it's not that common, why ask me about it?"

Padman shuffled uneasily, this was the part he hadn't wanted to talk about. He had no idea how Jake would react to the video in his hands, and he knew that showing him the footage was breaking every rule in the book. If Jake stormed out and told anyone, Silicate could be exposed. Padman hoped that their romantic encounter, however brief, would be enough to not let that happen.

CHAPTER 13

"And a glass of red wine for me, please," Shira said as she handed her menu back to the waiter.

Abby looked up from her phone with a quizzical expression. Her mother rarely drank alcohol.

"Well, we're on holiday, and Silicate are paying for our meals, so I thought I should treat myself."

Abby smiled; it was nice to see her mother in such good spirits.

"Did you have fun today?" Shira asked. "What did you think of Silicate?"

Abby chewed her lower lip while she considered her response.

"Those reflection pods things were a bit scary at first, but when Doctor Sharma showed us how they worked . . . it's just a bedroom with glass walls really."

"I expected to get wet when he opened the door."

"Me, too!" Abby exclaimed, smiling.

"And what about the Red Room?" Shira had asked enthusiastically.

"I want to live in there! Those reclining sofas are so comfy. They've got every games console in the world, Mom — even Japanese ones I've never heard of."

The waiter returned with their drinks, and Shira raised her

glass to make a toast.

"To my beautiful daughter — I'm so very proud of you."

"You, too, Mom."

They clinked their glasses, and both took a sip.

"Doctor Sharma seems nice. It's a shame he had to rush off," Shira said, placing her glass back on to the table.

"Yeah, he is. A bit kooky, but I like that. I wonder why he had to go so quickly, though?"

"He's a doctor, darling. Who knows what type of emergency he gets called out to attend. We'll see him again tomorrow. That is, if you want to go back?"

"I do."

"I'm so glad you said that." Shira grinned. "I was so worried about this trip, but now that I've actually seen the place and met the staff, I feel a lot more at ease about leaving you with them."

"Me, too. If they can help stop these horrible dreams then my life — *our* lives — can start over, sort of."

Shira reached for her daughter's hand.

"I really am so proud of you, you know."

The waiter arrived with their order, and they continued chatting casually over their meal. It was night-time when they left the restaurant and as they walked down the street, Shira noticed that Abby was smiling and laughing like she used to. The past few years had been extremely difficult for both of them; now, for the first time since Oren had disappeared, there seemed to be a sense of hope.

London was awash with lights, colours and sounds. Wanting to see more of the city, they walked to Tower Bridge and stared out across the River Thames.

"I can't believe we're actually in London, Mom. This is amazing!"

Shira slipped an arm around Abby's shoulders.

"I can hardly believe it, either, darling."

They stood there for what seemed a long time, drinking in the view and relishing this rare feeling of contentment.

Happier than they had been in years, they made their way back to London Bridge and their hotel. For a long time, Shira had gone without in order to provide for Abby, so it made a nice change living this luxurious lifestyle. Whatever the week ahead held for them, it was a welcome respite to be able to relax and not have to worry about money, even if only for a few days.

The bathroom in the suite was twice the size of their own. Shira ran a hot bubble bath and read a book while she soaked. Abby was glued to the television, amazed by how few channels there were compared to back home, but immensely enjoying the British offerings.

Not long after, Shira joined her and, together, they watched a comedy on the BBC.

"Isn't it funny how people here say 'Mum' instead of 'Mom'? Doctor Sharma said it, too. It sounds strange." Abby yawned; her eyes were only half-open.

"Are you tired, sweetheart? I'll turn off the TV and let you get some sleep. You must be exhausted."

"Thanks, *Mum*." Abby yawned as Shira laughed.

"You're right — that does sound strange, but maybe the way we say 'Mom' is just as bizarre to English people." She tucked her daughter into bed.

Abby sank into the bedclothes, her eyes already closed.

"I love you, Mommy," Abby said, almost under her breath, as she drifted off to sleep.

Shira kissed her daughter's forehead, switched off the television and climbed into her own bed to read another chapter of her book. Once she sensed that her daughter was asleep, she too, settled down for the night.

Bang! Bang! Bang!

Abby bolted upright in bed, her heart racing. She switched on the lamp and looked over to her mother's bed, but it was empty. She tried to keep calm, telling herself that her mother must be answering the door.

Another thirty seconds passed, and the banging hadn't stopped.

The thought occurred to Abby that it was her mother trying to get back into the suite. Perhaps she had locked herself out, somehow. She swung her legs out of bed and pulled on her dressing-gown.

"It's OK, Mom — I'm coming."

As Abby reached to unlock the door, the handle suddenly turned from the outside. It swung open, flooding the room with blinding light.

Standing in the doorway wasn't Shira, but the Shadow Man. He stepped forward, opening his arms as he approached the terrified girl.

Abby screamed as the banging sound amplified, mirroring the pounding of her heart. She fell backwards on to her bed, the silhouetted man inching ever closer. Pulling the bed-sheets over her head, she screamed at him to go away, covering her ears to silence the banging noise.

Suddenly, the bed-sheets were pulled away from her.

"Shush, Abby. It's Mommy, you're dreaming. Shush . . . shush . . ."

Abby closed her mouth and opened her eyes to see Shira standing over her. She was startled once again as she heard the banging from her dream within the room.

"It's OK, Abby — it's just someone at the door," Shira re-assured her.

"Hello? Is everything all right in there?" the concierge called.

Shira opened the door and explained that her daughter was having a nightmare. Abby's screams had been so loud, the concierge looked genuinely shaken and concerned.

It was past three in the morning when the two women finally fell back to sleep.

Ryder and Isabell chatted all night, and when the former soldier had started to feel tired, Isabell offered to share her bed with him.

Sally entered the room a few hours later to find them both fast asleep. She switched off the TV and closed the door softly before retreating back to the nurses' station, down the hall. As with all rooms in Silicate, cameras were installed so that everywhere and everyone could be monitored from stations around the building. Back at her desk, the nurse could keep an eye on Isabell and her new friend. She smiled at how the two had fallen asleep, entwined with each other.

Sally had moved her attention to a second screen to check her emails. She regularly worked the late shift, usually observing patients in Hygge as they slept in the pods. On nights like this one, when there were no pods to monitor, she could catch up on her paperwork and take advantage of the many leisure activities Silicate provided. Sally had become a force to be reckoned with in the video game world, but was just as happy to watch the latest films with her co-workers.

Another nurse walked into the room.

"Are they still talking?"

Andrew had joined Silicate soon after qualifying as a nurse. His family owned shares in the company, which had gone a long way in getting him this job. He was a good nurse, but his work ethic wasn't always on par with the rest of the staff.

With an extremely wealthy family, he would have preferred not to work at all; part of him would never understand why he couldn't be snowboarding in Switzerland with his friends instead of working the graveyard shift.

His mother had been a nurse before meeting his father and she had steered him into the profession. After only six weeks in the job, his smoke-breaks were lasting up to thirty minutes a time, something which had been noted by his co-workers. The only occasions he kept up the pretence of being industrious was when he was on the same shift as Sally.

She may have been the head nurse, but she was only a few years older than Andrew. What they differed in personality, they shared in interests. Andrew found that he looked forward to them being scheduled to work together.

"No, they're fast asleep now. Come and see how cute they look together."

Andrew walked over to Sally's desk and laughed as he saw the camera-feed from Isabell's room.

"She's drooling all over his face."

The two laughed as Sally zoomed in on them.

"I put a sedative into her IV to help her sleep, and her friend was just tired, I guess."

"Is that her boyfriend, then?"

"He's staff! Apparently, he started work here yesterday. They've only just met."

"Wow, he's a fast mover."

"They're only sleeping in the same bed together and I think it's cute."

"You want to watch the lovebirds sleep all night or do you fancy beating my arse again on the PlayStation?" Andrew asked.

Sally looked up from the monitor and smiled.

"Always."

"You're the only girlfriend I've ever had that's better than me at gaming," he stopped suddenly, looking flustered. "I — I mean, *friend* who's a *girl*, not —"

"Oh, shut up. I know what you meant." Sally moved from the desk to an adjoining room known as the den. This room was used exclusively by the nurses for breaks or quiet periods, like now. A huge TV was set up on the wall with different-coloured bean bags scattered across the floor. To one side were food and drink facilities, and comfortable sofas lined the opposite wall.

Above the TV were three smaller monitors showing live camera-feeds. The middle one constantly changed between the rooms; one showed their office feed, in case anyone was looking for them; and Sally had set the final one to show the feed from room 38, Isabell's room.

After three games, Sally had lived up to her reputation and won every round. It wasn't until she jumped up and did a mock victory dance that she noticed the centre monitor was flashing red.

"Shit, shit, shit," she muttered as she ran back to her desk.

Andrew put down his controller more leisurely and followed her.

"What's up?"

"The silent alarm's been tripped." She clicked on the screen and was presented with a password command prompt. "That's not good."

"What? You don't have the password?"

"No — I do, it just means that the alarm's from a high security area."

"I thought this whole place was a high security area?"

"It is," Sally said, tapping in a convoluted series of letters and numbers on the keyboard, "but there are even higher security areas that only management have access to. Sorry, but I have to ask you to stand at the other side of the desk, please, so you can't see my screen."

Sally didn't look up as Andrew raised his eyebrows and moved out of the way. He'd never seen her this flustered before. What could be more secretive than this place was already? As he stepped back, he noticed the reflection of Sally's screen on the glass wall behind her. Although he couldn't see the password being entered, he could clearly make out what was being displayed.

Sally was confronted with hundreds of thumbnails showing live camera-feeds from every part of the building, a small series of which were flashing red. Sally clicked on the first one and moved closer to her screen. The bar at the top of monitor informed her this was *Archeus, Camera 001*. She could see the door to the room was open, which was unusual; but everything inside and out appeared normal.

To her knowledge, she and Andrew were the only clinical

staff on duty tonight. Suspecting one of the security guards might have opened the door on their nightly checks and forgotten to close it behind them, she called the security station. There was no answer. She placed the phone on loudspeaker as it rang, while she clicked through the other camera-feeds from Archeus. Everything inside appeared to be as it should be; she couldn't see anything out of place. Not being able to contact the guard station, she ended the call and made her way out of the room.

"I'm not sure what's going on downstairs, but I'll have to check it out. Keep an eye on the patients, and call me immediately if there are any problems."

"What's going on?" Andrew asked.

"Hopefully nothing."

Sally left the room, leaving a rather perplexed Andrew alone in the nurses' station. From the reflection, he could see that she had forgotten to log out of the system and moved over to her desk to see what the emergency was. He scanned through the ten cameras in Archeus and could see nothing out of the ordinary except for the door being open. The room looked to be a large pod, like the ones in Hygge, but the equipment was significantly different. Glass was only used on one part of the room and black covered every other surface.

He tapped the keyboard mindlessly, scrolling through the different cameras positioned around Archeus, talking out loud.

"Is that a bed? Why are there huge cannons hanging from the ceiling? What was *that*?" He stopped. He was sure he had seen movement on one of the cameras. Slowly scrolling back through the live-feeds, he paused on camera 005.

There was nothing, yet he remained convinced that something had just moved. A foot, maybe? It could have been Sally entering the room, he guessed — but if so, where was she now? The door was still open and everything in the same place as before. He began to zoom out on camera 005, pushing the focus wider. Archeus remained still, but in the reflection on the wall, he could see what looked like a leg moving very slowly across the floor, as if the person was lying down. He picked up the phone and called Sally; interrupted by the mobile resting at his side starting to ring.

"Really?" he exclaimed, hanging up. He squinted at the screen, but the leg was now gone, and the room was still once more.

"You're imagining things, Andy. Get a bloody grip," he muttered to himself, moving away from the desk and collecting his jacket. He patted his packet of cigarettes within the pocket before walking down the corridor towards the emergency exit.

Using the staff elevator to get out the building and smoke was a hassle he didn't need. After his first few days working here, Andrew discovered the fire escape at the end of the corridor. It was secluded, unmanned and out of camera range . . . with the right adjustments. In short, it was the perfect place to smoke and to bunk off work.

Tonight, in that concrete stairwell away from prying eyes, leaning out of a small window, Andrew's mind felt so full it was overflowing. As the smoke escaped his lips into the cool, night air, he thought about Archeus. What was this secret room? Why was access to it so restricted? Why didn't *he* have access to it? What on earth could require even more security than the rest of Silicate?

The images he'd seen on the monitors earlier played on a loop through his mind. Though it had been a momentary glimpse, he couldn't seem to rid himself of that brief image of a moving leg. Suddenly, he gasped, inhaling the smoke too rapidly, causing him to cough and splutter as he threw the cigarette butt out of the window and raced back to the nurses' station.

Seated in front of the monitor, he accessed camera 005 and zoomed out, trying to find the same view as he had before. There it was: a foot. Only for a split second, and then it was gone. The camera continued to zoom out for a few more seconds and then stopped at its outer limit.

Frame by frame, Andrew zoomed back into the image, resisting the urge to blink as he stared at the wall. On the tenth click, he gasped in shock, standing up and staggering back from his chair, staring at the screen in disbelief. On the monitor, a man's leg could be seen clearly laying on the floor, sticking out from behind some piece of equipment. Was he injured? Had he been attacked? Was Sally in danger?

Andrew right-clicked on the screen to check the room information. A map of the whole facility was displayed, a highlighted section showing the camera's specific position and where Archeus was situated within the building. He could see from the display that the security doors leading to the room were also flashing red, indicating these, too, were open. Perhaps Sally had left them that way?

Andrew bolted from the room; he didn't know what was going on, but if Sally needed backup, he wanted to be there for her.

It was the sticky substance congealed on his beard that first roused Ryder. As his senses began to wake, he became aware of warm air blowing gently up his nose. As he opened his eyes, he could see Isabell, fast asleep with her face nuzzled into his. Her mouth was wide-open, the warm air her exhalations.

Not wanting to move and wake Isabell, he reached for the call button. Several pushes and over five minutes later, a rather frazzled-looking nurse rushed into the room.

"I'm so sorry," the nurse said, straightening his clothes and trying to regain a steady breathing pattern. He wasn't used to seeing people sharing beds at Silicate, but as strange occurrences went, this wasn't even close to some of the things he'd witnessed. "I'm not actually due on shift for another twenty minutes, but I could hear your alarm from the changing-room —is everything all right?" he asked anxiously.

Isabell groggily woke up and raised her head.

"What's going on? That had better be my breakfast."

CHAPTER 14

At seven a.m., Terrell woke with a start. He switched his alarm off, stretched, and sat up in bed.

"Good morning, sweetheart. Are you all rested and excited?" Beth came bounding into the room holding a tray of tea, orange juice and a dinner plate overflowing with pan-fried rashers of bacon, sausages, eggs and baked beans. On a side plate was a stack of buttered toast and jam.

Rubbing sleep from his eyes and yawning, Terrell looked on in astonishment.

"Morning, Mum. What's all this?"

"You're not going to be here for the next few weeks, so I thought I'd bring you breakfast in bed. Your father and I were up at six, getting everything ready."

Terrell smiled, feeling a little overwhelmed as he took the tray from his mother.

"Now, don't let that go cold. Felix said the car will be here at nine and I want you showered, dressed and ready to go when it arrives. Make sure you eat all your breakfast."

"Mum, you've made enough food for all three of us."

"Yeah . . ." Beth looked sheepish. "Your dad and I were too excited to eat, but that doesn't mean you get to skip the most important meal of the day."

Terrell smiled. Seeing his mother so flustered was a humbling and heart-warming sight.

"I don't know about you," Beth continued, "but I'm equal-parts nervous and excited . . . I knew you'd be leaving us one day; I just didn't expect it to be so soon."

"Mum, it's only for two weeks."

"They said two weeks *initially*. Initially, Terrell — once they realise how clever you are, they'll not want to let you go." She ruffled her son's hair, dropped a kiss on his forehead and left the room. "I know I don't," she whispered under her breath as she closed the door behind her.

Their transport arrived at nine precisely. The family were peering out of the living-room window waiting for a taxi. Instead, a large, oddly shaped van pulled up outside the house. It was jet-black and looked like it had armoured plating instead of side windows.

"What on earth is that?" Ghalen's eyes were like saucers.

A well-dressed chauffeur exited the vehicle and walked up the garden path to their front door. Beth opened it before the young man even had a chance to ring the bell.

"Ah! Good morning, madam. I'm here to take you and your family to London. Do you need any assistance with your luggage?"

"No, you're OK, thanks. I've got it." Ghalen dragged two heavy cases to the back of the van. "Is there a boot on this thing?"

The confused-looking chauffeur recovered himself swiftly and, after a brief discussion with Ghalen about who should be putting the luggage into the vehicle, they compromised and lifted one case each.

"What have you got in these things, Terrell? You're only going for two bloody weeks," Ghalen huffed, sounding out of breath.

"I packed him a few extra things in case he gets hungry," Beth replied.

"That makes sense." Ghalen grinned, the excitement of the day overriding his grumpiness.

"Your mother will have put food in there to last you until Christmas."

The family laughed as they walked to door the chauffeur was holding open for them. As they peered in, they gasped in astonishment; it looked like the first-class section of an aeroplane. There were seven seats, four facing each other and three in a row behind, with large TV screens at the front and back of the van and personal, in-seat monitors, along with individual tables and a central mini-bar. What had appeared to be metal plating from the outside was, in fact, tinted windows, offering protection from external attention and sunlight.

As the Princes stepped inside, there was headroom for even Ghalen to stand tall. They took their seats, still staring, wide-eyed, at the opulent environment they'd found themselves in.

"What kind of vehicle is this?"

With his parents uncommonly mute, Terrell chatted with the chauffeur.

"This is a Mercedes-Benz Sprinter JetVan, sir. If you need anything while we're on the road, there's a communication system by your seats.

"The journey usually takes around an hour-and-a-half, but if you need a rest-stop on the way, please let me know. The mini-bar's stocked with drinks and light snacks and here —" he pointed to an envelope on Terrell's table "— is a letter from our director welcoming you to the company. Will there be anything else, sir?"

Terrell smiled. It was the first time in his life someone had called him "sir" and directed a conversation to him, rather than to his parents. He was actually being treated like a grown-up. It was a new sensation; he didn't feel sure about it yet.

"No, that's all, thank you," he mumbled.

The chauffeur nodded, closed the door and the family buckled their seatbelts.

"Wow! Look at this place. It's absolutely beautiful. I didn't even know things like this existed — it's fancier than a limousine," Beth said, admiring her surroundings.

"When have you been in a limo?" Ghalen asked.

"I haven't, but we've seen them on the telly."

Terrell was engrossed in his phone and began reading from the webpage he was looking at.

"Apparently, these JetVans are quite rare and *extremely* expensive. They cost around three hundred grand each, and are completely customisable."

"Oh, look, my seat reclines!" Beth exclaimed, pressing a button by her chair.

Ghalen was checking out the mini-bar and retrieved a bottle of champagne.

"It's too early for that, Ghalen!" Beth gave him a look, and he quickly replaced the bottle with a can of cola.

The vehicle pulled away from the house and started its journey towards London. Terrell gazed out of the window and watched his street disappear from view. He didn't know what lay ahead of him, but he reasoned this was one of those moments he would always look back on and remember; he wanted to absorb every image into his memory bank. His father's snoring broke him away from his thought process and, with a smile, he, too, settled into his seat to enjoy the ride.

While his parents slept, Terrell stared out of the window most of the journey. As they ventured into London, he was mesmerised by the number of people milling around Central London. The JetVan turned left past Temple Station, and Terrell was greeted with his first view of The Particle building. A wave of nervous excitement rushed through him; they were nearly there, and he had no idea whatsoever about what was waiting for him.

As if sensing his growing excitement and nervous energy, his mother awoke and turned to her son.

"What are you looking at?"

Terrell spun around with a beaming smile, pointing out the window.

"Look!"

As Beth blinked and opened her tired eyes, she saw the majestic building in front of them. She smiled back at her son.

"That might be your fancy new home for the next few weeks —just don't forget where your real one is."

The vehicle slowly weaved its way through the mid-morning traffic. Ghalen woke up, yawned loudly and stretched.

"I thought it would be quieter on the roads today," he murmured.

"I guess it's because there's no congestion charge at the weekend," Terrell replied.

"It's a beautiful day, too," Beth chipped in. "I'm sure a lot of people will be driving down to the coast — we're not far from Brighton here, are we?"

The JetVan pulled up in front of The Particle. With the engine still running, the chauffeur stepped out and opened the side-door for his passengers.

"If you would care to walk this way, please. The porter will fetch your luggage and assist you upstairs." The chauffeur shot a look at Ghalen as he said this, but he was too overwhelmed by his surroundings to argue.

With Terrell's luggage stacked on a trolley, the three of them moved into one of the fastest elevators in the world, making Ghalen's ears pop. Within seconds, they had reached their floor; the doors pinged open to a magnificent reception area with stunning, elevated views of the city below them. The whole family looked around in a dazed awe.

An exquisitely dressed Chinese woman approached them and addressed Terrell.

"Good morning, Mr Prince. Welcome to the Apogee Hotel. My name is Yu Yan and it is my pleasure to assist you today."

"Nice to meet you. I thought I would be going to Silicate this morning?"

Yu Yan smiled.

"I was asked to show you to your room first and let you freshen up before your meeting."

"Cool, thank you."

"It's my pleasure. If you would like to follow me, the porter will bring your luggage separately."

The family followed the petite woman as she led them up to the fiftieth floor.

"We have prepared the Apex Suite for you. We have five suites here at the hotel; I think you'll find the Apex extremely comfortable." As Yu Yan opened the door to Terrell's temporary home, the family gasped.

"You've got to be kidding!" Ghalen exclaimed.

"Is this all for me?" Terrell asked.

"This is your accommodation for the next two weeks, yes, sir. Would you like me to show you around?" Yu Yan gave a running commentary as she led the family through the spacious suite.

"The Apex Suite has a floor space of a hundred and twenty-five square metres. The windows are floor-to-ceiling, offering guests unparalleled views of the city. The accommodation also provides separate living, working and sleeping areas. The marble-clad bathroom is really particularly special, if you don't mind me saying. Again, it offers views across London."

Beth pointed to the bath, which was positioned in front of a huge window.

"But can't people see you when you're, you know, *naked* in there?"

Yu Yan smiled.

"Being the tallest building in world has its benefits. You can be assured that no-one can see you this high up."

"Don't use the bath," Beth whispered in her son's ear.

Terrell shrugged her comment off as he continued to drink in the view of London's skyline. It's a good job I don't get vertigo, he thought.

Yu Yan continued to show them around, pointing out the private dressing-room and under-floor heating.

"The suite also comes with a butler, available twenty-four hours a day. It will be his pleasure to arrange anything you may need during your stay with us."

On cue, a smartly dressed Chinese man walked into the room carrying a tray of refreshments.

"This is Tee-Cheng," Yu Yan introduced the man. "He's your personal butler for the length of your stay," she said, addressing Terrell directly. "Whether you need a shirt ironing, a bath running or a snack, whatever time of day or night, Tee-Cheng will be able to facilitate your needs."

Tee-Cheng bowed his head before offering the family a welcome drink.

"Bloody hell . . . bloody, bloody hell," Ghalen muttered under his breath, trying to take everything in as he sipped his ginger tea.

Beth took his hand, giggling nervously. She, too, was feeling overwhelmed. Turning to each other, they grinned before clinking cups and taking a seat together on one of the plush sofas.

"I'll let you settle into your room now. If you need anything at all, please don't hesitate to contact Tee-Cheng."

The two Asian figures left the room; Tee-Cheng closed the door softly behind them.

"Well . . ." Ghalen exhaled, shaking his head gently. "I can't quite believe all this, son. I thought they'd be putting you up in a bedsit or something."

Terrell, sitting at the desk, scrolling through his phone, looked up at his parents.

"I'm on the website for the Apogee. This room we're currently in costs three thousand pounds *per night*. That means it'll cost *forty-two thousand pounds* for the two weeks I'm here." Shock was audible in Terrell's voice.

"Don't be ridiculous, Terrell. Even this nice a room can't cost that much. Are you sure it's not three thousand for your whole stay? Even that sounds like too much money . . ." Beth shrugged.

Terrell passed his phone to his mother, who stared at the screen before handing it to her husband.

"That's more money than I make in a year." Ghalen laid the

phone down and scrunched up his face, pausing before he spoke.

"Son, these past few weeks have been life-changing. I don't just mean the money or you coming to London — I mean what you discovered, and how valuable you must be to this company. I doubt they put everyone up here, regardless of how fancy and posh this Silicate company is. I know we haven't always seen eye-to-eye, and I can't say I really understand everything that's happening, but I want you to know how very proud I am of you —" he looked over to Beth, catching her eye "— how proud we *both* are of you.

"Whatever happens from here on in, remember that we love you very much. However things turn out, we'll always be there to support you."

Terrell welled up at his father's words; when he tried to respond, he found he was too choked to speak.

"But be careful," Ghalen continued, snapping the family out of their emotional reverie. "Fancy room, chauffeur-driven Jet-Van-wotsit, personal butler? They're buttering you up for something, Terrell. You've obviously got something they need, and it looks like they'll go to pretty much any length to get it. Don't give them all your ideas straightaway — play this right and this could set you up for life, son. Just be savvy. You know what I'm trying to say."

"I do. If I give them everything now, there'll be no need for them to keep me around."

"Precisely."

The phone on the desk next to Terrell began to ring.

"Hello?"

"Hello, could I speak to Terrell Prince, please?"

"Speaking."

"Hi, Terrell. I'm Doctor Sharma's secretary. He'd like to meet you at midday — here, at Silicate. Will that be convenient?"

Terrell looked at his watch and saw it was just past eleven.

"That'll be fine, thank you." Terrell put the phone down and looked at his parents with a smile. "We're meeting them in fifty minutes, so I've got just enough time to try out that bath!"

Mrs Prince looked at her son in disbelief before rolling her eyes and laughing.

"Good morning, I'm Shira Rosenberg. This is my daughter, Abby. We have an appointment to see Doctor Sharma at midday."

The usually bustling reception area was quiet on this Saturday morning. Abby looked around at the spacious, stark, white room accented with red sofas. The huge, semi-circular reception desk spanning the whole right side of the room had only two members of staff behind it today; one of them, the cheery man Shira was now speaking with.

"Good morning, Mrs Rosenberg. Doctor Sharma will be with you shortly. If you'd both like to take a seat, I'll let him know you've arrived."

"Thank you very much." Shira and Abby sat on the nearest sofa, letting their eyes be drawn to the cookery programme playing on the muted television.

"It's so quiet here today," Abby whispered to her mother.

"Well, it is Saturday, sweetie."

"It feels a bit creepy after it being so busy yesterday."

Shira smiled at her daughter and held her hand as they both turned back to the TV.

The door behind them opened and loud voices could be heard coming from the elevator. The Rosenbergs turned around to see three people walk up to the desk.

"Hi. My son's starting work here today. We're meant to be meeting someone at twelve," Ghalen announced.

"What's your son's name, please, sir?"

"My name's Terrell Prince. We're meeting Doctor Sharma at midday."

"Very good, sir. If you'd all like to take a seat, the doctor will be with you shortly."

The Prince family sat on the sofa opposite the Rosenbergs. They nodded politely to each other before waiting in silence, no-one sure what to expect.

Terrell's leg jiggled slightly and he chewed his lower lip, sure signs that he was nervous.

"It'll be all right. We're here with you," Beth comforted, gently resting her hand on Terrell's leg.

Shira looked over and smiled reassuringly at Beth.

"Abby was nervous yesterday before we met Doctor Sharma, but he seems like a wonderful man. He's not one of those stuffy doctors."

"Oh, that's good. We don't know anything about him."

"Haven't you spoken to him on the phone?"

"No. Felix organised everything with us, but the welcome letter said that we would be meeting Doctor Sharma today."

"Oh, OK. Well he seems lovely — you've no need to worry."

"Thank you."

Terrell looked up from the ground and smiled.

The large doors at the far end of the room opened as Dr Sharma, Jake and Ryder entered and made their way towards the two families.

"Ah, how lovely, we're all here and you're already acquainted." Dr Sharma looked over at the Prince family. "I'm so glad you could make it, Mr and Mrs Prince. And Terrell — I believe you'll be joining us for a little while? I've been following your research with great interest. It's a real pleasure to meet you — all of you." Padman shook everyone's hands before introducing his small entourage.

"This is Jake Hampton, and next to him is Ryder Braighton, our head of security."

Jake and Ryder exchanged greetings with the two families.

"Now we're all here, let's get started, shall we?"

The group stood up and followed Padman as he led the way into the heart of Silicate.

CHAPTER 15

"And finally, this is Chez Reves, our in-house restaurant," Padman announced, showing the group to their table. The past couple of hours had been a whirlwind tour of the facility and everyone welcomed this chance to sit down and relax as they tried to process all they'd seen.

Chez Reves was big enough to host gala events for Silicate's financial backers and guests, but most days it was used by the staff as a kind of up-market canteen.

"Even this room's high tech," Abby commented as everyone sat down at a large, circular table in the centre of the room.

Floor-to-ceiling, moveable, glass walls surrounded the seating areas positioned around the restaurant. They acted as partitions, partially shielding them from the rest of the room and giving diners privacy as they ate, with the option of being moved to the sides to create an impressive, open space for large events.

The maître d' walked towards Padman, who was hovering over the table as everyone took their seats.

"Hello, Matías. Could we have eight menus, please, and some water for the table?"

"Of course. Right away, sir." Matías hurried back to his station.

"Are you not eating with us, Doctor?" Beth asked.

"I'm afraid not. I have to nip back to the office to catch up on a few things, but I'll be back before you finish your meal. Matías will take good care of you."

Jake looked over to Padman with rising panic in his eyes. The doctor kneeled down next to him to whisper in his ear.

"Sorry about this. I've got a staffing crisis I have to sort out. You can stay here and get something to eat, or you can sit in my office until I'm done? I shouldn't be too long."

Jake wasn't really the social type. He'd spent years on his own working the farm. He wasn't proficient at small talk; the idea of sitting around a table with a bunch of strangers was more than a little intimidating. However, his empty stomach and the wonderful aroma from the kitchen made the decision for him.

"That's OK, I'm pretty hungry, to be honest."

"Me, too. Sorry — I should've made us breakfast this morning."

"If you're hungry, stay and eat with us."

"I wish I could. I'll have to grab something from the machine on the way."

Jake looked around the table at the families conversing and turned back to Padman.

"Just don't leave me here too long. Deal?"

Padman rose, with a smile, and placed his hand on Jake's shoulder.

"I promise." He turned to the rest of the table. "Thank you, everybody. I'll leave you in Matías's very capable hands." He gave a slightly awkward wave as he left the restaurant and Matías brought over menus.

"He's an odd fellow, isn't he?" Beth announced to the group, receiving a startled look from most of the table.

"Mum!"

"Don't Mum me. We were told you were starting work here today and now they're checking you into the hospital?"

"Doctor Sharma explained on the tour. He wants to record my apparition with the equipment here and then I can help study it over the next few weeks."

"Sounds fishy if you ask me. I think there's a lot that doctor isn't telling us."

"I have to agree with you there, he did dodge quite a few of our questions during the tour," Shira agreed.

Both Terrell and Abby looked devastated by their parents gossiping.

"There's only so much he can tell us in one day, Mom." Abby spoke gently. "He's probably playing it down so as to not over-load us with information."

"You're probably right, darling. I just worry, especially where you're concerned. You'll be spending the night here alone — I want to be certain you'll be OK."

Ryder had been listening to the conversation, but decided it was time to interject.

"As head of security, I can assure you your children will be in good hands. I'll be staying here at Silicate tonight to keep an eye on both Abby and Terrell."

"No offence, but what could you do if there was an emer-gency? You're in a wheelchair."

"*Ghalen!*" It was Beth's turn to feel embarrassed.

Ryder smiled.

"Please don't let the chair fool you, Mr Prince. I served in Af-ghanistan and other warzones. I would willingly throw myself in front of a bullet if I had to."

"I didn't mean anything by it."

"I understand. People see the chair and they instinctively think I'm incapable of doing anything. I assure you — I may not have the strength I once had in my legs, but the rest of me is in perfect working order."

Ghalen, humbled, sank back into his chair. Beth shook her head, turning away from her husband towards the only person who'd hardly spoken the whole day.

"And what about you, Jake? Do you work here as well? Or are you a patient?"

Jake looked up, a slight flush rising to his face. He didn't really know how to answer. Why *was* he here? It seemed that one minute he had been drinking tea after an amazing night, and the next, he was sitting around a table with people whose names he couldn't even remember. When Padman had showed him the footage, he hadn't been able to believe what he was seeing. The doctor had explained that the bedroom was once an office, and he must have inadvertently switched the camera on when he had plugged his charger in. Jake's mind recounted the events which had brought him to Silicate just a few hours before.

"I totally forgot that camera was even there," Padman said, removing it from the mount behind the wardrobe. "I'm so sorry this happened. Let's go downstairs and I can try my best to explain what you've seen."

Sitting back at the dining table, Jake stared in disbelief at the video.

"Is this some kind of joke? Did you edit this together before I woke up?"

"I promise you — this is the raw footage. I've only just seen it myself."

"How is this possible? I can see both of us asleep and then this ghost thing in between us."

"It's called an apparition, and we believe it's a version — a dream version — of you. It's what the company I work for studies."

"Other people have these as well?"

"I believe we all have them, but not all are as prominent as yours. It's only the active ones we can monitor, though that might change as the technology develops."

"Do you have one?"

"I hope so. Unfortunately, mine is one of the shy ones. Are you OK?"

"I guess." Jake pushed the tablet away. "It's a lot to take in." His brain hurt. He rarely had conversations this intense or confusing, especially so soon after waking up. He poured himself more tea before pulling the tablet back towards him and replaying the video. "Did you know about me last night, when we were in the pub?"

"I wasn't certain, but a few things you said, did make me wonder."

"Like?"

"You're an only child, aren't you?"

"Why would that matter?"

"Apparitions seem to be more pronounced in patients without siblings, so that was my first clue."

"What else?"

Padman reached across the table and picked up his phone.

"Remember that picture I took of you?"

"Yeah. I was pretty drunk by that time, though — I probably look a total mess." Jake grinned awkwardly at the hazy memory.

Padman handed him the phone, the picture displayed.

"Yup. Just as goofy as I thought I'd be." The photo showed Jake holding up his pint and smiling, his eyes closed. "Why do you want me to look at this?"

"Take a look at your reflection in the pint glass."

Jake squinted at the image, staring at the partial reflection for a long moment. He suddenly gasped, almost dropping the phone.

"My eyes are closed, but they're open in my reflection. How's that possible?"

"It's nothing to be scared of, it's just your apparition."

"Easy for you to say. You're used to this stuff." Jake stood up and rubbed his arms, breathing hard.

"Sorry, I should have eased you in to all this. I get carried away sometimes."

Jake sat back at the table, trying to compose himself.

"I thought you were pulling my leg about the whole ghost thing in bed with me. I went along with it, seeing how it would play out. I was sure you'd edited it together and were just winding me up — but you weren't, were you?" Jake's breathing had become chaotic, which the doctor recognised as the start of a panic attack.

Padman leaned over, held Jake's head in his hands gently but firmly, and kissed him passionately. Shocked, Jake kissed him back. This pulled him out of his panicked state.

"I hope that's not what you do for all your patients who freak out." Jake chuckled.

"Only the hot ones."

They both laughed, and Padman placed his hand on top of Jake's.

"You're not alone, you know. I can help you."

"If I'd never met you, I wouldn't even know I needed help," Jake had responded.

"That's true, I suppose." Padman looked dejected.

"Oh, man, I was only messing with you," Jake reassured him. "I wouldn't change last night for anything, even with this ghost stuff."

"Apparition."

"Yeah, that."

"I feel the same," Padman admitted, smiling shyly. "I don't meet many guys. I don't want to screw this up before we've even started, but it wouldn't have felt right not telling you about the video."

"I'm glad you did, but I also wish that I didn't know, if that makes sense?"

"It does." Padman picked up the tablet. "I need to go into work now. Sorry. You're more than welcome to come with me, and we could discuss it all further, or we can meet up tomorrow and chat then? Though I would like to monitor you properly with Silicate's technology rather than my father's old camera, if you're up for it. What would you like to do?"

"You can't leave me hanging — I need to know more. And spending the day with you doesn't sound so bad." Jake grinned. "I've got nothing to wear, though."

"You can borrow some of my clothes, if you like. You grab a shower and I'll get everything ready."

"Cool." Jake jumped up from the table.

"Just to be totally transparent, I do have to show two patients and their families around the facility today, if you don't mind joining the tour? After that, we can spend some one-on-one time together." Padman's large, beaming smile made Jake laugh.

"Look at you, like butter wouldn't melt. OK, fine — I'll tag along. It's not like I had any other plans today. It's not really the perfect second date I was hoping for, though . . ."

"Oh?"

Jake raised an eyebrow, indicating he meant upstairs. Padman smiled and checked the time on his phone.

"Let's make Silicate date *three*, then. We've still got time for our second one."

Jake kissed him on the lips before running upstairs excitedly.

That had been six hours ago and now Jake was eating lunch with a group of strangers with Padman nowhere to be seen. He looked up at the mouthy woman, staring intently at him, waiting for his response. The rest of the table turned towards him, interested to hear what he had to say.

"I'm a patient, I guess."

"You guess? What does that mean?" Beth asked.

Jake shifted in his seat nervously. He wasn't used to all this attention from so many people at once.

"Well, erm. Padman, the doctor, he's . . . my friend. I only found out about this place a few hours ago when he showed me a video of me sleeping." He swallowed hard, all eyes on him. Had he said too much? Not enough?

"How could he film you before you knew about this place?" Beth quizzed.

Jake didn't know what to say. Ryder, sitting next to him, could tell the Yorkshire man felt deeply uncomfortable discussing the matter.

"Jake's a friend of Doctor Sharma's, and has only recently discovered that he, too, has an apparition. The doctor invited him along to the facility today to join you on the tour. As you can see, this is all very new to him and he's still adjusting to it. I don't think he needs to be interrogated any further, Mrs Prince."

"I was only asking," Beth huffed, feeling suitably chastised.

"We can't all be as socially open as you are, Mrs Prince." Ryder smiled at Beth, taking the sting out of his words.

Jake nodded to Ryder in thanks before turning to the group again.

"It's all very new to me. It's quite overwhelming, to be honest."

This disclosure seemed to appease the group. Only Terrell realised the nature of Jake and the doctor's relationship, deciding it was best to keep this information to himself. His mother was indeed "socially open", as Ryder had termed it. A bit of a busybody at times, Terrell thought wryly.

As the rest of the table continued to converse, Jake leaned over to Ryder.

"Thanks for that. I'm not used to being under the microscope."

"No problem, I've faced army men less aggressive than some of this bunch."

The two men grinned at each other in understanding as Padman walked back into the restaurant. Wearing his trademark beaming smile, he waited for the staff to remove the last of the empty plates before stepping forward.

"Perfect timing, I see. Did you all enjoy lunch?"

Everyone talked over each other, praising the food.

"I'm glad to hear it." He looked at his watch. "We're approaching five, and I'd like to get our patients settled in for the night. Parents, you're welcome to stay here for more drinks or something more to eat?"

Abby looked at her mother, her eyes brimming with worry. Shira reached across, hugging her tightly.

"Come on now, my brave girl," she whispered in her daughter's ear. "I'll be back in the morning and you can tell me about all the amazing things you do tonight. There's nothing to worry about."

Abby held on to her mother, squeezing her eyes shut in an effort to hold back her tears.

Despite the nerves Terrell felt starting to build, he was determined to act like an adult as he addressed his parents.

"Have a safe trip back home. I'll call you in the morning when I get in to my room," he informed them.

"Come here, you." Beth started to well up as she grabbed her son in a bear hug. Ghalen joined in, embracing them both from the side.

"We're going to miss you, son."

Abby allowed herself to look over at the Prince family. The sight of Terrell squirming between his parents made her laugh out loud. She looked up at Shira.

"I think you're right — I'll be fine."

As his parents finally released him, Terrell walked over to Padman, indicating he was ready to leave. Abby followed suit, leaving the three parents at the table.

"I think that's our signal to shift ourselves," Beth announced.

"The JetVan's waiting for you outside, whenever you're ready to go," Padman told them with an understanding smile.

As the group moved towards the exit, Shira fell into step alongside Beth.

"What on earth's a JetVan?"

"We'll show you when we get downstairs — you won't believe it."

Abby and Terrell waved to their parents as they crossed the reception towards the elevators. They were still waving as the doors closed and they disappeared from view.

A nervous tension hung in the air in the elevator. Padman, standing behind the teenagers, leaned in.

"Right, now they're gone, the real fun begins. Who wants to go to the Red Room?"

Abby and Terrell spun around, wearing huge smiles.

"I thought we were going to bed so you could monitor us?" Terrell asked.

Padman checked his watch.

"Who goes to bed at four forty-five on a Saturday afternoon? We've got *hours* of gameplay to get in first. That's why we had to get rid of your parents so early."

Abby looked at Terrell.

"I think I love this place."

"Me, too!"

They walked back into the facility, Ryder and Jake bringing up the rear.

CHAPTER 16

As Terrell, Abby and Jake battled for the title of Supreme Gaming Champion, Padman was in his office explaining the day's events to Ryder.

"They've vanished?"

"Apparently."

"What about the cameras? This place has more security than Fort Knox."

"Scrubbed. We found evidence of smoking on the fire escape next to the nurses' station. The camera there was turned towards the wall, and the footage deleted."

"Who was it?"

"We can't be a hundred per cent sure, but there were only a handful of staff in the building last night. We believe it was Andrew, one of our soon-to-be-*ex* junior nurses."

"What about the other cameras?"

"Wiped."

"All of them?"

"Our tech guys say it was probably accidental. These files aren't meant to be deleted and the programme's difficult to navigate, especially for someone not trained. It's possible that by trying to delete one file, they ended up binning the entire folder."

"How would this junior nurse even have access to the security systems?"

"He wouldn't, but his co-worker, Sally, did. It's been suggested that they were romantically linked, and she was in on it with Andrew." Padman looked thoughtful. "It's strange, though. I interviewed her myself and I've worked with her for over a year now. She's always seemed so trustworthy. I personally appointed her head nurse. It's so out of character for her."

"Love can do strange things to a person, or so I'm told. What about the security guard who was on shift last night?" Ryder flicked through the files on his tablet. "Fred Randal?"

"Who knows. Three-way, maybe?"

Ryder looked up from his screen.

"It says here he's sixty-seven and married with three kids, all of them older than these two nurses. Surely you're joking?"

"I hope you're not being ageist, Mr Braighton?" Padman pulled a stern look before breaking into a smile. "Yes, I'm joking. But his disappearance does add to this mystery. I just can't wrap my head around two of my staff becoming romantically linked and running away together after doing something stupid. As for Fred, I've no idea how he fits into all of this."

Ryder paused.

"I'll see what I can find out. With no video surveillance, it looks like I'll have to do this the old-fashioned way."

"Which is?"

"Go room to room and check for signs of foul play."

"What kind of foul play are you suggesting? We're a non-intrusive scientific research facility. What could possibly go wrong here?"

"I don't know, but I'll find out."

Ryder moved towards the office door, Padman following closely behind.

"OK, but please do it subtly. The staff were already spooked today. Conspiracy theories flying everywhere. I let the more talkative ones leave a few hours early to try to quash the rumours. My main concern's patient welfare — they're already nervous about sleeping in the pods tonight . . . the last thing we need is Inspector Clouseau interrogating them."

"*Aucun probleme.*"

"*Merci*," Padman replied with a smile.

As Ryder reached the door, he turned back around to face the doctor.

"Not that it's any of my business, but is Jake your boyfriend?"

Padman's face flushed bright red.

"No, he's just a friend . . . for the moment."

"A friend who slept in your bed last night?"

"What? How did you —?"

Ryder smiled.

"Mrs Prince gave him the third degree over lunch."

"Oh, no, the poor guy. I knew I shouldn't have left him in there alone, but I had all this stuff to deal with."

"Don't worry, I saved him."

"What did he say?"

"Enough to make me realise you were sleeping together, but not enough for the others to realise."

"Thank you for stepping in. I shouldn't have brought him here today. I thought I'd have plenty of time after the tour, but then all this happened. I was so excited after meeting someone nice and then discovering he has an apparition, it just seemed like the right thing to do."

"How did you figure the apparition out?"

"He slept in my bedroom which used to be my father's treatment-room before The Particle was built. There was a camera behind the wardrobe with a water filter in front of the lens — pretty primitive stuff, but it did the job back then. Jake accidentally switched it on before going to bed last night, and it streamed to my tablet this morning. Can you imagine how shocked and embarrassed I was when I saw it?"

"How did he take it?"

"Well, I think. To be honest, it all went over his head. That's why I wanted to spend more time with him today and explain it better."

"Where is he now?"

"In the Red Room. That's where I'm headed."

"I won't keep you, then." Ryder moved out of the way, allowing Padman to open the door.

"Oh, one more thing, while I remember. What's this about you sleeping with one of the patients?"

"It's not what you think." Ryder looked mortified.

"Don't worry, Isabell told me everything." Padman smiled as they moved along the hallway. "I'm aware it was all above board and you stayed at her request.

"I was going to talk to you today about keeping personal and professional relationships separate, but as Jake's here, I don't want to sound hypocritical. Just, please, no more sleeping in the same bed — I don't think your grandfather would approve. You're lucky there isn't any video evidence from last night."

The doctor turned the corner and walked into the Red Room.

"That's not fair!"

Terrell and Jake were sitting, arms folded, watching Abby celebrating yet another win.

"You just need a little more practice and maybe you'll be as good as me, in say, five years' time!" Abby laughed.

Terrell pulled a face, making her laugh even more.

"Having fun, guys?" Padman walked over to the group.

"Oh, hey. We are, though Terrell's a bit sore because Abby keeps beating us."

Abby turned around.

"Do you want to play me? These two won't, any more."

"Maybe tomorrow. I've got to get you into the Blue Room."

Jake looked at Padman questioningly, but it was Terrell who spoke.

"But it's only nine. I don't usually sleep 'til after midnight."

"You'll be going individually — the Blue Room will help you relax before entering Hygge."

Abby spun around.

"Can't I stay up a bit longer? Please?"

"Sorry, Abby, this is on your mother's instructions, I'm afraid."

"OK." Abby stood up and walked over to the doctor.

"I suppose . . . you could use the spa for an hour before going to bed? As long as Shira doesn't find out."

"Oh, yes, please! I promise I won't say a word."

"OK. Go and get changed in the Blue Room and one of the nurses will take you down to the spa.

"Terrell, would you mind going with Abby and keeping her company please?"

"Of course not."

"Thank you. Off you go, then, and I'll come and see you both before you enter your pods."

As Abby and Terrell left, Jake looked up at Padman and smiled.

"You were always going to send them to the spa, weren't you?"

"We always do. We find that the pods can be intimidating for some patients — especially children. The spa helps them relax before they go to bed."

"Does Abby's mum know this?"

"I told her yesterday. It was Shira who suggested the ruse of getting her to bed on time."

"Clever!"

From the back of the room, Ryder signalled to Padman.

"I'm going to head down to the security office."

Padman turned to Ryder.

"Great, thank you. Buzz me if there's any news."

"Will do," Ryder said, leaving the room.

The doctor walked over to Jake and sat down on the sofa next to him.

"Sorry about earlier. Ryder told me about what happened at lunch. I shouldn't have put you in that position."

"It's OK. I was totally tongue-tied. I didn't know how to respond. Thankfully, Ryder was there."

"In hindsight, perhaps bringing you in today wasn't my smartest move."

"I'm here now and I'm not having the *worst* time. I just wish

I could have seen more of you, and I still don't exactly know what's going on. I was chatting with Abby and Terrell, and it seems they know as much as I do, which isn't a lot, so that actually kind of helped, in a weird way."

"'Weird' sums up what we do here." Padman smiled and reached out to hold Jake's hand. "Thanks for being so understanding. My biggest fear is scaring you away before we get a chance at really knowing each other. You seem like a genuine guy; I would like to see more of you."

"The feeling's mutual." Jake leaned in and kissed the doctor.

"Have you been all right in here? Sorry for leaving you with two kids."

"Terrell's not really a kid, and Abby's more grown up than most adults I know. It was cool kicking back and playing games. I've not done that in a long time. I get that you're worried about me, but there's no need. This is your place of work — I understand you have to actually do some work." Jake grinned. "Let's face it. it's not the worst place to be — sitting in a room playing video games."

"If you get bored or want to leave, you can, you know. You don't have to sit around waiting for me if you need to go."

"Honestly, I'm fine, stop worrying."

Padman leaned in and gave Jake a huge kiss.

"I'm so glad I met you."

"Me, too."

"Once I've got the kids — sorry, Terrell and Abby — into their pods, you'll have my full, undivided attention."

"Do I have to sleep in one of those things?"

"If you were a regular patient, yes. You would sleep in a pod and would be monitored by the night staff while I went home and got some sleep. As you're my, well, friend . . ."

"Potential future boyfriend?"

"Boyfriend?"

"I said *potential future* boyfriend. All I know about you so far is that you like to secretly film strangers in your bed. I'm still assessing you."

Padman chuckled.

"Fair enough. Well, as I already know that you emanate apparitions when you sleep, I thought I would monitor you personally tonight, from Archeus."

"What's that?"

"It's a singular lab in a different part of the building. Only a small number of people have access to it, so I can stay with you all night, undisturbed."

"Don't you need sleep, as well, though?"

"I'll be fine. I work a lot of all day, all night shifts. It's pretty standard in medicine."

"If you're sure, I'm up for that. I feel better knowing I'll be with you."

Padman looked at his watch.

"That gives us about an hour before I get the others into their pods."

"Are you thinking what I'm thinking?" Jake asked expectantly.

They both jumped up from the sofa and landed on two bean bags facing the TV.

"There's no way you're beating me — I've had three years of practice working here," Padman announced as he switched on the game console.

"Tsk! I'm fifteen years younger than you, my reflexes are better."

"Youth doesn't trump experience."

"We'll see."

"Wait! You have a butler?"

Abby and Terrell were sitting in the jacuzzi. There was no-one else in the spa and conversation flowed between them.

"Yup. His name's Tee-Cheng. I haven't had a chance to talk to him yet, but he seems all right."

"Tee-Cheng… what a cool name! I thought the hotel we were

booked into was swanky, but yours is next level."

"My dad says they're trying to butter me up."

"Who are? The hotel?"

"No, Silicate."

"Oh, yeah. They probably are. I wish I'd thought about filming myself, then I could be staying in a suite like yours."

"It was a total fluke I captured anything. Who'd have thought to record themselves through water?"

"That's probably why no-one else has. Actually, I've got a lava lamp by my bed. You think that would work?"

Terrell started laughing.

"If it did, imagine what the apparition would look like?" He waved his arms above his head, pulling a funny, distorted face.

Abby joined in with her own rendition, making them both fall about in the water, laughing hysterically.

Abby's face suddenly changed into a worried look. Concerned, Terrell moved closer to her.

"What's up?"

"I haven't seen my apparition yet. To be honest, I don't know if I want to."

"Why not? It's just you. It's not scary or anything. My dad calls it my ghost-self, but I think it's my soul or something."

"It's still a bit creepy, though."

"I guess. Hopefully we'll know more tomorrow, once they've monitored us sleeping."

"That's the other thing I'm worried about. What if *he* appears?"

"You mean that shadow figure?"

Abby nodded.

"I don't want to be trapped in that glass box with him."

"From my footage, there was only me and my apparition, and it didn't do much of anything. This Shadow Man is probably just in your dreams. I doubt they can capture those."

Abby paused, her lower lip quivering.

"I saw him again, today."

"Here?"

Abby nodded.

"I'm sure I saw him at the other side of the restaurant, but when I looked again, he was gone."

"It was probably just your imagination. All the things we've seen today have had my mind racing, too. Just in case, I'll make sure they put me in the pod next to yours tonight. If anything happens, I'll rush in and help you. There's a team of people monitoring our every move, so they'll probably see anything before we do. If you think about it, this is the best place we can be."

Abby forced a smile.

"I didn't think of that. If the Shadow Man does appear, maybe they can even get rid of him for good. That would be amazing."

"If anyone can, it's these guys. They really seem to know what they're doing. Buttering me up or not, I've never been treated so well in my life."

"Says the man with the butler!" Abby splashed Terrell play-fully, who retaliated, both teenagers laughing and relaxed again.

CHAPTER 17

"Shall I get another round in?" Ghalen drained the contents of his glass and stood up before the two women had a chance to answer.

As Ghalen wobbled to the bar, Beth turned to Shira. They were all quite drunk.

"He'll be asleep and snoring the whole way home. He always does after drinking."

"I think I'll be having an early night. I don't usually drink this much. Actually, I can't remember the last time I got drunk. I had a few glasses of wine on the plane, but nothing over the top."

"You know, I've never been on an aeroplane before."

"Really?"

"Nope. Furthest I've ever been is a train to Aberdeen when I was a nipper."

"What's a nipper?"

The three of them had left Silicate and decided to get a drink before heading home; one drink had turned into many and now, five hours later, they were all a little merry. The crowded London pub was busy and noisy, but as they had arrived much earlier, they had secured a table at the back of the room.

"Here you are, ladies — a white wine spritzer, and a brandy and Babycham for my lovely wife." Ghalen plopped the drinks on to the table, some of the liquid spilling from the top of the glasses, before half-falling back into his seat.

"You're drunk, Mr Prince, if you're calling me your 'lovely wife'."

"You *are* my lovely wife," Ghalen mumbled, sipping his pint.

"I think this'll have to be my last one. I don't want to be hungover when I pick Abby up in the morning."

"It's early!" Ghalen looked at his watch, moving his eyes closer and further away from the face but still unable to read the time.

"It's ten, Ghalen," Beth informed him, placing her hand on his. She turned back to Shira. "We'll walk you back to your hotel. You don't want to be roaming the London streets at night on your own."

"Thank you, that's very kind, but I'm sure I'll be fine. The hotel's just around the corner."

"It's not a problem at all, is it, Ghalen?"

Ghalen's head was resting on his left shoulder and his eyes were closed.

"*Ghalen!*"

He startled awake.

"What? What's wrong?"

"You fell asleep. Come on, we have to take Shira back to her hotel."

"But I just bought us drinks."

"That was an hour ago," Beth lied. "We finished them." She quickly moved all the glasses to table next to her.

"Did we? Oh. Right, then." Ghalen stood up and stretched his arms before stumbling past the patrons to the exit.

Beth grabbed her handbag and motioned to Shira.

"We'd better go after him before he collapses on someone."

When they arrived at the hotel, Shira invited them into her room for a coffee to help sober everyone up, which Beth agreed was a good idea. Ghalen collapsed on to Abby's bed and fell asleep immediately. Both women tried and failed to rouse him. In the end, it was decided that the Princes would stay in the hotel overnight.

"Honestly, it's fine," Shira reassured a flustered Beth. "The room's big enough for all of us and, to be honest, I'm glad of the company."

"Thank you. We'll be out of your hair first thing in the morning."

"Oh, hello. I didn't know if I'd see you again." Ryder moved into Isabell's room. She was sitting up in bed with her laptop resting on the covers. "I thought you were being discharged this morning, otherwise I'd have come by sooner."

"I'm being kept in for a second night. Doctor Sharma's worried I might have another episode. At least they're letting me work while I'm here."

Ryder closed the door and moved over to the bed.

"Are you sure they're OK with this? Your books are based on the guy who keeps attacking you — won't writing about him make him more likely to appear?"

"I think that's *why* they're letting me write. They want to know if thinking about Vincent conjures him up. I've told them it doesn't work that way. It's totally random when he appears. Still, at least it's quiet here and I can actually get some work done."

"Sorry, should I leave?"

"No, don't be silly. Unless you start pawing at me for food."

Ryder gave her a puzzled look and Isabell laughed.

"My cat — Megara — always pesters me for food when I write. I don't really mind, though. She's beautiful, and she's been such a comfort through all this horrible stuff with Vincent Gast. My neighbour's looking after her tonight."

"Vincent Gast — that's the guy who attacked you?"

"You've not read my books, then?"

"Oh, sorry, I . . ." Ryder was embarrassed.

"I'm teasing. They're not really aimed at the ex-soldier market."

"You'd be surprised what us soldiers read. It's not all porn mags hidden under the mattress, you know," Ryder responded, grinning. "You'd better believe I'll be reading all of your books as soon as I get home."

"In that case, without giving too much away, I describe him in intimate detail in my books, but I still don't think my readers understand just how terrifying he is."

"I think I understand. I saw what you were like yesterday."

Isabell closed her laptop and placed it on the bedside table. With her palm resting flat on top of the computer, still gazing, unseeingly, into space, she spoke softly.

"I thought I was going to die. I honestly thought — this is it. If that had happened anywhere else, I wouldn't have survived." She turned to face Ryder, tears filling her eyes. "I know I put a brave face on, but I'm truly terrified. That's the reason I didn't fight Doctor Sharma when he said I had to stay here another night. To be honest, I don't know if I ever want to leave." She broke down, sobbing into her hands.

Ryder moved closer to the bed and reached over to hold her. Isabell clung to him and cried on his shoulder.

"I'm so sorry. I'm not usually this emotional," she said, pulling herself away and wiping her face on the sleeves on her hospital gown.

"No need to apologise. I'm sure anyone would be the same in your situation. I'll have a word with Doctor Sharma and see what can be done about you staying here a little longer. At least until you're ready to go home."

"Thank you. I'd even rather sleep in Archeus than my own bed at the moment. In fact, don't tell him that, he might take me up on the offer."

"What is this Archeus I keep hearing about?"

"Urgh! It's horrible. Have you ever seen those old Hammer Horror films with Doctor Frankenstein's lab?"

Ryder nodded.

"Well, it's creepier than that. You get sucked into this huge bed so you can't move and there's medical equipment every-where. They usually sedate me, but they don't like doing that when I've had one of my episodes, like last night. Thankfully, I was so out of it, I didn't know I was in there. It gives me the creeps."

Ryder looked on, concerned. He was sure Isabell's descrip-tion was tainted from the extreme conditions that brought her there, but he would need to check the room out himself to make sure.

Nurse Phoebe led Terrell and Abby from the spa up to the Blue Room, allowing them to change into their night-clothes.

"Doctor Sharma will be with you in five minutes," she called as she left the room.

Terrell was the first out of the changing-room and took a seat in a large hammock-chair near one of the TV screens.

"Where do we put these?" Abby entered the room, carrying her bag of clothes.

"The lockers behind you," Terrell informed her, not divert-ing his gaze from the TV. "Is it just me, or is there something wrong with this telly? It looks blue."

"Really? You sure it's not from the walls reflecting on the screen?" Abby replied, securing her belongings before joining Terrell.

"I didn't think of that. You know, you're pretty smart, for a kid."

"Hey! I'm fourteen — you're only three years older than me."

"Four next week." Terrell smiled cheekily as Abby sat down next to him.

"Not to detract from your intelligence, Miss Rosenberg, but it's not the walls."

Terrell jumped, startled by Padman's silent entrance.

"Whoa! You scared me."

"Who's the kid now?" Abby mocked, grinning.

Padman picked up the TV remote and flicked through the channels.

"All the TVs here and in the spa have a blue filter. It's been proven to help your brain unwind and give you a good night's sleep. Although not watching TV at all is even better." He switched off the screen, making both Abby and Terrell groan.

"Sorry to be the 'evil doctor', but it's time for bed, I'm afraid. I'll take you to Hygge and my team will monitor you throughout the night as you sleep in your pods."

Abby started to fidget as they followed the doctor through the large doors and into Hygge.

"You've got this," Terrell reminded her gently as they walked through the dimly lit room. "You're going to be fine. Remember, I'm in the next pod if you need me."

On hearing their muted conversation, Padman smiled to himself. They reached the first pod and stopped.

"Terrell, this is your room for the night." Padman held up two lanyards holding credit card-sized keys. "These cards allow you to enter your rooms." He placed one over each of their heads. "Simply scan your card on the panel at the side of the door." The doctor moved aside for Terrell to enter his room.

The door opened with a whooshing noise and cool air lapped at their faces as they entered the glass cube. A large bed with fresh, white linen stood in the centre. A small table connected to the bed at the side held a bottle of water, earplugs, a control panel, and an eye-mask.

"This panel allows you adjust the air-conditioning, select a white noise sample — Niagara Falls is my favourite — and the red button's for immediate assistance, if you need it for any reason. Some people like background noise, others don't, so there are earplugs as well. We recommend using the eye-mask, though — these lights stay on all night. The bottle of water's more for the morning, so only small sips now and during the night if and when you need it. We don't want your bladder disturbing your sleep."

"Phoebe drilled that into us earlier," Terrell said; Abby nodded in agreement.

"She wouldn't let us drink anything for over an hour."

"I know it seems a bit extreme, but it is for your own comfort."

"It's cool." Terrell pulled back his bed-sheets.

"We'll let you get some rest."

"Erm —" Terrell looked at the doctor "— if I need to go out for any reason . . ." he motioned towards Abby ". . . would that be OK?"

"Yes, of course. Just press the button by the side of the door to open it. You only need the card to get into the room, not out."

Abby smiled at Terrell.

"Shall I show you to your room, Abby? It's right next door."

Padman motioned for Abby to lead the way.

"And this is your home for the night," the doctor said as they entered Pod Two.

Abby leaped on to the double bed and bounced up and down a few times.

"It's really comfy. I was expecting a hard mattress like the hospital back home."

"Well, it's still technically a hospital mattress, albeit a luxury one. Only the best for our very special patients."

Abby laid down on top of the covers, gazing up at the glass ceiling.

"It's so cool in here."

"Would you like me to adjust the temperature."

"No, I mean it's really cool to look at, like I'm a fish in an aquarium. And it's a lot bigger than it looks from the outside. Why all the space?"

"To make you feel more comfortable. The last thing we want is for you to feel claustrophobic."

"I like it!"

"I'm glad you approve," Padman said, smiling. "Would you like me to explain the buttons on your panel?"

"It's fine, I was listening in Terrell's pod. Air-con, waterfalls, earplugs and only sip the water."

"Very good — I'm impressed. In that case, young lady, if there's nothing else, I'll leave you to sleep. If you need me or one of the team, just buzz us from the panel."

"Or I could just wave at the camera."

"You could, indeed. Goodnight, Abby — sleep well."

"Goodnight, Doctor Sharma."

The door closed, and Abby turned to look through the wall to wave at Terrell, but she couldn't see anything but water. She climbed out of bed and pushed her face against the glass, but couldn't see anything outside.

Padman was walking away when he heard a door slide open behind him.

"Doctor Sharma?" Abby called.

"Yes Miss Rosenberg?"

"Why can't I see outside when I'm in bed?"

Padman walked back towards her.

"We installed one-way glass for better privacy and to minimise distractions while you sleep. We can still observe you through the cameras, though."

"Oh, OK."

"Is there anything else?" Padman smiled warmly; Abby was a genuinely likeable girl and he wanted her to feel completely at ease trusting both him and his work at Silicate.

Abby smiled, the slight shadow of worry disappearing from her features.

"No. Thank you, Doctor Sharma. Goodnight." She stepped back and pressed the card around her neck to the panel by the door. Once inside, she waved until the door closed in front of her. Padman watched as Abby stared at her reflection in the door, squinting to try to see through it, to no avail. Padman continued to watch, smiling faintly to himself, until she finally relented and climbed into bed.

CHAPTER 18

Ryder wheeled himself out of Isabell's room and down the corridor towards the staff elevator. Inside, there were only four floors listed: the level he was on, *The Spa*, *Archeus*, and *Ground*. He pressed for *Archeus*, but nothing happened. Repeatedly pressing the button, the doors stayed stubbornly open. Frustrated, Ryder admitted defeat and radioed the security station.

"Dani here."

"Hi, Dani, it's Ryder. I'm trying to do my rounds, but the lift won't take me to Archeus."

"Did you scan your pass?"

"My pass? Oh, of course. No, I totally forgot." Ryder felt every inch the new-start he was.

"That'll be why, then, sir."

Ryder scanned his pass and the door closed.

"Yep, that worked. Thanks, Dani."

"No worries, boss."

Ryder could hear the smile in her voice as he placed the radio back into his pocket. He felt the elevator descend before stepping out into a small room, with a double door in front. He moved over to the panel and scanned his pass. Nothing happened.

"Oh, come on!" he groaned, reaching for his radio again.

"Dani here."

"Hey, Dani, it's Ryder. Again. I'm in the entrance to Archeus but —"

"You can't open the door?"

"I scanned my pass this time, but it's still not working."

"Hold on." The camera in the corner of the room rotated. "OK, I see you. There's a camera to the left of the door, above the panel . . . look into it and hold your pass over the panel at the same time."

"Are you messing with me?" Ryder followed Dani's instructions and stared into the camera lens, and the door opened. "Whoa! It's like being in a sci-fi film."

"Pretty cool, eh? The ID camera we use for the security pass also scans your retinas and adds them to your file."

Ryder stepped into the hallway, letting the door close behind him.

"You're one of the chosen few with access to Archeus," Dani continued. "I've never even seen it."

"I'll tell you about it when I get back," Ryder replied. "Thanks for your help, Dani."

"Anytime." The radio clicked off.

The wheels on Ryder's chair trundled over the textured metal covering the corridor. Lights flickered on overhead as he reached each new section, disguising the true length of his journey. Doors on either side indicated laboratories, offices and meeting-rooms lay behind them. He pushed along further until he reached a door spanning the width of the corridor. Above it, embossed metal letters spelled out the name of the room: *ARCHEUS*.

Looks like I'm in the right place, then, Ryder thought, scanning his pass. The doors opened into a room he recognised as a sound and light buffer, much like the one upstairs leading into Hygge. He headed for the door at the other end, this time not requiring Dani's assistance as he scanned his pass and eye at the same time.

"Still cool," he murmured aloud as the doors glided open, revealing a dark space in front of him. This was such a contrast from the rest of the building. At first, Ryder waited for the lights to flicker on, as they had in the corridor, but as his eyes adjusted, he realised they already *were* on.

He moved into the room, his wheels sinking slightly into floor. He brushed his hand against the ground before pressing his fingers into it. The floor was entirely covered in rubber.

As his pupils dilated, he adjusted to his new surroundings. Before him was a huge, glass wall, arching in a semi-circle. To either side was an office, but the main event here was beyond the glass. Pushing himself forward, Ryder realised that Isabell's description, far from being exaggerated, actually did this room a disservice.

Black and silver were the dominate colours, and while all very clean and clinical-looking, there was a hard kind of beauty to it, as well. At the very back of the room was what looked to be some kind of futuristic bed, surrounded by equipment Ryder had never seen before. Between the end of the bed and where he stood was a huge, open expanse. Everything seemed to be crammed into the back of the room — why, then, he wondered, was there all this space here?

Ryder let out a yelp as something brushed the underside of his foot. He looked down, expecting to see a rodent, but there was nothing. He moved his chair around in a circle, staring at the black, rubber floor.

"It's just your imagination," he muttered under his breath, trying to calm his heart, which was beating rapidly. As he moved back towards the glass wall, he noticed something from the corner of his eye, darting around the curve of the circular perimeter. As quietly as he could, he eased himself forward. As he neared the corner, the thing raced past him in the opposite direction. He spun round, amazed to see a tortoiseshell cat with a white front paw sitting with its head tilted to one side, staring at him quizzically.

"Hello, there. What are you doing in here?" Ryder stretched out his hand and rubbed his fingers together. "How did you get in?" Inching forward, the cat stayed perfectly still. "It's OK, I'm not going to hurt you." Just as he reached down to pat its head, the cat sprinted to the opposite side of the room. Frustrated, Ryder followed the cat, now pawing at the glass door leading into the central lab.

"You want to go in there?" he asked the creature, who continued to stare at him and paw the glass. "Well, unless your retina is on file, you'll need me. Now, are you going to be nice and let me stroke you?" he murmured quietly as he reached down.

This time, the cat brushed its head against his hand.

"That's better. I'm not really that scary, although I know my chair can be a little daunting." He tried to reach the name-tag on its collar, but the cat was far too interested in having its head stroked. "Do you want to come up here?" He patted his lap and the cat leaped on to him. Now with both hands available, he adjusted the collar while continuing to stroke the cat's head. His gasp shocked both of them as he read the name tag: *Megara*.

Isabell's mobile rang. She ignored it, finishing the paragraph she was working on before checking the call register. She smiled.

"Missing me already?"

"Can you describe your cat for me?"

"What?"

"Please, can you just describe her."

"Erm, yeah. She's a tortoiseshell with a white front paw and she wears a red collar. Why on earth would you want to know that?"

There was a long pause.

"Ryder? What's going on?"

"Wait right there, I'm coming back to get you."

"How are they both doing?" Padman walked into the nurses'

station. Phoebe and Zane were monitoring the screens of the two patients.

"The pods are pressurised, and we've reduced the humidity, so they should be asleep any time now," Phoebe replied, not taking her eyes off the screens.

"Good, good. Contact me if there's anything unusual or any sort of emergency."

"Will do."

Padman returned to the Red Room and to Jake, who paused the game he was playing.

"They're both settled in for the night. Do you want me to walk you down to the spa?"

"Is it OK if I stay here? I've just found a version of Shivers 3. I didn't even know there was a third game!"

"Big kid! Fine, but I'll have to do this." Padman picked up a remote control from the table and activated the blue tint on the screen. "If you don't have the filter on, you won't be tired when we get down to Archeus."

"That's cool, I can still see it clearly. Want to join me?"

"I have to go back to my office and catch up on some work," Padman admitted apologetically. "You can come with me if you like?"

"Sit and play computer games or sit in your office listening to you typing up notes . . . I'm fine here, thanks."

Padman smiled as he kissed Jake.

"I'll be back as soon as I can."

"Take your time, no rush," Jake called as the doctor left the room.

Padman was still smiling as he entered his office, locking the door behind him. He hung his suit jacket on the hook behind the door and slipped off his shirt, walking over to the white, leather sofa. He yawned and stretched as he sat down, wiping his tired eyes. Another long day, but overall, a good one, he thought.

By the side of him was a series of drawers, all protected by a thumbprint scanner. He reached across and placed his thumb to the top drawer, which opened to reveal a lock-box. He lifted it out and placed it on his lap. After scanning his thumb again to the panel on top, he heard the lock release and he lifted the lid. Inside was a long, white cylinder.

Padman placed one end of it to his neck and pressed a button on its base. A sharp, short hissing noise caused him to flinch and tears welled up in his eyes momentarily. Pulling the cylinder away revealed a red mark on his neck. He rubbed it for a few seconds until it disappeared. His eyes widened, and he shivered slightly.

Holding on to the cylinder, he threw his crumpled shirt into a basket behind the sofa and reached to place the cylinder into the inside pocket of his jacket. He opened the wardrobe and retrieved one of the five identical, freshly pressed shirts inside. He dressed again, checking himself in the mirror before sitting down at his computer and opening his emails.

Isabell was slipping on her shoes when Ryder arrived, his brow furrowed.

"You can't wear those!" he exclaimed, looking at her red stilettos.

"I don't have anything else to wear. Well, apart from these things."

She picked up a pair of white, hospital-issue, disposable slippers.

"Perfect, wear those."

"No way." Isabell pulled a face of disgust. "They're awful. What do you have against my shoes?" She changed her features into a comical sad face.

Ryder moved his chair up to the bed.

"Nothing — they're lovely, but the floor in Archeus is made of rubber . . . therefore, these —" he picked up one of the shoes, pointing to the seven-inch heel "— would pierce holes right through."

"Rubber? That's a peculiar choice."

"That's what I thought. It's all over the walls, too."

"That's why it's so dark in there, like some freaky sex dungeon," Isabell said, sliding her feet into the slippers. Sitting on the edge of the bed, she kicked up her right leg and placed it on Ryder's knee, rotating her ankle to show off her footwear. "They really bring out the colour in my sclera, don't you think?"

Ryder looked confused.

"Sclera — the whites of my eyes."

"Yes, they bring those out beautifully," Ryder replied wryly. It was the first time he'd smiled since entering the room, and Isabell was relieved.

"Now you're in a better mood, are you going to tell me why you're dragging me down to my least favourite place?" Isabell removed her leg from Ryder's and sat upright.

"Sorry. I wouldn't ask you to do this if it wasn't important."

"I'll take that as a 'no', then. Right, come on, the faster we do this, the faster I can get back to bed."

"Did I wake you up?"

"No, I'll just feel a lot safer up here than down there in the sex dungeon."

"It's not a sex dungeon."

"You don't know that, and I'm always out of it when I'm in there ... Who knows what they do to me?"

"It's not a sex dungeon," Ryder told her sternly.

"Why else would they need rubber floors and walls?" Isabell stood up and walked to the door.

Ryder shrugged as he followed her.

"Easy cleaning, that's all I'm saying."

They both laughed as they descended in the elevator. Through the high security door and along the hallway, the closer they got to Archeus, the more nervous Isabell became. She shivered.

"Are you cold?"

"No, I'm OK. I thought you said the floor was rubber?" Isabell asked, purposefully deflecting the question.

"It is, in here."

The doors opened and Isabell stared at the glass wall surrounded by black. As they moved inside, she could feel the change beneath her feet. The doors closed behind them, and Isabell began to hyperventilate. Ryder just managed to catch her as she collapsed on to her knees right in front of his chair.

CHAPTER 19

"I shouldn't have brought you here. I'm so sorry."

Isabell's head remained lowered and her eyes closed as she tried to regain composure. With her hands on her legs, she felt something brush against her. Instinctively, she began to stroke the cat, which brought an instant wave of calm. Surprised, she opened her eyes and watched as Megara danced playfully around them. Continuing to pet the cat, she looked up at Ryder, confused but delighted.

"How?"

"This *is* your cat, then?"

"This is Meg — I'd know her anywhere. How did she get in here? Jackie's meant to be looking after her. Did you do this?"

"Not me. I was on my rounds when I found her."

Isabell stood up with Megara in her arms. She peered around the room.

"There's no-one around and I can't see a litter tray or food. Why would someone lock my cat inside Archeus?"

Megara leaped out of Isabell's arms and ran towards the lab door, pawing at the glass.

"She was doing that when I called you."

"Why does she want to go in there?" Isabell kneeled down and stroked Megara, examining the panel at the side of the door. "Do you have access to get in here?"

Ryder pulled out his pass.

"Excuse me, ladies," he said, scanning his pass and eye.

The door slid open gently and Megara ran in, jumped on to the bed and looked at Isabell expectantly.

"Maybe she's tired?"

"No, I know that look. She wants something. Usually, that's the look I get before she leads me to her empty food bowl or a dead mouse. She's probably hungry."

"I doubt we'll find cat food in here," Ryder said, looking around the huge space.

"Who knows *what* we'll find in here." Isabell moved to the side of the room and started opening cabinet doors.

Ryder looked up.

"What are those?" He pointed to four massive, cylindrical objects attached to the high ceiling. "They look like rockets."

Isabell joined him and pulled out her phone. Activating the camera function, she zoomed in and took a series of photographs with her flash.

"They look like laser cannons," Ryder said.

"Laser cannons aren't real," Isabell replied, putting her phone away.

"The military use them."

"Of course they do! I should have known amazing sci-fi tech would be invented by the army."

"I doubt we — sorry, *they* — invented them, but they definitely *use* them."

"Whoever invented them, what are they doing here? It doesn't make any sense." She walked over to the bed, and after giving Megara a few more strokes, went back to snooping.

"I've found something," she announced a minute later.

Ryder joined her behind the bed in front of a wall panel containing a myriad of buttons, secured with a scan lock. Isabell looked at Ryder.

"Open it."

Ryder scanned his pass but nothing happened. He tried a few more times before moving away.

"I guess I don't have clearance for whatever that is," he said apologetically.

"But I do."

Isabell and Ryder spun around to see Padman and Jake standing in the doorway.

"You scared us," Isabell said, clutching her chest.

"What are you two doing down here? And why — how — is there a cat in my lab?" Padman was clearly displeased.

Ryder recounted the events that brought them to Archeus.

"That still doesn't explain how your cat got in, Isabell. Have you called your neighbour to ask if Megara is missing?" Padman asked.

"I'll do it now." Isabell, feeling a little bit like she had been told off by a parent, dialled Jackie's number but couldn't get a connection. "It's not working. I don't have a mobile signal," she informed the group.

Jake, Ryder and Padman all checked their phones, discovering no-one had signal.

"That's strange, I called Isabell from here less than an hour ago," Ryder said, moving his phone around in the air. "Actually, I wasn't in here, I was still behind the glass wall when I made that call." He moved back into the antechamber. "Nope — still nothing," he called to the others.

Padman sighed and exchanged his phone for his radio.

"Hello, Dani? Are you there?"

Static.

"Phoebe — can you hear me?"

More static.

"Hello, this is Doctor Padman Sharma. Can anyone hear me?"

Static.

"Fan-bloody-tastic! Ryder, could you go back upstairs, please, and inform Dani we have communication problems down here?"

"Sure thing." Ryder moved to the exit, but the door wouldn't open. "I think the electrics are down — the scanners aren't working, either."

"That's impossible. Silicate runs solely on renewable energy, generated in this building. Electrical outages simply can't happen. Let me try."

Ryder moved out of the way as the doctor tried to open the door, to no avail.

"This is most unusual," Padman muttered, pacing the floor. "We have enough stored energy for years. We've got backups for our backup generators. This shouldn't be *able* to happen."

"But it has happened," Isabell said gently.

Padman stopped pacing and looked at the group standing in front of him.

"Actually, I don't think it has. If the electrics had gone down, we wouldn't have lights."

"If the lights are on, maybe the cameras are still working. Can we signal to Dani?" Jake started waving his hands around in the air.

"Dani can't see these cameras. You need high-level access to view them, and there's only one person in the building tonight with that access — me."

"Well, that's great," Isabell said, Megara dancing at her feet. "What about the emergency exit? There must be one."

Megara miaowed loudly. Isabell reached down to pick her up, but the cat ran back into the lab, bounding over the bed to paw at the far wall.

"What's gotten into you tonight?" she asked, following Megara in.

"How is your cat here at all?" Jake queried, catching up to them.

"Your guess is as good as mine." Isabell spun around and offered her hand, with a smile. "Hi, I'm Isabell, by the way. Nice to meet you — although probably not the best location for a first encounter."

Jake snorted a laugh.

"No, probably not." He shook her hand as they both smiled. "Nice to meet you, too."

Ryder and Padman walked into the lab.

"What's she doing now?" Ryder asked, diverting everyone's attention back to Megara.

Isabell pulled out her phone and activated the torch. She directed the beam to where the cat was pawing at the rubber wall.

"I can see a gap at the bottom." Ryder reached down and ran his finger along the underside.

"What are you doing?" Padman asked.

"I'm trying to see if there's a door hidden back here. It's the only thing that makes sense."

"Does any of this make sense?" Isabell asked.

Ryder was too busy searching to reply.

"Nothing. It's a solid wall — well, a rubber wall. Why is everything covered in rubber, anyway?"

"Sex dungeon!"

Everyone stared at Isabell.

"Sorry — just trying to lighten the mood."

Padman turned to Ryder.

"Rubber is a non-conductive material. Some of what we do in here requires a lot of energy and this keeps it all contained in a safe environment."

"It's not very safe for us if we're trapped in here."

Padman half-smiled at Jake in an attempt to reassure him, but it was obvious the doctor was also anxious.

He turned to Isabell.

"How are you? I mean, how have you been feeling today?"

"Fine. Great, actually," she replied, a little startled.

"Have you had any episodes since your treatment here, in Archeus?"

"None. Which is rather strange. I was writing earlier and usually I can visualise Vincent really clearly, but today, I couldn't. I put it down to being on the ward and not at home, but it was —"

"You're saying you haven't seen Vincent since your attack?" the doctor interrupted.

"No — not at all."

Padman resumed pacing, deep in thought.

Isabell turned to Jake and Ryder and shrugged.

"What's going on?" she mouthed.

"May I examine your cat, please?" Padman asked.

"Of course. She's not usually good with strangers, though."

Padman picked up Megara and touched his nose to hers. He stared into her eyes for almost a minute before passing the cat back to a confused Isabell.

"Hmmm," he murmured, walking over to one of the computers at the side of the lab and sitting down in front of the monitor. The screen came to life at a touch of a button. "Just as I thought — the computers are also working," Padman announced as he started to type.

"If the electrics aren't down, why aren't the doors working?"

"That's what I'm trying to figure out, Ryder," Padman snapped in reply.

"Sorry, Doc." Ryder turned to Isabell and shrugged.

Padman checked the security protocols first; every door seemed to be working except for the one connecting Archeus to the higher floors. It was the same story with the cameras and communications. He picked up the phone to his left, but there was no dial tone. He slammed it down in frustration, causing the others to jump.

He continued writing lines of code in an attempt to regain access. This can't be happening, he thought. Opening folders within folders, inside more folders, he eventually found a system backup automatically recorded less than an hour before. He checked the code carefully. Everything was in order. Silicate's security system was one of the best in world; for this to happen to an isolated section of the building, suggested to Padman that either the software was corrupted or someone had trapped them in here deliberately.

He opened one last programme. It was room-specific, so wouldn't be affected by a possible system or network collapse. It showed the air quality of the room. It was dropping. A cold shiver ran down his arms and then a warm hand touched his shoulder gently. He spun around and found Jake peering at him, looking concerned.

"Are you OK?"

Padman stood up and hugged him, before leading him back to the others, so he could address them all together.

"I'm sorry for snapping at you, Ryder; I apologise to you all for my erratic behaviour."

"Think nothing of it." Ryder smiled.

"OK, first, the *somewhat* good news. Two of our nurses seemingly disappeared last night and Ryder has been looking for them all day. I imagine that's what brought you to Archeus?"

"It is, sir."

The doctor nodded before continuing.

"I received an email from one of the missing nurses informing me that he and Sally are tendering their resignations with immediate effect. He apologised for their swift and secretive departure. According to Andrew, they're madly in love and have eloped. He believes his father won't be happy with the relationship, so they've run off together in a somewhat foolhardy or romantic move, depending on how you look at it.

"I've contacted Jeremy, Andrew's father, who's on our board of directors, but with it being so late in the day, I imagine we'll have to wait until tomorrow for a response."

"What about Fred, the security guard?" Ryder turned to Isabell and Jake to explain. "Fred also went missing last night."

"They could be a throuple?" Isabell suggested.

"That's what I said," Padman responded, chuckling.

"What's a throuple?" Jake asked.

"A three-way relationship," Isabell announced, a cheeky glint in her eye.

"How do you know about all this stuff?"

"I'm a writer — I have to know a little about a lot."

"Discounting the throuple idea — because it's ridiculous — where could he have gotten to?" Ryder asked.

"He could simply be ill," Padman replied, "but I can't understand why his wife would lie about that. He could have quit without telling us, or it could be something more sinister."

"You mean, he could be dead?" Isabell asked.

"I suppose that's also a possibility, but I was thinking more along the lines of him being the reason we're now locked in this room."

"Why do you think that?"

"Archeus is one of the most secure areas in the building. Only myself, heads of departments, and certain members of the security staff have access. Fred was one of them."

"That doesn't prove he's guilty."

"I agree, although it doesn't mean he's innocent, either. I have to look at all options here. The only other person with access last night was Sally, but as she and Andrew have eloped, I think we can discount her.

"This isn't just a process of elimination, though. I've always had my suspicions about Fred. He was here when I joined the company and we've never seen eye-to-eye. I frequently found him in restricted parts of the building with no explanation as to why he was there. When I raised my concerns, I was told he was doing his rounds, carrying out his duties."

"I hate to side with him on this, but that does sound like he was doing his job," Ryder responded cautiously.

"While taking photos?"

"Huh?"

"I would sometimes catch him taking pictures on his phone. When I confronted him, he denied everything, of course, but I know what I saw. Our relationship became even more strained when I reported him to the board, with evidence from the video surveillance. His phone was searched as part of the enquiry, but it was clean."

"Did he know you were the one who reported him?" Ryder asked.

"It was never disclosed that I'd made the complaint, but he knew. After that, we kept our distance from each other as much as possible."

"And you think he's trapped us in here out of spite or something?" Isabell asked.

"I can't say I understand his motives, but the system logs show he was the last person to enter this room before today. Until we have more information, that's the only explanation I can come up with."

"What do we do now? Just wait until someone lets us out?" Jake asked.

"I'm afraid that's not an option. The nearest washroom is on the other side of that locked door, along with the kitchen, so we have no food or water. The next person with access to Archeus won't be on duty until six a.m."

"You're saying we have to hold our bladders for another six hours?"

"Sorry, I meant six a.m. on *Monday*."

"What?" Isabell, Jake and Ryder cried in unison.

"And that's assuming we're reported missing and they come to check Archeus."

"That's insane. How are we going to manage that long?" Isabell asked.

"That's not even our most immediate problem."

"What do you mean?" Ryder looked hard at Padman.

"I can't access the main network on the computer, but I was able to search through the folders specific to this room. In the system logs is a live-feed measuring the air quality. It's dropping. I checked why that might be, and I believe the air circulation system has been manually switched off. This is a vacuum-sealed room and as you can see, there are no windows to crack open."

"How long do we have left?" Ryder asked.

"There are stores of air to feed this room and as long as we —"

"How long do we have, Padman?" Jake asked nervously.

"A little over an hour."

Panic set in for Isabell and Jake, whose eyes were now darting around the room, searching for an opening of any kind. Ryder maintained more composure.

"Do you have any suggestions?"

"Only one, and I would use it in a heartbeat, but —" the doctor turned to Isabell "— your cat being here terrifies me more than the thought of us all suffocating to death."

CHAPTER 20

"We're getting images from Pod Two."

Phoebe was sitting in front of a set of monitors showing all five cameras from Abby's pod.

Zane, at the next station along monitoring Pod One, pushed his chair over to Phoebe's station.

"Whoa! Look at that. I've never seen so many clear images before."

The two nurses watched as powder-blue, smoke-like strands wisped from Abby's head, multiplying and dancing above the sleeping girl, flowing effortlessly; extending to the full height of the pod. As the strands collided, they combined, and from the chaos, images created by Abby's mind began to form. A young man's face, the Transamerica Building, a flock of birds; the wisps created these scenes in real time. Illusions of thoughts and dreams brought to life for the briefest of moments before reforming into the next beautifully crafted image.

Suddenly, the wisps stopped dancing and the images disappeared as a deeper shade of blue raced from Abby's head, engulfing and saturating the apparitions.

"What's that?" Zane asked.

"I think this is what we're looking for."

On the monitor, a silhouetted figure emerged.

"Is that him?"

"I think so. Padman said she calls him the Shadow Man," Phoebe replied, not taking her eyes off the screen.

"This has to be him. He gives me the willies. No wonder she can't sleep."

They watched as the Shadow Man stretched out, extending his wispy arms and legs fully until he reached the ceiling of the pod. Finally, red swirls of smoke formed in his head.

"Yes, that's definitely him. Padman mentioned he had red eyes — if you can call them eyes."

"What's it doing?" Zane asked, moving closer to the screen.

"I have no idea. I've never seen anything like this."

Dark smoke circled in the centre of the Shadow Man's body. The black mass grew, radiating down through his wiry legs and back into Abby's head, forming a rope, of sorts, from his stomach. His blue arms glided towards the rope. Grasping it with both hands, he began tugging and, in the process of doing so, pulled on Abby's head.

"How's this even possible?"

"I don't know, and I don't care. I'm purging this, now." Phoebe began the shutdown procedure.

"You need to see this."

"In a minute Zane, I just need to —"

"Phoebe!" Zane shouted, causing her to look back at the screen.

The Shadow Man was staring directly into the camera. His red eyes burned as he shook his head slowly.

On the main monitor, Phoebe switched from camera to camera; each time she did, the figure moved, too, so that it was always staring right at them.

"How is he doing this? It's a young girl's dream. It doesn't have *consciousness*; it doesn't know we're here. It's not even *alive* — how can it be doing this?" Phoebe frantically typed in the shutdown code. As she entered the final command, the Shadow Man rushed towards the lens with his mouth open, as if roaring at her; and then it was gone.

"I'm going down there." Phoebe jumped up from her seat.

"I'm coming with you," Zane responded, racing out of the office in pursuit, and missing the images which were now being streamed from Pod One.

"What's so terrifying about Megara? I know she's not the friendliest at first, but that's only because she's a rescue cat. It takes time for her to warm to people." Isabell was clinging to Megara and stroking her gently as she spoke.

"Isabell, I don't mean to upset you, but that's not your cat you're holding," Padman said, as gently as he could.

"Of course it is. Don't you think I know my own cat?"

"Please, put your face up to hers — I want you to feel specifically for her breath."

Isabell frowned in confusion.

"I can feel that she's breathing, in my arms, right now."

"I know you can feel her chest moving but humour me. Please, Isabell."

Sceptical, Isabell brought Megara up to her face and rubbed her nose against the cat's. Everyone paused, expectantly.

Isabell stood for over a minute before lowering the cat and cradling her back in her arms.

"There's no air. No breath." Isabell looked tearful. "But there has to be — look!" Isabell held a squirming Megara up, showing everyone the movement of her chest. "See? She's breathing."

"Simulating breathing." Padman spoke softly and calmly. "You clearly love your cat very much. So much so, in fact, that you've created the perfect facsimile. One that even its owner can't tell apart from the real thing."

"Padman, what are you saying? This makes no sense at all." Isabell felt angry, confused and upset, and it wasn't helping that the doctor was giving her answers in bite-sized chunks.

"I believe we may have inadvertently created a copy of your cat when you were here last night."

"How?"

The doctor walked closer to the group to address them all.

"Do you know what we do here?"

"You analyse people's dreams, and —" Ryder struggled to remember the word "— and look for apparitions."

"That's correct, and to be able to monitor and analyse those apparitions, we need to be able to see them as clearly as possible. We've experimented over the years, we've advanced our understanding, and we've pushed — we continue to push — the limits of technology. And we have, in some cases, been able to give those apparitions corporeal form." The doctor looked at Isabell, trying to determine how she was coping with all this information.

"No way. You're saying this is a dream-cat?" Ryder couldn't believe what he was hearing.

Neither could Isabell, who clung even tighter to Megara.

"How do you give a dream form?" Jake asked, trying to understand but feeling as perplexed as everyone else.

"I know this is a lot to take in — it was for all of us in the beginning. We live in a world where these types of things are almost impossible to comprehend. Before all of you came to Silicate, you had no idea thoughts and dreams could be seen and studied, yet you have seen it with your own eyes and accepted it as the truth. Is this any different?"

"It's one thing to see blurry, blue smoke making shapes, but you're trying to convince us that this —" Ryder moved over to Megara "— is made from a dream. I can touch it. I can stroke it. I can feel it *moving*."

"Ryder, everyone, please — I need you to open your minds to this possibility. Perhaps we should all sit down?" The doctor guided them over to the chairs at the side of the room. "Please, take a seat and I'll do my best to explain everything."

As Jake and Isabell sat down, Ryder moved over to Padman and crossed his arms.

"No offence, Doc, but do we have time for this? You've just told we're running out of air. Shouldn't we be looking for a way out of here, instead of having story-time?"

"Rest assured, I'm not about to put our lives in danger, I promise. What I'm about to tell you relates to our situation."

Frustrated and unconvinced, Ryder joined Isabell and Jake and waited for the doctor to speak.

"Archeus is much more advanced than the pods in Hygge. This room generates the majority of our funding. In fact, I'd go as far as saying it is the sole reason Silicate still exists at all. The ability to see people's dreams was a huge discovery and helped, initially, to save one life —" he turned to Ryder "— your grandmother's life.

"A small team was formed, and Silicate was founded. We started out believing this information could benefit the whole world, but we needed money to do that, and so we invited investors to see our research. They were shocked and amazed, at first. As the novelty wore off, they decided they needed more than some grainy camera footage of apparitions from one patient. They wanted to know how they could profit from it."

"Wasn't saving lives enough?" Isabell asked.

"We believed so, but the investors needed a guaranteed return on the huge sums of money we required to get the company up and running. Things got worse when we started clinical trials and discovered our technology only worked with a small percentage of patients, those with similar cognitive disfunction to Lady Braighton." Padman looked pained at the memory. "Our foolhardy estimated one hundred per cent of the population plummeted to a mere two per cent.

"From the hundreds of *potential* patients we monitored, only those in heightened emotional states showed any signs of an apparition, and of that group, only patients without siblings displayed results we could actually use.

"The investors, of course, threatened to pull all their funding."

"I have a brother and you can see mine," Isabell stated.

"We've come a long way since those early days. We've refined our tech and our understanding. Today, we can treat a much larger proportion of the population, although we do still get the best results from patients who are only children."

"How did you manage to keep your investors? You said it had something to do with this place?" Isabell was struggling to keep Megara on her lap as she questioned the doctor.

"A few of us had been developing technology to capture an apparition in a glass case. It was wildly unsuccessful, but I was convinced we could do it, given time. At the board meeting, the investors demanded answers and, feeling we would lose them, I . . . well, I lied." Padman looked mortified. "I told them we had successfully captured an apparition and given it form. In the presentation, I applied a tagline intended to sell the idea: Silicate, where dreams become reality."

"What is this, Disney World?" Jake asked with a smile.

"I meant it literally, not figuratively."

"But it was a lie, you can't actually do it," Ryder pointed out.

"We couldn't back then, but we can now." The doctor stood up and walked into the centre of the room. "These —" he pointed to the ceiling "— are particle beams."

Everyone stared at the four cylinders.

"This one pumps out proteins. This one is carbohydrate." Padman pointed to each in turn. "This one lipids, and, the last one, nucleic acids."

Isabell audibly gasped.

"The building blocks of life."

"Precisely."

After a long pause, Ryder broke the silence.

"Bull! You can't just bombard a thought or dream or whatever with some molecules and, hey, presto! You've made life."

"Not *life* — I never said that — I said we make *dreams real*. The cat in Isabell's arms is proof of it."

Ryder motioned to Isabell, who held Megara up cautiously to him and then to Jake. Both men checked for breath but couldn't detect any.

The doctor stroked Megara's head.

"From outward appearances, this is your cat, Isabell. It'll move, behave and even simulate breathing like the real Megara at home with Jackie. But, in essence, this is a dream clone."

"I still can't get my head around this. She's my cat." Isabell retrieved Megara from Jake's arms.

"Smell her — she won't smell of anything. Feel her tongue and it won't be wet. She's a perfect recreation, but a recreation, all the same."

"I don't believe it."

Padman turned to the ex-soldier.

"I understand this is difficult to process, especially for someone with your training and experience, but, please, humour me for a while. For argument's sake, imagine I'm telling you the truth. Let's say that these four cylinders can give form to a dream. Let that sink in for a moment. Now, imagine what could be done with such technology."

Ryder played along.

"Well, if — hypothetically — you could create a cat which could fool its owner..."

"Hey!"

"Sorry, Isabell, *convince* its owner..."

"Much better, thank you."

"If you could do that, I suppose you could create anything a patient dreams."

"Yes. Now, let's take this hypothetical situation a little further. If we could make a cat, what else could we make? And who would benefit the most from it?"

"Everyone, I suppose ... you could have cartoon characters for kids or bring dead family members back to life." Ryder paused and let his imagine roam. "Or dragons, or celebrities, or stormtroopers or — oh, no!"

"What? What's wrong?" Isabell kneeled down beside Ryder, releasing Megara, who ran to the back of the room again.

Ryder turned to her with a look of pure anguish.

"If this were real, and I'm not saying I believe it is, but if it *were*, then surely the military would gain the most from it. They'd be able to create soldiers out of nothing. Unstoppable monsters who could tear up whole cities — countries, even — without being able to be killed."

"And that's precisely what I won't let happen. It's the reason Silicate is so security-conscious. If the military ever got their hands on this technology, it would create chaos around the globe. It has the potential to destroy us all." Padman said seriously. "Billions of pounds have been pumped into this place by countless investors on the promise that we're working on a technological breakthrough that every country in the world will be interested in."

"They think you're working on military tech?" Ryder was concerned.

"We wouldn't take money from such people and your grandfather would never have allowed it, even if we were desperate."

"But in the beginning, you said you *were* desperate."

"Isabell, you've known me a long time now. Do you really believe I would hand over my life's work to someone I knew would attempt to use against or harm innocent people in any way? Even if I needed their money?"

"No, you wouldn't."

"So how did you get them to invest?" Jake asked.

"They'd seen apparitions in the pods emanating from the patients, but I had no proof we could actually give dreams any sustainable form, although I did have a real-world example; one they could all understand. That gave us time to back up my grandiose claims."

"What real world example?" Ryder asked.

"Ghosts. People have sightings of them all the time, usually in dusty, old houses. We surmised that they're leftover strands of thoughts and dreams. Over time, they collect dust, skin, glass and water particles, building a somewhat visible mass. Obviously, with so few active molecules, ghosts are mere glimpses of someone or something, but with the information we had gathered, it made sense to us that what some people identify as ghosts, we know now are actually apparitions."

All three remained in a stunned silence as Padman continued.

"Working on that assumption, and with a hefty sum of money invested, I helped design and build Archeus. Our small team had a lot of creative ideas and all wanted to contribute, so we tried everything.

"You have to remember — we were working blind in a field that no-one else had ever attempted. We crammed this room full of every piece of equipment and technology we could find and tested day and night. We didn't have time on our side and sleep was a luxury we could not afford for those first few months. Eventually we had our breakthrough and have been constantly refining our research and technology ever since.

"The glass wall in here is unnecessary. We added it to appease the investors — they wanted a viewing gallery, somewhere they could stand and watch their money at work. It only took six months before we were ready to invite patients into Archeus. The first few trials failed and we couldn't understand why. We were almost at breaking point, when a flock of seagulls were borne from the mind of our third patient, Arturo, a young boy from Mexico. They circled the room four times before disintegrating into a cloud of dust. It lasted only a matter of seconds, but we had succeeded. It was the best day of my life.

"We were able to work with Arturo more closely over the coming weeks. He was such a great kid; my heart went out to him. He'd suffered so much trauma already in his young life after witnessing his father's murder when he was only five. The horror of it caused some of the worst night terrors I've ever seen. We vowed, to his fraught mother, to do everything in our power to try to help him."

"And did you?" Ryder asked.

"Yes, unfortunately."

"Why *unfortunately*?"

"In Arturo's second week here, we invited the investors to come and see for themselves how well we were progressing. We'd made massive leaps forward in the space of a week — extending the duration of the apparitions to over five minutes. That may not sound particularly impressive, but we were giving form to thoughts and dreams and, with more time, we believed we could extend that half-life indefinitely." The doctor walked over to the security panel on the far wall.

"I tried to open that earlier, but it wouldn't accept my pass," Ryder said.

"Your pass wouldn't work here. Neither would mine, actually." Padman placed his hand on the panel. The wall to his left opened, revealing a compartment with an extendable tube inside. The group looked confused as he pulled the tube out of the wall, brought it up to his mouth and breathed deeply into it.

After a few seconds, there was a bleep.

"Hello, Doctor Padman Sharma," a computerised voice said as the panel opened, revealing a switchboard.

Padman pressed a series of illuminated, coloured buttons, activating a spring-loaded charging dock. He reached inside and retrieved a tablet, switching it on as he walked back to the stunned group. The entire glass wall became a giant TV screen, displaying the contents of the tablet. The doctor opened a video file; the time stamp showed it had been filmed three years ago.

"What I'm about to show you is harrowing, but it'll lay to rest any doubts you may still have about this place."

The doctor clicked *Play*, and the video came to life.

CHAPTER 21

Three years earlier

Padman stood in the centre of Archeus wearing white hospital overalls and holding a tablet. Looking towards the viewing gallery, he addressed the congregation of investors.

"Hello, everyone, and thank you for joining us. As you'll know from the communique we sent, this is the breakthrough we've all been waiting for. After today, I guarantee there will be *no question* regarding the legitimacy of this programme and the vital nature of our work." Padman paused for a reaction.

There was stirring amongst the crowd. Some of the investors appeared nervous and apprehensive, but most were smiling with excitement, reflecting Padman's own mood. He had dreamed about this day. Working around the clock, he had poured his life and soul into this project.

"Archeus was a thought, a mere dream, just a few years ago. And now, we make thoughts and dreams a reality, *literally!*"

There was a light chuckle from the audience, everyone's attention fixed firmly on the doctor.

"For many of you, this is your first time seeing Archeus, so allow me to show you around." He moved closer to the glass wall. "Unlike the pods, we pump water molecules into the room rather than fill the wall between us, meaning we can now do things like this."

The doctor pressed a button on his tablet and videos, live-feeds and medical information appeared on the glass wall; with another click, it was gone. The investors applauded. Smiling, Padman spread his arms wide and circled the space.

"This means that instead of being limited as to how we can see the apparitions, we can now make them appear to all of us, in real time, right here." Padman walked to the back of room. "On either side we have our workspaces. It's not your usual medical equipment here. Everything's been specially designed by our in-house team."

He picked up an item that looked like an oversized fly swat.

"This, for example, may look like a common household object, but it is far more sophisticated. It is used to dissipate any unwanted apparitions. The holes are surrounded by an electrical charge, which disrupts the pre-rendered form." The doctor placed the item back on the tray.

"And electrical charges are something we need to be wary of, which is why Archeus is covered entirely in non-conductive rubber. Electricity from the brain is what gives the apparitions form. We take that energy and render the apparitions into stable matter. Beneath the rubber walls are wooden panels underpinned with plastic insulation, all which dampen the electricity, keeping everyone inside safe.

"Our bed, Meditati, is made of fibreglass." Padman rested his hand on the intimidating-looking device. "This is the most advanced piece of technology in the entire building, if not the world. With a fibreglass shell and thick rubber coating, we've developed the perfect vessel to bring our patients' dreams into our world."

Padman pressed a series of buttons, moving the bed into an upright position facing the audience.

"As you can see, this isn't standard, hospital issue." Padman passed his tablet to one of the nurses and stepped into Meditati. Automatically, the bed began to adjust slowly around his legs, arms, body and head. "Don't worry, it won't crush me."

The audience tittered as they watched the bed secure the doctor. Once he was in place, the machine stopped moving.

"Meditati has hundreds of built-in sensors. It's stopped at the point where I'm completely secure but also perfectly comfortable. We need people to experience as little stress as possible, and we also need to keep them still, during the procedure."

Padman nodded to the nurse standing next to him holding his tablet. She clicked on the screen and the bed began to release the doctor. When it finished, he stepped out and retrieved the tablet before addressing the audience again.

"We've designed Meditati meticulously. It's adjustable for all our patients, big and small." He pressed a further series of buttons, causing the bed to elongate and contort into different shapes before settling at a considerably smaller size than before.

Padman walked behind the bed and brought the audience's attention to the head recess.

"This is where our technology really comes alive." He pressed another button and beams of light roamed over and around the front of the headrest. "This floating screen is made up purely of light energy and yet is totally interactable. It's similar to an X-ray screen, minus the glass. This helps us target every part of the patient's brain in real time."

Using his fingers, the doctor interacted with the floating screen.

"Here we can monitor automotive functions and access the apparitions directly before they even enter the ether.

"We believe in a few years' time, we'll be able to refine this technology to be used on everyone, regardless of their background or brain activity. If you dream it, we'll be able to see it. The ability to delve into all those nooks and crannies and retrieve any thought or memory the patient may have, even those suppressed for years... just think how amazing that will be."

Padman switched the screen off and returned the bed to its

usual position.

"At least, that's our vision and hope, with your continued support." He smiled widely.

Using the glass wall as a screen once again, Padman brought up images of previous patients.

"For the past few years, Silicate has been helping people with — and even curing them of — their nightmares. The ability to show the patient the source of their trauma has been highly effective and impactful.

"We have an incredible team of therapists who work one-on-one with all of our patients to help them deal with what they're seeing and why. They work with them to determine why they're dreaming these images, which can sometimes be very harrowing. This is not just about peace of mind — here, we save lives.

"In itself, that's incredible, but we wanted to push ourselves even further. With Archeus and specially designed technology, like Meditati, we can now not only see these apparitions, but remove them from the patient's brain entirely."

The audience broke into applause.

"Thank you. None of this would have been possible without the tireless efforts of Silicate's staff, your faith in us . . . and, of course, your money."

There was a ripple of laughter, which was abruptly interrupted as two nurses wheeled a hospital bed into Archeus.

"This is Arturo, a ten-year-old boy from Mexico." Padman introduced the patient. "Five years ago, his father was killed in front of him by a man named Carlos, a member of a drugs cartel. Since that tragic event, this innocent little boy has struggled to sleep. We've been working with Arturo for a number of weeks now and believe that, today, we should be able to finally rid him of his nightmares, and the terrible man who haunts them."

The nurses positioned the boy into Meditati, which instantly adjusted around the small, unconscious body.

"To minimise any potential distress this room or the apparitions may cause, we've given our young patient a sedative." Padman checked on Arturo and spoke briefly to his staff before walking back to the centre of the room. With one press of his tablet, four huge cannons descended from the ceiling.

"Ladies and gentlemen, these hold the building blocks of simulated life." An electronic grid made up of beams of light spread out across the empty space. "Any apparitions will be moved into the centre. The computer will calculate its exact size and will add a mixture of molecules from these four cannons. If all goes to plan, the apparition will be given corporeal form right in front of your eyes."

Padman was pleased to see the looks of awe and wonder on the investors' faces. He nodded to his team and walked back to Meditati, where Arturo was sleeping soundly.

"Our patient has entered REM cycle, so we're ready to show you just how effective Archeus is."

An air-powered pop emanated from the side of the headrest aimed at Arturo's neck.

"Rather than rely on syringes, Meditati's been equipped with air injectors. These can administer medication faster, more effectively, and without breaking the skin. We've just given our patient a mixture containing sodium amidotrizoate and meglumine amidotrizoate. It's a reformulated version of gastrografin — the liquid a patient may receive before a CT scan. Used with Meditati, this helps give us a clearer image of the apparition."

The investors stepped closer to the glass to get a better look at what was happening, but quickly jumped back as a hissing sound echoed throughout Archeus.

"No need to panic, that's just the introduction of the water molecules."

A fine mist was pumped into the centre of the lab, creating a light fogginess in front of the investors. This soon dissipated, giving way to the images beginning to form above Arturo's head. Initially patchy, the apparitions danced through the air, wisping and waving around the bed.

Padman brought up the floating screen over Arturo, and began interfacing with it.

"What this console does," he said, addressing the audience while working on the screen, "as well as accessing Arturo's brain, is also enhances the apparitions and enlarges the images we see. Using a combination of the brain's own electricity and our newly designed systems, we can now do this . . ."

The doctor brushed his hand over the screen, clenched his fist and drew it away from Arturo, pushing it towards the grid beneath the cannons.

A mass of gathered light and data swam around in a jumbled mess. As it darted around the room, it combined together, steadily growing in size, assembling and ordering itself, until creating an apparition ten times larger than it had been before.

As the image settled, it formed a life-size man, who stared at the audience. Still in a wispy, dream-like state, the only movement produced was by the smoke-like texture, waving and weaving.

"Ladies and gentlemen, meet Carlos," Padman announced with glee. The surrounding grid of lights began to move and change colours. Lights darted over the apparition, checking for size and consistency. Once the lights had settled, the cannons came to life. All four moved around the apparition, shooting a steady stream of gaseous molecules. In front of their eyes, the body began to fill . . . First a foot, then a hand, an eye, a leg . . .

Padman watched the percentage of the gauge rise as the cannons automatically controlled the flow of each precise molecule being added to the apparition. When it reached one hundred per cent, the cannons stopped, retracting back to the ceiling.

Everyone held their breath, staring at the fully formed man in front of their eyes. No-one spoke, for what seemed an eternity, waiting to see what would happen next.

The man collapsed to the floor.

Padman and his team rushed forward while the investors pushed closer to the glass. Two nurses raised the man up, supporting him beneath his arms. Padman moved in front of Carlos and checked him over.

Why did something have to go wrong today, of all days, he thought. He lifted Carlos's head and checked his eyes — they were there, that was good. He checked the pulse, even though not alive, he should at least simulate life. There was nothing. Keeping his fingers around the man's wrist, he whispered to him.

"Come on, you bastard, wake up."

Carlos's eyes fluttered open and he looked confused as he observed the doctor. He glanced from side to side and then at the sea of people pressed up against the glass wall. Carlos smirked. He shook off the two nurses holding him, then smiled at Padman before clamping his hand around the doctor's neck.

Carlos squeezed hard as he pushed him against the glass, lifting his feet off the floor as he did so. The investors screamed and jumped back. Some of them raced for the door but were unable to open it. Panic ensued while Padman remained in the killer's grip, struggling to get free. The medical team rushed to take down Carlos, but he was too strong for them and refused to loosen his grip.

"¿donde esta el?" Carlos demanded.

Padman was beginning to blackout. He couldn't breathe and his face was turning blue. He could barely register what was being asked of him as his eyes pleaded with Carlos to let him go.

"¿DONDE ESTA EL?" Carlos smacked Padman's head against the glass.

With his oxygen depleted, Padman struggled one last time in a futile attempt to fill his lungs with air before blacking out, his head flopping to one side.

Enraged, Carlos threw the doctor to the ground. Five nurses were now on top of killer, attempting to restrain him. He pushed the nurses to the floor, turned around and saw Arturo.

With a sinister smile, he marched over to the bed, sneering at the sleeping child before spitting on the boy's body.

Carlos needed a weapon, but looking around the room, he found nothing of use. The nurses were helping each other up, two of them tending Padman while the other three cautiously approached Carlos. Raising his arms, he roared at them and bared his teeth like a rabid dog.

It was when his arms fell back to his sides again that he felt something instantly recognisable. Smiling, he stuffed his hand into the waistband of his jeans and pulled out a bloodied machete. He pointed it at the nurses, who immediately backed away. Carlos moved towards the sleeping boy, raised his knife-wielding hand, and with a roar, plunged it down.

Just before it touched the boy's skin, one of the nurses tackled the murderer to the floor. Still holding the knife, Carlos began slashing at the air. He missed several times, but he only needed one hit. As the knife sank into the nurse's stomach, he laughed maniacally.

"Get off him!" Padman screamed.

Carlos looked up at the doctor, who was now standing over him, a fire extinguisher in his hand.

"¿Lávame?" Carlos smirked.

Padman squeezed the trigger and released the white, powdery smoke. Carlos roared and jumped to his feet. He ran to the opposite side of the room, with Padman following, emptying the contents of the fire extinguisher into his back. Carlos looked possessed as he pounded on the glass wall, eyes fixed on the frightened investors, now huddled against the exit. The white powder began to destabilise the killer, dissipating parts of his newly formed body. As his fists hit the glass, they turned to powder and fell to the floor, followed shortly by his arms and torso. The last thing to go was the killer's face, leaving his cold, evil eyes burning into the minds of the crowd, before crumbling to dust.

Padman stood, staring at the pile of white powder on the floor, breathing heavily, his fist still clamped tightly around the trigger. Eventually, he loosened his grip and threw the empty cannister to the ground. His bloodshot eyes filled with tears as he stared into the lens of the camera.

Present day

Padman stopped playback and turned to the group.

"I'm sorry if that upset you."

"Upset us? Scared us half to death, more like," Isabell remarked.

"What happened to the nurse, the one who was stabbed?" Jake asked, clearly moved by the events he'd just witnessed.

"He made a full recovery, though he could never work here again. What happened traumatised him — understandably. The company arranged an early retirement package and he has access to medical help around the clock, should he need it. None of that changes the fact he almost died at the hands of something he helped create. It's the same thought which haunts all of us."

"Do the other medical staff still work here?" Jake asked.

"Some, but not all. Two of them moved to one of our other facilities, and the rest work within Hygge, although Fatima has been back to Archeus a few times."

Padman noticed Ryder was looking ahead, at the glass wall.

"Why didn't the security team barge in and apprehend Carlos? It was just you and a small team of medical staff against a knife-wielding murderer. The security guards in the footage were cowering in safety with the investors."

"They were *protecting* the investors. Once the process of apparition realignment begins, the room is sealed automatically. We initially designed this to prevent contamination or a partial apparition escaping Archeus. I was the only person who could have opened the door that day, and even if I hadn't been incapacitated, I still wouldn't have."

"Why not?"

"You saw how strong he was. He had me in a death grip while brushing off five grown adults. If he'd gotten out, he could've killed everyone in that hallway and who knows how many others. I couldn't let that happen. If we couldn't stop him, at least he would have been trapped in this room."

"You were willing to sacrifice yourself and your team on the assumption that your security guards couldn't take him out."

"Correct."

Ryder pondered this information.

"You would have made a great army captain."

Padman snorted.

"In another life, perhaps."

"Wait!" Isabell moved closer to the group. "Why did you show us this?"

"You needed proof of what we did here, and —"

"Yeah, I understand that. But you also said there were *successful* trials. If you wanted to show us proof, surely one of those would have done that same job without all the horror? Why show us this particular one?"

Padman paused, choosing his words carefully.

"You're making me nervous now, Doc. Is Carlos back or something?" Isabell asked.

"No, I don't believe Carlos has returned. That apparition's molecular structure was destroyed by the chemicals in the fire extinguisher."

"Was that a special extinguisher designed to do that?" Jake asked.

"Just a regular one. At that point, we didn't have anything that could take out a fully formed apparition because we never imagined something like that could happen. Knowing the chemical make-up of the extinguisher, I just hoped it would work."

"OK. If our situation has nothing to do with Carlos, why show us?" Isabell pressed the matter.

"Carlos was a turning point for the company. I tendered my resignation, but Ryder's grandfather and the board of directors refused to accept it. They were shocked by what had happened, of course, but they saw the potential in my research and appreciated how far my team had come. So, we re-evaluated everything we did here at Silicate — especially inside Archeus."

"What about the investors? Did they want to pull out?" Jake said.

"Some of them did; but they realised what this could mean in terms of profit margins. They insisted on extra safeguards and higher security measures. We now boast some of the most stringent safety protocols of any company in the world.

"We redesigned Archeus, too. Apparitions no longer form in this room — they're converted into digital energy and sent to a secure location before realignment begins. Now, the patient's safe, the staff are safe, *and* we have a specimen we can evaluate and study without being in any danger. The computer analyses the data and composites an image on Meditati's screens, so we know what's being sent.

"The cannons were too big to move, so we left them where they are. At this point, they're mostly decorative."

Padman began pacing in front of the group, choosing his next words carefully.

"This has worked for the past three years. We've had hundreds of patients in that time, all of them discharged happier — in most cases, cured. We're careful, we're *so careful* . . . I just don't understand —"

"Padman, what is it?" Jake moved closer to the doctor.

"I don't know how this could have happened. It can't have been a glitch—I would've been alerted. The only other option is too terrible to consider. I keep asking myself, could someone do this intentionally? And if they did — how?

"For this to happen, every single one of our safety protocols and procedures has to have been bypassed. That has to be deliberate."

Isabell was shaking. She knew this was to do with her. If Megara wasn't really Megara, Padman must be talking about her apparitions.

"Please, Padman. Just tell us what's happening here."

"I'm trying to, as delicately as I know how." Padman returned to pacing as he spoke. "While you were watching the video, I looked through the Archeus files on my tablet. Yesterday, we brought you in here, Isabell, during your attack. As usual, we went through the full procedure, but according to the log, no digital transfers were registered.

"Megara was one of the apparitions which failed to transfer and yet somehow she was found roaming Archeus. That should be impossible, yet here she is."

"What was the other image?"

Padman stopped and looked directly at Isabell, his face full of fear.

"No! Oh, no. Please. Please don't tell me he got out."

"I'm so sorry, but if your cat's here —"

"You're telling me he's here, right now? Somewhere in this building?"

"Who? Who's here?" Jake looked intently at Isabell.

"Vincent. The man who's been trying to kill me for the past ten years."

CHAPTER 22

"I'm not letting you go in there alone," Zane said, catching up with Phoebe.

"You should be upstairs monitoring the cameras. Doctor Sharma will have a fit if he finds both of us gone."

"After that creepy thing we saw on your screens, you need backup. Anyway, from what I've heard, Doctor Sharma's busy entertaining his boyfriend this evening." Zane grinned.

"What? Padman has a boyfriend? I thought he said he didn't have time to date?"

"He's obviously made time. They were seen at lunch together. Matías told me."

"Bloody Matías — don't believe a word that comes out his mouth. He's such a gossip. And you should know better than to soak it all up."

"You're probably right. The way Matías told it, though . . . it sounded really juicy."

Phoebe shook her head.

"It's a shame he can't inject some of that juice into his moist-free chicken."

They walked into Hygge.

"What's happening in there?"

"I told you not to leave your desk." Phoebe walked closer to the glass. "You'd better run back and initiate the abort procedure for Pod One, too."

"On it. Will you be OK with—"

"Zane, go! And make sure you're recording all of this."

Zane scampered back to the nurses' station, leaving Phoebe staring into the pod.

Terrell was sound asleep, while above him monsters and horrific-looking beings were fighting for supremacy.

"What goes on in that kid's mind?" she mused aloud. Edging around the glass perimeter, still transfixed by the apparitions, she eventually turned to face the door to Pod Two and scanned her pass. The door opened, and a wave of cool air hit her face, temporarily blinding her. Eyes closed; she missed the dark mass which floated out of Abby's pod and into the open air beyond. Phoebe wiped her eyes and walked over to the now-calm child.

As the nurse reached the bed, Abby opened her eyes.

"Hello. Is it time to wake up already?" she asked, smiling.

"Not yet, I'm afraid. I was watching you through the camera. It looked like you were having a bad dream, so I thought I'd check on you."

Abby sat up and rubbed her eyes.

"I don't remember dreaming tonight. I feel fine, actually, which is unusual for me."

"That's good to hear."

"Is my mom here yet?"

Phoebe smiled.

"You've only been asleep a few hours. Aren't you still tired?"

"I feel like I've had the longest sleep ever."

Phoebe checked her watch.

"It's only twenty-five to one."

"How strange." Abby's eyes were wide and bright as she looked at the nurse. "Do you think I could go back to the Red Room for a little while? Just until I feel sleepy again?"

"OK, but not for too long."

"Yay! Thank you."

Abby jumped out of bed and moved through the door. As she

reached Terrell's pod, Phoebe worried she might be alarmed by the disturbing images. Luckily, they were gone, replaced by wispy strands of blue smoke.

"Wow! Are they his dreams?"

"They're the start of dreams, yes," the nurse replied, pleased to see that Zane had purged the room so quickly.

"Can we stay and watch? It's so beautiful."

"I'm afraid we can't. You're supposed to be asleep — it's the Red Room or the bedroom for you."

"Red Room!" Abby paused another second to admire the blue smoke one final time before following Phoebe out of Hygge.

Isabell was huddled up next to Ryder's chair. The ex-soldier was stroking her head, trying to soothe her. Jake stood next to them, not really knowing what to do.

"Is Vincent as bad as Carlos?" he asked eventually.

"Much worse. Much, much worse." Isabell sobbed.

Padman was deep in thought, desperately trying to formulate a plan.

"He couldn't have gotten out of here. He would've been trapped, just like us. He could have opened the door to the lab, but wouldn't have got further than the antechamber."

Padman raced around the glass, shouting his findings back to the group. He checked the office and store room, both empty. He moved to the exit door.

"There's damage here — it looks like he's tried to punch his way through, unsuccessfully, of course." Padman scanned the walls, following them back into the lab, around the sides and over to the far wall, near to where the group were huddled. "Look at this!"

"What is it?" Jake asked.

"If the lab door's left open, it triggers a silent alarm which notifies any staff on duty who have clearance for Archeus or its cameras. I wasn't here last night, so the only person who would have been alerted was our missing nurse, Sally . . ."

"I'm not liking the sound of this," Ryder muttered.

"Indeed. Sally was one of the few people I could depend on entirely. When I promoted her, I entrusted her with the access codes to Archeus as well as every camera-feed in the building. She had unrestricted access to everything, including this." Padman pointed to a panel on the wall. "If Vincent managed to gain access through here, it would be disastrous for every living thing on the planet."

Isabell looked up, wiping her eyes.

"What does it do?"

"After the incident with Carlos, we needed a new, separate facility to store the newly formed apparitions . . . a place where we could monitor them safely. Originally, Lord Braighton wanted Silicate to be based underground, so he added space to the original blueprints beneath The Particle. It took a lot longer than expected, and so we moved into the main building while construction was still being completed.

"Over the years, we've expanded some of Silicate's operations underground. I think that's where Vincent has gone. Hopefully, the computers in my office down there will still be working, meaning we can call for help."

"What if we bump into Vincent?" Isabell asked shakily.

"Then I'll deal with him," Ryder assured her.

A loud bleeping noise perforated the tense silence in the room.

"What now?" Jake shouted, covering his ears.

Padman sat down at the computer, typing into the keyboard until the screeching stopped.

"That delightful noise is informing us we're out of air."

Panicked cries were directed at the doctor, who held up his hand to quiet the group. He stood up and walked over to the panel on the wall, pressing a series of the buttons. There was a loud clanking noise as the entire far wall retracted, opening to reveal a large elevator. Air rushed into the room as lights activated from the roof.

"I knew there was a door there," Ryder said triumphantly as he watched the elevator doors open.

"We could have had air at any time, and you chose to wait until the alarm went off?" Isabell asked, annoyed.

"I needed to arm you with information before we left Archeus. I wasn't going to let us all suffocate, but you needed to understand exactly what we do here, and you needed to believe it. If Vincent *is* down there, he could be a danger to all of us. You needed to know the threat is real."

"I suppose that makes sense," she said, grudgingly, nodding.

"It's big enough to fit a couple of elephants inside," Jake said, sizing up the elevator.

"Actually, you could fit a couple of *mammoths* inside," Padman corrected.

Isabell entered the elevator and looked down at the floor. Megara was already sitting in the centre, waiting patiently. Isabell reached down and picked her up.

"Hello, baby dream-cat. You've been trying to tell us about this from the start, haven't you?"

Meg looked at her and miaowed. Ryder moved inside and pulled his chair next to Isabell.

Before Jake could follow them, Padman pulled him aside.

"I'm so, so sorry for all of this."

"Hey, it's cool. Just make sure we don't get murdered down there, OK?" Jake pulled Padman close before he could respond, kissing him passionately.

Isabell peered around the door.

"Come on, you two lovebirds." She turned to Ryder, rolling her eyes but grinning delightedly.

"I think it's sweet," Ryder whispered.

Padman and Jake stopped kissing and rushed into the elevator, embarrassed.

"Sorry," they said in unison.

With everyone inside, the doctor reached out to press the *Down* button, pausing just before touching it.

"What's wrong now?" Jake asked.

The doctor turned around to address everyone.

"When we get downstairs, I want you all to stay inside the elevator. If Vincent is down there, it could be dangerous. I don't want any of you to get hurt. There's enough air in here for a few days — it recycles from the shaft."

"I'm the head of security — you need me with you."

"But you've just started working here, Ryder. With every respect, you have no idea the scale and potential dangers we could encounter. I very much doubt your grandfather expected you to be in a situation like this when he offered you the job."

"Perhaps not, but he employed me to keep you safe — *all* of you — and that's what I intend to do. I'm coming with you, Doctor."

"Me, too," Isabell added. "If he's down there, I want to be the one to take him out. He's tortured me for years. It's payback time."

"Count me in, too," Jake chimed in. "I may not be army-trained, but I'm strong from working on the farm and I'm handy in a scrap. I can help."

"Are you sure about this?" Padman looked relieved and a bit overwhelmed.

They all nodded.

"Then, thank you. I'd be grateful for the company. There's something else I haven't told you about, though. Downstairs isn't just rooms housing medical equipment. We've built a museum, of sorts, and it's a lot bigger than you're probably imagining."

Isabell, Jake and Ryder looked perplexed as they watched the elevator doors close.

CHAPTER 23

The doors opened into a dark corridor leading off to the left. As the group stepped out, lights automatically came to life above them, illuminating the long, wide hallway. The walls were stark white and free from any adornments; the floor was covered with a grey, riveted metal.

"This is the staff entrance, or at least, it will be, when it's finished," Padman explained as he led the group through the white expanse. "We've completed most of the work on the museum. The final phase will be making the spaces behind the scenes more pleasing."

"It certainly needs work," Isabell commented as they passed door after door painted the same stark white, blending them into the walls.

"It's a big space to cover. In fact, we believe it's the largest basement ever built," Padman announced proudly. "Lord Braighton didn't know how much space Silicate would need, and so asked the architects to draw up the biggest plans they could. The result is a sublevel almost half the size of the entire Particle," he explained.

"So, the tallest building in the world has another fifty percent of it under the ground? That's wild!" Jake exclaimed.

"That's my grandfather," Ryder added. Padman nodded in agreement, leading them into a sub corridor. Ahead of them, their path was blocked by wooden pallets, paint cans and scaffolding.

"Perfect," Padman muttered sarcastically. "Could someone help me move these please?"

Try as they might, though, everything was either too heavy or too jammed in to be removed without specialised equipment.

"Now what?" Isabell asked.

"If we can't take the short cut, I suppose we'll have to go through the museum," Padman replied, wiping the build-up of sweat from his brow.

"I need a drink" Jake gasped.

"There are vending machines around the corner and facilities for anyone who needs to freshen up" Padman announced.

"That'll be all of us, then." Ryder said, moving in the direction the doctor was pointing.

Five minutes later, the three men were waiting patiently in the main corridor, when they heard Isabell giggling.

"Are you alright in there?" Padman called.

Isabell exited the small room carrying a hessian bag on her shoulder.

"Where did you find that?" the doctor asked.

"There was a box full of them by the side of one of the machines. I thought it would be useful for carrying supplies, but someone had other ideas."

Megara popped her head out of the bag, looked around and then ducked back inside.

"That is so cute!" Jake exclaimed.

"You don't mind me using the bag, do you?"

"Not at all. They're promotional stock anyway." Padman smiled.

The group continued down the long corridor.

"It shouldn't take too long to get to my office this way. If I'm being totally honest, I'm excited to show you the museum."

"What have you got in there?" Jake asked.

"Sex dungeon."

"Isabell!" the men shouted at once, all laughing as they neared the end of the corridor.

"What's that over there?" Ryder asked as he looked ahead. Even against the stark white, it was difficult to see what Ryder was pointing to. "It looks like a man."

"Hello? Are you OK?" Padman shouted, as they sped up.

As they closed in, Isabell let out a sharp gasp.

"That's him! That's Vincent!"

"Or what's left of him, at least," Padman said, kneeling down next to the fading body of Isabell's tormentor. "He's demateri-alising."

Vincent was but a faded image of a man. Unmoving, he appeared to be a ghost or projection. His eyes were closed, and his body slumped in the corner; propped up by the locked door behind him.

Megara began hissing at the figure.

"I don't understand what's happening. Why is he a ghost?" Jake asked.

"The older mix couldn't stabilise apparitions for very long. A few hours, maybe a few days, but definitely no longer than that. We spent months working on the formula until finding a mix that could stabilise the apparitions indefinitely. If Vincent was created in Archeus last night, as I believe, that would mean he was assembled using the old cannons and the old, unstable mix of molecules. This would explain his rapid de-cellularisation."

A wave of relief washed over Isabell.

"He's dead? You're absolutely positive? He can't come back, can he?"

"You've no need to worry any more. He's gone for good."

"We still don't know who created him, though," Ryder pointed out.

"I believe we do. My theory is that Fred's been taking money from another company in the hopes of selling our research to the highest bidder. I've said as much to the board in the past.

I think he's tapped into the Archeus network last night and created Vincent to come down to the museum and collect the data he couldn't . . . You've got to admit the timing of his disappearance raises suspicion.

"Luckily for us, Vincent wasn't able to access the security panel so ended up stuck in here; left to disintegrate." Padman rose to his feet and beamed his trademark smile, order restored. "The threat is over. When the security team arrive in the morning, they'll investigate it all fully . . . but my bet is that we'll finally see Fred put behind bars, where he belongs."

"Does that mean my little baby will fade away soon, as well?" Isabell asked, hugging Megara closely.

"Dematerialisation happens quicker in larger apparitions. As Vincent's structure has only just collapsed, I should think it'll be quite a while before Megara befalls the same fate. We've got a lab down here where I can give her a dose of the new formula."

"Will that keep her alive longer?"

"Indefinitely. Although you must remember that the real Megara is still at home waiting for you, and I'm afraid you can't leave Silicate with this version . . ."

"I understand, but dream-cat or not, I can't bear the thought of her fading to nothing. Will she be able to stay here?"

"I'm sure we'll find room for her in the museum and you can visit her whenever you like."

Isabell smiled, squeezing the cat and making her squirm uncomfortably. Megara looked at Isabell and miaowed. She placed her gently back into the bag. Once settled, Megara rested her head on the side, staring ahead with her ears pointing straight up on alert.

Calm washed over the group as they watched the image of Vincent fade to nothing before their eyes. No-one spoke for a few moments as they let themselves relax. Jake yawned, becoming the catalyst for everyone else to notice how exhausted they felt. Adrenaline had kept them alert; now that the danger had passed, their bodies began to shut down. All except Padman.

"I don't suppose you have sleeping quarters around here, do you?" Isabell asked as she stretched.

"We do, but we would still need to access them through the museum, I'm afraid."

"How long until we reach your office?" Ryder asked.

"If we race through the exhibits, maybe an hour?"

"An hour!" Jake exclaimed.

"And that's if we 'race through'?" Ryder added.

"I did warn you, it's a large place," Padman replied, grinning.

"I don't think I'll make it," Isabell said. "I'm exhausted already." She turned to Ryder. "Can I sit on your lap and you carry us there, please?"

Padman dug into his inside pocket and produced the white cylinder he had used earlier, in his office.

"What's that?" Jake asked.

"It's something I developed in the early days of Silicate. Sleep was getting in the way of our work and so we developed a solution to combat it."

"Adrenaline injection?" Ryder asked.

"Nothing so primitive. This is a full night's sleep without the need for a bed."

"Seriously?" Jake asked. "Though I don't know why I'm shocked by anything after today," he added.

"I know the military have been trying to formulate something like that for years." Ryder looked sceptical.

"They have, indeed, and Silicate have perfected it. It tricks the brain into believing it's had the rest it needs whilst also reinvigorating the cells, giving you a boost of energy. It's quite safe, I assure you."

"You're saying you could use that every day and never have to go to bed again?" Isabell asked.

"It's possible, I suppose. Although nothing beats a good night's sleep in a comfy bed." The doctor smiled at Jake.

"I don't know, it all sounds a bit sci-fi to me." Isabell pulled a face.

215

"This whole place is a bit sci-fi. I'll do it." Jake stood in front of Padman. "I trust you."

"Bleugh, give it a rest, you two," Isabell mocked gently.

"It stings a little, but that passes quickly." Padman injected Jake in the neck.

"Whoa! I feel so warm . . . so tingly!" Jake ran his fingers through his hair, his eyes widening. "That stuff's amazing. I feel wide-awake, like I've just woken up from the best sleep ever."

"My turn next," Ryder said, grinning.

"And then me!" Isabell set aside her sci-fi concerns.

Reinvigorated, the group were ready for the journey ahead.

There was a relaxed sense of freedom running though the group. The past few hours had been fraught with impending doom and now, with the memory of Vincent fading faster than his apparition and bolstered by Padman's injection, they felt happy and carefree.

"I really think you'll be bowled over with the museum," Padman said. "You'll be the first people to see it. I can't wait to hear what you think."

The doctor pulled out his pass and used the scanner above where Vincent had lain just moments before. The doors opened slowly, showering the group in light and colour. Padman led them inside, then turned and stood in front of them, spreading his arms wide.

"Welcome to Somnio."

As the group looked around the expansive entrance hall, their mouths opened wide in astonishment. A soaring dome rose up at least five storeys above them. At its the centre, there was a projection of Earth, almost filling the entire dome, complete with an orbiting moon.

"It's a one-one thousandth scale replica of our home planet. We wanted everything to be believable here, as that's really the point of Somnio." Padman talked as he led the group towards the centre of the room, all four of them entranced by the immense projection ahead. New Zealand passed before their eyes, followed by Australia.

"Would you like to see how it'll look to guests when they first arrive?"

The group nodded, still captivated by the globe, as Padman bent down and pressed his pass to the scanner hidden at the base of the projection. Earth disappeared, and the room fell into a soft darkness. There was silence for a few moments before a single point of light appeared, shining brightly. The point exploded into a billion particles shooting out in all directions. A soothing, female voice began to narrate.

"The Big Bang. This is where our story begins. The beginning of everything. It all started right here."

Particles danced overhead, swirling around before joining together, forming hundreds of galaxies as the soothing voiceover continued.

"There are as many galaxies in the observable universe as there are grains of sand on Earth. But to us, there is none more important than this one." A spiral galaxy grew in size, dominating the space and circling above the group's head. "This is the Milky Way, home to billions of stars and trillions of planets."

Bright balls of burning gas illuminated the map as the galaxy circled a supermassive black hole at its centre. The group stood in wonder, watching the projection focus on an outer branch of one of the spirals.

"And here, on the edge of the Milky Way galaxy, is our solar system." In a smooth, fluid motion, the projection zoomed in, bursting through the outer heliosphere, dodging asteroids, the Voyager telescopes and dwarf planets in the Kuiper belt, only slowing as it reached the first planet.

"Neptune, a frozen world on the outer limits of our solar system and one of four ringed gas giants, the second of which is its neighbour, Uranus." They sped over Neptune's largest moon, Triton. "Tilted on its side, from behind Uranus, we can observe the planet's rings glimmering in the sun's rays. As beautiful as these are, nothing compares to the rings of the next world." Off again, the group were carried along on their interstellar journey.

"Saturn is the shining gem of our solar system. This gas giant may look beautiful, but with no landmass, it is totally unfit for human habitation; unlike its moon, Titan — one of the only other worlds presumed to sustain life outside of our own." Skimming Titan's surface, the projection continued, bringing into view a mass of light and colour.

"Jupiter — the largest of the planets — is the final gas giant on our journey home. As we travel past our sister planet, Mars, we can wave at the man-made machines we currently have mapping and surveying the surface, preparing for our future visits."

The group watched as the projection carried them over the red, dusty landscape and into the path of a Rover ambling across the rocky terrain. Up and out, through the thin Martian atmosphere, they caught their first glimpse of Earth. Pushing forward, towards our moon, the projection slowed as it passed over the Apollo 11 landing-site.

The familiar view of Earth now filled the dome entirely, rotating slowly before them.

"This is Earth, our home and where life as we know it began, four billion years ago. In that time, ninety-nine per cent of all life has been lost, but it doesn't have to be forgotten." The camera slowly moved forward, passing satellites, the International Space Station and into the ionosphere. The United Kingdom could be seen through the clouds. The projection pushed down into London, following the Thames and passing landmarks: Westminster, the London Eye and Tower Bridge. It veered to the right and towards The Particle, and then down beneath ground-level to the entrance of the museum.

"Welcome to Somnio, where dreams become reality."

The presentation ended, and the main lights rose. Padman looked at his guests expectantly.

"What did you think?"

"That was incredible. It felt like I was actually there, flying through space." Ryder was awestruck.

"How did you do it? I mean, how could it look so real without wearing VR helmets?" Jake asked.

"It's all to do with the projectors — most of the technology in this place was invented right here by our in-house tech guys. We have some of the greatest minds in science and technology working for us." Padman's pride in his work was obvious.

"It shows. I'm not usually impressed with new tech and graphics and stuff — give me a pen and paper and I'm happy — but that blew me away," Isabell said. "I don't think Megara was impressed, though," she added, peering down into the bag, where the cat lay sleeping.

Padman smiled.

"There are actually ten shows currently programmed into the projector."

"Can we see one of the others?" Jake asked enthusiastically.

"As impressive as the entrance hall is, the museum is where we've focused most of our time and effort."

"And no-one else has seen this place yet?" Ryder asked.

"Only staff with clearance. No-one outside of Silicate's payroll."

"Won't you get into trouble for showing us around?"

"We're soft-launching Somnio in a few weeks anyway, and when I explain about being locked in Archeus, I think we'll be fine."

"OK — let's do this." Ryder smiled.

"Yay!" Isabell and Jake couldn't contain their excitement.

"Honestly, you two are like a couple of kids," Padman said with a beaming smile. "Which, as it happens, is the perfect mindset for our first stop: the World of Animation."

CHAPTER 24

Abby and Phoebe were watching a film in the Red Room when the phone beside them rang.

"Hello?" Phoebe answered, still half-watching the romcom playing on the large screen.

"Hey, Zane, what's up? What? Are you sure? OK, OK . . . Begin the purge procedure and I'll be right there," she ended the call and turned to Abby. "Will you be all right in here on your own for a few minutes? I've got to help Zane with something."

"Yep," Abby replied, not taking her eyes away from the TV.

"Great, thanks. I'll be back soon. Oh, and let me know if they get together in the end," the nurse called as she raced out of the room, unwittingly leaving the door open behind her.

"Yep," Abby responded, not really hearing what had been said.

Only when the credits started to roll did Abby's attention move back to her surroundings and noticed the noises emanating from outside the room. She switched off the TV and walked to the open door, looking down the hall towards the nurses' station. That door, too, was open. Inside, Phoebe and Zane were frantically pushing buttons and talking animatedly.

Abby tiptoed towards the station and peered inside. On the screens in front of her were multiple views of Terrell's pod.

Squinting to get a better look, she could see her friend asleep, blue smoke weaving above him. As she watched, smoke engulfed the pod and began to change colour and transform into semi-recognisable images.

A pallet of grey and black smoke created what looked, to Abby, like an old man. His face seemed to be distorted and wizened, with wisps of black smoke forming a body with arms and legs. Abby was fascinated. Was all this really coming from Terrell's head?

The old man reached down to pick something up from the floor. Abby covered her mouth to stifle a scream as the man forcibly yanked up the blue head of a young woman, her mouth widening as if screaming, though there was no sound. The man began to drag the woman across the floor by her hair, as she continued to scream.

Abby had seen enough. She stepped backwards, ready to run; but in her haste, she tripped over her hospital gown and stumbled, falling to the ground. The disturbance caused Zane to spin around in his chair. He jumped up to help the girl. Phoebe finished the purge of Pod One quickly before joining Zane and Abby.

"Are you OK?" Zane asked, clearly startled.

Abby was crying, not from any injury from falling but from the horror she'd just witnessed.

"She's in shock."

"Let's get her back to the sofas." The nurses guided Abby into the Red Room. Once seated, Phoebe crouched down in front of her.

"I'm sorry you saw all that, I should've closed the door behind me. Try to remember — they were only dreams, and they're gone now. We got rid of them, didn't we, Zane?"

"Yep, they're gone."

"Just like we did with your nasty dreams."

"You got rid of the Shadow Man?"

"Doctor Sharma will need to review the footage in the morning before he gives you his full diagnosis, but we saw him, and we purged him. We watched him disappear, didn't we, Zane?"

"We did."

"Does that mean I'm cured?"

Phoebe looked at her colleague cautiously as Zane started to talk.

"He may very well be gone for good, or there might be other versions of him stored in your head. Doctor Sharma can explain it better than we can, but over the years, your brain will have imagined many different variations. The more dominant apparitions are the prominent ones, like the one we saw tonight. By purging him and the rest of the dominant apparitions, we're subconsciously retraining your brain to discount the weaker versions. Over time, even when you're back at home, those apparitions will simply cease to exist, and you can finally get a good night's sleep."

Abby looked frightened.

"Are you saying there could be millions of versions of the Shadow Man in my head?"

"Zane! You're scaring her."

Zane moved aside, looking chastened.

Phoebe smiled and spoke in a calm voice.

"No, it doesn't mean that. The human brain isn't big enough to hold millions of dominant versions. I've worked here for a few years now and have monitored a lot of patients — every single one of them has left here without their nightmares."

"All except Isabell."

Phoebe looked angrily at Zane, who responded with an embarrassed, apologetic look.

"Who's Isabell?" Abby asked, her voice shaking.

"Isabell's a writer and a patient here, but her problem is very different from yours. She writes about her 'shadow man', creating new versions of him all the time."

"Does that mean if I ever think about the Shadow Man in the future, he'll come back?"

Phoebe stroked Abby's hair as she glared at Zane again, furious with him. Zane backed away and headed to the nurses' station, realising he was more of a hindrance than a help in settling Abby. Phoebe turned to the girl and smiled.

"No, it doesn't mean that at all. When you leave here, the Shadow Man will be gone, never to return."

"But what if he does?"

"I promise you — he won't," the nurse said, firmly but comfortingly.

"Phoebe, you need to see this!" Zane called from the nurses' station.

"What's up with him now?" She rolled her eyes, making Abby smile. "I won't be long. I still need to know how that film ended." She winked as she left the room, this time making sure to close the door behind her.

Abby didn't particularly want to be alone, but it was preferable to seeing that scary, old man on the screen again.

"No way. He's back? I just purged him." Phoebe said as she took her seat.

"He's a tenacious one, all right."

"What's he doing?"

"Nothing, he's just lying on the floor, motionless."

"Let's not wait to find out. Initiate purge procedure."

"Already on it."

As Zane hurriedly typed in the commands, another apparition appeared in the pod. It looked like a young man in a nurse's uniform.

"That looks like one of ours," Zane said, his key-strokes slowing.

"You're right, it does. It even has our logo."

The apparition nurse looked around the pod cautiously, oblivious to the man below him. After a few moments, he stopped in front of the old man's right leg and crouched down to inspect it. As he extended his arm, the wizened man kicked up his leg, his foot landing slap-bang in the centre of the young man's face. The nurse collapsed on to the floor, red wisps shooting from his nose and coating his uniform.

Zane entered the final commands and pressed *Enter*. The last thing they witnessed on their screens was the wizened man dragging the nurse across the room before both were purged out of existence.

"Let's hope that's the last we see of him," Zane breathed, sitting back in his chair.

"It will be, for a while, at least — Terrell's waking up."

"I'll go down there this time. You're better with Abby, anyway," Zane said, rising from his chair.

"That's the understatement of the year," Phoebe replied, following him out of the nurses' station.

"Can I see him?" Abby asked when she heard that her friend was awake.

"Not just yet. Let Zane check on him first. Depending on how he feels, he might be joining us for our film fest."

"I'm not sure Terrell's a romcom kind of guy." Abby laughed. "He was geeking out about Lord of the Rings earlier."

"Hey! I love Lord of the Rings *and* I love romcoms; it is possible to like both, you know. Come on, how about we get started on the next one?"

"Can I get a drink, please? I'm really thirsty."

Phoebe checked her watch, seeing it was past four in the morning.

"I didn't realise it was so late. How tired are you?"

"Not at all."

"Usually, Doctor Sharma likes patients getting a full night in the pod, but I'll explain to him about tonight's events. I'm sure he'll understand."

"Drinks and popcorn?"

"Popcorn? Really?" Phoebe laughed. "I suppose you can, as long as you promise to stay in bed for the full eight hours tomorrow night."

"I promise."

"OK, come on, then. There's a Julia Roberts film I've been wanting to watch."

Abby looked at the nurse quizzically.

"Who's Julia Roberts?"

"Who's Julia...? Wow! You're in for a real treat."

Zane entered Hygge and walked towards Pod One, pulling out his security pass and opening the door to find Terrell pacing the room frantically.

He stopped, focusing on Zane as he entered.

"I need to speak to Doctor Sharma, right away," he declared. "I think he's in danger."

CHAPTER 25

"The hall can hold up to five hundred people."

"Five hundred? Why so many?"

"We expect to attract a lot of visitors; the entrance and central hub had to be large enough to accommodate them all. We'll have shops and information booths as well as the projection shows. They're scheduled to be installed next week."

"How far down are we?" Ryder asked, gazing up at the domed, glass ceiling.

"If you're asking, does the dome crest on the surface? It doesn't. We have lighting to mimic times of day. We're actually a hundred and fifty metres underground."

"That's a long way down," Isabell noted, peering up.

"We're further down than any other structure in London — the space is so big it had to go that deep in order to bypass the Tube, sewers, and the Lee Tunnel, which is eighty metres underground."

They stopped in front of the exhibition entrance.

"If you expect a lot of visitors, how will they all get in? Surely the elevator from Archeus can't fit five hundred people?"

"We have our own underground line. We'll have trains running every thirty minutes to and from Waterloo Station bringing them practically to the door." Padman activated a panel by the tinted-glass door and scanned his security pass. As the door opened, he turned to the group.

"I should warn you — it can get quite loud in here."

Everything was dark at first, and then, from nowhere, a swirl of light formed and grew in size. Jake reached out to touch it and, as his finger made contact, it exploded into a sea of colour, as if a boulder had fallen into a swimming pool, splashing luminous paint over the walls. Beneath their feet, wooden boards appeared, and large, red curtains swung down from the sides, covering the walkway in front of them.

An orchestra started to play, making Isabell jump back and Megara duck down further into the bag. From behind the curtain, Betty Boop stepped out and addressed them.

"Welcome to the World of Animation, it's so good to see you all. Are you ready to meet the gang?" Betty asked.

"She looks so real," Jake commented.

"Hey! Watch your manners. I'm as real as a girl can be." Betty winked.

"That told you," Isabell whispered to Jake.

"Why, hello, Doctor Sharma," Betty smouldered. "I didn't see you there. How are you today?"

"I'm good, thanks, Betty. I've brought some friends along with me."

"Any friend of yours is a friend of mine, Doctor. Follow me."

Stunned, the group followed the black-and-white, animated character through the red curtains and further into the room. Beyond lay a seemingly endless world of animation. Characters, buildings, roads, and even sky were all in cartoon-form.

They gazed in awe as they marvelled at the scene in front of them; even Padman, who had helped create it and watched it grow, couldn't contain his excitement.

"Are these projections as well?" Jake asked.

"Only the sky is procedurally generated. Everything else you see are apparitions."

"You're telling us someone dreamed up this place?" Ryder asked.

227

"Not just *one* person, but by hundreds. Children and adults from all over the world."

Betty was waiting for the group; her head tilted to one side with her hands on her hips. She pouted as she spoke.

"Are you guys coming, or what?"

"Sorry, Betty, it's their first time here. Perhaps it would be better if I showed them around today."

"Suit yourself, Doctor." Betty blew a kiss towards Padman. From her hand, cartoon lips bounced through the air and landed on his cheek, leaving a black smudge. Betty laughed and skipped off into the distance.

Smiling delightedly, Isabell passed Padman a tissue to wipe his face.

Megara poked her head up and scanned the room nervously.

"Oh, hey, puss. Are you OK, baby?"

Megara looked up at Isabell and around the room before sinking back into bag again.

"Very wise, puss — stay where it's safe."

Jake was mesmerised. He was watching a group of hand-drawn rabbits pass by his feet, which he recognised from Watership Down; in the sky above him Aladdin and Jasmine rode a magic carpet; and directly behind them, Superman was flying through the air. To his left was Gotham City with the bat symbol shining overhead; to his right — Springfield, with a host of Simpsons' characters meandering around. Right in the centre of the room was the classic Disney castle.

"Is that a life-size castle?"

"It's big enough to walk through, yes. Each exhibition room is as big as the entrance hall. In some cases, larger."

"How many exhibitions do you have?" Ryder asked.

"Currently, we have twelve, with space for a few more in the future."

"I still can't get over just how realistic it all is," Jake said as he watched Wile E Coyote chasing Road Runner. Road Runner stopped to paint a tunnel on to the side of the Disney Castle before running through it. Wile E followed, only to hit the side of the castle and collapse on to the floor. Jake chuckled as he turned back to Padman.

"What about the buildings, vehicles, fields, mountains?" He looked at his feet. "Even this cartoon floor we're standing on … They can't be apparitions, can they?"

"Think about your own dreams. You don't just imagine people and characters — your brain conjures up whole worlds and everything within them. It's taken time, but we try to preserve as much as possible. As time moves on and we treat more and more patients, the exhibits we'll have will increase."

"I could spend a lifetime in this room," Jake said, unable to tear his eyes away from the animated characters all around him.

Ryder was startled as Stitch jumped on to his lap and began chattering nonsensically at him.

"What's happening?"

"Stitch! Get down from there," Padman ordered.

Stitch stuck his tongue out, blowing a raspberry at the doctor. Isabell started laughing, reaching to stroke Megara, who had popped her head out of the bag to see what the commotion was.

Jake reached across slowly to touch the apparition, shocked to find his hand didn't go through it.

"I can feel his fur." Astonished, Jake proceeded to stroke Stitch, much to Megara's annoyance.

"Of course, you can — you can touch Megara," Padman pointed out.

"That's different, she looks so real … but these are *animations*, and I can touch them."

Stitch was enjoying the attention. Even Ryder was getting involved, joining Jake in petting the creature.

"There you are!" Lilo appeared and grasped her arms around the struggling alien. "What have I told you about running off?" She looked up at Padman. "Sorry about that, Doctor." She carried Stitch away, while Megara hissed in his direction. Stitch retaliated by sticking out his tongue at the cat over Lilo's shoulder.

"It's OK, darling. He's gone now," Isabell soothed, stroking the cat's head.

Ryder burst into delighted laughter.

"That. Was. Incredible!" he panted, trying to steady himself. "When you said museum, I thought stuffy antiques behind glass, not this. What else is here?"

The others smiled, all feeling Ryder's enthusiasm.

"There is plenty more to see."

Padman led them on through the exhibit.

"I know you said there are eleven more rooms, but I can't imagine any of them being more wonderful than this," Jake breathed as they moved passed Pixar Village.

"I'll admit, this is one of my favourite exhibitions as well." Padman stopped walking and turned to his left. "This is our comic book section. We've recreated as much of Gotham City as was possible. Amazingly enough, all of this came from one nine-year-old American boy who had a comic book obsession.

"Unfortunately for him, the Joker had infiltrated his psyche and caused him terrifying nightmares which were bleeding out into the real world. He was here for almost a month, but by the time he left, the Joker had gone, and he and his parents decided it was time he found a new hobby."

Spiderman swung past their heads, waving at the group. Asterix and TinTin were eating sandwiches on a park bench, watching Aquaman swimming in a lake. The Batmobile streaked down the main street as Batman and Robin chased after the Penguin and Cat Woman.

"If we had more time to watch the scenes play out, you'd see that the villains — including the Joker — are always captured and thrown into Arkham Asylum. We did it as a tribute to the little boy who dreamed all this up, and to avoid any more children having nightmares like his."

They continued walking, passing Bedrock, where the Flintstones shot past in their cramped vehicle, Dino peering out from the roof and pawing at the Jetsons, flying overhead.

"And this is Dillydale. It's a small exhibit populated by the Mr Men and Little Miss characters. I believe it was one of *your* favourite shows as a child, Ryder. Lord Braighton insisted we include it in memory of you and your mother," Padman said as the ex-soldier wheeled himself closer to the small, cartoon town.

Ryder eyes watered as he watched the characters from his childhood come to life in front of him. Mr Bump and Little Miss Sunshine skipping down the road together . . . Mr Happy and Mr Messy on the swings in the park, and Mr Nosey peeking out from behind his curtains. He laughed and wiped his face before looking up at Padman.

"This is perfect," he said sincerely. "Thank you."

There was a door to the left with a *Coming soon* banner strung across it.

"What's in there?" Jake asked.

"That'll be adult animations, which kids won't be allowed into. Rick and Morty take you on a journey to visit different realities, with the guests able to visit the characters from Family Guy, American Dad, BoJack Horseman and South Park."

"Sounds awesome!" Jake said.

"It will be when it's finished. Unfortunately, it's taking longer than we anticipated to get it ready for the public. Let's just say the characters are a bit more mischievous than we want them to be."

"Does that mean you can change the apparitions? I thought whatever people dreamed is what appeared?" Isabell asked. "We all saw that Mexican guy stab a nurse and try to kill you."

"That's exactly why we have to alter the apparitions. The refined molecular mix giving them corporeal form has electronic markers running through it. Everything is catalogued and monitored by the system, so we can modify the appearance, speech, actions, and track their movements. We had to make sure that the mistakes we made with Carlos would never be repeated. Now, every apparition is totally safe."

Padman continued walking, pausing at the back of the castle.

"Here's our main Disney section, though as you've seen, the characters are free to wander throughout the exhibit."

"Do you have all the Disney characters?" Isabell asked.

"Not yet, but I'm hoping to finish the collection in the next few years, once we've advanced the technology and are able to monitor all individuals. I know I've got some of the missing characters locked away in my head."

The magic carpet carrying Jasmine and Aladdin flew over the group, landing just ahead of them in Agrabah market, the Sultan's palace shining brightly beyond the stalls. As Isabell looked further, she could see ancient Greece, the setting for her favourite film, Hercules.

Megara, who had been watching cautiously, now leaped out of the bag and sauntered casually through different Disney lands. Scooby Doo began to bark at her, but was held back by Velma, Megara hardly flinched. Characters made way as she strolled along the cobbled street and through the palace gates before jumping over the back wall, landing in Athens. The group raced after her, opting to enter Greece via a gate behind the palace rather than scaling the wall. Megara eventually halted in the middle of a small square, between two characters. Hercules noticed the cat and picked her up.

"Hello, there — what's your name?"

Isabell was unable to control her emotions as tears streamed down her face. She stepped forward.

"This is my cat," she said, her voice breaking. "Her name is Megara."

Hercules smiled and looked at his wife.

"She has your name."

As the animated couple stroked the cat, Ryder looked at Isabell inquisitively.

"I named my little puss after Megara from this film," she explained. "It's my favourite and Megara is the greatest heroine *ever*."

Padman held out his hand.

"Should we go and say 'hello'?"

Isabell's eyes widened, and she nodded quickly. They walked forward to meet her heroes.

"It's pretty surreal, don't you think?" Ryder whispered to Jake.

"I know what you mean. We all grow up watching cartoons and now, here we are, surrounded by real-life versions of them. It's like being in a dream."

"We kind of *are*, if you think about it."

"True. Did you like Disney films as a kid, or was it just Mr Men?"

"Mr Men was something Mum and I used to watch together when I was really young. When I went to school, I got into the more action-themed cartoons . . . He-Man, Defenders of the Earth, and BraveStar were my favourites."

"You were always destined to be a soldier, then?" Jake grinned.

"I never thought of it like that before." Ryder laughed. "Perhaps they were preparing me for later life."

Isabell and Padman returned to them with huge smiles on their faces. Even Megara looked content, now returned to her nest in the bag.

"Have fun?" Ryder asked.

"That was the single greatest moment of my life. Thank you, Doctor Sharma."

"You're very welcome." He beamed, turning to Ryder. "I overheard you talking about Eighties cartoons . . . On the other side of the castle we have an area devoted to some of them — Eternia, Thundera, and the realm of Dungeons and Dragons. You can always come back through later though, if you like, and check them out properly."

Ryder nodded as he followed the group through Zootopia, Ancient China and an old-fashioned version of London where some of the princesses were picnicking in Hyde Park with Mary Poppins flying overhead. Further down, Mickey and Minnie were ice-skated on a frozen lake created by Elsa's magic and Jessica Rabbit was singing to Roger in the band stand.

Isabell, Ryder and Jake were so engrossed in the scene that they almost missed Maleficent, Jafar and Hades who appeared, blocking their path.

"Halt! You are trespassing on our domain," Jafar announced.

"Leave now or feel the wrath of the titans," Hades declared.

"And the wrath of me." Maleficent transformed into a mighty dragon and reared up, threateningly.

Three pairs of eyes turned towards Padman. He smiled and reaching for a magic lamp lying on its side on the ground. He picked it up and rubbed. Suddenly, Genie flew out.

"Wheeeeee! Boy, was it getting cramped in there! Ah, hello, Master Sharma. How may I assist you today?"

"Genie, I wish for you to clear our path please."

"Your wish is my command."

Genie zapped the three villains, who vanished in puffs of smoke. His task complete, he bowed to the doctor and shot back into the lamp, which Padman returned to the ground.

"That's one of two exit scenes we have in this room. On the opposite path, there's a standoff with Skeletor, Venger and Lord Tirek. He-Man and She-Ra save the day with help from the My Little Pony gang."

"Aw!" Ryder whined comically.

As the group neared the far door, they discovered Bugs Bunny standing by the exit, gnawing on a carrot.

"What's up, Doc?"

"Hello, Bugs. Staying out of mischief?" Padman asked.

"You betcha! Leaving so soon? I hoped you would stay to see Daffy and Porky's new show. It's a real stinker, but someone's gotta watch it."

"I can't today, I'm afraid — I'm showing my friends around the museum."

"You be careful if you're going in there. They have them laser guns that smart if they hit ya."

"We'll be careful. Thanks, Bugs."

The group waved goodbye to the animated rabbit and

moved towards the door, on to the second exhibit.

CHAPTER 26

"I'm telling you the truth. Doctor Sharma is in the museum right now. He's with Jake, Ryder, and a woman called Isabell. They entered through a secret door in Archeus and now they're all in danger. You have to believe me!"

"How do you know about Archeus?" Zane asked. He, Phoebe and Abby were all gathered around Terrell in the Red Room as he explained what he had seen in his dream.

Phoebe spoke in the calmest and most soothing voice she could muster.

"We do believe you, Terrell. We saw for ourselves just how intensely you dream. But don't you think it's possible that what you saw was just that? A dream?"

"This wasn't a normal dream — it was a premonition. I've had them before. I know the difference."

"We deal with some unbelievable stuff," Zane responded, "but premonitions aren't a thing. I understand you truly believe what you saw was real, but it can't have been. We don't even have a museum here — we're a hospital." The conversation had looped like this for thirty minutes, and Zane was losing his patience. He stood up and walked to the back of the room to make himself a coffee.

"It's pretty late." Phoebe checked her watch. "Actually, it's pretty early in the morning. Why don't you both try to get some sleep? I know you keep telling me you're not tired, but after everything that's happened tonight, I think you'd both benefit from getting a few hours' rest."

"Back in the pods?" Abby asked.

"You can sleep here on the ward, if you like?"

"Yes, please."

"Great. Zane, could you collect their things from the Blue Room, please?"

Zane nodded and left, taking his coffee with him.

Terrell sighed, stood up, and walked towards the door.

"Do you know where you're going, Terrell?" Phoebe called after him.

"I'll find it," Terrell replied, already in the corridor.

"I think he's upset," Abby said.

"I think he is, too. Once I've shown you to your room, maybe you could go and check on him? I think he'll respond better to you."

Abby nodded in agreement. They rose from their seats and walked along the ward, meeting Zane on the way, who followed behind, bags in hand. As they passed Terrell's room, they saw he had tinted the window, so no-one could see in.

"I'll leave you with Terrell's bag — gives you an excuse to check on him."

"Good thinking. Thanks, Phoebe." Abby looked up. "Thanks, Zane."

After the nurses had left, Abby knocked on Terrell's door. He peered out and, seeing Abby was alone, ushered her inside before locking the door behind them.

"I brought your bag."

"Great, thank you." Terrell fished out his clothes and started to get dressed.

"Are you not going back to bed?"

"Are you? I thought you were wide-awake?"

"I am, but Phoebe said to try to sleep."

"They also said I was lying."

"No-one said you were *lying*, they just said you were dreaming."

"I know the difference between a dream and reality. This was more like a memory — like I was actually *there* when it all happened. Which, of course, is impossible. Until I went to sleep, I didn't even know about Archeus or the museum."

"I heard Doctor Sharma mention something about Archeus earlier today when I was eavesdropping. I don't know what it is, though, and I know nothing about a museum." Abby wrinkled her nose. "Zane had never heard of it."

"There's a lot more going down here than a few hospital beds, and not all the staff are in on it. I'm positive something bad's happened, or is about to, but I can't get anyone to believe me."

"I believe you."

"Really? I thought you were just being nice to keep me company."

"Of course, I believe you."

"Thank you." Terrell slipped his trainers on to his feet.

"Does this have something to do with that old man with the wrinkly face?" Abby furrowed her brow in worry.

"How do you know about him?"

"I saw him on the screen in the nurses' station when you were sleeping. It looked like he was attacking a woman."

"That was Sally — she works here. She was in Archeus last night, and that's why I need to get down there."

"What about that awful man?"

"He's long gone by now. I'll explain everything later. The sooner I can warn them, the better." He jumped up from the bed and headed to the door. "Do you mind covering for me if Zane or Phoebe check on us?"

"Wait!" Abby fixed Terrell with a look of pure determination. "I'm coming with you."

"No, it's too dangerous. You should wait here until I get back."

"Is it because I'm a girl or because I'm a kid?"

Terrell didn't know how to reply without hurting Abby's feelings.

"I'm fourteen, not much younger than you. If you're going, I'm coming with you."

"Are you sure? My premonition didn't tell me everything, just snapshots, really. Maybe Zane's right — it could have just been a dream."

"You don't believe that."

"No, I don't."

"Wait here." Abby left the room for a few minutes. When she returned, she was fully dressed.

"I've stuffed my bag under my duvet so if they do check, it looks like I'm curled up in bed. You should do the same."

"Clever," Terrell said, following Abby's instructions.

"See, you do need me around." Abby grinned nervously. "What's the plan?"

"First thing we need to do is get into Archeus."

"What even is it?"

"It's a lab, two floors down. The problem is, we need a security pass to get in." Terrell put his hand into his pocket and pulled out Phoebe's staff pass.

Abby gasped.

"You stole it?"

"I borrowed it. I promise I'll give it back when I'm done, but with four lives at stake, I had no choice."

"I don't like this, Terrell. Maybe if we both explain to Phoebe and Zane what you've seen, they'll understand?"

"You just saw me try that — they won't listen. Look, I totally understand if you don't want to come with me. I don't want you to get into trouble."

"No way! You're not ditching me that easily."

"Suit yourself, but we need to leave. Now."

Switching off his bedroom light and walking silently out into the corridor, Terrell led the way to the staff elevator. He gained access with the stolen pass and pressed the button for *Archeus*. As the doors closed and they began their descent, Abby felt a sinking feeling in the pit of her stomach.

The doors opened into a small room with more security

scanners.

"Oh, no."

"What is it? What's wrong?" Abby asked.

"It's a biometric scanning system."

"What does that mean?"

"It scans your eye and only lets you in if you're registered on the system." He placed his eye to the scanner and waited. Nothing happened. "I knew their security was tight, but this is next level."

"Can I have a try?"

"Sure. Knock yourself out."

Abby looked into the biometric scanner and waited. She stared at the electronics sitting at the back of the screen.

"I can see something moving inside."

"Yeah, it's scanning your eye, but it won't open because you're not on file."

"There's another scanner below it."

"It's for the security pass. I'm guessing you have to do both at the same time."

Abby grabbed the pass and pressed it to the bottom panel before returning to staring into the glass well.

Terrell scanned the room. In the corner was a dark mass, like a black raincloud hovering above them. As he stepped closer, it swept down towards Abby, dimming the lights of the room as it shielded the ceiling from view. It rushed towards Abby's head and into the glass well.

"Abby! Watch out!" Terrell cried, just as the door opened.

"I did it!" Abby shouted triumphantly.

"I don't think it was you. It was that black, smoke thing."

"What thing?"

The door began to close.

"Quick, get in." Terrell pushed Abby into the long corridor just in time. The door closed behind them.

"Terrell? What's going on?"

"I don't know, but I think something's trying to help us."

◆ ◆ ◆

Dani opened her eyes and chastised herself for falling asleep on the job. She usually avoided working nights but had agreed to pull a double-shift to cover Fred's absence. Still half-asleep, she reached over and took a sip of her now-cold coffee. She grimaced at the taste of the mug's stale contents before pushing the chair backwards, over to the coffee machine.

Revived with fresh, hot caffeine, she pulled herself back to the desk and checked the monitors. As expected, everything appeared normal. She had witnessed the fuss in the Red Room earlier and had spoken to Zane briefly. He had mumbled something about "kids" as he collected their belongings and Dani had watched as they had walked to their rooms. She now checked the ward cameras and saw what looked like Abby and Terrell-shaped lumps in their beds. Sipping her coffee, she flicked routinely through the many cameras.

One had gone dark. Her eyes widened as she read the room name: *Archeus lobby*. That was strange. She knew the camera had been working correctly earlier in the day. She picked up her radio and called Padman and then Ryder, receiving no response.

They're probably asleep, she thought, scrolling through the contacts on her phone for Ryder's mobile number. By the time her eyes returned to the screen, the monitor was no longer dark, and everything seemed normal. She put her phone down and recorded the glitch in the security log before returning to her coffee.

CHAPTER 27

"You need to jump over the barrels!" Jake panted.

"I'm trying, but they're too fast," Isabell replied, out of breath. "Are you OK down there, Ryder?"

"Ah, don't worry about me. Megara's keeping me company."

"We won't be too much longer."

"I'm fine, honestly."

Isabell looked down at the former soldier and started to giggle.

"What's so funny?" he asked.

"You remind me of Doctor No with Megara on your lap."

Another barrel hit Isabell, knocking her down to the bottom level.

"Bugger!"

"You need to concentrate," Jake shouted, now climbing the ladder two levels above her.

The group were playing a life-size version of the original Donkey Kong, trying to reach the top with Mario. Wheelchair-bound, Ryder was watching the action from the stands as the other three bounced around.

Padman, right on Mario's heels, was almost at the top, ready to rescue Pauline from the clutches of Donkey. He looked down to see Jake breathing heavily below him as he pulled himself up the ladder; Isabell was all the way back at the start, laughing loudly. Padman grinned in anticipated victory as he and Mario climbed the final ladder, only for Donkey Kong to grab Pauline and escape to level two.

With the game paused, Jake called up to the doctor.

"This isn't fair! You've had a lot more practice than us."

Padman and Jake climbed down, collecting Isabell, who was still laughing as they exited the platform.

Ryder clapped his hands as they approached him.

"You all seemed to have fun up there."

"Sorry you couldn't join in. We couldn't find a way of creating the game with wheelchair access. Most of Somnio is accessible, though," Padman informed him.

"Don't be sorry. I had a great time living vicariously through you all. Especially you, Isabell — you didn't stop laughing once."

"I thought I hated video games, but it's a totally different kettle of fish when you're in one." Isabell collected Megara from Ryder's lap and placed her on the floor to walk alongside them.

"Are you hurt?" Ryder asked.

"Not at all, actually. How is that?"

"Everything here is safe to use. We can't have people falling over and hurting themselves, so we installed a shock-absorbent floor, padding on the walls and the barrels are basically balls of air which blow players backwards."

"Kids are going to love this."

Padman grinned.

"We think this room will appeal to just as many adults, if not more."

"I can't see my grandfather playing Donkey Kong." Ryder laughed.

"No, neither can I, but he has played the next game. Many times, actually . . ."

The group followed Padman further into the Gaming Exhibition. A full-scale pirate ship was docked in front of them and beyond that, an island in the middle of an ocean.

"We used forced perception to create the illusion of space."

"Do you need to, in a room this size?" Jake asked.

"You wouldn't believe how vast the gaming world goes. Almost every patient we've monitored has added to the collection, and it's still growing. When you walk in, the guests start with arcade classics and early types of gaming. Some are playable, like Donkey Kong, Q*bert and Pacman, then others are interactable, like Sonic and Space Invaders.

"This is our nod to the origins of gaming. As everyone boards this pirate ship, they sail over to Monkey Island, based on the original Lucas Arts game from Nineteen-ninety. There's a whole host of other adventure game characters and themes . . . Broken Sword, Life is Strange, Gabriel Knight . . ."

"No way! I've played the entire Broken Sword series. They were the only games my parents would play with me." A memory of his family sitting around the shared computer made Jake smile.

"Me, too, and all the Monkey Island games. I loved those as a kid," Ryder added.

"Are they Lemmings?"

Everyone turned in the direction Isabell was pointing. A long line of blue characters with green hair were queueing on the side of the dock and individually jumping into the water below.

"They are. Another nod to early gaming. They float down into a cave just beneath our feet where players can control their actions using old style controllers."

"Cool!" Jake exhaled as he watched the last Lemming leap over the side.

"That's actual water?" Isabell asked.

"It's simulated. We needed something which could also double as the sky for the exhibitions on the level below, which is how we arrived at the ocean idea. We have so many gaming apparitions, we're still struggling to incorporate everything inside. There are plans to add a third level in the near future."

"What have you got in here?" Ryder asked excitedly.

"From Monkey Island you can choose your own path. In this room we have adventure games, real life SIMS, rollercoaster creators and a section dedicated exclusively to Lego. We've also teamed up with YouTube and brought some of the more popular gaming shows into the exhibit. My favourite is the Game Theory Lab with its presenter MatPat.

"Downstairs, via the central ramp, is tailored more to hard-core gamers. As you walk in, you are presented with an FPS arena and sports pavilion. The rest of level two is dedicated to action games and MMOs past and present. I didn't know much about World of Warcraft before we started building the museum, but now, I'm a top-level mage with legendary gear." He glanced towards Ryder. "All of which is accessible."

"Really? Can I live here?"

"This is a geek's paradise," Jake said.

"What's an MMO?"

Everyone looked at Isabell.

"What? I told you — I'm not into gaming."

"Maybe we should press on," Padman said, stepping on to the wooden plank leading up to the ship's deck.

"We can come back, though, right?" Ryder asked.

"Whenever you like." Padman smiled.

The former soldier felt as giddy as a child on Christmas morning as they sailed over to Monkey Island. Guybrush Threepwood was waiting on the dock to greet them as they disembarked. He introduced the group to George Stobart and Nicole Collard, who informed them they were working a case and needed their help.

"Sorry, guys — not right now. We'll be back later to help, though," Padman told them, ushering the group past.

Ryder and Jake lagged behind, desperately wanting to stay amongst their childhood heroes.

Eventually, Padman got everyone herded through the exit and into the next room.

They were standing in a desert. All around them was sun-baked sand. In the distance, a lone figure walked towards them. It was a thin, black woman; scantily clad and holding a baby in her arms. As she neared the group, she bent down and dug into the sand, producing what appeared to be a primitive bottle, holding fresh water. She poured the contents into her baby's mouth before taking some herself and continuing forward. She stopped in front of the group and spoke.

"Welcome to the history of humankind."

A flash of light from the sun partially blinded them. When their eyes readjusted, in front of them stood the Pyramids of Giza, still under construction.

"We spent a long time working on this exhibit," Padman told them as they journeyed towards Egypt. "This is the only room not quite finished. We're having to use a combination of apparitions and projections at the moment, just until we have all the materials we need. Our plan is to have all human history in this one space. As you can imagine, it's a pretty difficult task to accomplish."

As they neared the Great Pyramid of Kufu, the group observed thousands of Egyptians building the mighty structure.

"Who was that woman at the start?" Isabell asked.

"She represents the first human, about one hundred thousand years ago. Human beings originated in Africa, surviving in some of the harshest conditions. As this is the start of our story, we felt skipping ahead a few millennia to Ancient Egypt would be a good segue.

"Eventually we will have a narrator guiding the guests through this room."

The desert gave way to a sprawling body of simulated water where, standing proudly, was the Lighthouse of Alexandrea. Excited, the group marvelled at the ancient wonders; walking under the legs of the Colossus of Rhodes, passing the Mausoleum of Halicarnassus, the Temple of Artemis and smelling the flowers from the Hanging Gardens of Babylon, all before stopping to admire the giant statue of Zeus, presiding over his temple.

"I wanted to add a whole section on Atlantis, but it was voted down," Padman told them as they moved into the common era of human life.

"I'm sure I read something about deep-sea divers finding the remains of Atlantis in the Mediterranean," Jake said.

"There are many sunken cities in our oceans, but sadly none have been authenticated as the fabled Atlantis. It's more likely Plato wrote it when he was angry, as a warning to the Greek world."

"Why was he angry?" Isabell asked.

"For the unjust condemnation and execution of the man he loved, Socrates."

"His love?"

"Platonically, of course. *Plato* is where we get *platonic* love from."

"Wow! Who needs a narrator when we have you?"

Padman flushed. He was proud of all he'd learned as a result of developing Somnio. It was one of the reasons he had pushed so hard to keep it as a museum instead of a theme park — he believed edutainment was the best use of his work. Thankfully, the board agreed with him.

A marching Roman army, headed by Emperor Claudius, guided the group through the rest of Europe and on to Great Britain, a pungent smell hitting them as they entered the capital.

"Ergh! What on earth is that?" Isabell asked, holding her nose.

"That's the smell of London in Forty-three CE, or a close approximation of what it would have been. Dreams don't come with smells, so we've added them."

"Can you un-add them?" Isabell asked, gagging.

"I've smelled worse," Ryder said, smiling at Isabell's over-the-top response.

"I haven't. I think I'm going to puke," Jake muttered, turning to the side and holding his hand over his mouth.

Padman looked concerned.

"Is it really that bad? Perhaps we went a little overboard with the sensory experience. I must've gotten used to it by now." Padman reached for his tablet, the smell disappearing at the touch of a button.

"Thank you. That's much better," Jake said, composing himself.

The group took in their surroundings. If this was London, there were no discernible landmarks they recognised. Poverty-stricken people appeared in abject squalor, a stark contrast to the wealth and happiness of the citizens they'd seen elsewhere in the ancient world.

"The Romans called this place Londinium. This is the birth of what we know as London today."

"You wouldn't believe it, would you?" Jake said.

"Everything has to start somewhere," Isabell responded.

"Didn't we have an army to defend us from the invaders?" Ryder asked.

"Nothing as formidable as theirs. We were just out of the Iron Age. Even though this area was colonised a thousand years before the Romans arrived, it was mostly used by tribes, not armies. Great Britain's been invaded many times, but it was this point in history that was the real catalyst to where we are today.

"The Romans leave in about four hundred years. Soon after, we create a monarchy, followed by government, banks . . . Pretty soon, we're sailing around the world invading countries ourselves."

"We were probably sick and tired of being pushed around by everyone else," Ryder said.

"Spoken like a true soldier," Isabell responded, half-joking.

"Hey!"

"Well, it's true. Just because someone bullies you doesn't give you the right to bully someone else."

"I agree that the indigenous people of places like America and Australia didn't deserve our arrival or the destruction we brought with us. I'm not justifying what our ancestors did, I'm just saying I can understand why."

"Hmmm . . . OK," Isabell replied, distracted by Megara playing with a mouse apparition on the floor. "Don't do that, puss," she said, scooping the cat up and placing her back inside the bag.

The streets of London grew and transformed as they moved forward, Megara peering out of the bag, fascinated by the ever-changing landscape.

"We won't go down that way," Padman said, pointing. "The building of Tower Bridge is one of my favourite sections, but we have to go through the plague area and a whole load of burning houses from the Great Fire to get to it, so we'll head this way instead."

From around the corner of a thatched house, a bearded man in pantaloons approached them.

"Hello, there. Could you help me, please? My name's William Shakespeare and my actors have gone missing. Could you please do me the kindness of filling in for them on the Globe stage?"

"Not right now, Bill — perhaps later."

Shakespeare bowed towards the doctor with a smile, before disappearing down a side street.

"That's so cool. Visitors can play a Shakespearean actor?" Jake asked.

"They can. A little further on we'll find Sherlock Holmes — he'll ask us to help him hunt for Jack the Ripper."

"Seriously . . . this isn't a museum, and it's not a theme park. I don't know *what* this is, but it's the best place I've ever been to," Jake enthused.

The group continued, surviving two world wars, sheltering in an Anderson shelter from the Blitz, having a quick sing-along with Noel Coward in the West End, and finishing their tour in modern-day London before being led to the door of the next room.

CHAPTER 28

Terrell explained to Abby what he had seen as they walked along the corridor, into the soundproofed room. Reaching the end, they were presented with yet another biometric scanner.

"Do you think the black smoke thing will let us in again?" Abby asked anxiously.

"I honestly don't know," Terrell replied, placing his eye in front of the scanner. "Keep a lookout for it, will you?" He stayed motionless whilst Abby surveyed the area.

"Nothing. I don't see anything."

Terrell moved away from the scanner.

"The door isn't budging. Maybe it likes you? It worked the last time."

"OK. Keep an eye out for the ghost of Christmas Future," Abby joked.

As soon as Abby's eye touched the glass, a black haze descended from the ceiling.

"There it is!" Terrell shouted, causing Abby to look up just in time to see the black cloud enter the aperture. The door glided open.

"Quick, get in." Terrell pushed Abby gently through the opening and into Archeus.

"What *was* that?" she asked, shocked.

"I have no idea, but I think it wants us to be here."

They walked around the glass wall; the black smoke hovered above, appearing to wait for them. Abby stopped.

"We need to leave," she said, her voice unsteady.

"We can't. We need that thing to get us through that door."

"What if it wants to hurt us?"

"It's just a cloud of smoke — what's it going to do? Choke us to death?" Terrell moved forward slowly. As terrified as he felt, he knew he had to be brave for Abby.

The smoke shimmered in front of him as he pressed the pass to the panel. The door opened, and the smoke floated inside. Terrell held his hand out to Abby, who was cowering around the corner.

"Come on, it'll be all right."

Her clammy hand held tight to his as they entered the laboratory.

The smoke hovered around the cannons suspended from the ceiling.

"What are those?" Abby asked, staring up.

"I recognise them."

"From your premonition?"

"I'm not sure." Terrell tapped his head. "Come *on*, brain. Remember!" He looked over at Meditati. "I think I need to get into that."

"What is it?"

"A bed, kind of. From what I remember, it sends people's dreams down to the museum and brings them to life."

"What?"

"I know. Pretty freaky, isn't it?"

They walked over to the moulded bed and Terrell tried to climb in.

"It's too small!" Abby exclaimed.

"Yeah, not sure why. In my dream, I was lying in it. I can't have grown half a metre in the past hour."

Abby was watching the black smoke cautiously as it moved across the room towards the wall panel.

"What's it doing now?"

Lights flickered on and the bed grew in size. Terrell, resting on top, fell into Meditati's recesses as it automatically adjusted to his body.

"What the . . .?"

The black smoke glided to the centre of the lab as the cannons descended. Abby rushed towards Terrell, who was struggling to free himself.

"Ouch!" Terrell cried as a sedative was injected into his neck, knocking him out.

Abby began to cry, trying unsuccessfully to free Terrell's arm. She looked towards the black smoke. It was static in the centre of the room, looming over them like an ominous presence.

There was a loud clanking noise followed by the four cannons lowering down. They began to spray molecules into the black smoke, and as Abby gazed, transfixed and terrified, the wisps reshaped, forming legs and arms.

"Terrell! I'm scared! Please wake up. *Please*!" she screamed, getting no response.

The black smoke pulled and stretched as it took human form. It wasn't until the cannons finished and retracted into the ceiling that she was able to look clearly at the man now standing in front of her.

"Daddy?" She managed to squeeze the single word from her choked throat.

"Abby."

The apparition of Oren ran towards her, his arms open wide. As the man approached, Abby found her voice and screamed, as loud as she could.

Oren stopped and brought his arms back down to his sides.

"Abby, it's me — or, at least, it's some *form* of me. I know this is a lot to take in but you have to believe me — I am your father."

"My dad's dead, and two seconds ago you were a cloud of black smoke. Stay away from me." Abby backed into the farthest corner of the lab.

There was a long silence, when neither of them moved nor spoke. Abby squeezed her eyes shut, wishing the thing in front of her would disappear. It was the gentle sound of singing which cut across the tension filling the room. The words were in Hebrew, but Abby knew every single one of them. Her eyes opened, spilling with tears.

As Oren continued to sing to his daughter, she was transported back to her childhood, when he would soothe her with his voice and guide her off to sleep. She knew every word and every intonation he used and had replayed it in her head thousands of times.

As a young girl, she had thought it just a simple lullaby; as she had grown, she understood that the lyrics had a much more powerful, deeper meaning—it was a song about the passage of time, and about how we are all powerless to stop it.

"You are my daddy. How is this possible?" Abby choked out the words through her tears.

Oren stopped singing and smiled at her, just like he used to.

"May I come closer?"

Abby nodded, but still felt a rush of uneasy emotions as he walked forward slowly. Now in front of her, he held out his arms in invitation once more.

"You have no idea how good it is to see you again, my beautiful girl. Oh, how I've missed you."

Abby fell into his arms and wept.

"I've missed you so much, Daddy."

Time seemed to slow down for them as they held on to each other, neither wanting to let go. Eventually, Oren spoke.

"Look how much you've grown. You're a young woman now."

"You look just as I remember."

"This was how I looked five years ago."

"I don't understand." Abby's brow furrowed.

"I know you don't, sweetheart. I promise I'll explain everything."

"You're not leaving me again, are you?" Abby asked in a small voice.

"I would never leave you, nor your mother. I was kidnapped by a company called BioLearn. They've held me prisoner for the past five years, forcing me to work for them and do as they say."

"Why?"

"They needed my expertise. I discovered some of their research and they found out. They invited me to work for them, and when I refused, they took me by force. They present themselves as a research facility, but their only goal for the past few years has been to take down Silicate.

"Through the work they've made me do and their own team of hackers, they've managed to access all of Silicate's research with the goal of destroying this site and passing the research off as their own."

Abby looked shocked.

"What can we do to stop them?"

"All our hopes rest on this young man, here."

They both turned to see Terrell, unconscious in Meditati.

"He has the ability to manifest his dreams and premonitions, and that's going to come in handy."

Abby realised her mouth was hanging open and closed it. This was all too much to take in. She had spent the past five years believing her father was dead, yet now, here he was, standing right in front of her. Or, at least, *something* was standing right in front of her.

"You were *smoke*. I saw those cannons *make* you. You're not really here, are you?"

"It's difficult to explain, sweetheart."

"Try." Abby folded her arms defiantly. "I'm not a little girl any more."

"I can see that, and I apologise. Here, sit down." Oren pulled across two chairs. "For the first few weeks of my capture, they kept me in a cell. I had no idea where I was. Eventually, they let me out into their bunker, giving me certain, specific tasks to do. I was under armed guard the whole time.

"I don't want to scare you, but they told me that if I didn't do as instructed, they would kill me and then come for you and your mother. I believed them. And so, to protect you, I became the perfect slave, for the most part.

"A team of us worked for months, learning all about Silicate's apparitions and how to give form to dreams. With this knowledge, BioLearn built their own version of Archeus and I was the first to test it out. Amazingly, it worked.

"The first thing I dreamed of was you and your mom. It made me miss you even more. Using their technology, I was able to make contact. It had to be *you*, Abby, because you're half my DNA — I don't have a genetic link to your mom.

"Pleased with my performance, I was no longer deemed a security risk and was sometimes left to work alone. It was in these brief moments I devised a plan to use this new technology to reach out to you."

"But it didn't work?"

"It did, and it didn't. I'm so sorry, sweetheart. I should have perfected the programme first . . . I should have tested it more, but I was so sure it would work." Oren looked pained.

"I don't understand."

"Abby, I'm your Shadow Man."

Abby gasped and placed her hand over her mouth, tears welling in her eyes.

"I never meant to scare you. I rushed the programme. In my arrogance, I honestly thought it would work. I sent my digital form, this form, in an email which, when opened, gave me access. I thought we'd be able to chat when you slept, but the files corrupted during transfer and you ended up with a nightmarish version of me.

"There was no way to remove it. I thought about sending another file, but I worried I would just make things worse. I've been with you, inside your head, since that day. I tried to communicate with you in so many ways, but nothing worked. I tried to keep myself awake while you slept in an attempt to stop your nightmares, causing you to see me when you were awake. No matter what I did, all you saw was a shadow figure with burning red eyes.

"I am so, so sorry, Abby. Please forgive me."

This was too much for Abby to take. To discover her father was still alive was incredible; to find out the Shadow Man, the nightmare which had destroyed her life, was actually her father all along . . . the mix of conflicting emotions was overwhelming, to say the least. She wanted to scream and thrash out; yet, at the same time, if what he said was true, he had simply been trying to connect with her. He had meant to be a comfort, not a nightmare.

Oren's eyes were filled with emotion as he regarded his daughter.

Abby wiped her eyes, composed herself as best she could, and reached out to take hold of her father's hands.

"I know you would never do anything to hurt me, Daddy. I can't say I fully understand all this, but I forgive you."

They hugged.

"Does this mean the Shadow Man's gone for good?"

"Yes, darling. You'll never see him again."

Abby smiled, but then her brow furrowed in concern.

"But if you're the Shadow Man, does that mean I won't ever see *you* again?"

"If all goes to plan tonight, you'll be seeing a lot more of me, but the *real* me and in real life. I'm still being held prisoner at BioLearn, but with you and Terrell, I think we can change that. We'll need to work quickly, but we can save Silicate and we can get me home to you and your mom."

CHAPTER 29

The door opened to reveal a canopy of vines and tree branches. The air felt hot and humid

"Bloody hell! Are we in a lizard's tank or something?"

"Not a bad guess, Isabell," Padman replied. "We've simulated the jungle atmosphere in this area, but it'll cool off once we're out in the open."

They pushed through the overgrown branches. Sounds of hundreds of animals surrounded them, yet nothing could be seen. After a short trek, the canopy opened, and they stood at the edge of the African savanna.

"Welcome to the Congo Basin. A world teeming with exotic life, and the start of our Wild Earth exhibition," Padman announced as Isabell, Ryder and Jake took in the view.

"Are they real lions?" Jake asked, pointing to a pride, ten strong, prowling the desert floor mere metres away.

"They're apparitions of lions, but other than that, they're real in every way. Of course, we've modified them so that guests can interact with them without losing body parts."

"You mean we can stroke a lion?" Isabell asked excitedly.

"And a tiger and an elephant, if you wish."

"I wish! I wish!"

"How many species of animals do you have here?" Ryder asked in amazement.

"Around three hundred, but that includes mammals, reptiles, fish and insects, so a miniscule fraction of the amount in terms of the real animal kingdom. We offer guests different safari adventures, but my favourite's the bear encounter. Every bear in the world in one place. You can actually sit in the arms of a grizzly bear and get your picture taken."

"Lions and tigers and bears? Oh, my!" Jake cried with a smile.

Isabell and Padman chuckled.

"What's funny about that?" Ryder asked.

"Come on! Even straight guys know this one," Isabell told the confused ex-soldier. "It's from the Wizard of Oz."

"Oh, OK," Ryder replied, evidently not understanding the group excitement. "I've never seen it," he admitted.

"What? You have to watch it!" Jake exclaimed.

"We can do better than that," Padman interrupted. "We have a whole Oz section here in the museum."

Jake's face lit up.

"You're kidding! Best. Day. Ever."

A family of chimpanzees swung down from the trees above them, landing on the floor.

"Hello, there," Isabell greeted the smallest chimp.

The baby observed her with his huge eyes, before darting shyly behind his mother.

"They're so lifelike," she breathed.

"The human brain's an incredible machine. Everything we do, see, or hear is stored away perfectly. We blame our memories for things like losing our keys or forgetting someone's name, but really, it's more a case of us not knowing how to access things properly."

Padman was met with uncomprehending faces. He tried again.

"Imagine the brain is the largest hard-drive in the world, and it contains all of human history within it."

"Google, then?"

"That's a better analogy. Thank you, Jake. Everything's there, but if we don't know what to type in to get to it, we can't see it. It's the same with our brains. If we don't know how to access specific memories, we believe they're lost. They're not.

"I've studied hundreds of brains, and the wealth of information and detail stored inside every single one is incredible. That's why this monkey, that lion and this tree, and, well, *everything* looks so authentic."

A large, female chimp jumped up on to Ryder's lap, feeling his face with her hands.

"Why is everything doing that today?" he questioned, and everyone laughed.

Leaving the primates behind, Padman led the group over the sandy grass towards the pride.

"He's so beautiful," Isabell murmured as they neared the male lion.

"This is Banjo. He was one of the first apparitions we made for the museum, so he's been with us for a few years now. We've become quite attached to each other, haven't we, Banjo?" Padman ruffled the lion's mane as the imposing animal nuzzled the doctor's chest. "Would anyone like to stroke him?"

Isabell squealed with excitement as she moved carefully towards the magnificent creature. Megara appeared less convinced, and hopped out of the bag Isabell was still carrying, taking shelter behind Ryder's wheelchair.

"Where did you store a lion before the museum was complete?" Ryder asked as he joined Isabell petting Banjo.

"In the Living Lab, behind the main hub of the museum in a totally secure area. It's now where all apparitions materialise."

Padman noticed Jake was standing on his own, slightly away from the others.

"Are you OK?"

"Yeah, I'm fine." He was staring at Isabell, now seated on a rock with two lions licking her face. "Are you sure these things are safe?"

"Completely safe, I assure you. If we were in the wild, our instincts would tell us to run away screaming, but as lifelike as these appear to be, they're not." Padman turned to a female lion, who was sniffing his hand. He crouched down and pulled her mouth open, sliding his hand inside. The lion stayed still, not biting, not even making a sound. He removed his hand again and stroked the lion. "You see? She can't harm me."
Aghast, Jake gave him a disturbed look.

"OK. I believe you. I still can't get my head round it, though. Can we move on, please?"

"Do we have to go?" Isabell asked, hugging Banjo's head.

"Jake's right, there's still plenty to see." Padman checked his watch. "And the security detail should be arriving soon. I need to inform them about what happened last night."

Isabell groaned, and kissed Banjo on the head one last time before moving away. Megara, who had been watching cautiously, now bounded over, deciding she could be as brave as Isabell. Banjo began licking and grooming her, making the domestic cat purr loudly.

"I think Megara's found a friend," Ryder announced.

"My gorgeous girl." Isabell beamed. "Come on, now, it's time to leave," Isabell called, but the cat was oblivious to her mother's beckoning.

"You could leave her here for a while. We can always come back later," Padman offered.
"Will she be safe on her own?"

"She's an apparition herself— she'll be perfectly fine."

"Doesn't she need a dose of new molecules or something?"

"Not for at least another twelve hours. We'll be back well before then."

Isabell ran through the possibilities in her head before picking the cat up and placing her back into the bag.

"Nope, can't do it. I know she's an apparition, but my emotional attachment is real."

They moved through the sand-dunes, coming to a halt at a beautiful, golden beach, beyond which was a seemingly endless sea.

"I should have brought my swimming costume," Isabell commented, looking out across the ocean.

Padman moved forward, into the lapping waves.

"I was only kidding," she called after him.

"This isn't real water. We need to enter it to continue. Come on in—you won't get wet."

Ryder, Jake, and Isabell followed tentatively, their brains struggling to assimilate the ocean their eyes perceived with the lack of wetness felt underfoot. They watched, mesmerised, as the doctor suddenly submerged and disappeared from view.

"Where did he go?" Ryder asked.

"Only one way to find out," Jake called, running into the water and disappearing beneath the waves.

Ryder looked over at Isabell and shrugged, manoeuvring his chair into the water.

Isabell closed the bag to keep Megara from jumping out and moved alongside him. She instinctively held her breath as they descended into the ocean.

Darkness gave way to flickers of light shimmering from the surface above, casting wave-like shadows on the ocean floor. Hundreds of tiny fish descended from the light, flashing a kaleidoscope of colours. Everyone oohed and aahed in wonderment and delight. Overhead, a pod of dolphins guided them forward, chattering noisily as they swam.

"You can touch them, if you like. They're rather playful, though—they rarely stay still for very long."

Padman smiled as all three reached up to stroke the rubbery-textured mammals.

"How are they swimming when there's no water?" Ryder was fascinated.

"Because they're not alive!" Isabell whispered to him.

The light dimmed suddenly, and they became aware of a massive object passing over them; at twenty-five metres long, the blue whale dwarfed everything else. Isabell gasped.

"Are you OK?" Ryder asked.

"Look at it — it's magnificent," she replied, staring up at the whale.

"It's not real, you know," he whispered, coyly. She glared at him before turning back at the majestic creature swimming above them.

They passed many other species of fish, sea mammals and sharks before exiting the immersive aquarium. Padman was delighted to see everyone's smiling faces.

"Sorry it's a bit of a whistle-stop tour, but it's really just a preview. If we turn left here, we can make a detour to the next exhibition and on to my office."

"What's down there?" Jake asked, pointing to the right.

"That's the Americas exhibit along with the bear sanctuary I was talking about earlier," Padman replied. "And ahead of us is the arctic section with Roald Amundsen and Robert Falcon Scott as guides, taking guests through the frozen landscapes of the north and south poles."

The ground beneath their feet suddenly changed from yellow to white as patches of snow began to appear, becoming denser. They pushed on towards the exit.

"Through here is the largest exhibit by far, and is sure to be a firm favourite with all our guests." Padman opened the door and allowed them to enter. "Welcome to the Mesozoic Era."

CHAPTER 30

Terrell slowly opened his eyes. The first thing he saw, through clouded vision, was Abby leaning over him. Behind her stood a man Terrell didn't recognise.

"What happened?"

Abby opened her mouth to speak, but no words came out. Sensing her hesitation, Oren spoke first.

"Hi, I'm Oren — Abby's father. I'm sorry I had to sedate you. It was the only way to activate the system which brought me here."

Terrell sat up, confused.

"Sorry, what?"

Abby and Oren proceeded to explain what had happened. It took some persuasion for him to accept that Oren wasn't a real human being.

"The real me is still in San Francisco. Imagine this as a video call with a three-dimensional image you can interact with," Oren suggested.

"I thought apparitions were dreams? Copies of our thoughts, not linked to the person who dreamed them?"

"They are, but I'm not. I've been working on this technology for years. Finally — *thankfully* — it works. This is one of the few areas where BioLearn's leading the way . . . though the research to achieve the tech was all stolen from Silicate in the first place."

Terrell reached out to touch Oren. His arm felt like skin, and as Terrell watched the man's chest move, it certainly looked like he was breathing.

"It's all simulated," Oren explained, pre-empting Terrell's question. "Everything you see is a perfect simulation of me. Well, actually — it's a perfect simulation of how I was when I first sent this form to Abby, several years ago." He turned to his daughter. "I have a beard now. Don't tell your mom."

Terrell stared in disbelief. Seeing the distrust in the boy's eyes, Oren walked over to the side of the room and scoured the counters until he found a hypodermic needle. He walked back over to Abby and Terrell.

"I suppose I should be flattered that you think I'm real, but we're running out of time and I need you — both of you — to believe me."

Without warning, he jabbed the needle into the palm of his hand. It pierced right through, causing Abby and Terrell to flinch. When Oren pulled it out again, he held up his hand for inspection. There was no blood; there wasn't even a hole, nor any indication the needle had ever touched his flesh.

"Apparitions are copies of what people see, remember and dream. As I didn't have a needle — or, indeed, a hole in my hand — when I sent this form to Abby, my apparition can't change to include that information. There's no blood inside me, so I can't bleed; and even though it appears I'm breathing, there's no air in my lungs because I have no lungs to fill."

"Does that mean you can't die?" Abby asked.

"This version of me can and will disappear when the molecular structure begins to degrade. The technology in this room is rather outdated. I may have only a few more hours before I start to decompile."

Abby eyes filled with tears again.

"I'm sorry, darling. That wasn't very tactful — I didn't mean to upset you." Oren comforted his daughter.

"Can we transfer you to the other lab?" Terrell asked.

"Possibly, but that won't matter if we can't eliminate the threat downstairs first. Once we've done that, we can expose BioLearn and get me — the *real* me — home to my family."

"Really?" Abby looked up at her father, eyes hopeful.

"Yes, really. But I can't do this alone. I need both of you to help."

"What do you need us to do?" Terrell asked.

"I need you to attempt something which has never been successfully executed before."

"Why me?"

"You're different from the others. In your premonition, what did you see?"

"I saw this place, that bed and me sending an apparition of myself down to the lab where the others are."

"That's incredible. We've been trying to create mirror apparitions for years. What you see here —" he gestured to himself "— is the closest we've gotten. Without an active link, this is nothing but an empty shell. If what you saw is correct, your apparition should be fully autonomous. It'll take your form along with all your thoughts and knowledge, without you having to control it."

"What if I need to tell myself something?"

"Once your other self is in the lab, we should be able to communicate."

"Won't you be going, too?"

"I need to stay here to keep you both safe by fending off any attacks from BioLearn. Once they realise what's happening, they'll try to stop us. Security here is tight, but BioLearn can get around it. Especially in Archeus — any areas where transfers happen are weak spots. They'll try to use this lab as an entry point. I'll attempt to keep them out of the system for as long as possible, hopefully long enough for you to warn the others and get them to safety."

"Will the real you be safe?" Abby asked.

"Don't worry about me, sweetheart. I've barricaded myself in an unused storage closet on the lower level. Even if they learn of my involvement, it'll take them quite a while to track me down."

"OK, I'm ready. What do I do?" Terrell asked.

"Climb back into Meditati. I'll sedate you and activate the panel. If your premonition is correct, you should be able to produce your mirror self. How detailed was it, exactly?"

"We're about to find out, it seems," Terrell said, walking over to the large bed and climbing back in.

Abby walked to his side and gave him a reassuring smile.

"Do you know what needs to be done down there?" Oren asked.

"Once I've materialised, I need to get out of the lab and find the others. In my dream, they were spread out across the museum."

"The first thing you need to do is find Doctor Sharma and explain in as much detail as possible what's happening.

"I don't know how long we'll have before BioLearn discovers what we're up to, so the faster you take action, the more lives we can save."

Terrell nodded, sweat beading on his forehead. Abby squeezed his hand.

"Right. Are we ready to begin?" Oren asked.

Terrell and Abby both nodded.

Oren activated the controls and the floating screen appeared above Terrell's face.

"Whoa! What on earth is that?"

"It's just an interface, nothing to worry about."

Terrell watched as Oren tapped on the screen floating in the air. He could see electronic recreations of the inside of his brain: synapses firing and darting around, as well as monitors for his vital signs like pulse and breathing rate. He watched as they edged up and up.

"Perhaps it's best you close your eyes," Oren suggested. "I think the light is overstimulating you. I'm almost ready to administer the sedative now, anyway."

"No, don't do that."

"Is something wrong?"

"In my dream, I wasn't sedated."

"You must have been. Apparitions only appear when the brain's in REM."

"I don't need to dream to create a mirror version. Let me try, at least?"

Oren looked sceptical, but nodded in agreement.

Terrell closed his eyes and started to breathe slowly and deliberately. The screen above his face showed his heartrate drop from ninety-nine beats per minute to just forty in a matter of seconds. Next, the activity in his brain increased dramatically, as hundreds of neurons began making new connections in rapid succession.

Oren watched, in muted amazement, as the screen cycled through thousands of varying images of the boy lying on the bed. After a few minutes, the images stopped, brain activity returned to normal and Terrell's heartrate began to climb again.

Across the centre of the screen, text unfolded from left to right: *Apparition sent.*

Abby, still holding on to Terrell's hand, now felt him squeeze hers.

"I think he's waking up, Daddy."

Oren retracted the screen.

"Terrell? Are you OK?"

Terrell opened his eyes.

"Did it work?"

"Something was sent down to the lab, yes. It'll take a few minutes for the system to recalibrate so we can see the image. I can monitor the codes from here, but we won't know if it's a success until your other self gets in contact."

Terrell nodded, pushing himself up out of Meditati. He joined Oren and Abby at the computer.

"How did you do that?" Oren asked excitedly, switching on the monitor. "I've been working with this system for years and I've never seen anyone do what you've just done. It defies everything we know about apparitions. You weren't even asleep!"

"I just repeated what I saw in my dream."

"You closed your eyes and started the process immediately. It was as if you put yourself into a meditative state."

"It was instinct . . . Like my brain already knew what it had to do. Because it's done it before, sort of. Or, at least, knew what I was going to do. Premonitions are weird."

"That's one way of putting it," Abby said, smiling.

Oren accessed the folder on the desktop.

"Good, everything's back up and running."

"Why wouldn't it be?" Terrell asked.

"Silicate has a mole. They hacked into Archeus, giving partial control to BioLearn. I was able to sever the connection and reactivate security protocols before you two arrived. It's a good thing I did, otherwise you wouldn't have had any air to breathe." Oren grimaced at the thought, pulling up a series of data files. "But that hasn't stopped them trying to sneak back in. Let's hope your mirror self is successful."

"MT will come through for us. I'm sure of it."

"MT?" Abby asked.

"MT — Mirror Terrell."

Abby smiled.

"MT. I like it."

Oren opened a file and dragged it across to the monitor in front of Abby. Strings of blue numbers ran up and down the screen. As she tried to make sense of what she was seeing, red numbers began popping up in the threads of blue.

"Daddy, what's this?"

"The easiest way to describe it is, imagine we, or this company, are the blue numbers and the red ones are BioLearn trying to hack into the system." He began typing in a series of commands, and one by one, the red numbers disappeared. "I can delete them from here manually, but I won't be able to deflect them for ever. Everything rests on MT's success or failure."

CHAPTER 31

Ryder, Isabell and Jake stood in amazement scanning the room, unable to comprehend exactly what they were seeing.

"You've created Jurassic Park!" Jake exclaimed.

Giant Argentinosauruses stomped the ground as a herd of Compsognathus ran through and around their legs. Two Tyrannosauruses prowled the green expanse, while an Allosaurus peered through the trees to one side. Pterosaurs soared overhead, while an Ankylosaurus slept under the artificial sun, shining from far above them.

Padman chuckled.

"Jurassic Park was fiction. These dinosaurs are not. They also won't try to bite your heads off. As with all of our apparitions, you can touch these ones. Interact with them . . . ride them, even."

"Do they attack each other?" Ryder asked

"They did, at first, but we've spent a long time carefully modifying their behaviour. Now they can comfortably share the space together."

"How many do you have?" Isabell asked.

"Currently, there are twenty-nine species; at least two of each. At the last count, we had seventy-three in total. That's not including the prehistoric sea creatures on the level below."

Ryder looked around for a body of water.

"There's a simulated lake beyond the trees," Padman explained. "By the side of that is the central hub of the whole museum and a viewing gallery for the underwater exhibits. Guests will be able to shop and dine whilst watching Plesiosaurs and Ichthyosaurs swim about. For our purposes, we can also access my office from there."

"I thought you said there were twelve exhibits?" Isabell asked.

"There are, the hub is just the midway point. Don't worry, there is still plenty more to see, including an age-restricted exhibition in the hub itself."

"Sex dungeon!"

"Do you have a nervous tick or something, Isabell?" Jake joked. He turned to Padman. "You don't have a sex dungeon, do you?"

"No, we don't. Though it's not the first time it's been suggested. Most of our patients dream about sex, as we all do. The amount of sexual imagery we have collated over the years is in the thousands.

"The board of directors is still divided on whether to build a sex exhibition or not."

"Wouldn't that be a breach of privacy, though? I know I wouldn't want my face or body paraded around a museum."

"We would, of course, change or remove any discernible features.

"For now, at least, we've decided to keep the focus more family-friendly, albeit for a few age-restricted areas. I mentioned the adult animations earlier, in addition to that, we've also built an immersive horror experience. Like a classic haunted house, only Somnio-style. Nothing *too* scary, but enough for it to warrant a strict PG13 rating."

Padman began walking forward, pointing out various dinosaurs and moving through ferns and overgrown plants. Near the lake, they came across a baby triceratops. Isabell reached out to touch it.

"You just can't help yourself, can you?" Ryder said, smiling.

"As if you don't want to touch the baby dinosaur," she replied, rolling her eyes in jest, as Ryder joined her in stroking the rough-textured creature.

Padman was looking around anxiously.

"Is everything all right?" Jake asked him.

"Probably. It's just that there should be a lot more dinosaurs here. This baby triceratops is never without its parents."

"Maybe they're in the trees?"

"Perhaps, but I haven't seen any gallimimuses or microraptors, either." Padman stood up on his tiptoes to try to see over the bushes in the distance. "Come to think of it, the Spinosaurus is missing, too."

"Could one of your team have taken them out for some reason?"

"I suppose so, if they had found a problem, they might have removed them for testing. Surely, they would have informed me, though."

"Maybe they didn't want to worry you?"

"Yes, you're probably right." Padman breathed deeply and made an effort to appear more relaxed than he felt. "I'll check the system when I'm in the office and see what's been going on." The doctor looked at Jake and smiled. "How are you doing, anyway?"

"I feel great, actually. That wake-up boost you gave us worked wonders . . . and this, this, *museum* is honestly the best place I've ever been to. You must be so proud."

"Thank you. I am. It's taken years and a lot of hard work from a whole team of people, but yes, I do feel very proud of Somnio. I just hope the public appreciate it."

"How could they not? This place is incredible."

Padman smiled and kissed Jake on the lips.

"Thank you."

"That was amazing! I touched a triceratops," Isabell exclaimed excitedly as she walked towards Jake and the doctor, Ryder following closely behind.

"What's next?" Ryder asked.

"Next up — a fun and exciting visit to my office."

The group descended the spiral slope leading into the hub, a circular, partially open area, flooded by light from the Mesozoic Era exhibition above. Around the perimeter were huge waves of glass walls, showcasing the magnificent, prehistoric sea creatures. Shops and eateries lined the walls with tables and chairs set against the ocean backdrop. To the north was a large door with the London Underground logo on it; to the south, the stadium.

"You have a stadium?" Jake asked.

"It's actually more of an amphitheatre. Ten thousand seats around a central stage. We plan to host events and shows using our apparitions."

"When Adele's concert sells out, people can see her here, instead?" Isabell asked.

"Actually, we'll be focusing more on artists *no-one* can get tickets for any more. The ones who are sadly no longer with us; Whitney Houston, Kurt Cobain, Prince, and Freddie Mercury could all perform here."

Megara lifted her head out of the bag and yawned.

"Hello, puss. You missed all the dinos," Isabell informed her.

"Probably for the best," Ryder said, reaching to pet the cat.

"The Living Lab's through my office. You can wait there while I tend to Megara, if you like."

"Can I come with you?"

"I'm afraid not. It's one of the most restricted areas in the building. She'll be completely safe with me, I promise. Once I've made the necessary calibrations to the system, the process should only take an hour."

Isabell reluctantly passed the bag to the doctor, kissing Megara's head repeatedly before relinquishing it.

"If I can't actually be there with her, do you mind if we continue looking around the museum? It would beat waiting in your office. Up for it, Jake?" Isabell asked.

"Yeah, if that's OK with you?"

"Fine by me," Padman replied, smiling. "Go and have fun. We shouldn't be too long. Once the security team's been brought up to speed on what's happened, we'll come and find you and finish the rest of the museum together."

As Jake and Isabell waved goodbye, Padman turned to Ryder.

"You could join them, you know — I can make the call myself."

"Duty first, sir — sorry, *Doctor.*"

Padman smiled.

"Come on, then. The sooner we do this, the faster we can join Starfleet."

"What was that I said about duty?"

The two laughed as they entered the office.

"Where are we going?" Jake asked Isabell.

"I spotted some maps over there. Let's have a see what else they have."

They walked over to the stadium entrance. There were stands of information pamphlets on the wall outside; Isabell took two and handed one to Jake.

"Why didn't Padman give us one of these at the start?"

"I guess he wanted to surprise us," Jake replied, unfolding the map. "I can't get over the size of this place, there's still tons more to see."

Isabell studied the full-colour visitor's guide.

"We're here," she said, pressing her finger to the paper, "so we've seen all the rooms on the left side and Fantastic Worlds, Future Lock, Danger Unlimited and Stage and Screen are on the right. We have the stadium in front of us, Myths and Monsters, over there and, ooh, this sounds good, Carry On Dreaming."

"What's that?"

"*Barbara Windsor and Kenneth Williams guide you onto the sets of your favourite Carry On films*" she read. "*This British pinnacle of comedy is filled with classic one-liners and an abundance of innuendos. Ooh Matron! Exhibition opening on December 1st."* Isabell's face dropped. "Oh no, it's not open yet."

"Good. It sounds boring," Jake replied.

"Have you ever watched a Carry On film?"

"Only when flicking through the TV. They're so dated."

"They're classics."

"That's just another word for 'old'."

"I bet I can change your mind with Carry On Screaming. It's a parody of early horror films."

"Who needs a parody when we can do the horror exhibition?"

Isabell looked worried. "Comedies are fine, but I really don't like being scared."

"Oh, come on, I'll be with you. Padman said it wasn't too frightening. We should at least check it out. If you don't like it, we can just leave."

"OK, but you're holding my hand."

"Deal."

The entrance to Myths and Monsters was under the canopy of the Mesozoic Era, partially hidden from view. A big, red sign on the wall stated this was an age-restricted area.

"Not that there's anyone policing it today," Isabell joked.

"You think you'd pass as an under-thirteen, do you? How old are you, anyway?"

"One should never ask a lady how old she is."

"I didn't, I asked *you*."

"Oi!" Isabell slapped Jake lightly on the back. "Cheeky. OK, I have a question for you. How long have you and Doctor Sharma been an item?"

Jake looked at his watch.

"About thirty-three hours."

"No way!"

"Way. We met in a bar last night."

"And he brought you here today?"

"It's a long story. Now stop stalling and take my hand."

"Bossy. I can see why the doctor likes you."

"Now who's being cheeky?"

Wrapped around the frame of the door was a host of fibreglass creatures; vampires, zombies, swamp monsters and aliens, all squaring off against each other and forming an archway guests could walk under.

"It looks a bit cheesy, actually," Isabell observed.

"PG13, remember. I doubt it'll be scary at all."

The door closed behind them as they entered a dark forest in the black of night. A sudden crack of lightning lit up the sky, illuminating a gothic manor house on a hill in front of them.

"I guess that's where we're headed," Isabell said, as they walked down a stone path overgrown with weeds.

Bats flew overhead, and ghostly sounds added to the cheesy horror movie feel. As they reached the front porch, the large, wooden door creaked open slowly.

"That creeped me out a bit," Isabell admitted as they stepped into the grand entrance. "Although apart from a door opening on its own, nothing's really happened yet," she continued.

"It's the antici . . . *pation* of it all." Jake tried to adopt a spooky tone but couldn't help laughing.

"Brilliant! You're a Rocky Horror fan, too."

"It's one of my favourite films. I would watch it secretly in my bedroom so my parents wouldn't know. I thought they might figure out I was gay if they saw me mouthing every word to Sweet Transvestite."

"My parents used to sing it along with me."

"You're a girl from London . . . I'm a boy from the country — two totally different worlds. I hope they have a Frank N. Furter character here we can interact with."

"If they don't, maybe we could add one."

"I hadn't thought of that. Do you think Padman would let us add to the exhibits?"

"I can't see why not. By the sounds of it, he's keen to find more content."

"That would be so cool."

The house was styled in a wooden and stone gothic theme, like something straight out of an early horror or Hammer House film. They both gasped as they focused on the ceiling, where three corpses — two men, and a woman in the centre — were hanging. They'd all been strung up by their arms with rope and were completely covered in blood. Their heads were slumped to their chests, hiding their faces.

Isabell hid behind Jake.

"That's gruesome. No wonder they don't want to let kids in here," he said.

"So much gore! It's way too much, even for teenagers."

Isabell watched, transfixed, as blood dripped from the corpses' feet, pooling on the floor.

"I mean, come on — that's disgusting."

"And it looks like we have to walk underneath them to continue."

"Nope!"

"You don't want to see the rest of the exhibition?"

"I don't want to be in here at all. It's far too realistic. Nope! Not for me," Isabell said firmly, turning back the way they had entered.

"Fair enough." Jake shrugged.

As they turned towards the door, they heard a voice whisper something. They looked back, and were sure they saw one of the corpses moving.

"Help me, please!" the voice whispered.

Screaming, Isabell and Jake raced out of the exhibit and clung to each other until their goose bumps had disappeared. Once they'd managed to slow their racing hearts, they looked at each other and burst out laughing.

"Do you think we should tell Padman?" Jake asked.

"Tell him that we ran away screaming? Or that we think it's a bit too scary?"

"The latter."

"Definitely, but not yet. There are still four more rooms I

want to see before we get kicked out. What's next?"

Jake pulled out the map and scanned the information.

"*Fantastic Worlds*," he read. "*Join Atreyu and Falkor on a journey to the Ivory Tower and visit the beloved characters of Fantasia. Meet up with the Fellowship of the Ring in Middle Earth, take a class at Hogwarts with Harry, Ron and Hermione and fly your dragon over Westeros in the battle for the Iron Throne; then follow the yellow brick road with Dorothy and her friends in the wonderful land of Oz . . .*"

"Love, love, love it all. Let's go!"

"You're not going to scream again when we see a dragon, are you?"

"I think you'll find it was *you* that was screaming. I was just keeping you company." They both laughed as they made their way to the other side of the hub.

CHAPTER 32

Ryder and Padman entered the office.

"Do you mind calling upstairs while I get Megara sorted?" the doctor asked. "That's my work station — there's a phone next to the keyboard. The extension list is under the receiver. I won't be long."

"No worries." Ryder pulled himself up to the desk and picked up the phone.

After a few minutes, Padman returned.

"All sorted. Did you manage to get through to the security desk?"

"I'm still trying to get hold of them," Ryder replied, a note of concern in his voice.

"Did you try the other extensions?"

"All of them."

Padman checked his watch.

"They should have been on duty over an hour ago."

The doctor walked over to another phone and dialled a series of numbers; all of them rang out.

"How strange. Let me try the staff-room in case they're getting coffee or something. It is Sunday — without me around, they might be taking it easy."

That number, too, rang out.

"Either there's some kind of emergency upstairs or no-one is at their post, which would be very odd," he muttered, as much to himself as to Ryder. He dialled the nurses' station. The phone was answered immediately. "Ah! Good, someone I can talk to. This is Doctor Sharma. I'm looking for —"

"Padman, it's Phoebe. What's happening with the doors? We can't get out of the building."

"What do you mean?"

"Our shift ended an hour ago, but we can't leave. There are metal shutters over all the exits and the staff elevator isn't working. Did you put Silicate into shutdown mode?"

"No, I've been trapped downstairs. We were stuck in Archeus earlier, but we managed to escape. We thought it was just our section."

"It's everywhere. If you didn't do this, who did?"

"I've no idea. Can you access the mainframe?"

"I can, but I don't have high enough clearance to see the security files."

"Grab Dani, she has access."

"She's not there. I haven't seen her in hours. Me and Zane have been calling every extension we can think of, but there's no-one around to pick up."

"Can you call outside the building?"

"Nope, only internal."

"OK. I'll see what I can find out from my end." Padman opened his desk drawer and grabbed a handset. "Are the radios working?"

"No, they're down, too."

"In my office, in my desk, you'll find a mobile phone. Switch it on and call me on it. My number is five, five, two, four."

"That's the whole number?"

"It's on the building's internal network and shouldn't be affected by outside interferences. It's a backup measure in case of a cyber-attack. I never thought we'd need to use it, though."

"Heading there now, Padman. Speak soon."

The doctor placed the receiver down and sat, waiting for the mobile in his hand to ring.

"What's happening?" Ryder asked.

Before Padman could reply, the handset rang.

"Good — at least we know this works. Could you and Zane move into the security station, please, and keep tabs on the monitors for me? Any information — call me. We'll do the same."

"Will do, thanks."

Padman ended the call and sat back in his chair, looking worried. He turned to Ryder.

"The whole building is on shutdown. No-one can get in or out, and the only security guard we had on shift has gone AWOL. This is bad. Really bad."

Opening his eyes, Mirror Terrell looked around. He was inside a glass pod. A haze of blue smoke and vapour was dissipating in front of his eyes. Realising that he was the mirror apparition of himself, he walked up to the door and pushed. Nothing. He stood for a moment, wondering what to do next, when the door hissed open. Shocked, he looked around, spying a small camera in the ceiling of the pod. He waved in thanks to Oren for opening the door, realising the tech master must be monitoring the cameras.

He stepped outside and looked around, finding himself a bit disorientated within a whole maze of pods — at least a hundred identical units on this row alone. He closed his eyes, trying to recall which way he had gone in his premonition. *Right.*

He ran in that direction, only to find another row of pods, at least twice the length of the one he had just come from. He squeezed his eyes shut again, remembering the way through, trying to trust his vision.

His journey took him past penguins, Amelia Earhart, sequoia trees and a submarine, all in some kind of stasis inside their own glass prisons; he noticed none of them, so intensely was he focused on his mission. Finally reaching the exit door, he stood in front of the first of many security panels. The door slid open as soon as he looked into the camera.

"Thank you, Oren," MT mouthed.

"It's so much easier to guide him through with access to the cameras," the real Terrell said gratefully, narrowing his eyes as he followed his mirror version on the screen. "This is so weird — he looks just like me."

"He *is* you. Well, the you from ten minutes ago," Oren replied.

"How does he know where to go?" Abby asked.

"Because *I* knew where to go. I saw all this in my dream. He's about two rooms away from the office, then he just needs to find the others."

"Didn't your dream show you where they were?" Abby asked.

"The nurses purged my premonition before it was finished. All I remember is that there was a lot of blood."

On a second screen, Oren opened a map of the museum.

"Take a look ... See if anything jogs your memory."

Terrell examined the map.

"I doubt they'd want dinosaurs dripping blood on the guests, so that's out. They could've added it to the Fantasy room ... but I think the horror exhibit's the best bet."

"Then that's where he needs to go," Oren responded, opening the single camera-feed from the office MT was heading for.

Inside, he could just make out Padman and Ryder.

"That's them!" Abby announced triumphantly.

Oren reached for his daughter's hand and gave it a reassuring squeeze.

"When MT reaches the room, he'll explain everything to Padman, and one of them will give us a call."

"Why can't we just call them now?"

"When Archeus was compromised, the network was corrupted. We have to use a different system and be on the same frequency to communicate."

"That's why you told me — MT — to call us on your extension when he gets there," Terrell chipped in.

"Daddy, MT's waving at you."

Oren looked back to the main screen and released the lock on the door MT had reached.

"He's making good time, he's only one door away from the office." Oren's brow furrowed. "Padman looks upset about something. Who's the guy in the wheelchair?"

"Ryder, the new head of security. He's nice," Abby told her father.

"Let's hope he's good at his job. If BioLearn do break through, they'll infiltrate Silicate in no time."

"You can stop them, though, can't you, Daddy?"

"I'll do my best, darling."

"He's at the final door," Terrell said, pointing to the main monitor.

Oren opened the door and MT rushed through the room towards the two startled men.

"Terrell? What? How? Where did you come from?" Padman questioned.

"I'm not Terrell. Well, I am, but not the real Terrell. I'm a mirror version of him."

Padman stood back and peered at the boy.

"A mirror apparition? That's impossible."

"Mr Rosenberg can explain it all. He's in Archeus at the moment — you need to call him."

"Abby's father? But he's dead. None of this makes sense, Terrell."

"Please, call Archeus. Oren will explain everything. The extension is five, five, nine, seven."

Tentatively, Padman picked up his mobile and dialled. Oren answered immediately.

"Hello, Doctor Sharma. I know we've never met, but I'm a great admirer of your work."

"Who is this?"

"My name is Oren Rosenberg. We have a lot to discuss."

CHAPTER 33

"Zoya and I knew that Devansh wouldn't take the news well, but I never expected him to go to such extremes." Padman was still reeling from the barrage of information Oren had given him. "There were stories of his tyranny, but my father always told me that, at his core, he was an honourable man. How could he commit such atrocities?"

"I wouldn't know — I've never met him," Oren replied over the phone. "The prisoners don't have contact with anyone except armed guards."

"How do you know it's him, then?"

"We receive internal messages and emails, all from his account. He's definitely the one calling the shots."

"Are you in some sort of prison?"

"In a way, yes. Devansh built an underground facility beneath BioLearn. Unlike Somnio, though, he has captured scientists and tech experts from all over the world, now working down here, unable to escape."

"How have the authorities not realised?"

"BioLearn's very good at covering its tracks. It pays endless amounts of money to anyone who gets close to the truth to buy their silence."

"This is terrifying."

"I know it's a lot to take in, but if we don't act fast, they'll do the same to you, obliterating Silicate in the process."

"You're right," Padman said, pulling himself together. "We can discuss this later." He had been staring at MT throughout the conversation. "I knew Terrell was unique, but I had no idea he was capable of such a feat. We've tried creating mirror apparitions for years without success."

"As have we. He's a special guy, all right." Oren looked over at Terrell, who was smiling proudly. "In his premonition," Oren continued, "he said he saw a lot of blood. We think it might have been the horror exhibition?"

"No, it can't be. We don't have anything too gory in there. Not even for the zombie scenes."

"It was thick, dripping blood," Terrell called into the phone.

"Did you hear that?" Oren asked.

"I did — it's very worrying. We just don't have anything like that anywhere in the museum."

"I'm still patching the camera network. When I'm done, we should be able to monitor the whole museum, and get a better idea at what's going on in the exhibits. We should keep an open communication link."

"Good idea. Are you safe — I mean, the real you?"

"I should be all right, at least for a while."

"Let's hope so. I'm still reeling at the thought of Devansh being behind all this. Kidnapping, manipulation, espionage ... Lord Braighton was right about him all along."

"From what I've heard, his one goal is to destroy you and your company. Once he owns all your research, he plans to release his own version of Silicate under the BioLearn brand."

Padman wiped beads of sweat from his brow. If everything Oren was saying was true, he and Silicate were in serious trouble. Could this be linked to his missing staff? If Devansh was capable of kidnapping, what else might he do?

"For as long as I stay undetected, I'll be here to help you. Hopefully, working together, we can stop BioLearn, and whatever else Devansh has planned."

"Thank you." Padman placed the phone on his desk as he

searched for a Bluetooth headset. Fitting it to his ear, he pocketed his phone and turned to a confused Ryder.

"Ready for this?"

"Ready for what?"

The doctor paused, looked at MT and then back to Ryder.

"To be honest, I have no idea."

"And that *isn't* the real Terrell?" Ryder asked, pointing at MT.

"I'm not the real Terrell, but I have all of his memories up until around thirty minutes ago."

Ryder stared at MT uncomprehendingly and shrugged.

He turned to Padman.

"Do we have any weapons down here?"

"The only guns we have are of the staple variety. We're just scientists operating a museum, the thought of arming ourselves never crossed our minds."

"Looks like we're going in with my nightstick and twenty years' experience, then . . . you two better stay behind me."

"Actually, I can't get hurt. Maybe I should be in front?" MT asked.

"Apparition or not, you're still a young man in my eyes. I'd feel more comfortable if I knew you were safely behind me."

MT nodded as he and the doctor followed Ryder into the hub.

"Goodbye, Dorothy, goodbye, Scarecrow." Isabell waved to the host of characters who had gathered to see them off.

"I don't remember TikTok or Jack Pumpkinhead from the Wizard of Oz."

"They were characters in Return to Oz. There was a film made in the Eighties. It's a lot darker than the original."

"It seemed it. That Nome King was rather sinister. Beautiful land, though. Especially walking through the Emerald City."

"Thank you for skipping down the Yellow Brick Road with me. I've dreamed of doing that my whole life."

"And you think I haven't?"

They linked arms and giggled as they neared the exit.

"I think my favourite part was walking through Hogwarts. No, actually, it was meeting Gandalf. That wizards duel was epic! The Goblin King was a bit intimidating though."

"You think? All I could see was the gorgeous David Bowie. I always understood why Sarah was taken with him in the film."

"I've not —"

"Don't say it!" Isabell interrupted. "We've already established you're young and not seen most of the best films ever made, Labyrinth being one of them. I'm mentally adding it to the list. We'll be moving into the Red Room for a month at this rate."

"It's a date." Jake laughed, as they moved into Future Lock, the science fiction exhibition.

The door opened on to the bridge of the USS Enterprise. They were met by apparitions of every Star Trek captain, seated, awaiting their arrival. As Isabell and Jake walked in, James T. Kirk approached them.

"Welcome to the Enterprise, you've arrived just in time."

"What's the situation, Captain?" Jake asked, glancing around the room. "*Captains.*"

Isabell looked at him with surprised amusement.

"Play along, it'll be fun," he whispered.

"Q's up to his old tricks," Kirk continued.

"This time, bringing all of us together in an attempt to find the greatest Starfleet captain," Pike interjected.

"In defiance of him," Janeway continued, "we've agreed to work together in whatever frivolous scenario Q tries to throw at us." The captain sipped on her hot, black coffee.

"Kathy, I'm hurt." Q suddenly appeared on the bridge in a brilliant flash of light. "You, the godmother of my son — I hoped for so much more from you. Do you honestly believe that I would demean myself with anything less than fantastical? Frivolous endeavour, indeed."

"They usually are!" Picard responded, frowning.

"*Mon Capitan*, I'm wounded." The omnipotent being

clutched his chest through his Starfleet uniform in mock heartbreak. "No, no, no. This endeavour is far from frivolous. In fact, you could say it's a matter of life and death. For you, of course."

"Q! I demand you tell us what you're up to."

"Look who's here — Benjamin Sisko. This must be quite the adventure for you, experiencing what an actual Starfleet captain does for a change." Q snapped his fingers and an image of Earth appeared on the viewscreen. "Why, look! It's your home. Beautiful, isn't it? No war, no famine, no pesky money lining greedy pockets... You've built your own Utopia. It would be a shame if, say, the Borg *armada* were to show up and assimilate the whole planet into their collective."

"Q, don't do this. Please!" Captain Georgiou begged.

"Look, I don't know who you are, but you're obviously a very powerful and misunderstood being, but if we could —"

Q silenced Archer with a snap of his fingers, rendering the captain temporarily mute.

"That's better. Now, where were we? Ah, yes — the Borg. What would you do? How would you stop them? Surely, if I put every Starfleet captain in history together, they could combine their knowledge and find a solution . . .? I suppose there's only one way to test this theory, isn't there?" Q snapped his fingers and disappeared.

On the screen, Borg trans-warp apertures opened up around Earth, allowing a fleet of Borg cubes and spheres through.

"Battle stations. Red alert," the captains announced in unison.

Jake looked at Isabell with a beaming smile.

"This is going to be great!"

"Is there any way you can turn the lights up in here?" Ryder asked as he led the way through Myths and Monsters.

"We're working on it." Padman checked his earpiece was in

place. "Do you have access to the camera feeds yet, Oren?"

"Just a few more seconds... Yes, we can see you."

"Brilliant. Can you look inside the house we're about to enter?"

"No, something's blocking the cameras. We're getting a live-feed, but it's a black screen."

"That doesn't sound good." Padman looked at Ryder. "There could be trouble inside — the cameras are blocked."

Ryder nodded as he pushed himself up the ramp and placed his ear to the door. After a few moments, he looked back to Padman and MT and shook his head. Padman nodded and the ex-soldier pushed the door carefully. It creaked loudly as it opened. Ryder shot a look of annoyance towards the doctor, who shrugged in response.

"Horror exhibition!" he stage-whispered.

Ryder, realising there was no way they could do this stealth-ily, swung the door open with force and all three moved in-side.

"That's it. That's what I saw in my dream," MT gasped, point-ing at the hanging corpses.

"Are they part of the exhibition?" Ryder asked.

"No, they're not." Padman shuddered. "They're our missing staff members."

The doctor began to retch, turning to run out of the door. It slammed shut, locking them inside. Padman pulled the handle with all the strength he could muster, but some force kept it closed. A sudden creak in the floorboards made every-one spin around.

"What was that?" MT asked.

"Probably just a sound effect," Padman offered, his words lacking confidence.

"It could be the killer." Ryder edged around the corpses, checking the handles of all the other doors. Each of them, locked. "Someone doesn't want us leaving this room."

"What do you suggest we do?" Padman asked, turning away from his former colleagues' cadavers.

Ryder sized up the wooden door they'd entered through.

"If we use our combined strength, I think we could force it."

"I consider myself to be quite fit and healthy, but even I'm not Superman. These doors are made of steel."

"They look like wood."

"That's the effect we were going for, but wood's easily broken, so we opted for something more durable. Ironic, given our current situation. Oren, are you hearing all this?"

"We're with you. I'm looking for a way to deactivate the locking mechanisms."

"Look for a central folder called *Somnio Ops*, or something like that."

"OK, give me a sec . . ."

Padman heard mouse clicks and a series of keyboard strikes.

"Did that work?" Oren asked after a few moments.

Padman and Ryder both tried the door, but it still wouldn't budge.

"Unfortunately, not. It seems whoever wants us trapped in here, made sure we couldn't escape."

"I'll keep looking for a solution," Oren said. "Can you locate the cameras in there and clear whatever's covering them? I might be able to find another way out."

Padman pointed out the four cameras to Ryder and MT. The lenses had been covered in gaffer tape.

"Someone's gone to a lot of trouble to hide what's been going on in here," Ryder said grimly.

"I think I can climb up there and remove the tape," MT offered.

"Are you sure? It's pretty high," Padman pointed out.

"If you give me a boost, I should be able to use the gaps in the wooden slats to climb up. I used to, well, actually, *Terrell* used to climb trees when he was younger. I think I can make it. Don't be alarmed if I fall — I can't get hurt, remember?"

The real Terrell felt a rush of pride as he listened to his mirror version speak. He'd never thought of himself as brave before, but he was starting to see himself in a different light.

With Ryder's help, MT positioned the wheelchair as a boosting platform. He scaled the final stretch easily and ripped off the gaffer tape.

"Houston, we have vision." Oren cheered through the headpiece.

"You might want to shield Abby and Terrell's eyes from the monitors?" Padman said, conscious of the hanging bodies behind him.

"Got you," Oren responded as he ushered younger eyes to the other side of Archeus. The camera darted around the room, searching for an alternative exit. "Whoa, that's worse than I imagined. I'll try to get you out as fast as I can. It must really stink in there."

Padman's face dropped.

"What did you just say?"

"It looks like they've been hanging there for a while and I remember the smell from when our dog died. It was terrible. Hey! What are you doing?"

Padman had stopped listening. Instead, he was tugging on the corpse of the male nurse, Andrew.

"Doctor, have you lost your mind?" Ryder asked, concerned and repulsed.

"Help me, please. We need to get them down."

"Why?"

"Just help me!"

Ryder grimaced as he and Padman took a leg each and tugged on Andrew's corpse until the rope gave way, the nurse tumbling to the floor. Padman knelt down and lifted the nurse's head. It was covered in congealed blood.

Ryder watched, sickened, as the doctor touched his finger to the blood and then tasted it, before forcibly prying Andrew's lips open, pulling out his tongue, and peering closely at the insides of his mouth.

"Hasn't the poor man suffered enough?" Ryder couldn't bear to watch the scene.

"This man has suffered nothing."

Ryder and MT looked at Padman in confusion.

"In fact, he's not a *man* at all." He wiped his fingers along the tongue before standing up and displaying them for Ryder to see. "No blood, no saliva, nothing. If that wasn't convincing enough, there's no oesophagus or any kind of throat, at all. This isn't Andrew. It is an apparition of him."

"What?" Ryder and Oren asked in unison.

MT walked forward, willing himself to look at the nurse on the floor.

"He's like me?"

"Not exactly. This is a rough copy. The tongue stops at the back of the mouth, there's no throat, no eyeballs, and no lacerations in the skin. The blood seems to have been added after he was placed here."

"Are they all copies?" Ryder was staring at the two corpses still hanging from the rafters.

"Without a doubt."

"How do you know?" MT asked.

"It was Oren's comment about the how the room smelled — if these were corpses, there would be an overpowering, acrid stench, but there isn't.

"I think they were created like this."

"Who would do something so sick?" Ryder asked.

"Oren, how much of our research has BioLearn stolen?"

There was a pause on the other end of the line before Oren replied.

"They have everything." He sighed.

"Everything?" Padman was shocked and angry. "Do they have the technology up and running to create apparitions?"

"They do."

Padman let out a frustrated yell.

"What is it?" Ryder asked.

"Devansh! He's the one behind this. Not content with stealing all Silicate's research and destroying the company, now he's abducting my staff, as well."

"How do you know that?"

"These aren't true apparitions, but as crude as these might

be on the inside, the outward appearance is incredible. You would need a genetic copy to create something so realistic-looking. If I'm right, they've suffered the same fate as you, Oren—locked away in BioLearn's basement."

"That's very likely," Oren agreed. "If they do turn up here, I'll let you know."

"Why would Devansh do this and lock us into this room with them?" Ryder asked.

"He's taunting us. By trapping us in here, he's made me examine the corpses and realise what he's capable of — what he's done . . . Silicate's secrets are now his secrets. He wants me to know he's in control. With our systems compromised and the building in lockdown, we're completely powerless."

Padman leaned against the wall, sliding down until he reached a seated position on the floor with his head lowered. A mixture of anger, despair and sadness engulfing him.

"There must be something we can do?" Ryder's voice was full of concern.

Padman remained looking down, silent. MT knelt in front of him.

"Doctor, we need you. Tell us how to fix this."

Padman looked up, his eyes red and full of tears. He observed the boy in front of him, the mirror apparition of Terrell. A perfect recreation of the boy upstairs, totally independent and uniquely original. He wiped his eyes, a rush of adrenaline racing through his veins. He burst into laughter as he stood up.

"Doctor, are you OK?" Oren sounded concerned.

"I've never been better, but we have to get out of here." Synapses in his brain, all firing at once, brought fresh ideas and energy to the doctor's brilliant mind. "Oren, can you access my personal folder? It's on the desktop of my computer . . ." Padman rattled off a series of codes and commands; Oren's typing kept up; the sound of the rapid keystrokes audible over the earpiece.

"I'm in."

"Good. Go to the Somnio backup programmes . . . got it?

Yep. Yep. Look for the source code for the exhibits. Perfect. Copy that — great, then click back to the compromised active folder and paste over it. That *should* open the doors . . ."

Everyone remained silent as Oren continued to carry out Padman's instructions. Each second felt like an hour, but the next sound they heard was the locking mechanism clicking and the door opening wide.

"Great work, Oren." Padman raced out of the house followed by MT, with Ryder navigating the pathway as fast as he could in his chair.

"Keep up, we don't have much time," the doctor called.

"Much time for what?" Ryder asked, just as a loud noise behind him made him stop still and turn around. He caught the briefest of glimpses of a large object flying towards his face, then everything went dark.

CHAPTER 34

Bright, white light blinded Ryder as he opened his eyes. In a clouded daze, he attempted to look around, but everything appeared blurry. His brain registered he was lying on a bed. He could just make out the shape of a man, sitting at his bedside.

The blurry man moved closer; his features still obscured.

"You're waking up. I'm glad to see you're all right."

"Where am I?"

"You're in hospital, resting. How do you feel?"

Ryder paused, scanning his body for pain. There wasn't any.

"I'm OK, I think. I can't see very well, though."

"Your sight will return the more you use your eyes. Look around. You're safe." The man spoke softly, in a voice Ryder recognised, but couldn't place.

He squeezed his eyes tight-shut then opened them wide, in an attempt to clear his vision. The crisp, white bedlinen came into focus, then the aqua-blue walls and large window with the curtains drawn . . . Were those holograms dancing in the corner of the room? No . . . a TV screen.

Slowly, the man by his side became clearer, too. His hands, arms, torso, head, and, finally, his face.

Ryder jumped in shock, now wide-awake. He was looking at himself.

"There's no need to be frightened," the man said gently.

"Whoa! What is this? Who are you?"

"My name's Yoxdiosine. I'm your Keeper."

"Yoxdiosine? But you look just like me."

"I am you — and you are me — in a way."

"What does that mean?"

"It means just that. I'm the other version of you — the other half of you, the one who resides here and within you to keep you safe when you dream."

"I don't understand. Are you an apparition?"

"Not exactly."

"You're not making any sense." Ryder felt confused and agitated. "I don't understand what's going on and riddles are the last thing I need right now."

"I apologise. I'll leave you to wake up fully and come back in a little while." Yoxdiosine stood up.

"No. Please, stay. I need to understand what's going on."

The Keeper resumed his position next to the bed.

Ryder was still reeling from having a conversation with a man who looked identical to himself, but he needed answers.

"I'm sorry, it's just a little weird having a conversation with myself, Yoxdiosine, was it?"

"You may call me Yox, if that's easier."

"Yox, yeah — that works. How long have you been here?"

"In this room? I've been here as long as you have."

"Am I in a hospital?"

"Of sorts."

Ryder raised his eyebrow, prompting the Keeper to respond more directly.

"Yes, this is a hospital, but not a conventional one."

"You're still not making sense. Tell me exactly what's going on. Don't sugar-coat it. I'm used to difficult situations."

"I suppose that's true." Yox paused, trying to find the right words. "This'll be a lot to take in. I'm not entirely certain you're ready for the answers you crave."

"After the past few days, I'm open to anything."

"Very well." Yox shrugged. "You're in a hospital, but we're

not on Earth. This is Aetheri, my home. It's a realm, a plane of existence, an entire universe different from your own, yet it's the place every human being comes to in their dreams. It's also where they reside when they leave their mortal coils behind."

Ryder shook his head.

"OK, maybe I wasn't ready for this."

"Do you remember the last thing that happened to you before you woke up here?"

"I think so." Ryder tried to focus. "I was in the museum. We were trapped in the horror exhibition. As I was leaving, I heard a noise behind me. I turned around and everything went dark, then I woke up."

"You were attacked. The blow to your head was fatal. You died, and I brought you here."

"I'm dead?"

"From your mortal life, yes. But the essence of you, your consciousness, is still very much alive and will continue on in Aetheri."

"For how long?"

"For ever. We have no death here . . . No pain, no suffering. It's a world of your making, a life you've only ever dreamed of."

"Is this heaven?"

"Many humans describe it that way, but this is not the heaven depicted in religious texts. There are no gods nor omnipotent beings presiding over you. In Aetheri, you're in control of your own destiny."

"Why would you do this for me?"

"This universe belongs to you as much as it does to us. You gave birth to our species and in turn, everything you see around you.

"Come to the window with me, I'd like to show you something." Yox moved towards the window, leaving Ryder to scan the room for his chair. "You don't need that anymore," Yox said, smiling. "Your legs work fine, if you want them to."

Ryder shifted his right leg tentatively. It moved. He applied more pressure and kicked it out over the side of the bed.

"How is this possible?" he breathed.

"Anything is possible here."

Carefully, Ryder placed both feet on the ground and raised himself off the bed slowly. A little wobbly, he walked over to join Yox.

"Do you know where we are?" the Keeper asked.

Ryder stared across the rocky, frozen landscape. He scanned the terrain towards the horizon. In the sky he could see the unmistakable rings of Saturn. Ryder had to hold on to the wall to balance himself as the realisation hit home.

"We're on Titan."

"We're actually on the version of Titan you dreamed as a child. We're standing in the hospital wing of the moon base your subconscious built on Shangri-La."

Ryder was speechless. The space buggies, the buildings, and even the giant rocket with his name embossed along the length of it. This was the place he had escaped to when he was younger, when his greatest dream was to be an astronaut.

He turned to Yox, a myriad of questions racing through his mind. The Keeper smiled knowingly. He pressed a button on the wall and the full-length window opened up, revealing the moon's terrain. Ryder recoiled at first, expecting them to be sucked into the vacuum of space. Instead, he found himself able to breathe; the temperature in the room remained unchanged. Following Yox, he cautiously stepped on to the moon's surface, finding that despite being barefoot, the coarse sand and jagged rocks didn't cause his feet any pain.

"We are the Qas'ihar," Yox began as they walked side-by-side. "When you sleep, we wake and when you wake, we sleep. We're two separate species, living in two different realities and yet we're tied to one another, each sharing the same body, the same consciousness.

"The Qas'ihar occupy a plane of reality separate from yours, but also connected. Billions of years ago, during the formation of your solar system, Jupiter was on course to swallow the then-developing inner planets. It was the newly formed

Saturn which had enough mass to pull it back into the orbit it resides in today. This interstellar tug of war of the gas giants created a substantial amount of gravitational friction, causing the very fabric of reality to tear. Although microscopic at the time, this rupture grew, eventually bridging our two universes together.

"While you built planets, suns and galaxies, our universe lay dormant, an endless vacuum of electrical particles and gases. Billions of years passed before life began. Venus was the first, followed by Mars and eventually Earth.

"During all that time, Aetheri had been bleeding through the tear — small amounts of our universe mixing with yours. Life evolved, giving birth to amoebas, dinosaurs, and mammals ... but on Earth, it wasn't until a hundred and fifty thousand years ago that there was enough material from Aetheri to boost your evolutionary process, creating a symbiotic species built from both of our universes. Humans and Qas'ihar are one and the same."

Ryder was sitting on a rock next to Yox, looking out over the sand dunes, towards Saturn. He desperately tried to assimilate what he was hearing.

"How do you know all of this? How do you know so much about us when we've never even heard of the Qas'ihar or Aetheri?"

"Every human knows of this place. This is where you dream. We have likely avoided detection due to our molecular structure simply being too alien for you to understand. Until that time, we'll remain an essential yet invisible part of you."

"How did you discover us?"

"We share the same body, the same brain. All human knowledge is Qas'ihar knowledge. By you learning about your universe, we learned about ours. We can't take corporeal form here, but we can use the electrical particles to create the illusion of form. You gave us life. In return, we give you this."

"Titan?"

"It doesn't have to be, we could be sitting on a beach or at the top of Everest. Anything you dream is possible. When a human dies, their Keeper brings them here — to their own, personal paradise."

"You're telling me every person who has ever lived and died is here right now?"

"Every single one."

"Where are they all?"

"The universe is a pretty big place. We have a population of approximately two hundred billion lifeforms, both human and Qas'ihar. Whereas your universe is made up of planets and galaxies, we have a constant, molecular body stretching out across the vastness of space. All connected, never changing. Only consciousness can survive here." Yox stamped his foot on the ground, making a thudding sound. "This feels like rock, but it isn't."

Instantly, the landscape changed, and they were surrounded by a dense, white fog.

Ryder almost fell to his knees.

"What just happened? Where are we now?"

"In the same place we were just a moment ago. This is Aetheri. Before joining with humans, this was all there was. Through your consciousness, you sculpt and mould the atoms all around us, creating anything you desire."

Ryder peered through the dense fog, trying to see anything beyond it.

"How does it work? How do I dream something into existence?"

"Imagine yourself somewhere and it'll appear."

The white fog gave way to the green grass of a London park.

"It worked!" Ryder spun around, taking in the scenery. "This is Kensington Park. Or, at least, how I remember it." Ryder stared with the intensity and wonder of a child, and then, just as quickly, his smile faded.

"What's wrong?" Yox asked.

"My mother. This place reminds me of her. We didn't have a good relationship, but she used to bring me here when I was a child. That's always how I've tried to remember her. I'd give anything to see her again. We left so much unsaid. There was so much I didn't understand . . ."

"Look behind you."

Ryder turned around to see his mother, standing mere metres away from him, arms outstretched. In amazement, Ryder embraced her and held her close as he wept.

"Here, anything and anyone you think of will appear. This is your home — you can create it just as you wish, with whoever you want," Yox explained.

Ryder couldn't take his eyes from Maria.

"You're saying she's not real?"

"She's as real as you want her to be."

"But if she's the mother from my own memory, she won't have the answers I need." Ryder watched as Maria faded away. "You said every human comes here when they die, so could I see her? My actual mother?"

"I'm sorry, that isn't possible. When someone dreams, they create their own pocket of reality here in Aetheri. Over time, that pocket grows larger. Eventually, it becomes a planet-sized home for their imagination. Our universe is as big as yours, only without the separation of galaxies or spatial clusters. Instead, we just have the fog you saw earlier. The chances of two humans inhabiting an area close to one another is infinitesimally small."

"Can we at least communicate?"

"Sorry. No."

"Could you contact her for me?"

Yox walked over to a park bench and sat down, indicating to Ryder to sit next to him.

"For a long time, when humans died and came to Aetheri, we would explain what this place was and how they had gotten here, very much like I'm doing with you now. It caused a lot of distress. Their Keeper would stay with them during their adjustment period, but many people never truly accepted being here.

"Millenia ago, the Qas'ihar decided to stop this practice, allowing their human counterparts to awaken in Aetheri, with no knowledge of where they are. There is disorientation at first, but eventually they adjust and are happy. With no-one to tell them otherwise, some believe the people and places they imagine are real, while others reason that they are in a constant dream-state."

"A dream that lasts an eternity. What if it's a nightmare?"

"Their Keeper still resides with them, acting as their own reflection to help and guide them."

"You stay with us, for ever?"

"We *are* you. Where else would we go?"

Ryder paused for a moment.

"Why tell me all this? What makes me different?"

"The brain of a soldier, always questioning." Yox chuckled. "I knew you were the right candidate."

"Candidate? For what?"

Yox looked serious.

"The Qas'ihar reside inside of you when you sleep, connecting our two realities inside every human being. That connection has been compromised. Our universe is being stripped away, slowly, bit by bit."

"The apparitions."

"Exactly. They're literal pieces of our home, extracted through the Keepers and into your world. It threatens to destroy our universe. If it does, it'll take your afterlife, too."

"What can I do?"

"Something that's been attempted very rarely. We have to send you back to Earth."

CHAPTER 35

Padman came to a halt as he reached the centre of the hub. The unmistakable sound of giant herbivores pounding their feet above him gave cause to look up. What's gotten into them, he wondered, before turning around at the sound of MT's footsteps behind him.

"You OK?"

"Yeah, I'm fine. It's quite exhilarating not having lungs to slow me down."

"I'll take your word for it." Padman smiled as he scanned the area for his chief of security.

"Where's Ryder?"

"He should be right behind me. Maybe his wheelchair got stuck on the path or something?"

"That seems a bit odd . . ." Padman walked back into the exhibition. "Ryder!" he called, passing through the door. "You aren't flirting with Sidney Prescott, are you?" The doctor chuckled. "She won't fancy you unless you're wearing a Scream mask, you know."

As he neared the house, his smile fell away. He could see something at the bottom of the path — Ryder, on the floor, his wheelchair on its side next to him.

"Ryder, what happened?" The doctor checked his wrist for a pulse but there wasn't one. He moved to the carotid artery in the neck, spotting the result of blunt-force trauma to Ryder's face for the first time.

"Ryder! RYDER!" Padman shouted, attempting CPR in a frantic yet futile attempt at resuscitation. Sitting back on his hind legs, Padman hung his head, defeated, unable to save the man in front of him.

Oren spoke into the doctor's ear.

"What happened? Is Ryder OK?"

"He's dead."

"What? How?"

"It looks like someone struck him. Did you see anything on the monitors?"

"I was following you. Hold on, let me wind back the footage."

Padman examine the body more closely.

"He's been hit in the head — hard. It's crushed his skull. He would have been killed instantly."

"I see Ryder falling, but whoever attacked him knew how to avoid the cameras." Oren's voice was choked with emotion.

"Damn!" Padman shouted, hitting the ground with his fists.

"Is the weapon near the body? It was moving too fast for me to see what it was. That might give us a clue."

Padman searched the area.

"Nothing. They've either taken it with them or it's lost somewhere in the scenery."

"Did you just say 'body'?" Abby's small voice piped up behind Oren.

"No, Abby. Don't look at this, sweetheart. Go and help Terrell — I'll be with you in a minute."

Noticing the quiver in her father's voice, Abby simply nodded and moved away. Oren turned back to the monitor.

"You need to get out of there, Padman. Whoever attacked Ryder is probably still inside."

Padman stood up slowly.

"You're right. I'm heading back to the hub now."

Oren followed him on the monitors until the doctor was reunited with MT.

"Where's Ryder?" MT asked, putting down the map of Somnio.

"He won't be joining us. I'm afraid someone attacked him and —" Padman closed his eyes, forcing himself to maintain composure.

MT swallowed hard.

The doctor laid a hand on MT's shoulder in a gesture of solidarity, inhaling sharply.

"Oren, I need you to find out where Jake and Isabell are, please."

"Checking." Oren scanned through the different rooms' cameras. "They're on a movie set with Emma Stone and Daniel Kaluuya."

"They're in Stage and Screen — we're on our way. Oren, I really need those house lights on and for you to shut down the exhibits."

"I am trying, but with so many corrupted files, it's made the system even more complicated to navigate. I'll double my efforts."

"Thank you. Come on, MT — we have to find the others before that maniac does."

"What do we have to do?" Isabell asked.

"You and Emma are playing girlfriends who are having a coffee together when you spot two men on another table who start flirting with you. Let Emma do the talking, follow her lead." Robert Zemeckis sat back in his director's chair and signalled to the camera operator to move closer to the set. "And . . . ACTION!"

The house lights came on suddenly. Not knowing if this was part of the scene or not, Isabell and Jake shot each other a sideways glance and shrugged.

Emma and Daniel stood up without saying a word and walked away, joining the other apparitions in the exhibition who were moving, en masse, towards the other side of the room.

"Hey! What's going on?" Isabell called, rising from her seat.

Jake walked over to her.

"Is this supposed to happen?"

"I'm not sure."

"I told you we should have done that Last Week Tonight skit with John Oliver."

A crashing sound behind them made Jake and Isabell turn around to see Padman and MT racing towards them.

"Good, you're both OK." The doctor was panting heavily.

"Is that the end of the tour? We haven't done the musical section yet. We were just about to act out a scene with —"

"Ryder's dead," Padman interrupted. "We need to get out of here."

"What?"

"Murdered. The killer's still in the museum somewhere. We need to get back to my office, where it's safe."

The walk back was slow. MT, unable to be hurt, positioned himself in the front of the group. Despite not having a heart, his felt heavy, as did the others'. Isabell wept for Ryder, reeling from the shock of his death.

The group walked cautiously through the museum. The rooms looked eerie in shutdown mode. The apparitions were programmed to take themselves to a storage bunker beneath the stadium, usually used for maintenance or repair.

Oren monitored the screens closely, investigating any anomalies or potential sightings carefully. Padman's heart was racing for the whole journey. He felt thankful to have Jake's hand in his as they made the long walk back.

They reached the door to the office but before Padman could scan his security pass, Isabell held her hand over the panel.

"What if he's inside? What if the killer's waiting there for us?"

"Impossible. They would need my pass to get in."

Isabell kept her hand where it was. Padman nodded.

"You're right, it's best to be cautious. Oren, could you scan the room for us please? Just to make sure no-one's in there."

"Already done. You're clear to enter."

The door opened and everything was how it had been an hour before. They pulled up chairs around Padman's desk as silence fell over the group. The immediate panic over, grief and shock began to set in.

"We can bring him back!" Isabell announced, standing up so fast that her chair whizzed backwards across the office. Everyone looked at up, aghast. She pointed to MT.

"He's an apparition of Terrell, right? We can do the same for Ryder."

"I was created by Terrell — I'm a mirror version, not an apparition," MT stated.

"He's right. Ryder would need to be alive to produce a mirror version. Even then, Terrell's the only person who's ever managed it," Padman added.

Isabell tucked her hair behind her ears and composed herself.

"OK, so we can't have a mirror version of Ryder. What if I dreamed about him and you made him real, or whatever you do here?"

The doctor stood up to join Isabell and spoke softly and patiently.

"Then we would create a version of him that only lives in your memory. You've only known him a few days — I fear it would be an empty shell of a person."

"Surely it's better than nothing? We talked for hours . . . I feel like I was really getting to know him."

"I understand how much this hurts. We've all bonded so much. It's cruel and unjust for Ryder to . . ." The doctor's voice caught in his throat, heavy with emotion. "Isabell, it could make the grieving process much harder. He'd become another apparition, tied to this museum, with only a limited amount of knowledge."

Isabell began to cry.

"I just don't want him to be dead."

Padman felt her pain. He looked at Jake, the realisation that he had known him for the same length of time Isabell had known Ryder dawning on him. What would he do, if the situation was different? He turned back to Isabell.

"If we do this, you must understand, Ryder will be bound to this facility. Apparitions can't survive outside the building. As soon as they leave, their molecular structure begins to break down. They look like a ghost for a short while before disappearing completely."

Isabell hung on every word, nodding her head in acceptance of what Padman was saying.

"Given all those limitations, are you sure this is what you want?"

Isabell wiped her eyes and took a deep breath before replying.

"Yes."

Padman exhaled loudly.

"OK, then." He resumed his seat at the desk and accessed a file on his computer. "Oren, I'm still locked out of most systems. Can you keep monitoring the museum while we're in the lab? And any chance you can apply your hacking skills to restoring my access?"

"Of course. All three of us are working hard up here."

"I know you are." Padman smiled tiredly. "Thank you. Sorry for putting everything on your shoulders."

"Don't worry about it — that's why I'm here."

"We're heading for Archeus Five — it's the closest one to us." He turned to Isabell. "I'll have to sedate you, if that's OK?"

Isabell nodded.

"Oren, we shouldn't be more than an hour, hopefully less." The doctor stood up. "Right, let's get Ryder back."

For the first time since hearing the news of the tragedy, Isabell allowed herself to smile.

CHAPTER 36

Oren was typing as fast as his fingers would allow. He was so concentrated on his work that he didn't hear his daughter approach.

"Daddy, can we talk, please?"

Oren could hear the emotion in her voice.

"Of course, darling—just give me one more second."

He finished typing and closed down the system folders. The word *sent* and, shortly after, *received*, flashed in the corner of the screen. Oren turned his attention to Abby, offering her the chair beside him.

"Now, baby, what's on your mind?"

Abby sat down, facing her father square-on.

"I know what happened to Ryder. Are we in danger?"

Oren reached his hands out, grasping Abby's as he looked into her deep, blue eyes.

"You really have become a beautiful young woman. I'm so proud to see how you've turned out. I'm sorry I wasn't around to watch you grow up. In my mind, you're still that little girl who wouldn't sleep without one of my songs.

"But you're not a child any more — you deserve to know the truth." Oren paused and let his eyes be drawn to the screen for a moment. The word *received* remained visible in the corner. Oren felt a renewed vigour.

"Ryder was attacked, but the others are safe. As for us, as long as I'm here counteracting BioLearn's assault, we're safe, too." Oren sighed. "Unfortunately, we won't be able to hold them off for ever, but I've got a plan."

He looked over at Terrell, working on a laptop at the other side of the room.

"Could you join us, please?"

"Sure, what's up?" Terrell walked over to them.

"I have just sent an email on an encrypted channel to every news, police and government address I could think of, both here and in the States; something I wasn't able to do at BioLearn." He smiled towards Abby. "I also sent one to Mom."

"Hopefully someone will see it in time and come to our rescue."

"We still can't use the phones?" Abby asked.

"Unfortunately, not. Those systems are corrupted beyond repair — BioLearn made sure of that, and we can't use the cell phones to dial out of the building."

"Won't an email look a bit dodgy, though?" Terrell questioned.

"I've also attached data files to add weight to it, which should be all the proof they need. We only need one person to follow it up."

"What if nobody does?" Abby asked nervously.

"I've thought about that too sweetheart. I created a system folder called *Activate Somnio* and placed it on Doctor Sharma's computer."

"What does it do?" Abby asked.

"It will give us the power to defend ourselves, and hopefully regain control of Silicate."

"Why don't you use it now?"

"It wouldn't help us. It's a last resort measure — only to be used if our backs are against the wall. And if I've been captured." Oren shuddered at the thought.

"Does Doctor Sharma know about this?" Terrell asked.

"Not yet. I don't want to risk informing him through internal communications, in case BioLearn has hacked into those systems, too. This information must be given to him in person.

"That's where you come in, Terrell. I need you to send another mirror version of yourself down to the lab and let Padman know about the folder. When the time comes, all he has to do to is open it up and enter his password."

Terrell nodded, rose from his chair and climbed back into Meditati.

"Let's go."

Abby and Oren approached the bed. Terrell closed his eyes while Oren monitored his heartrate on-screen. It stayed the same.

After a few minutes, Terrell opened his eyes, looking at Oren and Abby in frustration before screwing his eyes closed and willing himself to fall to sleep. He stayed like that until his face hurt.

"Why's it not working?"

"I'm not sure. Your heartrate isn't dropping — if anything, it's gone up. Perhaps it's the stress of the situation," Oren offered. "Take a few moments to relax."

Terrell closed his eyes, gently this time, inhaled deeply and exhaled slowly. After a few moments, he sat up.

"Bloody brain. I think you're going to have to sedate me."

"You didn't need sedating before," Abby pointed out.

"I need it now," Terrell snapped.

Abby looked hurt.

"Sorry, Abby. I think you're right, Oren — I am stressed." Terrell looked at Abby apologetically as he lay back down.

"Okay, Terrell, injecting you now."

There was a sharp, short hissing sound, knocking Terrell unconscious instantly.

Oren hugged his daughter.

"Don't take it personally, darling — he didn't mean anything by it."

"I know, Daddy. I'm not upset about that, I'm worried that if this doesn't work, the killer will attack again."

He held his daughter tight; the same thought had been running through his mind.

"You shouldn't think like that. This will work. We're going to save everyone, and before you know it, you, me and your mom will finally be together again."

"I hope so, Daddy." Abby turned to the monitor. "His heartrate's dropping."

"You see? What did I tell you?" Oren replied with a smile.

Terrell jumped up from the bed, gasping for air.

"RYDER!" he screamed, before falling back down and into a deep sleep.

"What happened?" Abby was clearly shaken.

"I'm not sure, but his heartrate has returned to normal."

"What does that mean?"

"It means he's not dreaming. We'll keep monitoring him and perhaps he'll return to his REM cycle."

A bleeping sound from the computer made them both turn around.

"Oh, no!" Oren raced back to his seat and began hammering into the keyboard. "They've almost broken through all my security countermeasures. I'll have to stop them manually."

"What about Terrell?"

"He's fine. He's just sleeping. He should wake up soon."

"What about telling Doctor Sharma about the folder?"

Oren was working intensely now.

"This is more important, Abby," Oren explained. "Doctor Sharma might not even need it. Sorry, darling, I need to concentrate on this."

Abby was standing in the middle of Archeus, at a loss as to what to do. She looked over at her father, who was typing furiously. Terrell was asleep and not likely to wake up any time soon, but at least he was safe, unlike the others. The doctor needed the information only the three of them knew. She looked at the laptop resting in front of her, remembering her father's words from earlier in the night.

"If I'm captured, they'll sever the connection I have with this form. If that happens, use the emergency folder I've created for you on this laptop. It'll open any door in the building," Oren had said.

Abby opened the laptop now, her eyes focusing immediately on the emergency folder, there on the desktop, ready and waiting for her. She had to do this; she was the only one who could. As she moved the cursor across the screen, she noticed the drawer below her was partially open. Inside were more of the same cell phones her father was using to communicate with the others. She carefully collected one and, noting the extension number, slid it into her pocket.

Oren was still immersed in combatting BioLearn's attack. Capitalising on his distraction, and without giving it a second thought, she accessed the folder on the laptop. The elevator door opened instantly and she rushed inside, repeatedly pressing the *Down* button before her father could stop her.

Oren looked up just in time to see the door closing, his daughter inside. She waved the phone at him.

"Five, five, nine, nine," she managed to rush out, breathlessly, as the doors closed between them.

Oren rushed over to the elevator, too late.

"Abby! No!" he cried, hammering the wall with his fists. Bleeping from the computer intensified. He had to prioritise, and fast. He couldn't stop the elevator, he couldn't leave Archeus and Terrell vulnerable, and he needed to continue his defence against BioLearn's cyber-attacks. While the thought made his stomach twist in anxiety, he was going to have to trust his little girl to keep herself safe, while he could only follow her progress via the security cameras.

Back at his desk, he clicked through to the live-feed from the elevator, ready to track Abby as she navigated through Somnio. He reached for his phone and dialled the extension for the handset Abby had taken with her.

"Abby? Abby — are you there?"

"Hi, Daddy."

"Abby, please come back upstairs where it's safe."

"I'm sorry, Daddy, but you know I can't."

Oren massaged his face as he thought. This was his daughter, the light of his life, who he hadn't seen in years. He wanted to be able to protect her; instead, here she was trying to protect everyone.

"I'll direct you through the museum," he said, sounding resigned. "If I tell you to stop — you stop. If I tell you to run — you run. Do you understand?"

"Yes, Daddy. Thank you."

"Please be careful. Promise me."

"I promise."

The elevator doors opened and Abby stepped out tentatively, looking up and down the long corridor. A shudder ran through her body.

Pull yourself together, Abigale, she told herself silently. You can do this.

"Where's all the rubber?" Isabell asked as they walked in to Archeus Five.

"Here she goes again. You're obsessed!" Jake said.

"If this is a duplicate of the room upstairs, how come the walls aren't covered in rubber? I thought you said they were needed to protect against electric shocks or something?"

"Now that we don't produce the apparitions in the same space any more, we don't need the rubber," Padman explained.

Isabell walked up and examined the bed.

"Found some! The bed is still lined with it."

"Are you happy now?" Jake asked mockingly.

"It's actually a breathable, non-conductive fabric which only feels like rubber. Sorry to disappoint." Padman adjusted Meditati and tilted it forwards, allowing Isabell to step inside it.

"Do you need me to undress?"

"That won't be necessary. As long as I can access your neck for the sedation, you'll be fine."

"It feels weird getting into bed with my clothes on," she commented, stepping into the grooves of Meditati.

As Padman tilted the bed backwards, it automatically adjusted to fit Isabell's body, securing her comfortably.

"Is it meant to do that? I've never been in this thing fully conscious before."

"It's just to keep you safe and secure," Padman assured her, bringing up the floating screen.

"Whoa! What's that?"

"It's a screen for me to monitor your vitals on . . . nothing to worry about, I promise."

Isabell stared at the backwards text.

"It's hurting my eyes."

"Close them, then," Jake called from the bottom of the bed.

"Shut up, you!" Isabell chuckled. She closed her eyes and tried to settle her breathing. "OK, Doc. Let's do this."

"I'm going to give you a small dose of sedative. You may feel a cool sensation on your neck." Padman injected Isabell, who fell asleep instantly.

"I hope this works for her," MT said, watching her heartrate slowly decrease on the monitor.

"We all do," Padman said. "It shouldn't take too long before —"

A notification on the monitor caused the doctor to stop speaking mid-sentence.

"What's wrong?" Jake asked.

"Nothing's wrong, as such, I've just never seen it work so fast before. We already have two apparitions coming through."

"She's not been asleep a minute yet." Jake moved forward to get a better view of the screen. "I know."

"How long before the apparitions materialise?" MT asked.

"It has to go through quite a few processors first. Isabell will likely have regained consciousness by that time.

"I'm sure she'll want to be the first to greet Ryder when he arrives."

"You said two apparitions were coming through?"

"It's probably a mistake with the system. It says two, but they both appear to be Ryder."

Jake and MT sat down at the back of the room while Padman monitored Isabell. As Jake watched the colours and images on the floating screen, his mind wandered.

"Do you think we should be doing this? I was as up for it as everyone else, but now we're here, what if it's not a good idea to bring him back? It won't really be *him*, will it?"

"No, it won't. And, perhaps, you're right . . . but given the circumstance, I had to try. To be honest, I'm not even sure it'll work."

"Have you done this before?" MT asked.

"Never successfully. Lady Braighton desperately wanted to see her daughter again. We tried repeatedly to create an apparition of Maria, yet she never materialised.

"We still don't understand why. There's a theory that perhaps it's our brains that won't let us do this. Grieving's a natural process — we all have to go through it at some point — and I suppose there's an argument to be made against whipping up a new copy."

"Maybe we should abort and tell her it didn't work?" Jake offered.

Padman thought for a moment.

"I couldn't do that to her," he said thoughtfully. "The least we can do it try." As he turned back to the screen, Isabell began to stir. "I think she's waking up."

"Already? Didn't you say it would take about an hour?" Jake asked.

"I did. I can't explain what's happening."

Isabell's eyes opened wide and locked on to Padman's.

"Did it work?"

"Welcome back." Padman retracted the screen and helped her sit up. "We won't know for sure until we get to the lab."

Still a little drowsy, Isabell hopped out of Meditati, aided by Padman.

"I really think you should rest a little longer."

"I'm fine," she replied firmly, leaning on the doctor. "Which way to the lab?" She swayed a little, Jake catching her before she collapsed.

"Isabell, you need to stay in bed, at least until the sedative has worn off," Padman suggested.

"No!" Isabell was resolute. "I want to be there when he arrives."

Jake and Padman exchanged glances, realising there was no use in arguing with her. MT opened the door as Jake and Padman, still supporting Isabell, edged their way out of Archeus Five and towards the Living Lab.

CHAPTER 37

"OK, sweetheart, I see you. This next door will take you into the main entrance. You'll see the first exhibition room over on the right-hand side." Oren had an eye on Abby's movements on one monitor whilst he simultaneously tried to suppress BioLearn's attack on another screen.

"And you're sure there's no-one on the other side of this door?" Abby's voice wobbled.

"Promise — it's completely empty. All the lights are on in the museum and you've got a clear path all the way to the doctor's office. If there's a door that needs opening, I can do it remotely."

"Thanks, Daddy."

"Who are you talking to?" Terrell was sitting up in bed, looking around, in a state of confusion.

"Is that Terrell? Has he woken up?" Abby asked.

"It is."

"Tell him I say 'hi'."

"Abby says hello," Oren said, looking over his shoulder briefly before turning his attention back to the monitors.

Terrell stretched, jumped out of Meditati and scanned the room as he made his way across to Oren.

"Where is she?"

Oren pointed to the monitor on his left. Terrell wiped his

eyes.

"She's in the museum! Why is she down there?" he demanded.

Oren muted the phone.

"While you were sleeping and I was distracted, she ran into the elevator, believing she was the only person left who could tell Padman about the programme I created. When you speak to her, please don't mention any of this over the call. We don't know who might be listening in."

"I'm going down there. She's not safe on her own." Terrell opened the laptop, looking for the emergency folder.

"Wait! Don't you go rushing off, too. I need you here to guide Abby through the museum. BioLearn have amped up their attacks — I'm struggling to keep them out and guide Abby at the same time."

"Why can't I just go down there and meet up with her?"

"We'd end up with the same problem, Terrell — I'd have to guide you both through," Oren replied, his fingers typing as he talked.

Terrell stopped and breathed deeply.

"I know you want to help her — we both do. This is the only way. If I can't stop BioLearn, they'll infiltrate the museum before you or Abby could even get to the doctor."

Terrell plopped down on the chair next to Oren's.

"OK. You keep them out, I'll keep Abby safe."

"Thank you. The guiding part's easy now all the lights are on. What's more critical is watching for anyone else who might be lurking about, but that should be easier with the apparitions in storage. Here — use this phone. I've been juggling two calls at once. How are you feeling, anyway?"

Terrell accepted the phone and inserted the earpiece.

"Physically fine, mentally upset. If I'd have created another MT, Abby would still be here."

"Don't blame yourself. There's nothing more you could have done."

"You're very quiet up there. Is everything OK, Daddy?"

Abby's voice sounded anxious in Terrell's earpiece.

"Apart from you going on an adventure without me, everything's peachy," he responded.

"Hey, Terrell! Good sleep?"

"Not really. I'll tell you about it later. Your dad's asked me to guide you through the museum."

"It's pretty straightforward, actually. The rooms are huge, but they're mostly empty, so I've just been looking for the next door and then walking through it. Even with the lights on, it's creepy, though. I keep expecting to see someone jump out from somewhere."

"That's what you've got me for — professional lurker-lookout services."

"That's reassuring, thank you."

Terrell saw the briefest of smiles flicker across Abby's face.

"I'm heading into the second room now."

"I'm with you," Terrell promised.

Oren looked over at the young man leaning forward, staring at the screen and studying every aspect of the room ahead. He knew Abby was in safe hands, he just hoped it was enough.

Isabell felt sick to her stomach, excited and still a little woozy. She questioned whether she was doing the right thing, reminding herself that this wasn't going to be *Ryder*, just a ghost of what he was.

What if it didn't work — would they try again? Did she want to try again? Should she be doing this at all? A never-ending cycle of thoughts and questions circled around her head as she sat on a chair Padman had pulled from one of the offices.

The doctor had sent the images to the first row of pods in the Living Lab. He still wasn't entirely sure what to expect; a dual image of the same apparition hadn't happened before — it was believed to be impossible. He had double- and triple-checked the readings, always with the same result. The computer wouldn't let him send just one, so he activated two pods, surmising it was potentially an error due to the system being compromised.

He gathered the group around Pod Twenty-two, choosing not to inform Isabell of the anomaly.

Both pods activated at the same time, shooting a mix of colours and gases into the glass cubes. The process was faster than Isabell had imagined; within seconds, an apparition was created in front of her eyes.

Padman's back shielded the group from a clear view of Pod Twenty-three, and while everyone watched Ryder and his wheelchair materialise, the doctor glanced behind him. His involuntary gasp caused everyone to turn around.

"Why are there two of him?" Isabell asked, confused.

As the smoke cleared, Padman stood back, revealing both pods. Twenty-two housed Ryder in his wheelchair; in Twenty-three, there was another Ryder, standing unaided, no wheelchair in sight.

"And why is that one standing up?" Isabell peered closely at the second Ryder.

"Perhaps your brain dreamed of the Ryder you know, and the Ryder you imagined without the wheelchair?" Jake offered.

"That shouldn't make a difference. They're still the same person. I don't know how this is even possible," Padman admitted.

MT walked up to the glass of Twenty-three and regarded the apparition closely before stepping away wordlessly.

Ryder in Twenty-two tapped on the glass and waved at the group as they turned their attention to him.

"What do we do?" Jake asked.

"They've both been through the system and wouldn't be here if they hadn't passed the security checks," Padman informed them.

"We let them out," Isabell said decisively, reaching for the handle and opening the door.

"Thank you." Ryder wheeled himself forward and wrapped

his arms around Isabell. "I knew you'd bring me back."

Isabell teared up as she held him. When they parted, Ryder turned to Padman.

"You can let him out, too — he's with me."

"What do you mean, he's *with* you?"

"That's my Keeper. He can explain it better than I can."

Confused, the doctor opened the pod door.

"Thank you, Doctor. It's nice to finally meet you all in the flesh, so to speak." Yox stepped out of the pod and joined Ryder, his smile never faltering.

A wave of confusion rippled over the group.

"What's going on?" Isabell asked.

"What we're about to tell you is pretty mind-blowing, but please try to keep an open mind." Ryder smiled and turned to Padman. "Didn't you say something similar to us earlier, Doctor?"

◆ ◆ ◆

"OK, I'm down the ramp."

"You're inside the hub. You'll see loads of doors. The one you want is hidden. Walk forward, past the shops and around to the right. The doctor's office is at the end of that path."

"Cool." Abby followed Terrell's instruction.

"OK, I see it. Is there anyone inside?"

"Yeah. There's only one camera in there, and it's a bit obscured by a plant or something, but I can definitely see someone sitting at a desk with two people standing next to them. I don't see me, though."

"You? Oh, you mean MT. Maybe he went to the toilet or something?"

Terrell laughed.

"I don't think apparitions need to pee."

"Oh, yeah, probably not."

"Your dad's shaking his head, so I think that's a no."

"Can I speak to him or is he still busy?"

"Even busier. If he were really here, his fingers would be bleeding, he's typing so fast."

"Nice visual of my father bleeding all over the keyboard, Terrell — thanks for that. Right, I'm outside. There's a sign on the door saying *office* and *staff only*."

"Sounds like you're in the right place." He nodded to Oren, who opened the door, allowing Abby to move inside.

She spotted people surrounding one of the desks at the back of the office.

"Hi," she called, "it's me — Abby. I just came down to speak to Doctor Sharma."

The two figures in front of her didn't reply.

"Abby, are you OK? The camera's gone dark. I can't see you."

"I'm just walking over to the doctor now. I thought you said there were three —"

The phone cut off.

"Abby? Abby are you there?" Terrell looked terrified.

Oren touched his arm, his eyes wide with panic.

"Go — now!"

Clutching the phone, Terrell sprinted to back wall, waiting for Oren to activate the elevator. He ran inside and looked towards Oren, adrenaline pumping through his veins.

"Save my daughter."

"I will. I promise."

CHAPTER 38

"You're telling me there's a Keeper inside my body — inside all of our bodies — right now?" Padman asked incredulously. He, Isabell and Jake were listening intently, yet not able to comprehend nor accept what they were being told.

"Only when you sleep. But yes, we're a part of you, a part of all human life." Even though they shared the same body and the same voice, the Keeper spoke in a much more deliberate, soft and calming way from his human counterpart.

"I'm trying to wrap my head around all of this. You're telling us we're in a symbiotic relationship with an alien?" Isabell turned to Ryder. "You died. The doctor examined your body. I don't understand."

"I woke in Aetheri and met Yox, my Keeper, but it was you who brought us here. Is this really any harder to believe than everything else we've learned over the past few days?"

"Yes!" Isabell replied.

"I'm struggling with this too, Ryder," Padman said. "We deal with *dreams* — you're talking about a fundamental change to our evolutionary process and an afterlife in a parallel universe."

"Not all humans have a Keeper inside of them. Not at the moment, anyway."

Everyone spun around and looked at MT, who had been listening, silently, from behind them. He was smiling.

"Well, no — not currently. But that will be rectified," Yox replied.

"What do you mean?" Jake asked. "Why do you say that?"

MT walked towards the group.

"Humans and Qas'ihar are bound together physically by a part of the brain known as the cerebral cortex. That link only separates when the body dies."

"How do you know that?" Padman asked.

"Because I'm Qas'ihar. I'm Terrell's Keeper."

Padman eyed the boy suspiciously.

"That's impossible."

"Doctor, you've worked here since the creation of Silicate. In all that time, how many mirror apparitions have you created?"

"We've never successfully achieved it ourselves, but that doesn't mean —"

"And why do you think that is?" MT interrupted. "You can create beings from dreams, so why can't you create other versions of yourself?"

Isabell stepped in front of MT.

"If you're trying to tell us it's impossible to achieve, how are you able to stand here and tell us that?"

"I'm here because Terrell needed me to be. Over the years, I've felt his mind grow in a way very few humans have ever managed to do. From a young age, he's been fascinated with his subconscious, taking the time to look beyond what's said to be possible." MT looked around. "Silicate has all this technology at their disposal, and yet a boy of seventeen was able to create me using only his mind." He turned to the doctor.

"You thought his obsession with death was the result of a troubled past, when in fact, he's witnessing the deaths of those passing over to Aetheri. This young man has connected our two realities, allowing for me, his Keeper, to be here right now. This is his awakening, and mine."

"Prove it," Jake said. "Prove that you, and Ryder's double, are

Keepers."

MT looked towards Padman.

"Can an apparition dream?"

"No — they're not alive. A dream doesn't have independent thought."

"Then please explain how three apparitions can concoct a story about aliens living symbiotically inside of you from a reality you go to in your dreams."

"I can't explain it at all."

"You believe him? This is the craziest thing I've ever heard," Jake exclaimed.

"I remember you having a similar reaction when you learned about what we do here. I'll admit, I don't fully understand everything, but in a way, it does answer questions I've considered over the years. What the apparitions were. Why we couldn't we make active duplicates. Why we couldn't project mirror images of ourselves."

"I know this is difficult to understand. If I hadn't seen it with my own eyes, I would doubt this, too. But we're telling you the truth." Ryder looked towards Isabell, who appeared to be in a state of shock and confusion.

"It's really you in there, isn't it?"

"It is. Thank you for bringing me back."

"Do you believe us now?" Yox asked the group.

"I'm willing to accept this is the truth, for now," Padman replied, shaking his head. "It'll need further research."

"Always the scientist." Isabell grinned and rolled her eyes in jest before turning back to Ryder. "I believe you."

Yox turned to Jake, who looked torn.

"I don't know. I guess so. Something's niggling me, though. Why did you come back?"

"That's a good point. People don't make a habit of coming back from the dead," Padman added.

Yox spoke softly yet authoritatively.

"Doctor Sharma, I'm afraid your facility is threatening the very existence of Aetheri and all of its inhabitants."

"How so?"

"Your apparitions are created from the molecules that make up our universe — pieces of Aetheri, pulled from our reality into yours. If this continues, we fear it'll annihilate our home and everything in it."

"It could also destroy the human race," Ryder added. "The Qas'ihar are part of us. Without them, we don't know if we would survive."

Padman straightened up.

"You're asking me to destroy my life's work? On what, blind faith? No, this smells like some elaborate ploy by BioLearn to put me out of business and steal my research."

"Terrell made me, not BioLearn," MT said.

"We're telling you the truth," Ryder added.

Yox stepped in front of the doctor and placed his hands on the side of Padman's head.

"What are you doing?" Padman brushed his hands away, stepping back.

"I'm showing you the proof you need. Perhaps we should sit down." Yox indicated to the chair opposite him.

"I don't know if I trust you."

"You will, I promise."

Padman looked over at Jake, who nodded, indicating he had his back. Cautiously, he sat in the chair, the Keeper kneeling in front of him, once again placing his hands by the side of the doctor's head.

"Close your eyes please, Doctor."

Defiantly, Padman kept his eyes open.

"Trust me. I only need to speak with your Keeper. He'll be able to show you all the proof you need."

Reluctantly, Padman closed his eyes.

"What's he doing?" Isabell whispered to Ryder.

"I think he's going to take the doctor to Aetheri."

"I thought you could only go there when you're asleep?"

"You can enter Aetheri whenever you shut out this world. Sleeping, deep thought or meditation can all work. It's where your imagination comes from."

"Please, I need silence to bridge the connection." Yox spoke softly, his eyes closed, facing the doctor.

Silence descended over the group, only broken when Padman gasped for air. The doctor opened his eyes wide, stood up from the chair and thanked Yox. Tears streamed down his cheeks as he looked into the eyes of the people standing around him.

"It's true, it's all true." He wiped his face and looked back at Yox. "I'm so sorry. I had no idea."

The Keeper smiled.

"I know."

"Wait! What happened?" Jake asked. "What did you see?"

"I saw the truth." Padman smiled.

A muffled voice seemed to emanate from Padman.

"What was that?" Isabell asked.

The doctor delved into his pocket, retrieving the earpiece.

"I forgot all about Oren. Hello?"

"They've got Abby in your office. You need to save her."

"Abby? What's she doing down here? Oren?"

Silence.

"Oren. Are you still there?"

Silence.

The doctor nervously looked up at the group. "They're here. Abby's been captured and I think they've got Oren."

"What do we do?" Isabell's eyes were wide open in shock.

"Follow me."

"Where are we going?" Ryder asked.

"Back to my office — and quickly, we don't have much time."

As the group raced down the row of pods, Padman reached out to hold Jake's hand.

"What did you see?"

"Everything they told us is real."

"How do you know that for sure? You only closed your eyes for a few minutes. How do you know this isn't BioLearn confusing you?"

Padman slowed down to look at Jake.

"When you go to sleep tonight, you'll understand." He leaned in and kissed him passionately. "Come on, we can do this. Together."

CHAPTER 39

Padman opened the door to his office with renewed enthusiasm. With what he had just learned, he felt powerful enough to stop BioLearn and take down Devansh. Whatever they had planned, he was armed with knowledge they didn't have.

Someone was sitting in his large, leather-backed chair facing away from him. Got you, he thought. The doctor put his hand up to stop everyone from moving any closer.

Padman smiled as he tiptoed nearer to his desk.

"Oren. Oren are you there?" he whispered into his earpiece. There was no response. Concerned but not shaken, he continued, a hand grabbing his arm from behind.

"Wait!" MT moved in front of Ryder. "I can't get hurt. I should be the one going."

"I'm head of security, I'm going." Ryder pushed forward.

MT bent down close to Ryder's ear and whispered.

"You may be in an apparition's body, but you're the real thing. Without a Keeper, you're the least safe amongst us. You've already died once today, let me do this."

Ryder recognised a seriousness and wisdom seldom seen in someone so young. The ex-soldier nodded, signalling for the others to stay back as MT walked forward slowly.

As he neared the chair, two armed guards swooped in from the sides, pulling him to the ground. Isabell screamed as a

SWAT team surrounded the group and pushed them towards the desk.

Outnumbered and overpowered, Ryder gripped the armrests of his chair angrily as he was moved forcibly along with the group. They gathered around Padman's work station; MT struggling on the ground under the boots of two men much stronger than he.

Padman's confidence wavering, he mustered up enough energy to speak out.

"It's me you want, Devansh. Let my friends go."

The leather chair spun around, revealing an impeccably dressed Indian woman.

"Hello, darling. Were you expecting someone else?"

Padman's mouth fell open in shock.

"Who's she?" Isabell asked.

"She? I'm not the cat's mother. That's more your style, isn't it, dear? I found your little rodent earlier, the poor thing was trapped in a glass cage."

"If you've hurt her —"

"Me, hurt the poor dear? On the contrary, I liberated her. It skipped off somewhere, no doubt looking for you. I do hope it didn't find that door I left open to the outside. I'm not sure apparitions can survive out there for very long. I know the other apparitions Flynn let out only survived a day.

"I suppose if you were really quick, you could bring her back, but it looks like you have other plans." She shrugged mockingly. "Oh, well."

Isabell lunged towards the woman but was pulled back by the SWAT team.

"You're a monster."

"And you're too funny. If it's a battle between my army and yours, I think I've already won."

Padman struggled to find his voice.

"How?"

"How what, darling? How is it that I still look so good? How much did I pay for these shoes? Nice, aren't they?"

Padman stared at her with contempt.

"Darling, you're no fun when you're all tensed up. I'd offer to give you a massage, but I'm sure you'd prefer farmer boy to be doing that sort of thing for you.

"Then again, that was always the problem, wasn't it? It wasn't *me* you wanted climbing on your back."

A sudden realisation came over Jake.

"That's your ex-wife!"

Zoya clapped, slowly and deliberately.

"And I thought all you yokels were as dumb as the pigs you tend. Congratulations for breaking the stereotype."

"How are you here?" Padman asked, seething with anger.

"Oh, darling, you're all confused. You should calm down—it looks like you might burst a blood vessel." Zoya swept her hair back as she continued, "In answer to your question—I'm not. This is my apparition form. Technology our company stole from you many years ago, but perfected through Oren Rosenberg's work. Speaking of which…"

She nodded a signal, and a man appeared, carrying a chair. Strapped down in the seat was Abby, looking terrified. Gaffer tape was covering her mouth, muffling her screams.

"Hello there, darling. Comfortable?" She turned to rest of the group, shaking her head. "You know, I don't think she is." Zoya nodded to the guard, who moved the chair closer to her.

"We figured out pretty early on that Oren was working with you," she continued. "It was only a matter of time before we tracked him down at BioLearn and were able to get into Archeus.

"This, though —" she placed her hand on Abby's leg, squeezing it "— was an added bonus. His only daughter walking right into my lap. I'm not sure what I'm going to do with her yet …

"She wouldn't talk to me, the silly girl, but it was quite apparent she had something urgent to tell you. I'm not a fan of gagging people, I quite like the repartee, but in this case, I couldn't stand listening to her whine any longer."

MT was struggling harder on the floor, trying to force his way out from the two men on top of him. Zoya watched the boy for a moment in morbid amusement, before fixing her stare on Isabell.

"Perhaps we should send him to look for your cat?" She laughed.

"You bitch!"

"No, that's a dog, dear. My goodness, the education system in this country really is atrocious."

Ryder was still gripping the sides of his chair. With a curled lip, he spoke up.

"If you've only just arrived, who attacked me?"

Zoya leaned back, as if assessing the man in front of her.

"It could be a number of people. You have one of those faces... You know, the type people just want to hit."

Rising anger seared through Ryder, a flush of red spreading across his face.

"Look at him — he's turning into a beet!" Zoya laughed hysterically. "Yes, it was me." The laughing stopped suddenly and the look in her eyes was icy. "I ordered the attack, and it was Flynn, here, who carried out my orders." She beckoned one of her team over.

A tall, bulky man stepped forward. He stood beside Zoya, looking out towards the group. In head-to-toe SWAT gear and his black mask covering all but his eyes, he was an intimidating figure.

"Take your mask off — let them get a good look at you," Zoya commanded.

Flynn obeyed without question, handing his gun to Zoya before removing his headgear. The man beneath the mask was no less intimidating. His cold stare seared into the minds of the group.

As they stood transfixed by Flynn, they didn't notice Zoya aiming the gun at his head and firing. Everyone recoiled in shock as the body crumpled to the floor with a thud. Zoya nodded, and two of the team stepped forward to drag him away, leaving a streak of blood on the floor.

"I ordered him to kill you, but he obviously didn't do his job. I don't like people disappointing me."

"How is there blood on the floor? Apparitions can't bleed," Padman gasped.

"Clueless to the last. Thanks to your former security guard, Flynn's been inside the building for days."

"You killed him," Jake mumbled.

"Did I?" Zoya rose from her seat, stepping over the blood to get closer to the group. "Are you sure? I was under the impression that Lord Braighton's bastard grandson was dead, but here he is, alive and well."

Ryder shifted and was immediately pinned back into his chair. Zoya pointed the gun at his head.

"I wouldn't miss." She paused, sensing the fear rise in the room, before bursting into laughter. "There will be time for that later."

Zoya retracted the gun and paced in front of her frightened captors, her stiletto heels tapping on the floor beneath her.

"It appears I'm not the only one who thought you were dead," she continued, stopping in front of Yox. "You have a doppelgänger. Did someone try to dream you back into existence? I notice this one can stand, that must have hurt. Sucks to be you."

"Stop this, Zoya," Padman begged.

"Or what?" She sat back down, staring at the doctor. He went silent. "That's what I thought." Zoya crossed her legs and glanced casually around the room. "We came in through Archeus and made our way to your office, giving me a chance to look around. I can't say I like what you've done with the place, darling. The greatest scientific breakthrough in human history and what do you do? Create a bloody theme park. No, no, no. BioLearn deserves to have this technology. In our hands, we'll change the world."

"You'll destroy it," Padman muttered angrily.

"Potato, po-tah-toe. I had hoped to be in and out, but I needed to see you before I left."

"I thought Devansh was behind all of this."

"Dear Papa? Didn't you hear? He's dead. Almost five years ago. I've been running the company in his absence."

"How did he die?"

"Of a broken heart." Zoya closed her eyes, feigning sobbing. "At least, it was broken after my knife left his chest," she scoffed.

"You murdered your own father?"

"Look around — does that really surprise you?"

"You're not the Zoya I thought I knew."

"And you're not the man I thought I married."

Realisation hit Padman.

"You're doing this because of me? Because of what happened? I thought you were OK with things. You told my parents with me."

"What else could I do? I was just a girl — immature, weak."

"You were my rock."

"AND I SHOULD HAVE BEEN MY OWN ROCK!" Zoya rose as she screamed the words at Padman. She inhaled and held her breath, calming herself down, before slowly resuming her seat.

"My father taught me that, after I returned home. He made me realise what a fool I'd been, how you'd humiliated him and I. He gave me a job at the company and treated me as his equal, something he'd never done before. I was finally my own person, I felt strong and capable.

"I was no longer a prize to be married off — I was the head of my own department, reporting only to him. He entrusted me with plans to infiltrate Silicate, take your research and build an empire together. After what you'd done to me . . . the shame and humiliation you'd caused . . . the failure I'd felt . . . I wanted nothing more than to make you feel that pain.

"Unfortunately, like all men, darling Daddy hadn't the courage of his convictions, so I took it upon myself to follow through with his plan. It was me who started the underground operations at BioLearn. I arranged to have Oren kidnapped and work for us and, when my father found out, do you think he thanked me? No! He threatened to turn me in to the police. Me! His own daughter. I had no choice — he had to be removed.

"With him gone, I've been free to develop the company the way I want — under his name, of course. Creating a scapegoat who can never be found."

"You're insane. He corrupted you and now you're more maniacal than he ever was."

"Thank you, darling. I think that's the nicest thing you've ever said to me." She looked towards Isabell. "And thank you, crazy cat lady, for opening the door for us. Who knew there was a brain large enough under all that hair to hold someone so complex and, dare I say, evil?

"Vincent was just the apparition we'd been waiting for. He was so bent on chaos and destruction that he barely needed any coercing from me. I stopped him from killing your staff — you're welcome, by the way — but the nurse's security pass came in very handy."

"Where are they now?"

"On their way to BioLearn. I know it wasn't strictly necessary to hang their corpses in the horror exhibition, but it was worth it to see the looks on your faces. I'll dine out on that for weeks."

Tired of hearing Zoya's self-congratulation, Padman scowled at her.

"Vincent didn't get very far, though, did he?"

"Why do you say that darling? Because you found him decompiling outside the door to the museum? That's where I wanted you to find him. I trapped you in Archeus, giving him time to get into your office and give me access to Somnio. On his way back, I made him block the corridors with whatever he could find and wait patiently by the door until you arrived.

"Poor thing thought I wanted him there to attack you — he didn't know he was going to fade away."

"Making us think he was responsible for all the problems we were having and continue through the museum, giving you time to break our encryptions and take Silicate." Padman's voice was filled with frustration and fear.

"But you didn't count on Abby's dad getting here first."

Zoya looked down at the boy on the floor who had just spoken.

"Do you know, I'd totally forgotten you were there. You don't make much of an impression, do you? Unlike those boots currently pushing into your back — I'm sure they will."

Padman side-glanced Ryder, who was looking back. They both realised at the same time that Zoya didn't know about MT.

CHAPTER 40

"Story-time's over. I'm in control and, soon, BioLearn will be launching their very own line of apparitions. It's all thanks to you, Padman. You made this possible. By throwing me to the curb, you took away my future, giving me no choice but to take away yours."

"There's always a choice."

"That's right, darling — and I *choose* to do this."

"So, what, you're a homophobe now?" Jake spat through gritted teeth.

Zoya laughed as she rose to her feet.

"A homophobe? Darling, I live in San Francisco with my boyfriend and my wife. Sexuality was never the problem — he was." She pointed at Padman, signalling to one of the SWAT team with her other hand. A guard grabbed the doctor and wrestled him into the leather chair Zoya had vacated, pushing it up to the desk.

"Now, Doctor . . . all that's left for you to do is to give me your access codes."

"And then you'll let us go?"

"What do you think? I'll tell you what — you give me the codes, and I promise to save the children."

Padman looked across at Abby, bound and gagged in the chair next to him, tears streaming down her face. MT was looking determinedly at Padman.

"What's it to be, Doctor? You give me the codes and the innocent little kiddies go free."

"And if I refuse?"

"You all die."

"Then you wouldn't get the codes at all."

"Perhaps not right away, but we'd crack the encryption eventually." She bent down to Padman, placing her hand on his chest. "With or without your cold, beating heart."

Padman shuddered at Zoya's touch.

"I'm so sorry my rejection turned you into this monster."

"I'm not," she whispered in his ear. "It's the best thing that's ever happened to me."

It was Isabell who noticed Terrell first. She nudged Jake, who followed her gaze. The darkness of despair which had all but consumed him now gave rise to hope for the first time since meeting Zoya.

Terrell was peering in from the window overlooking the hub, careful not to be spotted by the SWAT team. He made eye-contact with Jake and pointed towards Padman, trying desperately, through rudimental mime, to signal that he had something to tell the doctor.

Jake and Isabell felt utterly helpless. They were being held captive by heavy guard with even heavier artillery. What could they do?

Jake coughed, loudly.

Zoya raised her head.

"What is it, farm boy? You have some parting words of flawed wisdom to share with us?"

Jake was shaking. The strong hands holding him had clamped around his chest, making it difficult to breath, and even harder to speak.

"I want to kiss Padman. If we're going to die, I would like to say goodbye properly." Tears fell from his eyes, soaking into the SWAT soldier's gloved hands, making him sneer in Jake's ear.

"How sweet. You want one last kiss with your lover." Zoya smiled. "Of course not. Do I look like the kind of person who cares what you want?" She spun back to face Padman. "Enough stalling. Enter your access code now, or the girl dies first."

Abby screamed into her gag.

"Please . . ." Jake stammered. "Please, let me say goodbye to him."

Zoya stomped her heel into the ground. She grabbed Padman's face and turned it to hers.

"You kiss him. Say your goodbyes, and when you sit back down here, you enter that damn code or watch all of your friends die, including farm boy. Do you understand?"

Padman nodded.

"Good." She motioned to the team, who yanked Padman out of his chair and pushed him roughly towards Jake.

As they locked eyes, both crying, Padman mouthed, "I'm sorry," before leaning in to kiss him.

"Terrell, window," Jake whispered just before their lips met. The kiss lasted only moments before the team were dragging the doctor back towards his seat. He just had time to observe Terrell standing by the window, looking directly at him, holding a piece of paper with words scrawled messily on it: *OPEN FOLDER: ACTIVATE SOMNIO.*

Thrown back into his chair, Padman stared at the desktop. There, amongst the many folders, was one he hadn't seen before. *Activate Somnio.*

"Now that gag-worthy scene is over, it's time for the final act. Don't worry, Doctor. Your creations will live on, under my superior care. No longer caged up underground, they'll be free to roam the world as valued members of society."

"You're planning on selling them to the military, aren't you?"

"What if I am?" Zoya tapped the screen.

Padman took hold of the mouse and hovered it over the folder.

"One last thing; after you kill us, how will you explain so many deaths?"

Zoya's smile changed into a smirk.

"I won't have to, no-one will know I was ever here, but your research gave me an idea. Details will emerge of your sexual deviancy, using this lab to create lifelike beings to perform your disgusting acts on.

"An unnamed colleague discovers what you're doing and tries to inform the authorities . . . in a rage, you kill them and destroy the building, taking you and everyone inside along with it."

"That's disgusting. Who would believe such a thing?"

"Have you never heard of tabloid journalism? When they see the amount of sexual imagery stored on your databanks, everyone will believe it."

"They aren't mine — they were extracted from patients."

"As of tomorrow, the whole world will believe they *were* yours."

Anger coursed through Padman's veins as a satisfied smile spread across Zoya's face.

"At least *you* don't have to live through your humiliation, Padman." She smacked her fist on the desk next to the keyboard, making everyone jump. "CODES. NOW!"

Padman had no idea what this folder was, but Terrell had just risked his life for it. He was out of alternative options and out of time. Whatever the folder did, he only hoped it would be enough to stop Zoya. He double-clicked it.

A text box appeared: *Hello, Doctor Sharma, please enter your access code.*

"Finally!" Zoya cried. She picked a phone smuggled in by Flynn and called BioLearn.

Slowly, Padman entered each letter, number and keystroke into the text box. He clicked *Enter*. Nothing happened.

Zoya spoke into the phone.

"Did you get that? Do we have his access code? What do you mean, scrambled?" Furious, she turned to Padman. "What did you do?"

A rumble from beneath them, shook the floor.

"I honestly don't know." Padman smiled as the rumbling intensified.

Zoya slapped him across the face.

"Tell me, damn it. What did you do?"

Smarting from the sting, Padman turned his head and looked out of the window.

"Maybe you should ask them."

Zoya followed his gaze as two pachycephalosaurs began ramming the glass with their heads.

"What the —" Zoya fell back into her SWAT team. "Get out there. I need to know what's going on."

More dinosaurs rushed down the ramp, followed by an army of apparitions from every exhibit. The SWAT team moved into position, facing off against the oncoming masses, but they were no match against the thousands of creatures descending on them.

"Aim your weapons. Fire on my command."

"They're apparitions, sir. They can't be harmed."

"Fire anyway."

Bullets didn't slow the apparitions, as a T-Rex charged towards the team, knocking the soldiers over like dominos. Zoya's heavies pulled back, trying to find shelter wherever they could.

Glass shattered as the pachycephalosaurs broke through the window of the office, followed by Jedi Knights, Daleks and Borg drones headed by Seven of Nine. They quickly overpowered the remaining SWAT team and effortlessly began rescuing the prisoners.

Padman helped MT up as the others rushed over to hug him. Terrell climbed in, followed by Link and Venger. He raced over to Abby and helped the others untie her.

"Are you OK?" Terrell asked.

"Let her catch her breath," MT added.

"Oh, yeah, sorry." Terrell stood back.

Abby pushed herself up.

"Weirdest day ever." She smiled, hugging both Terrells.

Outside, arrows flew through the air, landing close to the

SWAT team as Hatshepsut and her army of Egyptian warriors took aim from the Mesozoic Era exhibit.

"This isn't working, sir," a soldier called. "There are too many of them."

"Stay at your post. We have to hold them off for as long as possible. Use hand-to-hand combat, if you have to." He glanced up to see a shiver of sharks approaching.

"How do we go hand-to-hand with *them*, sir?"

"Where is she? Where's Zoya?" Padman spun around, scanning the crowded room.

"Did the Jedis get her?" Jake asked.

"No, she's not here," Isabell replied.

"Won't she have gone back to BioLearn?" Ryder asked.

"That's what a sane person would do." Padman's head continued to dart around the room. "Perfect!" He cried and disappeared into the mass of apparitions. A roar parted a group of Stormtroopers as Falkor nudged through them; Padman seated on the back of the white dragon.

"You're not going after her, are you?" Jake asked.

"I have to stop her."

"Wait!"

Jake spun around and grabbed the Nimbus 2000 which was resting at the side of a desk. He pulled it under him and started to levitate.

"Not alone, you don't."

"You should stay here with the others, where it's safe."

"Someone needs to look after you. Come on, let's find that bitch."

Huge spiders descended from the ceiling, crawling into the SWAT teams' uniforms, making them jump and wriggle around. Distracted, they didn't see the herd of mammoths charging at them. Their huge feet pinned the team to the floor as Mulan and her army joined forces with the Egyptians, overwhelming the soldiers.

"Retreat, men. RETREAT!"

One by one, the team vanished as they disconnected the link

to their apparitions.

Padman and Jake flew out of the office and into the hub, just in time to see the apparitions cheering in triumph.

"It's not over yet," the doctor shouted to Jake over the noise.

They sped through the crowds and hovered above the hub, scanning the area. The large doors to the amphitheatre were open.

"Over there!" Padman shouted, as he and Jake soared down and through the entrance.

A series of bullets missed them narrowly. As they looked ahead, they could see Zoya standing on the centre of the empty stage, holding a Kalashnikov rifle in one hand and a semi-automatic in the other.

"Stop this. It's over, Zoya."

"It's not over until you're dead," she cried, aiming the gun at the doctor and firing.

Falkor weaved, missing the bullets before ducking down behind the seats. Padman nodded to Jake, who swept left while he swerved right, using the seats to shield them from Zoya's onslaught of bullets.

She stopped firing and swung round, searching desperately for the doctor.

"You think this has stopped me? You and your two-bit circus freaks? I already have all your research, your staff, and don't forget — your porn stash. Whatever happens after today, you're finished. Silicate is finished, and I'll walk away unscathed."

Padman raged. He wanted to respond. He wanted to scream at her, but he knew if he did, she would kill him. Falkor stealthily floated behind the seats, keeping low to the ground. In this position, they were able to edge closer to the stage without making a sound. Looking through the stands, he could just make out Jake on the broomstick on the opposite side of the theatre.

The closer Padman moved towards the stage, the more restricted they became. Falkor was simply too large to get any further.

"I'll have to walk the rest of the way," he whispered to the dragon.

"I'll distract her while you get closer."

"How are you going to avoid the bullets?"

"With luck!" Falkor replied, smiling as he flew high into the air, weaving towards the door.

Zoya immediately began firing in the direction of the dragon, pulling down sheets of glass and plaster from the roof. Falkor successfully dodged them all as he made his way back through the theatre doors.

With Zoya distracted, Padman ran towards the stage, ready to jump up and stop her. Hearing his footsteps, she quickly spun around, her face twisted into an evil smile.

"I've got you now," she cackled, pointing both guns at Padman and pulling the triggers.

A huge crash suddenly reverberated around the auditorium. The bullets stopped. For a moment, there was complete silence. Padman dared to peer up from the stands and look across to the stage.

A wooden house was standing where Zoya had been. As the doctor pulled himself up, he realised it was Dorothy Gale's house from the Wizard of Oz.

His racing heart began to normalise. He looked around for Jake, calling out to him.

"It's all right — she's gone."

The door to the house burst open. Zoya was standing in front him, smiling, the gun pointed directly at his chest.

"I win," she breathed.

At that moment, Jake, riding the Nimbus 2000, pounced on to the stage, pinning her on the ground. A shower of bullets flew through the air, one hitting Padman in his shoulder and knocking him off his feet.

Jake tumbled to the floor and shuffled over to the doctor.

"Hey, hey, stay with me, all right? Stay with me."

"Zoya?" Padman asked.

"She's gone, disconnected."

"Good." Padman smiled before falling unconscious.

CHAPTER 41

"*These were the emotional scenes captured earlier today in Central London. Police officers arrived in droves to rescue employees and patients from a facility inside The Particle.*

"*According to an unnamed source, a mysterious tip alerted law enforcement to a potential threat inside. When they investigated, they found the entire site barricaded. It took three hours to break through the security and rescue those trapped inside.*

"*It's yet to be determined what caused the shutdown, but there were tears and laughter as friends and family, who'd waited outside for hours, were reunited with their loved ones. Let's go live to Jessie, who's outside The Particle right now . . .*"

Jake switched off the TV and settled into his chair next to the hospital bed. He held on to Padman's hand.

"We did it. Everyone was rescued from Silicate and the FBI arrested Zoya. The amount of evidence they've got will keep her imprisoned for life.

"Oren and the others have all been released. I spoke to him earlier — he's fine. He's been giving evidence about BioLearn. I don't think we need to worry about them any more."

Jake looked across at the abundance of medical equipment keeping Padman alive. He had waited outside the operating theatre, then kept a bedside vigil ever since. He gazed lovingly at the sleeping doctor, a tear escaping his eye as he spoke.

"The bullet's been removed and you're going to make a full recovery. All you have to do is wake up. Please, wake up."

❖ ❖ ❖

"Hello, Doctor."

"Hello, Ryder. Or should I call you Yox?"

"Names . . . they're a strange concept to the Qas'ihar."

"You don't have names?"

"We do, but we tend to use our Aetheri designations when communicating with others of our kind."

"You're known by your address?"

"A crude comparison, but, yes, I suppose we are." The Keeper smiled.

Padman looked around. A blanket of white fog surrounded them.

"Is this Aetheri?"

"Your home away from home."

"It's a bit sparse."

"Surely you, of all people, know how to change that."

The landscape transformed and they were standing in the clearing of a forest.

"Somewhere you're fond of?" Yox asked.

"Castle Rock. The village in India where my grandparents lived before moving to the UK." Padman looked around in awe. "The detail is incredible." He led them out of the shade of the trees and into the village. "I can feel the sun on my face."

"You don't have to."

"No, I want to." Padman continued down the dirt path towards a large, wooden building. "This was theirs." He opened the door and walked into his grandparent's home. He smiled as he looked around, sitting down on a chair facing the open fire.

The Keeper sat next to him. They listened to the crackling flames as they watched them leap and dance. It was Padman who broke the silence.

"What will happen to you now?"

"Once my work is done, I'll return home."

"Work?"

"Yes, Doctor. I've been tasked with overseeing the dismantling of Silicate."

"Oh, of course." Padman felt sadness grip his heart.

"I'm sorry, that was tactless of me. This was your life's work —it must be difficult for you."

"It is. But not as troubling as the knowledge that if I'd continued, it would have destroyed your world and possibly the future of our species. Believe me, I understand the gravity of the situation, I just don't know how I'll be able to explain this to my employees, the investors, or Lord Braighton."

"The Qas'ihar will help. Whatever you decide to tell them, we can show them here in Aetheri. Usually, people discount their dreams far too easily, but if we work together, perhaps we can get through to them. They may be more inclined to believe you."

"I hope you're right. We don't just need to stop Silicate — we need to make sure no-one else uses this technology in the future."

Padman noticed a picture on the mantelpiece. It was a photo of him as a young boy.

"What will happen to the apparitions already in the museum? Will you take them back?"

"Unfortunately, that's not possible. The process your machines put them through distorts their original make-up. They're no longer compatible with our universe."

"How is Aetheri?"

"We're recovering. This isn't the first time this has happened, and it won't be the last. Thankfully, we were able to reach out to you in time."

"It's a shame that Ryder had to die to give me the information. What will happen to him?"

"As his apparition wasn't modified in any way, he's free to return to Aetheri whenever he chooses. Although I believe, at least for the moment, he's not ready to leave his life behind."

Padman collected the photo from the mantelpiece, holding

it in his hands.

"I don't know what I'd do if I were him. This is paradise of our own making, but Earth is where our friends and family are. It's a tough choice."

"Thankfully, one that isn't available to most people. Ignorance, in this case, is bliss."

Padman nodded in agreement.

"What of you and Jake?"

"I'm not sure. I've certainly turned his life upside-down. I don't even know if he'll want to be in the picture after all of this."

The Keeper stayed silent, gazing as the flames lapped the stone surround. Padman noted the silence.

"What do you know? If Terrell could have premonitions, does that mean you can see things before they happen?"

Yox laughed.

"Human emotions really do baffle me. It's been an illuminating exercise, living amongst you and witnessing your many interactions. It's fascinating."

Padman watched him in anticipation.

"In answer to your question, he has a lot of love in his heart for you. He hasn't left your side since you were shot, and I don't believe he'll ever want to leave your side again."

Padman smiled happily, and the Keeper chuckled.

"Perhaps it's time you got to know Jake on a more personal level, away from all the apparitions, guns and psychopathic ex-wives."

"Perhaps you're right."

The doctor closed his eyes and smiled. When he opened them again, he was lying in bed, Jake by his side.

"Hello, beautiful man."

"You're awake!" Jake leaned in and kissed him gently. "I thought you were . . ." He stopped, shook his head, and kissed him again. "I'm so glad you're all right. We should get a doctor."

"You already did."

They kissed slowly, both savouring the moment.

The nurse entered the room to check on her patient. Jake sat back in the chair, a huge smile on his face, and breathed a sigh of relief.

"I'll be waiting at the airport for both of you. I can't wait to see you in person."

"You, too, Daddy. Mom wants to speak to you." Abby passed the phone to her tearful mother.

"Hello, darling."

"Hey — we said no tears. At least, not until we're in each other's arms."

Seeing Oren's face again, even on this small screen, was something Shira had dreamed about for years.

"I never gave up hope on you. Never."

"I'm sorry it's taken so long. Only a few more hours, and the three of us will be together for ever."

A Tannoy announcement echoed throughout the airport.

"They're boarding our flight now. We've got to go. I love you. See you soon."

"Love you, Daddy! See you soon!" Abby called into the phone.

"I love you both, so very much," Oren called, waving into the camera.

"Are you sure you want to do this?"

"What do you mean? Isn't this every girl's dream?"

"Isabell, I'm serious."

"So am I. This place is literally everybody's dream." Isabell walked over to another box and began unpacking. She could feel Ryder's gaze on her back. "I know what you're trying to say, but this is my choice. I want to do this."

"Who would choose to live underground, like an armadillo

or something?"

Isabell turned around, chuckling.

"Armadillo? Where did that come from?"

"I don't know. I saw one earlier and it was the first thing that sprung to mind."

"If it's that bad, why are you still here?"

Ryder hung his head.

"I don't know. I'm not ready to go yet."

Isabell sat down next to him.

"We might be underground, but we're not living like armadillos or moles or even badgers. Padman's old office makes a huge living-space for both of us, and it's not like we're ever going to get bored."

Ryder wasn't convinced.

"I can't leave here, but you can. I don't want you giving up your life for me."

"I'm not. I'm doing this for me. I can write in peace, I can get all the inspiration I would ever need, and conversation from a good friend."

"You're telling me, if I decided to go back to Aetheri, right now, you'd still live here?"

"Are you kidding me? Do you know how much an apartment this size would cost to rent in London? I'm not a prisoner and I don't feel guilted into this. I want to do it."

"Promise me."

"I promise. Come on! The endless fun we can have here. Flying a spaceship, picnicking in in the savanna and jumping off buildings with that assassin guy."

"Ezio."

"Yeah, him. I've spent my life running away from the ghosts of my past — now, I want to run towards the apparitions of my future."

"I hate that."

"What?"

"You always think of the perfect thing to say."

"Comes as standard with a writer's brain."

Megara miaowed from the corner of the room.

"Come on, then, baby — let's get you some food."

"Did you kiss her?" Cody nudged Terrell, causing some of his chips to fall to the floor.

"Ergh! Gross! That's like asking if you've snogged Pippa."

"That's not cool, man. She's my sister."

"Exactly. That's how I feel about Abby."

"How old is she?"

"Fourteen."

"Ah, OK. Sorry, man, I didn't know she was still a kid. The way you've not stopped talking about her, I thought she was our age."

The two friends were sitting at the side of a bandstand in their local park, eating fish and chips out of the wrapper. The last of the day's sun was beaming down, causing the trees to cast long shadows across the path leading to Bedford Pavilion.

"Abby and I are friends, probably the best of friends."

"Hey! I thought I was your best friend."

"You are. Can't I have more than one?"

Cody pondered the question.

"What happens if we're both with you. Who's the best, *best* friend?"

"What are you on about? That's not a thing."

"It's me, though, isn't it?"

"Yes, it's you." Terrell chuckled.

The two smiled as they ate their chips, appreciating being together again.

"You still haven't told me what happened with that company you were working for."

"They had to downsize. Laid off most of the staff, including me."

"That sucks, man. I guess having all that media attention really killed their reputation. It was all over the news, how you were trapped inside and stuff. Did they ever find out what caused it?"

BioLearn hacked the system, trapped us in there, killed Ryder and threatened to kill everyone else, including me ... the response ran through Terrell's head, but he knew he would never share it.

"No idea. System malfunction or something," he replied.

"Miss it?"

Terrell would have loved nothing better than to tell his friend all about what Silicate did, how amazing Somnio was ... not to mention MT and Aetheri and the Qas'ihar, but he couldn't.

Cody took his silence as confirmation.

"Don't worry, mate, there'll be other job opportunities. At least you had a bit of an adventure and got your face on TV."

"Only the back of my head. Mum was smothering me the whole time."

"Why don't you start uni with me? Think of all the girls we'll pull. You remember Dave, from the year above? He said university's amazing. No rules, wear your own clothes, tons of parties and, best of all, everyone gets a shag on freshers' week. It's like an official rule, or something."

"I thought you weren't going to uni."

"Changed my mind after speaking to Dave. I need to protect my future."

"You're just going for the girls, aren't you?"

"Too bloody right I am. I suppose it won't hurt if I get an education, as well, though."

Terrell laughed as he threw his empty wrapper in the bin.

"I've been telling you this for years. I go away for a week and suddenly David-*bloody*-Staines is the fountain of all knowledge. He failed art and design. Who fails art and design?"

The two friends burst out laughing as they jumped down from the wall and began walking home through the park.

"I don't know if I want to go to uni. I've been thinking I might start my own company. I made some contacts in London — I think I could make a go of it."

"Yeah? Cool. I'll come and crash on your sofa as your one-of-a-kind, can't-live-without, non-rent-paying roommate." Cody grinned.

"In your dreams," Terrell replied with a smile.

EPILOGUE

"Celebrated crime novelist Isabell Porra's new book, The Keepers, was released last month to critical acclaim, even though there isn't a whodunnit in sight. Isabell joins us in the studio. Hello, Isabell."

"Hello. Thank you for inviting me."

"I know a lot of fans were sceptical at first — no crime, no murder, no Vincent. Tell us, what made you change direction?"

"I believe a lot of fiction writers get pigeonholed these days. Many of them would prefer to try other avenues. I'm a writer, not just of crime fiction, but of everything. I didn't know how people would react to me trying something new, though."

"Very positively, it seems. You're currently at number one, both here and in the States."

"Yes, it's quite extraordinary."

"Although, it hasn't all been praise. There have been public book burnings in the American south with religious activists calling your book blasphemous. How have you reacted to those claims?"

"I can't stand hate in any form. If people don't like my writing, that's for them to decide, but this public shaming of someone they don't know, haven't met, and for a book I doubt they'll ever read . . . well, I think it tells you more about them than it does about me."

"Well said, Isabell. I've read the book — loved it by the way — but where on earth do you get your ideas from?"

"My dreams," Isabell replied coyly.

The presenter laughed.

"Very good. I wish I had your imagination."

"You do, we all do. If you think about it, our brains are capable of so much." Isabell looked directly into the camera. "For those of you who have read my book, think about it, discuss it with your friends, keep it fresh in your memory when you go to bed. Make sure it's the last thing you think about before falling asleep, and when you dream, maybe you'll be able to see Aetheri for yourself."

The camera pulled out into a wide shot.

"You do know I'll be trying that tonight, don't you?" The presenter chuckled, peering at her notes.

"Now, my viewers will kill me if I don't ask you this ... what's happened to Vincent? At the end of your previous book, he fell into the river. Did he survive? Will he be back in a future novel to terrorise yet another poor, unsuspecting woman?"

"Vincent is dead."

"Wow! I wasn't expecting that."

"He's gone, never to return."

"Well, folks," the presenter said, looking into the camera. "You heard it here first."

She turned back to her guest.

"Does that mean you won't be writing anymore Detective Oslo books, either?"

"Not for a while, at least. I feel it's time to breathe life into new characters, ones who don't always meet a grisly end."

"Well, The Keepers was a fabulous read and I, personally, can't wait to see what comes next. Thank you for talking with us today, it's been a real pleasure having you in the studio."

"Thank you, I've enjoyed being here."

The presenter looked into the camera as it moved closer towards her.

"After the break, Ben Holmes will be presenting a very special edition of Eco Watch, live from Spurn Point in Yorkshire. See you in a couple of minutes."

A producer rushed to un-mic Isabell as she left the set. Her agent was there to greet her.

"Fabulous as always, darling — the teeth, the glitz, the glamour ... they loved you out there."

"Jeff, you would say that even if I was terrible."

"And I'll keep telling you that as long as those cheques keep coming my way." He kissed her on both cheeks. "Love you, but I'm rushing to Elstree. Megan Hilty needs me, but who doesn't? See you soon."

Cameras clicked and flashed as Isabell left the studio, her driver ushering her into the limousine. As they neared The Particle, security guards held off the paparazzi outside, giving them access to the underground car park. Isabell closed her eyes and smiled.

I'm home, she thought.

THE END

NON IN FINEM

ENTER THE REFRACTED WORLD

www.refractedworld.com

www.twitter.com/RefractedWorld

www.facebook.com/RefractedWorld

ABOUT THE AUTHOR

Born in Derbyshire, raised in Yorkshire, resides in London.

Terry Geo wrote and directed his first play at age eleven. At sixteen, he started work in television, writing scripts and becoming the youngest director in the country. After a short stint in a boyband, Terry went back to writing, editing two national publications. He toured the world as an actor, moved to London and in 2017, wrote and directed an award-nominated musical for the London stage.

Refraction is Terry's first published novel.

ACKNOWLEDGEMENTS

I wasn't sure whether to write an acknowledgments page or not. I'd read some scathing reviews online about how they were only self-serving and listed names of people the average reader would have no knowledge of or indeed interest in seeing. I could see their point, on one hand, but on the other, if you don't like reading acknowledgements pages, don't read them! Personally, I believe it's a nice way for the author to offer thanks to those people who have in some way contributed.

It's said writing is a very solitary profession. As true as that is, I find the connection with the characters I create can be very engaging and entertaining. I'm bringing to life people that only exist in my head and the more I write and develop them, the more they evolve into the characters you read about. On average, I spent nine to twelve hours a day writing Refraction. I took most weekends off to spend with my husband, but through the week, this was my full-time job.

"It must be nice working from home," says every single person I've ever met.

The truth is, it gets lonely and sometimes stifling. I work, eat and sleep in my flat, often not seeing the outside world for days on end. I don't have 'water-cooler' moments, giggling lunch breaks or extended bathroom time playing 'insert mobile game here'. It's just me, a playlist of instrumental music I've heard a million times and Microsoft Word, beckoning me in to create more of the world I'm forming and demanding I finish the book.

The person who has helped me survive throughout it all, is my husband, Ken. Not only has he pushed me to continue, bolstered me when I felt lost and even whisked me away for the weekend when my brain needed a rest. He has also had to put up with me needing total silence for hours on end, live with months of distracted conversations and me, totally spoiling every twist and plot development before he even had a chance to listen to the finished book. Yes, I did say listen. He hates reading, so I read every chapter aloud to him – I'm his own, personal Audible!

He's also funded my life while I wrote Refraction. I guess most of us don't think about that, but for us first time authors who devote their full time to writing, there is no income until the book is released – which can take a long time. Even when you've finished writing the story, the book is still not done. Month of editing follow from a group of people who will read the book countless times until we all go word blind and miss the odd spelling error or erroneous comma. Which brings me on to my next acknowledgment – Rachel.

I met Rachel years ago on holiday in Turkey. When I announced on social media that I was looking for a copy editor, she offered her services. For over a month we worked together and although I didn't agree with some of her more aggressive edits (losing the seven wonders of the ancient world – what was she thinking?), it was a great help to have her on board and I even learned a few things about the pacing, tenses and paragraph formatting.

The next person to read through the book was my brother, Max. In its pre-release state, he managed to spot those spelling errors and even noticed a missing word. I was very grateful to have a fresh set of eyes looking over the book just before release. Max and I share a lot of the same interests, so his input at this stage was crucial.

I would like to thank my Mum, Spange and many others who offered their support and advice in the early stages of writing, especially for the first few chapters.

I also want to thank the entertainment world and beyond. Refraction is full of pop-culture references, historical people and places and species from the natural world, all of which I have a genuine love for. I'm a proud geek and have many interests, a lot of them now apart of my first novel. Thank you for the thousands of hours of tears, laughter and emotional engagement.

And finally, you. If you've read my book and got to this point, thank you. I really hope you enjoyed the story, the characters and the world(s) I created. If you want more; in the words of James Bond:

Refraction will return...

In loving memory of Megara

48213258R00223

Printed in Poland
by Amazon Fulfillment
Poland Sp. z o.o., Wrocław